FLESH

FLESH

Khanh Ha

Black Heron Press
Post Office Box 13396
Mill Creek, Washington 98082
www.blackheronpress.com

ISBN 978-0-930773-88-5

Jacket art and design by Bryan Sears

Black Heron Press
Post Office Box 13396
Mill Creek, Washington 98082
www.blackheronpress.com

for Nguyên Phuong Thúy, Hà T. Khoa and Hà T. Duy
in memory of my father

ACKNOWLEDGMENTS

The author would like to acknowledge the following books as his research sources: *From the City Inside the Red River* by Nguyên Đình Hòa (MacFarland & Company, 1999); *From a Chinese City* by Gontran de Poncins (Doubleday & Company, 1957); *War and Peace in Hanoi and Tonkin* by Dr. Édouard Hocquard (White Lotus Press, 1999); *Around Tonkin and Siam* by Henri d'Orléans (White Lotus Press, 1999); *Black Flags in Vietnam* by Henry McAleavy (The Macmillan Company, 1968); *Black Opium* by Claude Farrère (And/Or Press, 1974); *East of Siam* by Harry A. Franck (The Century Company, 1926); *Little China* by Alan Houghton Brodrick (Oxford University Press, 1942); *Vietnam: Mission on the Grand Plateaus* by Dourisboure and Simonnet (Maryknoll Publications, 1967). The hymn on page 31 is from *At Even When the Sun Was Set* by Henry Twells, 1868. Last, the author would like to thank his brother, Hà T. Trí, for his spiritual support and encouragement.

Yes, I am no longer a man, no longer a man at all. But I have not yet become anything else.
—Claude Farrère

When the world is reduced to a single dark wood for our four eyes' astonishment — a beach for two faithful children, a musical house for one pure sympathy — I shall find you.
—Arthur Rimbaud

THE OLD ME

In my twilight years, my possessions are sparse.

Among a few things I keep, there are two items that have been with me for who knows how long. You see, like most Annamese I don't keep track of my age. In fact, a French priest I knew once remarked to me that most members of my race did not even know their own birthdays. Like being born into this world was enough of a burden, he said. But they are old, these articles, at least sixty years or so since I got them at sixteen.

One of them is a pocket watch. You open its cover and on the inside there's a woman's black-and-white picture. She has been dead for many years now, but it still stirs me to gaze at her. She looks fifteen or sixteen—I'm not good at guessing a person's age—and her black hair, parted sharply in the middle, coils in a long braid over her shoulder. I say my father was a lucky man, and I'm his fortunate son who has survived everyone in the family, including my angelic little brother. This watch belonged to a man who betrayed my father so he could step into the woman's life—my mother's. They were part of a gang of outlaws led by my father. All of them were beheaded except the traitor, who was rewarded handsomely and disappeared thereafter.

The other article is a human skull. It sits on my window ledge looking out from its empty eye sockets at birds, trees. Sometimes moths get into the eye cavities and flutter around until they give out and die. But there it sits on my window

ledge, aged in ivory yellow—the traitor's skull—and I bear
him no more hatred. I polish him now and then, for I know
his occult neatness. He used to arrange his slippers outside
his sleeping chamber, so precisely even that you could draw
two parallel lines on either side of them. Only then could he
sleep. His loveless, enigmatic life happened to cross mine.

HANOI, 1896. ON THE EXECUTION GROUND

A horde of people thronged the clearing, all hushed and bunched up.

The quiet made my stomach queasy. Lined across, the doomed men faced the crowd. My father was the last one on the far left, where a French priest stood leaning against an outcrop, alone in his black robe and black hat, like Death itself. Clad in coarse white cloth, the men crouched on their knees, their hands roped behind their backs at the wrists, each wearing a cangue.

Watching them, I felt humiliated for my father. Gritty man, if you knew him. Dark-skinned, high forehead. He wore his long black hair in a chignon just like an Annamese woman. His face was unshaved. He could grow a full beard in a few days—unlike most Annamese men, who had no facial hair or only a few whiskers over their lips like a sullen cat. Now he was down on his knees, cinched to a wooden stake. While his men all kept their heads low, he flexed his neck a few times and then gazed at the sky, bluest of blue.

Why didn't he look our way? Then I saw the mandarin slowly crawling out of his hammock. He now stood thin and hunched in his white turban while the guards moved the parasols directly over his head. But there was no sunlight, only a hazy glow through the gaps in the foliage. The old man scratched himself on the cheek with his talon-like fingernails as he stood like a geomancer about to determine an auspicious burial spot for those about to die. The spectators lowered their gaze. My father threw him a glance as if he were merely a bothersome sight.

Up high a parakeet croaked, then another. Beyond the death line in the long shadows, guards were peeling back the burlap covers of the coffins and now pushed them right up to the stakes and flipped open the lids. I felt damp under my arms and between my legs, and I could hear a churning in my stomach— it wasn't from hunger. A few heads turned our way—they looked at me standing next to my mother, who carried my little brother on her hip no more than twelve feet away from my father, who didn't even look at us but stared at something above the trees.

The guards unbuttoned the collar of each bandit's blouse and yanked it back to bare each man's torso and shoulders. Then they stepped back into the shade. The onlookers wearing hats took them off and clutched them in their hands. The priest, too, removed his and pressed it against his heart while his other hand held the black rosary. Then the executioner—Granduncle—was at the first man. If you ask me why the crowd was so large, you are about to know.

Granduncle bent and pulled the bandit's long hair over the top of his head. Then he spat the quid of his betel chew into his palm, daubed the nape of the man's neck with this red cud, and shoved it back into his mouth. The man turned up his face, and his glazed eyes looked into Granduncle's hard eyes, graphite black. What he saw was a wrinkled face, sinister-looking because of the pointed chin and the hooked nose. He dropped his head. Down the line his fellow men squirmed on their knees.

Granduncle barked out an order. The man thrust out his neck and chest and opened both knees. Granduncle rolled up his white trousers past his knees, walked back two steps on an angle, and gripped his saber against his chest with both hands. The parakeets had gone silent. In that eerie quiet the mandarin's order rang out abruptly: *Chém!*

The slashing saber shot a white gleam, and the bandit's head fell like a coconut, rolled once on the ground, and rested with its eyes open skyward. The neck gaped, spewing blood. The onlookers cringed and many hid their faces behind their huge hats as the blood darkened the ground quickly. One guard ran up, grabbed the severed head by its ponytail, and dropped it inside a rattan basket. The priest muttered a prayer, clutching his rosary. My throat was dry.

Suddenly the bandit next to the dead man broke down crying. He turned his face toward Granduncle and then toward the mandarin who stood placidly fingering his gray whiskers. "Mercy...Your Highness!" he stuttered. "I have a wife and three children...not a bad person...never killed no one...swear to Heaven...Your Highness...look down, I beg you...have a heart... I'm forever in debt of your compassion." Someone cried in the crowd. Then the sounds of sobbing made me clench my jaws. I can tell you this: It would kill me if my father went to pieces like that man.

My father shouted across, "Stop crying, idiot!"

But the man didn't stop and now turned his face skyward pleading with Heaven and all the buddhas and bodhisattvas. Two guards rushed up, seized him by the head. One told him if he did not keep still, it would be messy when the blade fell on his neck. They restrained him as Granduncle quickly marked the spot with his quid of betel chew, then they cleared out. Already the man had wet his pants, and his crotch went dark. His knees were spread out, his neck jutted, his whole body shook because of his sobbing.

The priest closed his eyes at the muffled sounds of women's crying. The mandarin's shrill voice rose, and I saw the saber swing. The head rolled on the ground, the body jerked sharply forward as if following the part just taken away from it. My stomach sucked in.

While his men cast a half glance toward the lopped head, my father kept his eyes on the ground. His face was stony. I'm sure he knew his end was near. I'm sure he heard the sniffing and sobbing all around him. But did he fear death?

In the heat I could smell the sweet ferns. I heard the mandarin again and again and I closed my eyes. But something told me not to.

I opened my eyes just as Granduncle stepped up to the last man on the row—my father. I observed my father's calmness as his uncle went about the preparation routine. Suddenly my knees knocked. Years later, I recalled the French priest's words on men's weak will. He said God created man with flesh imbued with weaknesses they must overcome. In moments like this the emotions they showed would not belie their nature.

Deftly Granduncle swept up my father's hair to expose the back of his neck, and my father took a deep breath and strained his neck forward so his uncle could mark the spot where the saber would fall. As Granduncle walked back, my father puffed out his chest, opened his knees wide in a V. Their casualness has stayed with me to this day. Like everyone wanted to see men revolt—in tears or violence—against Death. How did Granduncle feel?

I shut my eyes. Unless you could feel the hollowness in my chest, you would never know how dead I felt that day. Something else you should know: I wasn't close to my father before he died, and his impending end, certainly gruesome, didn't bring me any closer to him. Eyes closed, I saw in my mind my mother, small and insignificant, standing several feet away from my father in her faded brown tunic, her head wrapped in a black turban, hugging my little brother whom she carried on her hip. The boy's cheek was pressed against her shoulder while he slept. The older boy—me—stood barefoot, bareheaded in his white blouse, patched here and there with brown cloths.

I opened my eyes, saw Granduncle step back. Just then my father flicked his gaze toward us as Granduncle swung his saber. An arc sparkled. Without a sound the head fell. I shrank back, seized by the sight of blood jetting like a spigot, my fists clenched so hard my knuckles hurt. In the stifling quiet Granduncle wiped the saber's blade against a white cloth hung from his belt, turned, and walked away into the gloom of shadows where soldiers stood holding spears, all standing in a daze like the rest of the crowd.

The priest remained by the outcrop while the soldiers deposited headless bodies into open coffins, except my father's, which my mother placed in one of the caskets with the help of others. The heads, as we found out, would be hung at the entrance of Chung, the village my father's gang robbed and partially burned.

When the soldiers headed back out, the parasols were at the front, the mandarin ensconced in the hammock. He was smoking a pipe and its strong smell stayed in the air after he had passed, trailed by soldiers who bore the coffins. The crowd gathered. Already flies came and touched down on the wet blood puddles. A column of huge black ants also gathered, perhaps for the sugar in the blood that had begun to dry.

Soon the crowd made its way out with several people carrying the coffin for my mother. We walked slowly, muted, in
black and brown, mostly brown, the color of our blouses,
like tribespeople on their way to a burial ground.

THE PLAGUE

Sometimes I wonder what it feels like being a white man who went to the execution ground and witnessed a decapitation—Annamese style. It had been many years now since we knew each other—this French priest by the name of Jules Danton and I—and even after he told me what he felt in his heart that day from watching such a lurid spectacle, I still ask myself what tempted him. Surely, I wish we could have traded places that afternoon so he could have lived my abhorrence, while I took his place by the outcrop and watched one head lopped after another.

One thing you should know about Danton: He was no ordinary priest. It wasn't because he didn't wear a long beard like all the missionaries, a choice that scared our people witless. It was his smarts. Of a few good things about him, I must say his knack for our mother tongue impressed me most. He had trained his tongue to the six tones of our singsong language. He had the patience to observe, the tenacity to succeed.

The death of my father left my mother in shock. She buried his headless body in the back of our hut and prayed for his soul not to be sent to Hell because the body was missing its holy head. I told her I'd bring back his head and make his body whole again. Hearing that, she just rubbed my head, as if I was full of nonsense.

A fortnight after the decapitation, Danton saw my father's head when he rode out on a black mule through the entrance of the Catholic village of Chung. He had visited with the victims who took refuge in the communal house while their burned dwellings, numbered in the fifties, were being re-erected and thatched over.

He could not tell which one was my father's as he passed under the banyan tree. Those were the same heads he saw in the rattan baskets, but now they had no eyes, only black sockets with grubs crawling in them. He spotted a hole bored under each jaw, and a rod was pierced through it to the top of the skull and into a limb. The heads looked out in different directions, and in the early morning light they bore a pinched look neither of hurt nor sorrow.

I hung onto his words, trying to imagine my father's face in vain. Until Danton concluded with a remark that brought me sympathy for my father, I had felt only anger. He said when he looked back at the heads curtained by the banyan's dangling aerial roots, he thought of God's way, of how things started and ended and progressed in between. Such was man's journey. Now when I remember his words I must say that of all the passersby, he was perhaps the only one who spared one brief moment to send his sympathy to the devils.

That day we met for the first time. Let me correct myself—he saw me and my family for the first time while he was on his way to the village of Ninh, another remote Catholic village in his parish a day on foot from Hanoi.

Ahead of him trotted his guide.

Danton heeled the mule. The animal's ribs were fishbone sharp, its hairless back covered with a piece of brown cloth, and its hide smelled sour. The guide was a young man, dressed in a maroon blouse heavily faded from sun and sweat. Slung across his shoulder were a short bamboo tube for his drinking water and his machete held inside a cowhide sheath. He ran barefoot, girded by a wide cloth belt, in which he carried his supplies. The only time he'd slow down was to fetch a cud of betel chew and feed it into his mouth.

He was one of Danton's many humble servants who had faith in him. He had acted as their confidant. He told me he lost count of how many marriages he had blessed, how many squabbles he had judged, how many times he had become the peacemaker between litigants.

But a boost of energy shot up in him just to think of their allegiance.

The sun was hot. Danton began to sweat under his cotton blouse and the mule's steaming flanks toasted his legs. Lack of sleep made his eyes water. He pulled the brim of his hat over his eyes. A rare breeze breathed on his back, bringing a smell of ordure from the mule's hindquarters.

At noon they made their way out of the forest, and before them lay a flat countryside trembling white in the heat. A low line of greenery bordered the land—another village. After harvest the fields lay yellowed with stubs, and over them ghosted the heat haze, staying with the men as they trod single file on an earthen dike barely wide enough for the mule. A miserable odor like iron baked in mud seeped into Danton's nostrils. He had been to the village of Ninh a long time before, but the land here looked unfamiliar. He called out to the man, "Where are we?"

"Lau village."

Ah. He felt disappointed. But Lau village? They told him of a squabble between the two villages—Chung and Lau. The district chief settled the case in favor of Chung village, perhaps out of their mutual affinity for Catholicism. Danton pondered the bandits' revenge that eventually led them to self-destruction.

Suddenly he thought of the outlaw leader's family who lived in that village while his head was hung on a banyan half a day from here. He saw them on the execution ground in Hanoi when someone whispered and pointed toward a woman who carried a little boy on her hip, and next to her stood an older boy of perhaps fifteen. He didn't see the woman's face clearly because of her large turban, only the boy's. His hair was cropped closed to his head, unlike most children his age, with a tuft of hair falling over their brows. His eyes were very black. There was a paleness about him, yet he looked ravishing as he stood barefoot, bareheaded, gazing at his father, waiting.

Now ahead the guide was down on his haunches by a pool, trying to grab a lily pad. He folded it at the edge and tucked its stem into the back of his turban and its tip into the front. He looked comical with this contraption on his head. As Danton rode up on the mule, the man plucked another leaf and offered it to him.

"Put this under your hat, Father," he said. "Will cool you off."

"Thank you."

The thick leaf seemed to ward off the heat and brought him freshness.

They entered the village on a narrow road, hearing the mule's hoofs clack away on the crudely cut blue stones, stepping over gaps filled with clods of dirt and grass. It was a short paved road going past a sorry-looking shrine with its missing tubular tiles. Shaded by a banyan, it stood doorless, like a dark mistrustful eye watching the men.

Danton dismounted and led the mule by the bridle. He

did not want someone to see him ride past the shrine, for such disrespect to the village shrine would make him bad company. After the broken paved road ended, there was yellow dirt narrowed to what looked like a path, hemmed in by tough, dried grass. A feeling of being watched alerted Danton.

There they were—the inhabitants. Squatting in the tall grass in that perpetual position, as if God gave them such uncommon suppleness of joints and limbs to sit for hours without tiring. Like apparitions materializing in ragged brown, they watched the strangers in silence.

He rode on, feeling their empty gaze on the back of his neck. Soon they came upon mud huts crouched under thickly thatched roofs, and the abodes shaped the path with their plots littered with broken vats and troughs. In the plots lay discolored wastes of fish guts and gooey rice. By a trough a naked boy sat holding a stick in his hand, fending off two deformed black pigs that nudged him repeatedly in the face with their noses. Behind a tree between two squalid-looking huts an old woman was squatting to relieve herself. Two scraggly dogs ready to claim her waste turned at the sight of Danton's mule and barked. The crone simply looked at them as if they were something out of a picture book. Her tranquility made Danton turn his head away.

An eerie feeling made him scan each hut again. Only a few had their narrow doors raised open with a wooden stick. The rest were shut. Outside each closed door dangled a pot of taro. Had it not been for its huge leaves, he wouldn't have noticed. Tense, he called out to his guide, "Did you see those taro plants?"

"Yup," the man said, not looking back.

"There's some kind of disease going on here."

"Yup. Better hurry through, Father."

They went round a hut, and the mule nearly rammed into a child playing by herself in a puddle of muddy water. The mule balked at the sight of three saddleback pigs running—*oink oink*—around the child. Where were the rest of the children? They always appeared when you least expected them. *Sir Father! Sir Father! Spare me one sapèque!* Half the time he gave in to their begging and dropped a zinc coin into the hands of those who were most persistent.

The huts leaned in toward the dirt path, so close he could see their mud walls laced with rotten, yellowed bamboo. The mule ambled through, twitching its ears to drive off the swarming flies, past each dwelling with its door closed. A taro pot dangled outside each door. One hut down the path had its door propped open. In the dark doorway stood a wizened woman carrying a child on her hip. Rheumy-eyed, she watched them while her toothless mouth masticated. Then she bared her dark gums and spat the chewed rice into her fingers. Like an automaton, the child opened her mouth to receive the fingers, the cud.

Danton halted in front of the hut and dismounted. While the mule shook its head in frenzy against buzzing black flies, he bowed to the old woman.

"*Chào cụ,*" he said.

She blinked. He saw her eyes shift, and then his guide's shadow fell upon his.

"What're you asking her, Father?" the man said, hand on his lily-pad hat.

The child stared curiously at his hat. The old woman stared too. Danton glanced at them, then at his guide, and then back at the old woman. "Madam, I'm looking for a family . . ."

"Father?" the man cut in.

"He was beheaded a fortnight ago," Danton said in an
even voice to the old woman. "I wish to see his family."

Already the old woman retreated into the dark interior of
her hut, and in that gloom the child's eyes gleamed, watching them. Danton stood, hands laced on his abdomen, waiting until he saw the woman turn and sink into the murkiness of her lair. The man spat. "You scared her, Father."

"How did I scare her?"

"That you might do something bad to that family."

He thought of the feud that led the bandits to their wicked ends. These people must have hated Chung village, its
Catholics. And he was a Catholic priest.

"I guess you're right," he said, and mounted the mule.

The young man walked at the mule's flank. "Why that
family, Father?"

Danton looked down. "Wouldn't you wish for God's
blessing if you were them?"

"They don't like Catholics."

"We haven't met them yet."

"But they don't like Catholics."

"Did you like Catholics before you were converted?"

"I had no squabbles with them. I was minding my own
business."

"You had no religion then?"

"I did, Father." The man swatted flies with his hands. "I
worship my ancestors."

"That's piety, not religion. You were brought into the light
of God because you discovered such a light within you."

"My light? Or His light?"

"There's no yours or His. Only one light. It's in each one
of us, coming from God. And it's always there—there when

you were born, and there when you die."

"It's always there? Hmm. Why didn't I see it before?"

"That is a great question."

The man suddenly laughed. His ringing laugh jolted the mule and made its ears jerk sharply. "You mean many people didn't see it before Lord Jesus came to die for them on the cross?"

"They carried the light in them without knowing it—until then."

The man peered up, shadowed eyes darting under his lily-pad hat. "I believe in Lord Jesus. But I believe in Him 'cause you didn't take my ancestor worship away. I mean my . . . my . . ."

"Your piety?"

"That thing."

"The love for one another all comes from that light. That is the reason why Catholicism allows you to keep your piousness toward your ancestors. Well, let's find that family."

Danton looked down at the young man and then up at a huge mud-caked buffalo rising from a pool's black water. The mule suddenly stopped, pitching him forward. The buffalo lumbered toward his side, swaying its giant scythelike horns. He could see its gleaming, pinched brown eyes, the wet nostrils snorting water, the dripping head. There was no place to hide. *Jump!* But his legs were lead heavy.

A shrill cry came from a nearby bush. The buffalo's head turned ponderously sideways just as his little master, a boy no older than ten, came running out of the bush. Danton sagged. They said these gentle beasts bore an occult animosity toward Caucasians, yet he had always doubted it. Then they said these beasts would come after white people because of their body odor. Now he watched the young man brush past the buffalo's murderous horns as its wet brown eyes gazed peacefully at him. Cattle drovers would tell you that these pachyderms reacted to odors. The little master and his Annamese kin had little body odor even when they sweated. He knew this about the Annamese.

The mule paid the buffalo no mind. On its back the boy sat crosslegged, hands on its withers, watching the strangers with his brown face full of sun. Wary, Danton eyed the monstrous horns. One false move from him or the mule could rouse the beast again.

He looked back and saw the boy calmly watching them from farther away. He pulled on the rope and turned the mule around. The buffalo was in its own world, grazing on a patch of withered grass. The mule joined it. They masticated wetly in unison. Danton pulled two zinc coins from the pocket of his trousers and held out his hand to the boy. "Take them," he said.

The boy took them and clenched his fist—they were his now, even if the priest changed his mind.

"Do you know the man who was decapitated, he and his friends—"Danton made a chopping sign with his hand against his neck "—a fortnight ago?"

The boy listened, taken by what he heard in his mother tongue from a beardless priest. He nodded. The priest said, "Can you take me to his family?"

The boy leaned forward and patted his buffalo on the head. "*Đi về*," he said.

Its mouth still cycling, the animal lumbered down the path, and Danton called out after the boy, "What happened to your village? The taro plants everywhere."

"Smallpox," the boy said, cocking back his head.

Danton's stomach turned. But he was vaccinated—like

all his parishioners—courtesy of the French authorities who sent French doctors and local practitioners every year to remote Christian villages to inoculate the Christian Annamese. What a pity, he thought with a twinge of guilt, to see villages like Lau falling victim to this scourge because they sat in backwaters. But the curse was not distance. It would have been different had a magnificent cross in these backward habitats been erected at their village entrance.

The boy led them on his buffalo. The man walked alongside the mule, spat, and, without looking up, said, "Why waste your time, Father?"

"God saved your soul once, did he not?" He looked away to avoid the man's scowl.

The mountain peaks toward the western horizon were sharp and ragged in palest blue. How different it was when one was free of preoccupation. Minutes before, the peaked range standing sentinel on the plain did not exist. What looked like black rocks submerged in the mud holes were heads of buffalos with nostrils above the water, blowing spray. Weedy graves stood among tall grass and shrubs, behind tattered huts. You could count the graves, one or sometimes two for every hut, and only then would you feel the presence of the dead as they walk among the living. Everything took on a hue of brown, as if colored by the sun. The birds, the fowls, and even the mongrels slinking away at the sight of the approaching men and beasts— they were all the cinnamon color of the dwellers' garbs.

Then they saw a cluster of huts in a banana grove where the barren fields came up to the edge of the treeless trail to meet tall yellowed reeds. The buffalo boy pointed toward a hut that sat low against a banyan. It had five trunks and spread its dark foliage like a giant pavilion over the hut. A curtain of its aerial roots touched the ground, and others lay curled on the hut's sun-faded thatch roof.

"Is that their house?" Danton raised his voice, pointing at the hut.

The boy nodded and rode on. Danton got down from the mule and handed his guide the rope. The man motioned with his head toward the hut. "You see that, Father?"

There was a taro pot outside the hut.

"It's everywhere, isn't it?" Danton said to himself.

"You don't want to go in there, Father."

"I was vaccinated. Were you?"

"Makes no difference, Father."

"Why no difference?"

"They ain't no Catholics. And late as we are—"

"It won't be long—Catholics or no Catholics. We're all brothers and sisters."

"Then why not the whole wretched village, Father?"

The man's rude voice made Danton ponder the question. "If we had time," he said, his eyes fixed on the man's, "I'd like to bless every unfortunate soul, dead or half alive because of this plague. In there—" he looked toward the hut, and the man followed his gaze, "you have the darkest side of life into which Jesus once descended to spread his love. Wait here."

The footpath followed the cactus hedge to the hut's door. He rapped on the bamboo crosspiece and stood waiting under the taro pot. The sight of it was a sore thing. Year in, year out, the plague swept through Tonkin like a foul breath from Hell. They said this curse affected the eyes if it failed to claim the body. Look at those beggars that walk in a queue, holding on to one another by the rod. Each one of them is blind, except the one who leads them—he has only one eye.

Many of the dead were children, and many more children were orphans who wandered like stray dogs in the market-place, on the mandarin-traveled roads, begging for food. Some brought to his church were clothed in tatters, with vermin crawling in their hair and bodies light as paper. One could count their ribs. Their eyes smoldered, haunted like souls denied the right of living, yet turned away by Death.

The rattan door was raised. He stepped back, looked down, and saw the bare feet of a woman who heaved the door over her head. Her knee-length, cinnamon-colored blouse was wrapped loosely about her. He knew the color well—that of the native earth—this tobacco-juice color. He felt a breath of hot air on his face and took off his hat and held it against his chest. The lily pad fell to the ground. Her eyes blinked.

"*Chào cô*," he said, embarrassed.

"Hello, Father," she said gently, and put her hand on her chest, which was covered by a white diamond-shaped hal-ter tied with cross-strings in the back.

"I'm sorry," he said, his throat suddenly dry. "I'm pass-ing through, but—"

"Are you thirsty, Father?"

"Yes, but I did not come for water. Thank you for asking."

"Are you lost?" Her head tilted to one side, and the braid of her hair, long and black and coiled once round her head, fell across her hip. "Where do you come from?"

She could have been a pious Catholic, and he could have been visiting with one of his parishioners. "No," he said, putting his hat back on, "I'm not lost. Thank God." Then he stepped up and lifted the bamboo door for her. She smiled thinly. Her teeth weren't lacquered black like those of most Tonkinese women.

"Are you here to teach the Gospel?" she said.

He didn't know how to say it. The woman who stood on the execution ground carrying her child on her hip, with her older boy standing at her elbow—the sight had left him with a wretched feeling that had been with him ever since. Now she stood in front of him in her earth-brown blouse, and loose, thin, black knee-length pantaloons held up by a cloth belt.

"I wish I could preach Gospel at this moment," he said, remembering her question. "I come from Hanoi. It was there, in fact, on the execution ground that I saw you."

Her eyes narrowed, she nodded. He said quickly, "How are your children? I saw the taro pot here—and everywhere."

"They're sick, Father." Her gaze fell.

"Can I see them?"

She lifted her face to him. Almond eyes the color of her blouse. She must be no older than twenty-five.

"The plague is contagious, Father."

"I'm aware of that," he said, still holding up the bamboo door above their heads. "I've been vaccinated. But I appreciate your concern."

She found a wooden rod nearby and propped up the door with it. Inside, the floor was packed earth, and sunlight reached only the threshold, casting a glimmer in the gloom. He stood hunched under the low roof. His nose picked up a stench and he shivered. The children lay side by side on two narrow cots tucked in a corner. She knelt there in the half-light, hands on the bamboo edging. He stood beside her, absorbing the sight of the victims. The blankets, which seemed like cloth covers, were pushed aside and holed as if gnawed by rats. There the naked bodies were in full eruption, covered with red pustules, the faces, too, peppered with dark red dots. The eyes were shut, the lips blistered. The smell of delirium and death filled the hovel.

There was a pan at the foot of a cot. She sloshed a piece of cloth in the liquid it contained and wiped each child from the neck down. An ammoniac odor seized him.

"What is that?" he asked.

"Urine, Father." She hung the cloth on the pan's rim.

He tried to speak, but words did not come. The smell became stronger. It did not come from the bodies but wafted up from under the bamboo cots.

He bent and looked.

Something dark and long and sleek lay under the cots. He moved beside her and peered under. The stench sent him reeling. God. He felt like retching and quickly touched the cross on his chest.

"What is that thing?" he asked, as he tried to collect himself.

"Eel." She canted her face at him.

"Live?"

"No. It has to be dead and let rot."

"What in the name of God—"

"Don't you know that it draws out the smallpox poison?"

This hushed him momentarily. What the children had needed was vaccine, but they were beyond that now. Resigned, he dropped his voice. "Let me pray for them."

She inched away on her knees and let him do what was entrusted to him by his God. He sank slowly to his knees. The air stirred. Sweat and sun. The familiar odor of men who had been out in the heat. He removed his hat and placed it on the earthen floor. A lock of straw-yellow hair slipped

onto his brow as he bowed his head. The air hung thinly in
the hut, permeated with the fetor of decomposed eel. He
seemed not to breathe while he held the gold-colored cross
in his hand against his chest, shoulders shaking. She heard
his words, the sound, in her native tongue:

*O Savior Christ, our woes dispel; for some are sick and some are sad;
and some have never loved Thee well, and some have lost the love they
had.*

*And none, O Lord, have perfect rest, for none are wholly free from
sin; and they who fain would serve Thee best are conscious most of wrong
within.*

*Thy touch has still its ancient pow'r; no word from Thee can fruitless
fall; hear, in this solemn evening hour, and in Thy mercy heal us all.*

Then he kissed the cross. "Amen." The way he spoke the
words soothed her. They sounded grave, but she understood them. He kept his head down and his eyes closed like
people who prayed and wished to be in communion with
a God she knew nothing about. The only Godlike presence
she knew intimately sat on a crate, covered in white clothing. It contained names on narrow tablets of teak, black
brushstrokes written in Chinese by the village schoolteacher
as a favor—the names of her deceased parents and, last, the
name of her recently deceased husband.

She too closed her eyes, taking in the stranger's solemn
figure, the glistening pale yellow stubble that lined the side
of his face. The faces of those who passed away. She never
dreamed of them. Even when she asked. *Hear my cries?* Always a void. Can the dead speak? Can they help? *I asked. I
prayed.* The last time she asked for help she returned home
with a headless body. Halfway home the coffin leaked blood
and did not stop, even after she had prayed in delirium. *If*

you are still angry, please hear my prayer and go away in peace.
Let me help. Hear me for the sake of the children. But blood kept
seeping, dotting the trail, and everyone wondered where all
the blood came from.

When she buried him in the back of their hut, under the
five-trunk banyan, she lit three sticks of incense and murmured to him, *Please do not forget the children, and be there for*
them not with wrath in your heart. She let the incense sticks
burn in a bowl filled with rice grains. *As they smolder may you*
not smolder in hatred. May the dead forgive the traitor and sleep
the eternal sleep in the cooing of mourning doves.

The priest turned to her and said, "What about you,
Madam? Have you been vaccinated?"

She shook her head.

"May God bless this house." He made the sign of the
cross with his left hand. "May nothing more than what has
just been be taken away."

He rose while she remained kneeling. The stench rose
with him. Sweat beaded on his brow, not from the heat but
from his effort to hold down his retching. The dwelling was
windowless. The air that one breathes must be refreshed,
but what could he do? Raise the wretched door? Incur the
village's wrath?

He extended his hands, and she let him pull her up to
her feet. Soft hands, long, tapered fingers. "I'm set to leave,
Madam," he said, letting go of her hands.

"You're a good-hearted man, Father." She hadn't seen
anyone for days, since the onset of the plague. *You are out-*
cast until you beat back this evil curse.

"Only because I'm more fortunate than you and your
children." He put his hat back on. "But God moves us
around in a mysterious way. I think he does that to spread

his light to every corner of this earth. Who are we but his lantern carriers?"

Outside on the footpath, his skin tingled in the stifling heat. He remembered his lily pad and turned back. The door had been lowered. A few feet from it he found the leaf, put it on under his hat, and stood briefly under the taro pot. He touched it, leaving it dangling behind him

THE LIVING AND THE DEAD

The frantic gongs woke Danton, who was sleeping in his curtained hammock. He cringed. Bandits? Through the tulle netting, the porters' torches spurted in blue, and red sparks swirled in the wind. Danton pushed aside the netting. Ghostlike figures hunched in their palm-leaf raincoats. A drizzle was falling in the night. "Something wrong?" he shouted to the pair out front.

One man tipped his head back and said, "*Ông Cop,* Father."

Jolted, Danton stared into darkness. Lord Tiger. "You saw him?" he said. "Where?"

"He was there, Father." The man gestured wildly toward the dense bushes where the forest thinned into tangled undergrowth.

"Saw his eyes, Father," the other man said. "Green fire. Was him all right."

The wind brought him a rancid burning brimstone, wet specks from the sky that burst on his skin. He could hear the porters talking to the man on the watchtower inside the stockade. This must be the village of Ninh, the closest Catholic village to Chung. These men from Chung village would return home once they were relieved at this village. They would take turns relaying him from one village to the next until he was safely home.

The gate opened to let them in, and the porters carried him into the communal house where they waited for relief from the next shift. He sat on a wooden bench in front of a huge drum hung from the ceiling beam with corded ropes. Dawn was coming. Just as he rested his head against the leather drumhead, the men showed up, five of them, bareheaded, without raincoats. The rain had stopped.

Sleep. The freshness of dawn. But he found it harder to sleep when the sun was up and shining brightly across the land, over sunburnt fields lumpy with mud graves and brown foothills bald and stepped like giant altars. He recognized the landscape. The bamboo grove tall and straight like ancient pillars of polished gold. The forest surrounding harvested rice fields. Glimmers of sunlight on scummy ponds. Anchored rafts like mammoth water spiders God made in time immemorial. He had ridden the mule through this land the day before, and now he saw the graves again, weeded humps behind the mud huts, eclipsed by cactus hedges, crouched behind wild pineapple shrubs. When they came upon the path, he saw apertures in the bamboo hedges where humans could crawl through, entering or exiting, like animals.

A procession of humans in brown garb came toward them. When God created a habitat, he gave every living creature the ability to adapt. Look at the brown color of every inhabitant's blouse. The color that came from the dye of the brown tubers. The color of the land must have been dyed into their souls before they were even born. One must blend with the earth, the soil that gives one crops each year.

The porters edged away from the trail to let the procession through. Out of the hammock now, Danton stood with them, watching the cortège go by. Under the shade of two giant umbrellas, a bier was hoisted on the men's shoulders. On it sat a large tray of food—white rice, golden roasted chickens, clay vessels of rice liquor.

He turned to one of the porters who was scratching his lower leg. "What is it? Where are they going?"

"They have smallpox here in this village."

"I know that. I saw the taro pots."

"Oh, you saw, Father?"

"Yesterday when I passed through here."

"Them people there, they're heading to the shrine."

Many dwellers must have died from the plague, he thought. But this was no funeral procession. "To the shrine," he said reflectively. Perhaps God would eventually look down on them.

"All those foodstuffs are for the genie." The porter slapped his leg and missed a fly that had crawled on his scratches.

"The village genie?"

"Yeah. Father, you know what'll happen if the plague goes away?"

"What if it does?

"The canton chief will hear it, the district chief, the prefecture chief, the governor. All of them, Father. Then the emperor. The genie will get promotion from the emperor. Hehe."

Danton chuckled. "He'll get elevated in some kind of spiritual hierarchy?"

"Well, if the plague goes away."

"And if it does not?"

"He'll get stripped of his rank. And gets whipped. Hehe."

"What in the name of God does that mean?"

"You never saw him? His statue, I mean. Yeah, they'll put chains around him, whip him. After the whipping they dump him into the river."

"So this procession'd better turn out well."

"Oh, always does, Father. Them people, they can't wait to get through the ceremony. To chomp on those dishes in the blink of an eye."

Danton tried to smile. He looked off toward the pond but the water buffalo wasn't there. The procession had gone farther up the trail toward the village entrance. He remembered the decrepit shrine where the road was paved with cut blue-gray stones. In a short time the place would be clouded with incense smoke, and people would prostrate themselves, seeking mercy and protection from their village genie. Like the tribespeople, they worship both evil genies and saintly genies. There was a commotion at the end of the rite. The flurry of chopsticks, the noisy smacking of mouths. Brown-garbed gourmands sat on their haunches, perched on their heels like a strange breed of bipeds born to squat, saving the bench for the elderly—those in long black tunics and turbans. But would the plague go away? How many had died in those huts with a warning taro pot in front? How many more would die if they had to drown their genie?

When the trail was empty, the porters shouldered the hammock and waited. The priest put on his round black hat, coughed into his clenched fist, and said to them, "I need to visit with someone. Take me there, please."

When she raised the rattan door, she looked very pale. Sunlight barely reached the door, much less the threshold, for it was early morning. But he noticed her chapped lips and her swollen eyes. The plague must have claimed her as well, he thought, pained. The moment he entered the dim hut he shivered. That evil stench still hung in the air. A sour smell of rice rose from a corner as they moved past. A clay pot overturned, a ceramic bowl broken. The glint of its shards caught his eyes.

"How are you?" he said, the moment she turned around. "How are the children?"

She glanced sideways at the two cots in the corner where the victims had lain side by side, convulsed with fevers, on the day he came. He cringed. The urine. The eel. One cot was empty. On the other cot, the younger boy lay naked without the cloth cover. There was something out of order there. He could feel it in his stomach. *Where's the older boy?*

"The boys—" he said, nodding toward the cots.

She shook her head. Her resigned look impelled him to step toward the little boy. A warm liquid wet his hands as he knelt down, touching the cot. The boy's urine dripped through the rattan mat, beading along the edge of the frame. His bony body had no life in it, one arm draped over the joined edges of the cots, the other bent under his buttocks where clumps of greenish dark matter clung to his thighs. *Dear God, when we are about to breathe our last, we defecate like animals.* He gripped the cross when her shadow fell on the cot. What else did she not see? This body she had given birth to, nursed, raised. It was punctured with red spots like lance cuts, many had ruptured yellow pus. *Almighty Lord, help me bless this child before he crosses over.*

He strained his neck so his ear was closer to the boy's nose. The odor of the child's shallow breathing gave him gooseflesh. He held his breath and then felt ashamed of his rejection. *Create in me a clean heart, O God.* Beside him, the woman knelt, taking the boy's feet in her hands and rubbing them as if to warm him, though his skin had gone cold like a fish's.

She watched him baptize the child with the water from his drinking bottle. The steady look in her eyes as he put the bottle back in his cloth bag made him ache with pity. No, he was not about to revive the boy with the magic water. Those eyes would never open again to see his mother, the world. "Hold this, little one," he muttered, pressing the boy's hand around his cross. Then he clasped his hands around the boy's, lowered his head, and prayed:

Hail Mary, full of grace;

The Lord is with thee:

Pray for us sinners, now and at the hour

of our death. Amen.

The little hand felt cold. He put his finger by the boy's nostrils and knew Death had just slunk away. When he turned to her she was still holding the boy's feet in her hands. He unclasped the little hand from the cross and gently rested it on the boy's chest, then lifted his body, unbent his other arm, and placed the hand on top of the other. He rose to his feet and said to her, "I can help wash him, and then you can dress him." He paused. She seemed oblivious to his words, and he understood. In moments like this, one must be left alone. The world shrinks to a pinhead, throbs with agony that cannot be shared with anyone. Then, afraid he might lose his thought, he said, "My porters can dig the grave. You only need to tell them where."

He stood, head bent, waiting. A hiss came from the corner where shards of the broken bowl lay, and a hairy round shape materialized out of the dimness. A rat crept closer to the shards and sniffed at the white rice grains that clung to them. The tainted air they shared, humans and rodents, the putrefaction that permeated the dwelling. If this was the threshold to Hell, then he needed no angels or God. *Sing,*

winged angels. Bathe in the pure light of love impregnable by pes-
tilent death.

She pushed herself up and said in a hushed voice, "I can
wash him, Father. You've done enough. I'm thankful."

There was a tremor in her voice, as if her pain was penned
deep in her guts. But wherever it was trapped, it shook free
in those almond eyes now filmed with tears.

"That is fine," he said. "What about a grave for him?"

"If you can help me with that." She leaned her head back.
"In the rear, next to his father's."

He opened his hand, looked at his cross. There was yellow pus on it. What he had wanted to ask her came back to
him. "Where's your older boy?"

Now her face became contorted with pain. "He went
mad," she said.

"Mad? What on earth do you mean?"

"Mad, Father. By fever. He crashed around, knocked
things over. Tore up his clothes. He ran outside, climbed up
the banyan, hung his clothes on their limbs . . ."

That made him glance toward the back of the hut, as if
the boy was still perched on the tree. She wiped the wetness
from under her nose with her fingertip. "He ran off," she
said. "I couldn't catch him."

"Mother God." He shook his head in dismay.

Her gaze fell. In silence they seemed to share a wordless
prayer.

"You know where he ran to?" he said.

"To the forest." Her chest heaved.

"When?"

"At dawn." She gulped. "Some of them never came
back."

"Them? Who?"

"Sick children. They jumped into creeks. The evil fever made them. And drowned."

His hands clenched.

"Some flowed into the river, all bloated," she said in an even voice. "Some got eaten by wild animals—their corpses, that is. What's left, we bury."

He nodded. Bones, skulls, a half-chewed leg. "Madam," he said.

"I've sent for their father's uncle. Maybe he could find him."

"Their father's uncle?" He frowned. "The executioner?"

She lifted her face at him. "Yes. You know him?"

"I went to the execution ground that day."

"Yes."

"How soon can he get here?" he asked, but then realized that she would have no way of knowing.

"A day."

"It'd be too late." Just as she looked up into his eyes, he said firmly, "I'll go find him."

"Father." Her calm eyes absorbed him.

"I have five men. Two can help dig the grave. The rest go with me."

"Father," she said.

"What do you bury the boy in?"

"I have the mat."

They looked down at the soiled mat. *It's better than nothing.*

THE YELLOW MONKEY

I ran splashing into a brook.

My body was singed with a wicked flame under my red-pimpled skin. My armpits, my neck breathed fire. I didn't care how deep the brook was. The water was swift. It rose quickly to my shoulders, then to my neck. I tiptoed, and then the pebbled floor was gone under me. The water got into my mouth and I gagged and blew. A smeary sky in blue-gray. Shaggy underbrush in patina green. Wet pins exploded inside my nose, my skull. Going. Going. Then suddenly my foot caught on something. I grabbed wildly with my hands, and then found a tree root.

The bank was steep. I was a salamander, half naked, creeping on the clay soil, seizing knotty vines that bulged across the incline. The dark odor of sundered organics. Lying flat on the ridge of the bank, I felt unusually warm, and then a suffocating heat hazed my eyes.

A dark, windowless hovel. A huge rat sat on its hind legs by the cot, cupping a tiny bowl of rice in its forefeet. It was trying to suck wet rice from the bowl but its snout was too big. On my belly perched a spider burying its head into a taut pimple. Sucking, sucking. That blood-red thing zigzagged across my abdomen and slowly grew to the size of a rice ball. It walked up my chest, hopped onto my chin, and sat down on my cheek. It had eight eyes in triple rows, gleaming. The two pincer-like fangs dug into my flesh. My cheek was aflame.

I opened my eyes. The sun was directly above my head.

Downstream, the brook frothed around odd-shaped twigs swirling like mindless things with nowhere to go. I plodded barefoot along the brook. A sharp pain stung my foot. I was walking on an ant trail. Hopping, I snatched a fly-sized red ant from the top of my foot and tore its body from my skin, leaving its mandibles in my flesh.

Just as I rounded the bend, a yellow monkey appeared before me. It looked human. The monkey stared, round-eyed, curious. Then it clapped its hands, grinned, and leaped into the dense vegetation that cloaked the bank.

At the mouth of the brook, where it emptied into a river, a felled tree trunk lay crosswise. Vaguely the compass in my brain stirred. I felt chills coming on. *Climb that tree.* My body shook. I slid down the slick bank and crawled on hands and knees until I reached the tree bridge. First I tried to tiptoe across, and my body shivered like a leaf and my knees knocked. Then I squatted, felt my blood cold as ice. I decided to lie down. Out on the river, waves glinted like fish scales, and farther down where its bed rose and the current was shallow, four silhouetted humans waded across, holding hands against the swift current. My teeth clattered. *Mother! Wrap me up. Who's standing by the cot? Dark, shapeless. Smells awful.*

The brook surged, frothing white. *Fall and you're gone.* I locked my arms around the trunk. My chin touched a fuzz of lime green moss growing out of the bark, and I smelled a spicy odor like beetles. Voices drifted upriver in choppy bits. I sensed that I was the prey they hunted. My body shook with chills, and in my delirium I was a king bark beetle watching a horde of females boring an egg chamber into a tree.

I woke to a glare in my eyes. The sun sat cockeyed and

the sky now hung with bean-curd clouds. I smelled rain in the wind. How long had I slept? When I looked down at the turgid brook, I wondered what had kept me from falling off the tree trunk. It took a while before I crawled my way onto the opposite bank. I stood among a habitat of scrub pines and oaks, the susurrus of the brook lulling my mind to quiescence, and in the brook a sky mirrored itself in fading blue.

I waited for the chills to come back. Nothing happened. I thought of home. The dark windowless hovel full of menacing shapeless shadows. Who did I see in my feverish eyes? Daddy? I wondered if my little brother saw that black thing, blackest of black. He would probably just stare at it. Sick as he was, he never screamed. He was so quiet that Mother had to check on him from time to time. *Sleeping angel.* That was what Mother called him. Everyone called him angelic baby. He looked like her, too. Mother kept warning me to set a good example. "You're the man of the house," she'd say. "Your daddy's never home. Whatever you do, your brother will follow you." Once she slapped me hard in the face when someone told her that I chopped a mongrel's head clean with Granduncle's saber. She didn't believe my story. "You lie like your daddy. Violence is in your blood." But the mutt had already been kicked in the head by a mule and was shaking its life out like an epileptic. It looked so loathsome, I killed it.

On old tree trunks I passed, moss was ribbed in glowing green. I felt as if I was being watched, and looked up. Three redheaded vultures were eyeing me, their naked necks sunk between their hunched shoulders. Little white warts stood on their bare heads. There must be carrion somewhere that attracted them. Their wretched look disgusted me. How could a bird look so ugly?

Walking, I thought of the yellow monkey. It looked so human, so cute. It would make a great pal for my little brother. That would be the first thing I told him.

But which way was home? I kept walking. Maybe something would tell me. Usually it was a clearing, or where trees were downed. The fallen trunks told of woodcutters' presence. I looked down to see where the path led. It must be a path, for it was bald, but it blended farther down with the moss-carpeted ground. My feet kicked up dried leaves and lumps of bark. I stopped. The path disappeared. A woodcutter once told me not lose sight of the trail when you are in the forest. If a trail is not used by humans, soon it would blend back with the forest floor. Someone must have been here. Like me. Under huge trees twining their gnarled roots, locking their branches so dense a felled tree was held up by a mesh of limbs.

I snapped twigs, crawling and burrowing my way through a passage opened in a cobweb of brambles. Red welts bled on my skin. I no longer heard the brook and felt weak from hunger. When I saw a footlog lying crosswise on a bed of bright green ferns I sat down. Between my legs crawled a sun-bleached slug squirming its way from left to right. *You must be lost too.* I rose, looking around. Just gray and brown and green things deader than dead. Boulders and rocks crusted with lichens. The wind felt dank. The sky, foretelling thunderstorms, was white like the skin of a fish's belly.

I plodded on. *No more chills, please!* My legs grew heavy when I came to a clump of briars. I looked at them dully and then covered my head with my arms and went through. Thorns pricked my flesh; I bit my lips. A wild pig darted in front of me. Then a snap. A spear shot through a bush, went through the pig's body, and knocked it over on its side. I dropped my arms and stood dead still. Boar traps. My eyes wide, I put one foot forward, then the other, looking down for a vine rope. *Trip over it and you die like that pig.*

A long time had passed when I came out of the grove of briars, limp and bleeding. My skin stung, my eyes teared up, I kept walking. Wings flapped overhead. The three vultures circled in midair, waiting.

Where's home? I heard my stomach growl. My body was soaked in sweat. There was a tree among tall timber and I thought I would climb it, the better to see my way over the surrounding brush. The sky sagged, as if being pulled down by the weight of the rain clouds. *Hear the winds?* The whole forest howled. My hair fluttered, my body dried instantly. Something was gouged out of my guts. With one foot on the tree trunk, both hands grabbing the branches, I put my weight on one leg to hoist myself up. Suddenly my body went cold, and I dropped in a heap.

When I came out of a mindless, dreamless, infinite vacuum, my limbs ached. I didn't know why I lay sprawled on the ground. Did I fall? I moved my arms. Stiff as a twig. My eyes clouded over. A bowl of smoking rice. *Go on home. Hurry before the storm.* Ten feet from me, the yellow monkey squatted on an uprooted tree, holding in its pink palms a pumpkin as big as its head. It grinned, scratching its cheek. I gawked. It rose suddenly to its feet, clapped its hands on its furry thighs, and hopped into the thicket.

I came to the uprooted tree and picked up the pumpkin. It was already cracked open and chewed around the edges, but the monkey hadn't nibbled the inside. I bit into the flesh and chewed hurriedly, hearing my teeth crunch the hard flesh. Then I sat down, face burrowed into the pulp, gnawing and sucking. Shadows gathered around me like a gigantic winged creature passing overhead. Strong winds kicked up dust and leaves, the air was dank on my back. When there was nothing left but the rind and seeds, I chewed all the seeds and threw the rind away. I felt the wind jerk it out of my hand as I stood licking my lips. *Where did that monkey go?*

A large raindrop pelted my face. Then more. Then sudden silence. Like the whole forest had gone dead. No chirping of birds, no sawing sounds of insects. A giant dark cloud stood directly above me. Night came before afternoon. I crouched under a tree, peeping at the sky, at the menacing cloud that was like some soot-black evil, and here came a whirlwind of dust. I curled up instantly, just as dirt and bits of leaves and twigs hit me. The forest groaned like it was hurt deeply. Winds hissed. They had teeth. *Run!* I wobbled to my feet and fell back against the tree. It was as if the winds wanted me nowhere but there. Trees tossed up their limbs, shaking like they were sick, and things broke and hurled around and crashed and snapped as rain fell, making a clattering noise as if falling on tin roofs. *Run!* I dashed out blindly and ran into the thickets where the monkey had gone. My feet caught on sprawling roots and I fell face down on the slick ground. I got up, ducking under boughs each time something crashed. Dark broken limbs tumbled around me. *Mother!* I crawled on the wet earth under a toppled tree and heard a thunderous noise just as a tree smashed down barely ten feet away. I saw the pale trunk where it snapped and then a white flash of lightning. Beyond the felled tree was a clearing and something shaped like a hut. I stared, waited. The sky flickered. *Quickly!* I ran, tripped, rose, hurled myself toward the hut, got in, and collapsed in a corner.

I wiped rainwater from my eyes and saw dark trees and the sky. Half the hut's roof was missing. In a corner that was still sheltered sat a pile of twigs, some still clad with leaves, and a tall stack of straw. I leaned my head on the bamboo frame, hearing rain pelt the thatched walls and water drip onto the dirt floor from above. Any place was better than being outside. The roaring winds whipped the trees and the trees writhed, bent, and snapped back. *Don't let this hut fall over*. I felt like crying, but terror numbed my skull. Then the chills came back.

I could feel them. The shaking of my limbs. The coldness under my skin. My teeth wouldn't stop chattering. I crawled across the clammy dirt floor and rested against the pile of dried wood. I doubled up, face buried between my knees, teeth clenched, but I kept shaking. I felt around and plucked all the leaves I could seize and shoved them into my mouth.

They came into the hut with drenched feet, stood panting in rain-soaked clothes that clung to their skin. The two dark figures were lit palely when the lightning flashed.

Through a gap in the straw stack where I lay curled in darkness, I thought they were woodcutters. But they carried no tools. The taller one wiped his face with the palm of his hand, took off his round hat, and squeezed water out. Next to him, the other fellow hunched up his shoulders, slipped out his sheathed saber, and leaned it against the wall. A blast of wind shook the hut, and in the thrashing of trees came a cracking of felled timber.

"When do you think this will end?" the taller man asked while wringing the front of his blouse.

"Not soon enough, Father," the shorter man said, peeping up at the leaden sky. "Will be dark in no time when this here's over."

"Your grandnephew will be gone by then, I'm afraid." The taller man shook his hat dry and worked it back into its original shape.

"He's done gone by now, Father."

Granduncle. So they came looking for me.

Perhaps Granduncle was right. I could have been dead by now. Much later, when I knew the priest, I was told that he and three men had gone into the forest and searched for me for a good part of that day before going back to our hut. Back to see my mother sitting under the shade of the banyan, tending the fresh grave in which my little brother was buried. The supreme resignation my mother felt when she saw them coming back, looking dejected. I wonder how the heart could harbor that much pain without a rift. Could it, unless one prayed? Maybe she did—to whom I do not know—because out of the waning day's sullen heat came Granduncle. He rode in on horseback, both man and animal dusty and spent after a day's ride.

Now the men looked around in the hut for a place to sit. Lethargy kept me from crawling out. The straw was warm. *Don't fall asleep*. Yet I felt a torpor deep in my bones that made me wish to be alone. Granduncle walked over to the pile of wood.

"Look'ere," he said. "Firewood."

"Must belong to some woodcutter."

"Mind if I make a fire, Father?"

"A fire?"

"A fire."

"Go ahead."

I was awed, hearing the priest speak in my mother tongue. If I had not seen his face, I would have believed I was hearing an Annamese. Granduncle fumbled in his cloth belt and came out with a round rock and some shreds of tree bark in his hand.

"Kinda wet," he said.

"Can you use the straw there?"

"Why not?"

Granduncle gathered some twigs and straw and I could feel the stack shake. The acrid straw smelled stronger when he pulled at it and then laid it in a corner. He knelt with his unsheathed saber in one hand and flint in the other. Danton squatted across from him. The saber was unweildy in Granduncle's grip, but he held it close to the side of his body, brought both hands down near the clump of straw, and whetted the saber's edge against the flint. The damp flint produced nothing. He struck again. There were sparks. Then he shielded the wind with his back and struck some more. The straw lit up and burned with a tiny blue flame, and he blew on it and set it down among the twigs. They watched the small fire glow. The twigs crackled and I smelled sap in the thin smoke. Strangely, I felt numbness ebb away in my head.

Granduncle stoked the fire with an armful of twigs. While shoving dried sticks into the fire, he peered at Danton, who was drying his hat over the heat.

"You want to sit, Father?"

"I'm sitting."

"You want a straw seat?"

"Much obliged. Make one for yourself too."

While Granduncle pulled straw, Danton reshaped the brim of his hat and tried it on. "What's your name?"

Granduncle walked back, holding a load of straw. Danton rose. "They call me Đôi Chém," Granduncle said, patting down the straw.

"Is that your name?"

"No. Name is Sang."

The man's sobriquet must have puzzled Danton for all of
a second. "So you're a beheading sergeant?"

"That's me."

Danton nudged a flaming stick back into the pile with
his foot. Then he sat down on the crude straw cushion and
watched the old sergeant rip another bundle of straw from
the stack that covered me. There he stood with an armful of
it half covering his face. He just looked down at the stack.
"You ain't got no place to sleep but here?" he said.

"What?" Danton raised his voice.

Granduncle dropped the bundle. "You little devil," he
said, grabbing my arm.

Danton stood behind him, staring, and laughed as I
squirmed. The way my eyes blinked and opened slowly, one
eye and then the other, like the eyes of roosting fowls, must
have amused him. Granduncle's hand reached for my jaw.

"Say, what's wrong? Your face don't look right, or me
seeing things?"

"He has something in his mouth, Sergeant," Danton
said.

Granduncle opened his own mouth and I did the same.

"What have you got in there?" he said. "Spit'em out!"

What came out of my mouth were chewed leaves.

"You sick or something?" Granduncle said, loud. "Only
dogs chew on these when they're sick."

"He's sick, sergeant," Danton said, studying my condition. "You should thank God that he's still alive."

"Yeah, Father. I know he's sick. Him eating leaves, that's what I mean."

I tried to sit up on my arm. Danton stared at the red dots on my body, my face—they had ruptured—but only the gashes looked fresh.

"Bless him," Danton said to Granduncle. "He's now out of smallpox danger. See if he still has fever."

I looked him in the face. Then I turned to Granduncle. "Granduncle, he speaks our tongue."

"Yeah," Granduncle said. "How 'bout the fever?"

"Just cold."

"Chills?" Danton asked. "How often?"

"They don't come often anymore."

"That's good," Danton said, nodding. He mumbled something to Granduncle about the pockmarks on my cheeks, which I'd have with me for the rest of my life.

An eerie feeling kept me silent momentarily. Would my little brother have permanent scars on his face, too?

Danton stepped back to the fire and sat down. "Come sit here and keep yourself warm," he said to me. "What happened to your shirt?"

"I got none," I said.

He and Granduncle lugged the whole bale of straw toward the fire and set it as a screen behind them. The fire suddenly burned brighter.

Granduncle looked at me. "You warm now?"

I nodded.

"Gonna dry this shirt here," he said, taking off his blouse, which was the color of tobacco juice. "You'll put it on when we set out for home."

Brooding, I watched the fire. I wanted to go home. The fire popped now and then, shooting sparks in our faces.

Danton leaned back, but I did not flinch, as if something belonging to me were lost among the embers. All I felt was a hollowness inside myself.

"What's your name?" Danton asked me.

"Tài."

Granduncle was holding his blouse over the fire, and each time he turned it, warm air breathed on my face.

"How old are you, Tài?" Danton said.

I regarded him out of one squinted eye. "Sixteen, I think."

"You think?" Danton grinned. "Is he sixteen, Sergeant?"

Granduncle shrugged. "How'd I know? Ain't keep no count even of my own age."

Danton looked across at Granduncle's thin torso and sinewy copper-brown arms. "Say," he said to Granduncle, "how long have you been in the service?"

Granduncle shook his blouse a few times. "Don't remember, Father. But long."

"Before the French came?"

"That's right."

"So you've been a soldier most of your life. . . ."

"That's right."

The howling wind cut through the bale of straw that served as a screen, and raindrops hissed against the fire. In our small quarters the straw smelled warm and thick, like a sunburned pasture.

"What made you take up the saber as a trade?" Danton asked Granduncle.

"'Cause I was good with em things even when I was just a little boy."

"Have you been busy with such a trade?"

He could have asked *How many heads have you chopped?*

but I guess, as a priest, he must be tactful.

"Pretty much." Granduncle bent, fanning the fire with his blouse, which he held by its shoulders. His sharp cheek-bones and receding chin had a simian look in the shifting shadows the fire made. Certainly he had nothing in common with my father as far as looks go.

"What kinds of criminals?"

"All kinds, Father." Granduncle blew his nose into the fire. "Bandits, mostly. Wartime breeds all kinds of bad seeds, ain't it? How long since you came here?"

"Five years and a few months."

"Been bad ways back. Very bad during those years with the Chinese Black Flags and Yellow Flags. You ever been up on em rivers? Clear River and Red River?"

"Both."

"Well, in those days you're gonna get picked clean by em Chinese pirates. I'm sure you know that. Em bastards bumped you with tax money so bad they ruined all the river trades. Once you get picked clean and you can't do your trade no more, what'd you do? Become a bandit is what you'd do."

"And the government? Didn't they do anything to help?"

"Which? Yours or mine? Oh, none could do nary a thing to em bandits. Our government even whipped up those bandits' greed to go loot rich provinces under your government's stronghold. Just to spite em. Even paid em Black Flags to take up arms against your government."

"I heard."

"So the country was full of robbers, bandits, pirates. Like vermin."

"Lots of executions, I imagine, if you go by the law."

"You heard of em execution schools, did you, Father?"

"Where they train people like you to become skilled executioners?"

"Skilled or no skilled—there weren't even enough of em is what I meant to tell you." Granduncle shook his blouse, eyed it like it wasn't his, and then dropped it into my lap. "Things just got worse."

"The banditry?"

"Yeah. The devil. After the Black Flags and Yellow Flags, there's this war on our soil between the French and the Chinese imperial government. You saw how it ended. The Chinese pulled back across the border. But look at who got left behind? Em Chinese soldiers that their army had no more use for. And em Black Flags were still hanging around. Hell. If it ain't bad enough with one kind of em, it's doubly worse having two kinds robbing and burning down homes of innocent folks all over the countryside. You know what, Father?"

"What?"

"We, the yellow race, live by the soil. Till the soil for a living. Yeah. All our lives. From the ancestors all on down. But here's this problem. Em Chinese bandits came and demanded crop taxes, just like in the older days when they robbed you blind on the rivers. They took most of your harvest, left you with a teeny bit of crops to survive. You ask what for? So you could carry on tilling the land and be a slave to em. And here's this other problem. There ain't enough food anywhere. And if being poor ain't miserable enough, there are plagues just about every damn year. If you don't die from em hellfire plagues, you just got poorer, that's all. What'd you do if you were them, Father?"

"I'd hate to be in their predicament."

"You ought to do something."

"I'm inclined to say yes."

"Like . . ."

"Yes?"

"Becoming a robber, a bandit your own self."

"I don't blame them."

Granduncle appraised me with his squinted eyes. "Can I blame his father? Yeah, for his stupidity of getting careless and getting sold like a hunk of meat, but not for his willingness to become an outlaw."

"They got no law to protect them. That seems the root of the problem."

"What can your government do about em?"

"Pray to God. Sometimes he's closer to you than your government."

"He might have an ear for you, Father. He ain't no kin to me."

"You don't believe in God?"

"I don't think I like him."

Danton took off his hat and held it against his chest. Both Granduncle and I looked at him curiously. Then I leaned back, hung Granduncle's blouse on the bale of straw and sat with my head resting against it. I didn't feel sleepy, but angry. At what? I didn't know. At something lost for good—and it wasn't my father's life.

Danton brushed back his hair with his fingers. "In dark moments, do you pray?" he asked Granduncle.

"Done that."

"To whom?"

"My ancestors, that's whom."

"So you do believe in communion."

"I believe in my ancestors."

"You believe in their spirits."

"That's right."

"God is the immortal spirit—immortal and timeless. As spirit, we're immortal but not timeless. Why? Because our spirits were created by God and then given flesh so we could experience temptation and learn to cope with it. That lesson is part of our evolution. Yet many of us are lost in this physical world, and many have become so lost, so blinded by their own folly they forgot the Maker who sent them to this world."

I regarded the priest quietly and said, "I've seen spirits."

Danton peered at me curiously. "Have you, Tài?"

I nodded.

"Who did you see?"

"Daddy."

"So you saw him?"

Again I nodded.

"What if it wasn't him?"

"Was him. Saw him in my fever. Just a black shape, that's all."

Danton turned to Granduncle, who was stoking the fire with a scythelike stick. "What about you, sir?"

"I ain't seen him." Granduncle poked and pushed the pile with his stick, sending up black ashes. "He ain't too fond of seeing me neither."

"I mean have you seen spirits?"

"Can't say I did. Can't see em when they're scared of you."

"In God's light they bear no animosity toward you."

"How d'you know?" I asked, propped up on my elbow. "That there's only love in spirits?"

"How d'you know that God's light does that?" I said.

"Because God is all love."

"Is he real—like spirits?"

"He's the Creator of all spirits. Yes. He's very real."

"How d'you know?"

"The Bible documented it."

Both Granduncle and I stared at him.

"In Buddhism you have the canon. In Catholicism you have the Bible."

"What if he's make-believe?" Granduncle said.

"Are spirits make-believe?"

"They're folks I know. I trust em. They're there, all right."

"So is God."

"People've seen spirits. Any of em seen God?"

"When you see his creation—the living things, the firmament—you see God."

"You pray to him, you said?"

"Yes. Like you pray to your ancestors."

"But I know em and they know me," Granduncle said, raising the glowing stick in his hand. "That's where help comes from."

"Sure. All of us are God's children and all of us can talk to him."

"He ever helped you, Father?"

"In every living moment."

Granduncle frowned. I just stared. His God seemed friendly.

"That I'm here in a foreign land," Danton continued, "living among people who don't speak my language, who share nothing with me in culture, in beliefs, and many of whom are atheists, and many of whom have come into

God's light because they found truth in what God intends for me to tell them. He helps me to help others, like you, to see the light."

"He ever take anything from you?" I asked, sullen.

"He did."

"Did he take my daddy away?"

"He gives and he takes away. That's the law."

"But you said he's all love." I felt hostile toward him.

"Tài, when your daddy died, it's not because God held anything against him, but because he had served his period of usefulness that he promised God in exchange for his stay on earth. He went out on his own. But because God is the Maker who's responsible for all things, he's held responsible for every death, every loss, every grief that befalls us."

"I don't believe it," I said, scowling.

"I don't expect you to just because I said it."

"My daddy didn't go out on his own. I know that."

"Yeah," Granduncle chortled. "Why would he? Man got a family. A madcap, but he ain't no hopeless case. That make any sense to you, Father?"

"Perfectly sensible." Danton put his hat back on. "When he died, his time was up. He only did what he was supposed to do as part of his learning through trials and tribulations."

Granduncle grinned as he tapped the ember off the end of his stick. "I sure want to know when mine is up. Wouldn't scare me none." He glanced at me. "Would it scare you, son?"

I shrugged. Sounds of rain and wind caught my mind, and I thought of the brook and the dead hog. Did those vultures make a meal of it before the hunter did? Next to me Granduncle was puffing on his hand-rolled cigarette. I'm sure he hid his sentiment for my father in front of the priest. How could he not feel for his nephew whom he helped raise when my grandmother died?

His cigarette lit and then went out. The tobacco was damp. I watched him press the red tip of his stick against the tip of his cigarette. The laborious puffing. I hated that burnt smell. It hung in our hut whenever my father was home. He smoked those stubby cigarettes down to butts and stuck them on the hut's mud walls—anywhere. A day or two after he was gone, I still smelled that odor on my mother's blouse. I wondered how it got on her. Perhaps it was from sharing the bed with him.

"I saw this strange monkey today," I said to Granduncle.

He got a good puff on his cigarette, and it glowed happily. "Yeah," he said, leaning the stick next to the fire.

"You ever seen a yellow monkey?" I said.

"Yellow all over?"

"Yep. He's bald too. Doesn't look like any monkey, that's what's strange."

"What did he do to you?"

"Did nothing to me. He was so cute—"

"Those yellow monkeys are bad," Granduncle spoke with the cigarette between his lips.

"He was no orangutan, Granduncle."

"Tell you something, son." He pinched the cigarette with his fingers and wet his lips. "In the old time, very old, those monkeys were humans. Yeah. Like you and me. Did that monkey look like a human to you?"

"Yes, Granduncle. I thought he was a boy my age."

"See? Still human after all these years."

"Who told you that?" I knitted my brow.

"Why they still look human?"

"No. Did they really come from humans?"

"You don't want to argue with those older folks, do you, son? Why would they make up these stories?"

"I don't know. They could be just a strange kind of monkey."

"They're dangerous."

"Not this one monkey."

"Was your lucky day, son."

Danton's gaze went from Granduncle to me and back. "This is interesting. A human type of monkey?"

"That's what's said, Father," Granduncle said, taking a quick drag. "See, this thing's been told from our great-great-grandfathers on down, so I'm gonna just pass it on to you. There this group of people who fell in bad company with the rest of the population, so the law told em to leave their land and hide somewhere, where law abiders wouldn't hunt em down and kill em. So they went deep into the forests. Yeah. Were never seen again ever after. By and by they lost their human speech, but here's this problem. They never lost their wrath against those who sent em away. And there's this other thing. They're mighty strong, known for their evil chokehold. Plenty of hunters found dead over the years. Of same kinda affliction. Broken necks. That's right. They ain't take so kindly to humans, it looks like."

Listening, I gazed at my body, my limbs. The red on them looked ghoulish in the firelight. I sat up and folded my legs under me. "Granduncle?" I said.

"Yeah?"

"Can man turn into beast?"

"Like those evil monkeys? Hell, sure. You seen it."

"He wasn't evil. He brought me a pumpkin. I was really

hungry."

Danton pushed his hat up and peered at me. "Brought you a pumpkin? How?"

I told them. "I saw him twice. He seemed to follow me around."

"Still human, still smart," Granduncle said, nodding. "Didn't I tell you that?"

"Maybe they took a liking to children," Danton said. "Certain breeds of dogs are also like that."

"Thái would like him," I said. "He loves em animals. When he's well again, like me—"

"Tài," Granduncle said.

Danton kept quiet. Granduncle put his hand on my shoulder. "Listen, son."

I peered up at him.

"Your brother died. He ain't so lucky. Damn shame like it is . . ."

Danton sighed, shaking his head. I cringed. Then I looked up at Granduncle. "He can't die. This thing didn't kill me. How could it kill him?"

"You were more lucky, son. You seen em new graves in your village?"

"But he can't die," I yelled. "He can't, Granduncle!"

"I know. Ain't it a shame?"

"He can't die, I'll kill . . ." I stuttered and sobbed.

"Kill what?" Granduncle asked quizzically.

"I'll kill . . . kill anything that has to do with him dead."

"Son, the plague is what got him. We ain't got no cure for it."

I shot a wild look at Danton. "You think God took him like he took my daddy?"

Danton held his breath before he spoke. "I think he came

back into God's light, to serve God."

"He never done anything wrong . . ."

"I'm sure he never had. But we don't question God's way."

"Why not? He got no right to take my brother away." I hiccupped from sobbing. "You said he's all love—"

Danton dropped his voice. "Things might not seem what they are sometimes, but things are done for a reason."

Granduncle flicked his gaze at the priest. "Huh?"

"That his innocent death might serve a purpose." Danton paused, pursing his lips. "I don't know what, but I've seen it."

I shrank back, staring at the priest morosely. Granduncle shot a glance at the dead stub between his fingers and then at the priest. "Seen it?" he said.

Danton nodded, took off his hat, and put it over the cross on his chest. "Yes."

"Someone your God takes away?"

"My little daughter."

"You had a daughter?" Granduncle's sinister grin made Danton nod with a forced smile.

"But you're a priest."

"Before I became a priest."

"'Fore you became a priest." Granduncle flicked his stub into the fire.

"She died when she was three years old."

I looked at him raptly. My brother was three.

"What happened to her?" Granduncle asked, raking the ashes to a fiery glow.

"She was a victim of typhoid."

Granduncle scratched his shin. "You left your wife and became a priest?"

"I was left with my baby girl."

"Did she die?"

"Who?"

"Your wife."

"We weren't married. She didn't want anything to do with our baby girl. So I raised her by myself."

We sat in silence. Then Granduncle rose and went to fetch more firewood. He stopped at the door and said, "Look at em eyes."

We went to the door, stood behind him with rain blowing in our faces, and looked where he was looking. On the edge of the clearing two green dots glowed, watching us.

"If it ain't for the fire in here," Granduncle said, snorting, "he might be gnawin' our bones right now."

It was already dark outside. Bushes and scrub trees tossed and twisted in the blowing rain, but the two green dots did not move. While Danton tried to make out the shape of the tiger, Granduncle dumped his bundle of wood by the fire and picked up a flaming stick. He came to the door, stood, and then hurled the burning stick toward the bush. It flew in an orange-blue arc and landed, spurting flames, and when we looked again the green dots were gone.

I lay down, resting my head against the bale of straw. Listless, I stared into the fire as it popped, throwing tiny glints before my eyes. Busy rolling another cigarette, Granduncle suddenly looked up at Danton, who sat with one eye toward the door. Outside, the wet dusk had darkened the bushes and trees.

"You smoke, Father?" Granduncle asked.

"No, but thanks."

"I always kinda wonder how you came around speaking our tongue so well. Yeah. Kinda made me rapt."

Danton let out a soft laugh. "It wasn't easy," he said. "But if there's a will, there's a way."

"There you go again. Said it better than me."

I watched Granduncle light his cigarette with a smoldering stick and saw the blissful aura that suffused his gaunt face when he dragged on it. Perhaps even food did not bring him this rapture. After he exhaled the smoke through his nostrils, he blew a ringlet toward the priest.

"I bet you can write like you speak, Father." Granduncle did not look as cynical as before. He got crankier as he got older, it seemed.

"That's part of my job," Danton said. "Your language isn't so easy to speak, and hearing it is another problem."

"You must be a very smart man." Granduncle appraised him with his eyes.

"I had help." Danton clasped his hands in his lap. "They had a very capable Annamese catechist who spoke Latin very well to work with me. Without someone like that, I wouldn't have progressed this far."

A bright white flash lit up the hut's entrance, and a thunderclap crashed so loudly that Danton grabbed his hat and hunched up. Granduncle did not budge, sitting with his arms around his knees, and I lay curled on my side, gazing at the fire. It kept me from thinking.

"Scared, Father?" Granduncle grinned. "Fold your hat up. Yeah. Em evil spirits might come hiding under it."

Danton pulled down the brim of his hat. "They might hide under an umbrella. This hat is too small for them."

Granduncle rose and walked to the hut's entrance. "You ever seen those struck by lightning out in the open?" He spoke without looking back. "Burned to bone-ashes, hat and all, 'cause em evil spirits came hiding under their hats.

Yeah. The thunder gods don't care who's who. If they want to hide under somebody's hat that's somebody's problem."

He stood at the entrance, his back toward us, watching the lightning flash and flicker in ethereal clashes. Soon the priest and I joined him at the entrance, and we all gazed at the turbulence in the sky.

"I want to get on home," I said, poking my head out in the rain.

"Look there." Granduncle pointed toward the electric worms pulsing across the firmament. "This here is the time thunder gods are out to get em evil spirits. Don't be a fool to get out there and get smashed like em demons."

I scanned the fringe of the clearing, peering at dark shapes of brush that swayed like mad. The distant rumbling reminded me of the last vicious lightning strike, which hadn't missed us by that much.

"Yes," Danton said, "it'd be suicide to head out while the atmosphere is so charged with electricity."

A blinding white bolt seared a black corner of the forest. I yelled, "Look there!"

Granduncle looked down at me. "Your daddy ever tell you how the thunder gods get em evil spirits during storms?"

"No."

"You ever seen em people go to the mountain before the rainy season?"

"Seen them carry tools, all kinds."

"Yeah. Farm tools, weapons. Offer em to the thunder gods. Now hear this. You come back to the mountain the next year, you won't find no more weapons there, not a trace. Where did they go? Well, look over there . . . See em lightning bolts? Yeah. Them. The thunder gods are pitching em weapons into the plains to kill em evil spirits. Yeah. Em things got buried so deep in the soil nobody could get to em. Nope. That's why they were gone without a trace. But you wait. Three months, ten days. Yeah. If you're lucky, son, you might come upon one of em, and when you do, consider yourself lucky."

My jaw dropped.

Granduncle nodded. "Yeah. Wish I'd come upon one of em kind and that'll be dandiest. No evil spirits will dare come near you. That's right, son. And they say when you kill a creature with such a weapon, there ain't no blood nowhere."

"Where'd the blood go?"

"I'm just a dumb person if you ask me. When that happens, you just don't ask."

I fixed my gaze on the firmament. Every flash became etched in my mind. Daggers. Swords.

Behind us the fire dimmed. Granduncle hauled more wood and stacked it by the fire, and the fresh wood burned bright. The hut was very warm now. I sat watching Granduncle stoke the fire. "Granduncle, are those stories make-believe?"

He stopped, glanced down at me. "About the thunder gods?"

"And the weapons."

"Why? You think em people ain't nothing but idiots? They do it year in and year out and come back and say the same thing year after year. The thunder gods do have some use for em weapons offered em. Yeah."

Danton smiled. "Listen, Tài, you don't believe it, do you?"

I crimped my lips and said nothing. Granduncle worked

his jaw back and forth and then said, "You believe it when you saw blood leaking out of your daddy's coffin? Ain't he trying to tell someone something?"

I grinned.

"You saw it, yeah?" Granduncle asked, his eyebrows raised.

"Yeah."

"What you make of it?"

"That was a cheap coffin they threw to him. I saw cracks in it."

"Yeah. You saw it. How much blood you think a man's body can hold, son?"

I shrugged.

"Most of it done spewed out when his head was gone. Yeah. On the execution ground, son. But that coffin kept on leaking blood till they got back home, ain't it?"

I felt like he just pinched my guts. I looked down into the fire. After a while I said, "You know who sold my daddy?"

Granduncle kept pushing the sticks into the pile and said "Yeah."

"What's his name?" I asked.

"Name? I believe his name is Lam." Granduncle coughed and spat into the fire. "You're too young to carry on with all this name crap. What you ought to do is help your mother. That's what you must do, hear?"

"I'll take care of her. I just needed the name, that's all."

"You got the name. Now forget it."

"I won't. Even after I kill him."

Granduncle guffawed, beating a stick in the pile several times. "If you're serious, son, I'll help you."

I peered up at him and tensed. "You will?"

"What?"

"You will?"

Granduncle let down the stick. "Damn, son."

Danton leaned his head to one side, squinting at us.

Granduncle looked down at me with a grin. "I might not be around anymore by the time you get to be old enough to swing my saber. But if I still hang around, yeah, son."

"I used your saber once, Granduncle."

"Say what?"

"I chopped a mutt's head with it."

"You did? That thing ain't light."

"I know. I want that saber to be mine."

"Yeah." Granduncle grinned and glanced back at his saber, which was leaning against the wall of the hut.

"That's all I want."

A thunderclap exploded very near the hut and the clearing lit up as if in daylight. Granduncle spat again into the fire. "Damn," he said. "Wish I could come upon one of em wonder swords in the fields someday. Yeah. Would make my job a lot easier."

DADDY'S SKULL

It was mid-afternoon when the ferry brought me to the village of Chung. Winter had returned and the sky was hoar-colored. The boat owner and his young daughter sat back as I climbed up the jetty into the shade of a weeping fig. I warded off the branches that hovered over the ground as Mr. Chim, the widowed boatman, called out to me, "Tài."

He had only one good eye. His dead eye was the sickly white-blue of a rotten egg. He stood at the bow, leaning on the row-locked oar, while his daughter squatted at the stern, resting her elbows on a paddle that was laid crosswise over the boat. I worked for him as an oarsboy. He gestured with his hand toward a bamboo grove upriver. "We'll be there, waiting for you. Don't do anything in there that I wouldn't do, hear?"

I squinted at him. "All I'll do is ask around."

I followed the path until I saw the tall dark banyan at the village entrance. My guts tightened. I was looking up at the giant tree when my feet tripped over a rock. It took me a moment to feel the pang. My big toe bled. I sucked in the pain until I felt the sting dim, as if it had left my toe and crawled into the ground. I wiped the blood with a clump of grass, daubed the cut with my spit, and walked on. Moments later, I came to the village gate and saw the watchtower behind the enclosure.

The banyan's long, gnarled branches cast a huge area of shade. Beneath the tree, I hopped among serpentine roots,

looking for skulls in the tree limbs. The only one who had
seen them was Danton, the priest. And I trusted him.

After walking around the banyan a few times—its trunk
was monstrously thick—I became irritated and came out of
the shade toward the watchtower. The lookout was watching me.

I stood in the sun and shouted to the man, "What happened to the skulls?"

The man took a good look at me. "You not from here,
ain't ya?"

"No."

"You have a place where you come from?"

"Lau." I spat. "What did you do with the skulls?"

The man poked his head out from under the straw roof.
"Why? Why d'you want em?"

"I want my daddy's skull back."

He scratched his chin. "So that's what you want, eh?
Well, em skulls been gone a long time now. Season comes,
season goes. Who knows where they went."

"They can't just disappear." I looked at the banyan and
then back at the man. "You have eyes, don't you?"

"Born with a pair."

"You see who took them?"

"I see a problem."

I shaded my eyes with both hands. "What problem?"

"You're from Lau. That's the problem."

I dropped my hands and looked down at my blood-
smeared toenail, and then looked up, grinning. "If you were
looking for your daddy's skull, what'd you do?"

The man smirked, shaking his head. "Hire a medium
dancer. She'll tell ya where to find his skull."

I narrowed my eyes to memorize his face before he pulled

back under the straw roof. Irked, I had the urge to cuss, but instead I turned abruptly and took the dirt path away from the watchtower. If every inhabitant of Chung village was like that oaf, they deserved to have their dwellings burned down. I wouldn't have blamed Daddy.

The path forked, covered with tall, tough grass. I thought of going back to the ferry but then turned to head in the opposite direction. Soon I came upon a pond that looked stagnant and brown. There were women washing clothes next to women who were washing rice in wicker baskets, and several feet away from the foaming current, some were fetching drinking water in their earthen vats. I stopped and asked a woman about the skulls. She stopped rinsing rice, looked at me with a sympathetic look, and shook her head. Next to her, a younger woman was washing her neck and face with a brown washcloth. After scrubbing the cloth in the water, she rose and pointed toward the rice fields beyond the pond. "Go ask those buffalo boys. They'll tell you."

The green of the rice fields was pale against blue-gray hills that fell away to a mountain range. The air was cool. I followed a dike toward a screen of trees, where cattle lolled in the shade. The dikes were black bars inked across the immense green fields. Near the clump of trees I saw black water buffalos grazing on the grass that edged the dikes. It was so quiet I could hear the leisurely munching of the beasts.

"Hey!" someone called.

I looked. A group of boys was lounging in the tall grass around the trees. I left the dike and went toward them. Four boys lazing under a kapok tree, each sitting with his back against its stout trunk. Before I opened my mouth, I saw what I was searching for. Each of the boys sat on a white skull. In front of them, two more skulls were turned upside

down and stuffed with yellow straw. The boys were smoking pipes, long bamboo tubes with small bowls fastened in
the middle. The way things appeared, I thought I'd better
keep quiet.

"What're you looking at?" one boy asked, taking the pipe
from his mouth. He looked older than the rest.

"Well," I said, "I heard someone call."

"Do I know you?"

"Don't think you do."

"You from here?"

"No."

"Where the hell you from then?" The older boy drew
deeply on the pipe and his cheeks puffed.

"From Ninh."

"Ninh?" Smoke curled from his lips. He was shirtless,
the others wore black blouses. On his chest dangled a small
wooden cross. He cocked his head and studied me. "You
Catholic, too, eh?"

That jolted me. I came up with the name because it was
the nearest Catholic village to Chung. But quickly I said,
"Yeah."

"Don't see you wearing a cross."

"That's right."

"Smart boy, ain't ya?" The boy leaned forward, elbows
on knees, his pipe smoking in his hand.

They all watched me as I stood in the sun in my calf-
length gray cotton trousers and long-sleeved indigo shirt.
Before I could say a word, the older boy said, "What're you
doing out here? Don't tell me you're sightseeing."

"Sightseeing?" I chortled.

"Or are you a buffalo thief?"

The boys roared with laughter. I looked away and then

back at them. "I'm just hunting field rats."

"That's a long way from Ninh to hunt field rats, ain't it, boy?"

"No, that isn't it. But since my uncle is visiting someone here, I wanted to kill time."

The older boy rose to his feet. He was taller than me, and he kept tossing back his head to clear long strands of hair from his face. Now he walked out of the shade and stood face-to-face with me, the stranger.

"Show me how to catch field rats. Maybe we can eat rat meat together, what do you say?"

I said nothing. I just nodded.

"Let's go then." The older boy squinted at me as he knocked the dottle out of his pipe.

The other boys joined us, walking behind me along the dike. One boy asked, "How do you look for a field rat?"

"You look for a hole," I said, eyeing the ground.

They all looked at the ground around us. The older boy said, "What're you gonna catch em rats with?"

I shrugged. "I usually catch them with a bag. You know the kinda cloth bags? You hold them open with a piece of round wire and smoke the rats into the bags."

"Let's see the bag."

"I don't have it here. I'll use my shirt."

"All right then. Let's look for em rats. Bet ya wouldn't have to look for em fat rats comes harvest time."

I said nothing. In two months when the fields were harvested, fallen grains would lure ducks and rats. For now, the rats just ate the tender roots of rice plants. I knew to keep off the fields. Between rice stalks, along the chinks in the fields, there were nasty traps. I told the boys and they said they knew. They said the rats were smarter than people, for very few got caught.

Then I saw a hole from where I stood on a dike. Several feet away in the field. I pointed it out and said, "Let's smoke it out."

"With what?" the older boy said.

"Straw. You got straw, don't you?"

The older boy scowled. "They ain't no cheap straw. See those damn skulls full of em straw over there? Took a whole day to pick that kind of straw. You light em up, they burn clean and slow." He tapped his pipe. "See this tiny bowl? Holds just a pinch of tobacco. You smoke it in two drags. So you don't want to mess around lighting it up with lousy straw. Use some damn grass if you want to smoke em out."

"You can't smoke them with grass."

"You haven't tried."

"It doesn't smoke like straw. And you have to wet the straw to get the kind of smoke that'll make those rats choke."

The older boy hawked up phlegm and spat at his feet. "Right over there." He pointed toward the two upturned skulls.

I strode to the kapok tree, my eyes fixed on the skulls. They bore the same features—dark empty eye sockets, a hollow for a nose, a jaw full of teeth. One of the skulls had black teeth, so I knew it wasn't my father's skull. But I couldn't tell which was which by just looking. I stood holding the black-toothed skull when the older boy came up.

"You got straw," the older boy said. "Go do it."

"Wet it," I said, giving him a fistful of straw.

"This better work." The older boy looked at his prized straw and went to fetch a jar of water he kept in a cloth bag hung on a limb.

We went back to where we found the hole. The boys watched me tapping the soil around the it. I listened as I tapped, and just a few feet from the hole I heard a hollow sound. I dug a second hole and poked my stick into the cavity below.

"Get ready," I said, taking off my shirt and tossing it to the older boy. "You ever caught a rat before?"

"Shut up! Just light up that hole." The older boy laid down his pipe as he squatted by the hole.

I held the damp straw over the hole while a boy lit it with a lunt. Black smoke quickly fouled the air. I fed straw into the cavity and then withdrew it to coax the flame back to life. Just as I coughed, the boys yelled, "Got him!"

The rat thrashed in my shirt, and the older boy deftly picked it up, swinging the catch around. "What now?" he asked me.

"Kill it, roast it, eat it."

"Let's see all that done." He swung the catch into my hand.

"Let's dump it into one of those skulls. You got a knife?"

The older boy handed me a knife they used to chop tobacco. I looked the skulls over. I didn't want to kill the rat in my father's skull, but which one was his? They all bore a similar morose, puzzled look. I picked up the skull that had black teeth.

"You mind if I kill this stupid rat in here?" I asked the older boy.

"I'd mind if you don't wash it clean after."

I dumped the rat into the empty skull and watched it hiss and wiggle in the hollow. A creature trapped. Like me. I stabbed it at the neck and held the knife firmly as blood streaked down its coarse, gray fur. When the rodent's feet jerked and its body went limp, I picked it up by the tail, laid it on the ground, and cut off its hairless tail and tiny feet. I ignored the boys who crouched, rapt, around me. After I slit the skin behind the rat's ear, I held its head down and ran the tip of the knife under its fur and rolled the skin back. I tested the sharpness of the blade against my fingertip and then drove the knife cleanly through the rat's neck. The head fell off. I stood up, the headless rat in one hand and the skull in the other.

"I'm gonna wash these things at the pond," I said to the older boy. "Make a fire while I'm gone."

The older boy ordered his underlings to build a fire and sat down on his skull, watching me as I walked toward the pond.

I cleaned the rat and the knife at the far side of the pond, away from the women. At this hour there were only a few left. One woman was washing her hair and a few others their vegetables. Then I washed the blood off the skull, feeling irate with myself. I could have made off with my father's skull if I had it instead of this one. Never have to deal with those idiots again.

I walked back into the warm odor of wood smoke, sat down, and made a bed of leaves. Quickly I cut open the rat and tossed out its guts. Then I spread it on upright sticks over the fire. The fire popped when pellets of fat dripped from the rat, and a musky odor rose. The air had become cooler. There was now a chill in the breeze. I put my shirt back on and turned the rat over. The flesh was browned, glistening.

We sat, each of us eating our share and blowing on the smoking meat. When I peered across at the older boy, I met his gaze.

"I'm set to leave," I said to the older boy. "What about you?"

"We'll be here a little longer."

"You gonna leave those skulls here?"

"Yeah. Why?"

"Where'd you get them?"

"Used to be hung on our village banyan."

It had been a year. How did they get those skulls so polished? "You cleaned those skulls yourself?" I asked the older boy.

"I got help." He wiped his greasy lips with the heel of his palm.

"How'd you clean them?"

"Boil em in ash water. Get all the craps to fall off and dry em in the sun for a couple weeks and then soak em in lacquer thinner to degrease em. Anything else?"

I licked my fingers. "What did they do?"

"Robbed our village." The older boy chewed and then washed the meat down with a drink of water. He reached for his pipe and squinted his eyes at me. "What happened to your face?"

"What about it?"

"All em scars."

"Aye. Smallpox.".

"That so? When?"

"Last year."

The older boy lit his pipe and dragged. "You'd better get going."

I stood up, looked the place over, and turned to leave.

"You going back into the village?" the older boy asked.

The word "no" rolled up to the tip of my tongue, but I

stopped just in time. "Yeah," I said, without looking back. I passed the buffalos that rested in the shade, though the sun was now mild and the sunlight fading. I could feel the older boy's gaze following me until I reached the pond and took the path to the ferry landing.

The boat owner and his daughter were lounging on the grassy bank covered with long shadows, and a pale blue mist rose from the water. I sat down beside Chim and told him what had happened. Then I told him that I would wait until dark and go back to get the skulls.

"You got me worried," Chim said, chewing on a stalk of grass. "Now I'm more worried."

"Why?"

Xoan, the girl, cut in, "He can't imagine how you're going to lug those skulls all by yourself. Think about it, Tài."

I glanced at her. She was a year older than me. She looked at me and formed a dimpled smile that lingered until I said, "I don't care about those other skulls. Only my daddy's. But I'll have to carry all those skulls unless I can tell which one is my daddy's."

They thought for moment. Chim turned to look at me. His dead eye was sickly white-blue, his good eye deep brown and kind. "Your bones don't change," he said. "Anything with bones. Think of his face. Now what comes to your mind?"

I closed my eyes and said, "His forehead."

"I'll give you that," Chim said. "He sure had a prominent forehead. What else?"

I shook my head. I could have recalled every feature about my mother, had Chim asked.

"You forgot about his eyetooth," Chim said.

I opened my eyes. Chim and his daughter were staring

at me. Xoan's lips curled into a smile. "Do you know what he meant by that, Tài?"

"I got it," I said. Perhaps I'd never noticed that when my father was around.

"Did your daddy smile much?" Xoan asked with a curious glint in her eyes.

"He never did."

"Did he, father?"

"When he was high on opium," Chim said. "A few times."

"You smoked opium with him?" I said.

"Tài," Chim said, "I wouldn't come near that stuff even if you gave me back my other eye."

"What happened to it?" I asked.

"Same thing happened to you. Smallpox. I was a young man when I fell sick."

"You saw my daddy smoke opium?"

Chim nodded. "In a den in Hanoi."

"You were there too? I thought—"

"I was a servant. Cleaned the addicts' pipes."

I nodded and then saw a cloudy look in Chim's good eye, as if he had second thoughts about something he'd just said. "You like my daddy, Mr. Chim?"

The boat owner pursed his lips. "Yeah," he said. "Just don't get on his wrong side."

"Did you?"

"He never bothered with a peon like me. He never told you much of anything, huh?"

"Told me what thing?"

"Nothing." Chim looked up at the vast, empty sky. Its gray had darkened and on a downriver boat passing by, a lantern glowed amber in the mist. Chim tore a grass stalk with his fingers and without looking at me said, "Go back in there. You need my help?"

"No." I rose. "What did he do, Mr. Chim?"

"He slashed this fellow's throat in an opium den."

"Huh? Really?"

"I was between them. The fellow came after me. That's when he met his end."

"Who was he?"

"This lout'd already gone through many pipes and he got delirious. Most folks became happy in their torpor after many pipes. But this guy became manic. Just when I brought him tea, things got crazy."

Xoan hugged her knees. I watched Mr. Chim.

"He took a sip and the next thing I knew he spat it in my face. 'You rascal,' he said, 'What's this? Dishwater?' 'That's jasmine tea,' I told him. 'Jasmine tea, my ass,' he said and grabbed me and forced me to drink the whole pot. That's when your daddy jumped in. He was lying beside the lamp and the tea table next to this guy. The guy snatched a cleaning rod—sharp little thing—and drove it into your daddy's guts. See, everyone was half naked in the den and this thing could've gone through his belly like rice dough. But it didn't, it bent. Not kidding you. Your daddy got the guy turned around in a chokehold and got out his knife from under his mat. He cut the guy's throat so fast I thought he let him go when the guy dropped to the floor. That cut went right to the back of his neck. You could see his artery like a busted pipe."

I frowned. "That rod . . . bent?"

"Yeah. Some kind of martial arts technique he used, I bet. But, hey, you go back in there."

I strode back toward the village. Dusk had fallen quickly.

There was no twilight. I hastened my pace toward the rice fields, and after a while I ran. I ran past the pond, now deserted, and when I made it to a dike I slowed down to a trot. I could see the canopy of the kapok tree among the greenery.

The fire had gone out but I could smell wood smoke. I put my hand over the ashes. They were warm. *Those idiots must've just left.* At the huge base of the tree, dwarfed by thick, level limbs above them, the six skulls sat in a straight line like shelved merchandise. I felt lucky. I came within a few feet of them and stood, my eyes darting from one to the next. The skull in the middle—where the older boy sat—caught my eye. Even in the dusky light I could see the high-domed brow, not receding like others, the left eyetooth. The face of my father hung in my mind. How could I have missed it before? Those idiots could have the rest, but that skull belonged to me.

I stepped up, and just as I bent, my right foot punched through the soil. An excruciating pain cut off my breathing, cut off my scream. I could not lift my foot. It was pierced by something wickedly sharp. The pain glowed like an evil fire in my abdomen, rising to my chest, my throat. I tasted bitter smoke in the back of my mouth and bits of teary light danced inside my eyes. I half stood, half bent, like a windblown scarecrow. I heard voices. The buffalo boys surrounded me.

"Welcome back, skull thief," the older boy said, tapping his pipe against his leg.

By now my face was dripping sweat and my fists were clenched in pain. My pierced foot jerked on its own. I saw a girl's face among the others.

"Why d'you want em skulls, boy?" the older boy asked.

I opened and closed my fists as I pulled up my foot. I looked down at my limp foot. There was something dark on its sole, and the smear of blood was darker. I had stepped on a bamboo spike, and the tip of it had broken off in my instep. The boy's pipe caught me under the chin and lifted my face up.

"You hear me, boy?"

I blinked away wet stars in my eyes. "I want my daddy's skull back."

"Daddy's skull?" the older boy said, and then tapped the skull with his pipe. "This?"

"That."

"It's mine."

"That's my daddy's skull you stole."

"I'm talking bout all em skulls here." The older boy snickered. "I own em."

"If it was your daddy's skull lying there, and I told you I owned it, what'd you do?"

The older boy rested his foot on the skull. "You got it wrong, boy. My daddy ain't no robber. He ain't never burned down innocent folks' homes. So his head'd never get hung. He'd never put me or his children in a bind like this. See?"

The girl, clad in a white blouse, nudged the older boy. "Ask him what he'd do for you if you give him back his daddy's skull."

"Hell," the older boy grunted. "I ain't gonna do that."

The girl inched up to me and asked, "What'd you give to get it back?"

Half bent, I braced myself, leaning on my knee with one hand. "You give me back my daddy's skull, I'll find a way to give you back whatever."

The older boy moved his jaw back and forth and clucked

his tongue. "Damn liar. You came here to steal em skulls. Your uncle visiting someone here? Bah! You never went back into the village after you left here, boy. What do you think we post a guard at the gate for? To keep an eye on thieves like you. You from Lau, ain't ya? Yeah, yeah. Half of you died from smallpox last year. Everybody knew that. Thieves and robbers." He spat on the skull. "God stamps your face with em scars so you can't hide."

I glanced down at my father's skull and back at the older boy. Hatred smoldered in my eyes as I stared at him. The girl whispered something into his ear and looked at me with malice in her glistening black eyes. The older boy picked up the skull and weighed it in his hand.

"I'll piss in your daddy's skull, and if you drink it up, I'll give you back his skull. Deal?"

My eyes narrowed to slits. "I can drink my own piss. But if you piss in my daddy's skull, I'll kill you. You can save yours for your little girlfriend there."

The girl screeched, "Hang him!"

The older boy glanced around. He looked annoyed. "What the hell are we gonna hang him with?"

The other boys just looked on dumbly. The girl appraised me with her eyes. "Just strip him off," she said, chortling. "See if you boys are clever enough to do a man's job."

"Yeah, yeah," the older boy said. He spat again at his feet, jammed his pipe down into the back of his trousers, and jerked the shirt off my torso. Then he barked to his boys, "What're you gawking at? Take his pants off."

I stood naked in the dimness, more wracked by the throbbing pain in my foot than by the chill. The boys worked my pantaloons into a loop and tested its strength by yanking it repeatedly. They then unknotted it. Now the older boy motioned to the girl with a toss of his head, and she grabbed my arms and bent them behind my back. They tied my wrists with my own shirt and then the older boy stepped back in front of me.

"You're gonna spend the night out here, pimple-face," he said. "We'll come back in the morning and our village council will judge you."

They looked at me. The notion of being hanged passed through my mind. I wasn't scared. Only miserably hateful. Helpless and naked in their gaze. The girl watched me, her head tilted to one side. In the weak light, her ponytail was so black against her white blouse it looked like a snake flung over her shoulder. Her skin was fair, her teeth white, her eyes wetly dark. I scrutinized her face so I could remember it later. Then I looked at the older boy and my jaws tightened.

The four boys dragged me to a horizontal limb a few feet over their heads. One squatted and looped my trousers round my ankles, threaded one leg between my legs and yanked it tight into a knot. My jaws locked in pain, and I looked down at my own nakedness. I saw my pubic mound, aware of the subtle changes of my body. I was soon to leave my boyhood.

Suddenly I felt even more vulnerable. She watched me. She did not flinch when I looked at her.

"You ready?" the older boy said, raising his voice.

"Yes," the boys said in chorus. My legs buckled when the older boy kicked them from behind. My whole weight slammed down on my injured foot, and tears blinded me. Three boys raised me by the feet, the older boy seized me by the neck and pushed. I saw the dark canopy of the kapok tree, a black sky, my naked body a faint white and my ankle streaked with blood. The hands were deftly knotting a leg of my trousers around the limb. Then I heard the older boy.

"I've got an idea. Change it up. I want him to look down, not up."

They held me, reworked the knot, and then flipped me around. The older boy was gone. When he came back from behind the trunk of the kapok tree, he held in his hands the skull. The eye sockets were plugged with clods of earth. By now my face was two feet from the ground, and I swung to and fro with my hands bound behind my back.

In that suspended pose, I saw the older boy stoop and place my father's skull upside down on the ground. What I saw inside the skull churned my guts with nausea. He had urinated in it.

"In the name of God," the older boy said softly, "you don't have to drink my piss. You thank my girl. She's a good Catholic."

"Fuck your God," I said. "Fuck all you Catholics."

The older boy squatted in front of me and lifted my chin up with his pipe. "Look, pimple-face. I'm gonna pull the tip of that spike out of your damn foot. And if you bleed to death, it's because God has no place for an ungrateful thief like you in his house."

The older boy stood up and the girl grabbed him by the shoulder. I could hear her hissing into the boy's ear. Then the older boy said, "Let's go." He stopped in front of me, looked me over, and said, "You'd better hope em wild hogs ain't showin' up tonight."

The boys and the girl walked single-file on the dike, leaving me to swing back and forth, alone, looking like a pale apparition.

For a long time I kept my eyes closed. My head felt like

a block of cement and my eyes bulged from the pressure in my head. The night hummed with the steady sawing of insects and the sporadic croaking of frogs out in the paddy fields, where fish vaulted from the water and fell back with quiet splashes. There was a chill on my damp skin, throbbing pains in my foot. Each time I opened my eyes, I looked down into a glossy pool of liquid. *Damn bastard.* I prayed that someone would find me.

Then, from my half-sleep, I heard my name called by voices that drifted across the vast, empty fields. I called back, pushing from my guts with all my might to send forth my cries. Moments later, I glimpsed them running into my murky, reversed world—Chim and his daughter.

They saw me and stopped. Neither said a word. They appeared to be looking upon a phantasmagoria that sucked their souls away. Then hands touched me, voices asked questions. The only answers were incoherent moans. My soul wept.

They got me down and laid me on my back. Chim worked the pantaloons on me. My leg lay lifeless and straight like a dead limb. Xoan buttoned up my shirt while she looked down at me. Through the slits of my eyes I saw the other girl's face, her dark, wet eyes. I shook.

"Can you walk, Tài?" Xoan asked.

"I haven't tried," I said.

Chim held my foot in his hand. After one look, he said, "Have to carry him. This spike's head will ruin his foot if he tries to walk to the river."

"You can't carry me, Mr. Chim."

"I haven't tried."

They stood me up single-footed like a heron, head drooping. Then Chim hoisted me onto his back, and wobbled to find his own footing. We were on our way out when I jerked on Chim's back. "My daddy's skull!"

Xoan turned back, picked it up from the ground, and emptied its contents onto the grass. We followed the dike out in the drone of insects, the boat owner a squat, black shape weighed down by its burden, and his daughter a slender figure behind him, holding a white skull.

A RESTING PLACE FOR THE DEAD

We rested our oars and let the boat drift in the late afternoon mist. The sole passenger stood amidships, leaning against a rattan dome. He was in his fifties, tall, lean, and dressed in a violet tulle gown that reached the calves of his white linen trousers. His frog eyes watched the sandbank and the land beyond it. The pale green of rice fields soothed the eyes. Among the clumps of fruit trees were myriad yellow dots that moved. The fields, too, were trembling with moving yellow specks.

"What are those?" the passenger asked, turning his head partially toward us.

"Those?" Chim said, squinting his good eye. "Canaries."

"May I ask why they all congregate there?"

"They're being let out to feed." Chim pointed upriver where the promontory was a misty shade of blue. "They're raised by those bird shepherds yonder. You drink, sir?"

"What did you have in mind?" The man narrowed his protruding eyes.

"Would you join us this evening?" Chim said. "Me and those fellows, we go sometimes, oh, way past midnight."

The man looked lost and then suddenly nodded, as if he felt foolish. "No, I don't drink like a buffalo. Mean no affront to you personally. But I'm more a connoisseur."

Chim appraised him quietly as the man watched the birds, tipping his head back slightly. Beyond the pale green fields, hill after hill receded until their ridges creased together in faraway blue silhouettes.

A horn sounded. All at once the birds rose and the air hummed and the sky tinged yellow as if littered with tens of thousands of windblown leaves. The passenger stood gazing until the rustling of wings died out. Somewhere beyond the sandbank, the boatmen who herded the birds were welcoming them back for the night.

Slowly the man turned to look at us and pointed toward the hills. "You think I can walk to those hills and be back before dark?"

I thought he could—by sunset. Chim must have thought likewise. He nodded toward the man. "You certainly can, sir," he said. "Just don't loiter."

The man picked up a haversack at his feet, worked his arm through the strap, and slung it over his shoulder. He watched the bank until the boat touched it and, with his sandals clutched in his hands, waded through water that was brown with sand. He walked into the mist that hung over the dike, a straight, blurred line in the far hills.

"What's he up to?" I asked.

"You know what I think?" Chim asked.

I stopped gazing into the misty hills and looked back to find him gone from the prow. I looked through the dim vault and saw him squatting on his heels, resting his forearms on the row-locked oars. His good eye followed the man as the sun broke through the clouds and the mist glowed. The man was a shade darker than the dike. Chim, squinting his eyes, said, "He's no land prospector. He's a geomancer."

"So that's what he is." I cocked my head. "What's that mean?"

"He prospects for gravesites."

"I thought he prospected for gold," I said. "Didn't you say yourself he was a gold prospector when he hired you?"

"He got us fooled." Chim coughed and spat over the ledge. "For almost a week now."

"Gravesites?" I said. "He buries people?"

"Hell, no. That's a gravedigger's job, son. A geomancer like him is a different breed. Kinda noble around here, if you ask me."

"What's so noble about looking for gravesites?" My mouth fell open. "I've been looking for a nice gravesite for my daddy and my little brother ever since Mother buried em in the back of our house."

Chim raised his gaze. "What's wrong with burying them in the back?"

"Flood." I rested my back against a plank. "Mushy soil gives me creeps."

Chim nodded. I guessed he knew how flooding could putrefy bones and flesh. Loathsome worms didn't disgust me. The damp soil did. But what complaint could the dead offer to Mother Nature as they shiver in the clammy earth? "What's his business looking for gravesites?" I said.

"To bury the dead." Chim stood up, resting one foot on the gunwale. "If he's good, wealthy people pay him handsomely for a good burial site. Believe it or not."

"You telling me they're no ordinary holes?"

"No, son. I'm not an expert in this, but if you were dead and got buried in a hole he picked out for you, they say your offspring will prosper, generation after generation. Don't ask me why."

I watched brown flotsam float by and saw a black water snake slicing through the water under the spume. "You believe in that, Mr. Chim?"

"Do I? Let me tell you a story." He hawked up phlegm and spat again into the water. "You've heard of the Lê clan in our village, haven't you? The richest in Lau. Back then, a century and a half ago, this one fellow who's their ancestor hired a geomancer and bought himself a nice burial place on a hill somewhere. He wasn't old or anything. Wasn't even rich then. He was just looking out for himself and his younglings by playing smart. But just after that, word came that he died." Chim cleared his throat, and you could hear a purr of mucus like a smoker's cough. "When they buried him, do you know what they said?"

I shook my head. My mind was blank.

"His body wasn't in the coffin. They said it was a home-less man about his size that lay in there."

I sat up. "Dead?"

"Dead. I don't know how he died though. But there he was. Laid out in another man's coffin and buried in a hole picked out by some geomancer. That beggar got a nice buri-al and nobody knew anything about this until many many years after. He left behind a son. Now, you'd think this little boy would follow in his father's footsteps. Right? No sir, he didn't become a tramp at all. Guess what he became? A mandarin. All cultured and dignified."

For a moment I thought of the mandarin who presided over the execution of my father and his cohorts. All my life I had never seen a cultured and dignified mandarin. I grunted.

"A beggar's son who became a mandarin," Chim went on. "That's news. But then when the son who was a manda-rin grew older, his own son became the youngest mandarin in the North, and word came that the Lê exhumed the beg-gar's bones and buried a deceased member of their family in that hole." Chim rested one bare foot against the struts in the bow. "That's when their fortune began to change."

I shook my head in disbelief. In fact, I didn't know what to believe. But one thing I knew for certain—this man, Chim, was no credulous fool. I'd listened to his stories countless times and had come to find out how wise and truthful he was.

"Then what happened?" I asked, grinning. "Any of them became a mandarin?"

"No," Chim said, chortling. "They were too dumb for that. What they became were silk merchants. One generation after the next. Best quality silk. They're still selling it today. After each flood, they'd air out their gold bars on their estate—if you believe it."

"What did they do with the beggar's body?"

"You mean his bones?" Chim shrugged. "That I don't know. Probably just chucked them out there for wild animals."

I thought about it. At least the bones of my father and little brother were safe in the clayey, soggy soil. To have your bones unearthed and tossed around made me feel sorry for the beggar. But if the burial hole was magical, what'd happened to his kin? Before I had time to ask, Chim said, "Wouldn't you want to be among that beggar's posterity?"

"What do you mean?"

"I mean their luck ran out. Just like that."

"No more mandarins?"

"No more mandarins. Their sons and daughters lived hand to mouth."

I shook my head and spat into the water. Perhaps I had picked up Chim's habit. To see someone fall from grace always takes something out of me. Then I thought of something else, something I'd forgotten to ask him.

"What on earth happened to that guy?" I asked, slowly raising myself up on the oars. "I mean the guy who hired the geomancer."

"Him?" Chim said. "There was nothing left of him when he died. That's why they couldn't give him a burial."

I clasped my knees as I looked at Chim, my mind again blank.

"He was struck by lightning," Chim said with a big grin. "You never seen a person frizzled by lightning? Bad. Bad for the family. Only cinders, if you want to bury those."

What foul luck. Imagine there is a nice resting place where you can lie down in eternal sleep waiting for you after death. But then you get trapped outside by the wrath of Heaven and become ashes. I thought of my mother, who worked as a midwife. There were nights she would come home in the torrential rain. You could see her sloshing across the rice fields under flickering bolts, hunched up in her palm-leaf raincoat. It hurt me to think of her suffering the same meaningless death by lightning.

Chim still grinned as he scratched the side of his neck. "I shouldn't tell you what I'm about to, but, hey, you'd find out later anyway and I wouldn't want you to blame me for not telling you. But that fellow who was struck by lightning . . . they said that he was out there humping a goat when lightning zapped him."

I grinned, and when Chim kept chuckling, I laughed. I wondered what happened to the goat.

Chim reclined, head resting on the thwart. His story got me thinking, not about the man and the goat, but of the magic burial hole that could change the fortune of a dead man's offspring.

I ducked my head under the rolled-up blind, entered the

dome and, stooped, groped my way through it. A bump in
the hard wooden floor stung my foot. It still hurt from that
booby-trap spike after three months. Inside, the smell of stale
tobacco came from a water pipe that sat on the narrow shelf
that was draped with a white cloth. A faint odor of fermented bean curd hung near the entrance where the geomancer
would sit at sunset and eat the dinner that Chim cooked. He
had been with us six days now. At night he would sleep in
the dome while we slept outside, both of us wrapped in a
blanket, using the thwart as our pillow. We had drifted from
place to place, going where the man told us to go.

The first day, we went upriver after a heavy rain. The
current was strong and forced us to keep close to the bank.
On the bank, three people were digging a well. Our patron
asked us to drift so he could watch. We knew they were gold
diggers and we said nothing. He might think they were digging wells. One man with a basket on his head was working
his way down the well. His basket was windlassed to the
surface and dumped on the bank. Another man dropped the
basket back into the well, and a third was on all fours, raking the yellow dirt with his bare hands.

Our patron stared, rapt. As we rowed on, he said, "You
think they found any gold there?"

Surprised, I looked over to Chim. He leaned hard on the
oars and his head bobbed. "You never know, sir," he said.
"Maybe a lump here and there if they dig that deep."

"They might want to try their luck somewhere else where
the soil is brown," our patron said, his gaze still on the men
at the well.

Later when we were alone I asked Chim about this com-
ment and he said land with yellow soil wasn't a good source
of gold. He said nothing afterward.

The next day as we passed a sandbank, we saw a family—a man, a woman, and four children—and our passenger again asked us to slow down so he could watch the people bent over the water's edge, feverishly working their feet in the sand.

"Would be pure luck if they find anything," our passenger said, squatting on his heels, hands on the gunwale.

"I don't know about pure luck," Chim said. "Maybe just gold dust, if you call that luck."

"I've heard this part of the region is rich with gold," our patron said.

"I've heard that too," Chim said. "Well, if you know where to find it."

When he hired us to take him around the region, the man had told Chim not to ask any personal questions.

Now I sat down on the gunwale and Chim opened his eyes, smacking his lips dryly. He must be dying for a smoke. A tobacco fiend like him would rather starve than be robbed of a smoke. He was only abstaining because of his daughter Xoan. He knew it bothered her. Not many people have his sensitivity. I had something on my mind I wanted to ask him, but instead I asked, "Why wouldn't anyone do what the guy from the Lê clan did? I mean to find that kind of burial ground for themselves?"

"Heck," Chim said, tapping his belly, "it ain't that simple. You don't find that kind of burial ground by just stepping outside."

I thought about it. For almost a week now, we had traveled the region, and our patron—whoever he was—had yet to find whatever he was seeking. Something dawned on me. "You mean places like that aren't nowhere near home?"

"Could be." Chim spoke with his eyes closed. "Could

also be right where you live, if all the elements come together. I'm talking about earth, wind, water. But nature has only a handful of spots like that for the taking. They're hard to find. And you must have a trained eye. Besides, folks don't want to travel too far to tend their family graves. And damn me to hell if any poor folk like us can afford a geomancer."

I didn't think of that. It dampened my excitement. "I've been thinking about my father and my little brother. I mean them lying down there in the soggy soil."

Chim just looked at me, his mouth puckered a little. Finally he said, "Find a drier place to rebury them."

"Yeah. But where?"

"Not around where you live," Chim said.

My mother had told me we could rebury the bones on a spot of unclaimed land. She said we could start looking now that the dry season was near. But around here there were just rice fields and owned properties and creeks and rivers. I thought of making the trek to the mountains. It wouldn't be easy.

"Mr. Chim," I said.

He opened his good eye.

"I'm gonna ask that man where to find a good burial spot," I said. "He won't mind, you think?"

"Who knows what he'd think. Trouble is, you don't know what you're talking about. You have the kind of money rich people pay him? You've seen how hard it is for him? But think for a second. If he'd simply show you a rare burial plot just because you ask him, then damn me to eternal hell with my own consent." Chim looked at the glowing horizon. "I'll have to cook dinner."

Our patron would eat his meal at about sunset. While he ate, he'd gaze at the sky, the flights of birds. Shapes of distant hills on the curved horizon took his attention. Sometimes he asked about the local weather and said, "Are you sure about that?" no matter what Chim's answer was. Sometimes he asked what the hills in the distance looked like to us. If you looked hard, your imagination would form shapes. Chim and I never agreed on what we saw. What looked like an elephant's back to me was a tortoise to him. A mountain range? While I could make nothing out of it, our patron said its peak was a dragon's head. He pointed out its feet and claws, far and bluish, stretching mightily across the misty horizon. It seemed to me the dragon was sleeping. Later, Chim laughed at this while the man wasn't around. He said our mind could play tricks on us. It could make us see things that weren't there. I chuckled. Chim could be right. Maybe that was how the old fart sold his idea to his clientele.

Then yesterday afternoon as we went down the river, our patron told us to moor before a ripple of hills looming over the land. They were dark, shrouded in wispy haze. Gazing at them, I suddenly felt a tremor in my stomach. Those hills had a ghoulish face. Our patron, too, was looking at the hills. I said to him, "Don't they look like an evil face, sir?" He glanced at me, his face impassive, and waved Chim to unmoor the boat. I could see him nodding, to himself perhaps. You wouldn't want to be buried there, I thought, unless you wanted to be damned to eternal hell. I looked back as we rowed on. The malevolent face of the hills bore down on me and my guts twitched.

Outside the dome entrance, Chim lifted a board and crouched over the pit to light up coals in the ashes. The black smoke rose from the bottom of the boat, and before it curled up in the air my brain already sensed its rancid smell. Chim stirred the pot of rice with a short bamboo stick and then sat down on his buttocks, watching the water bubble in the pot. He churned the rice patiently, like nothing else in the world mattered. He was a self-absorbed toad. I always savored his cooked rice and knew that the care he put into its preparation had a lot to do with it.

The setting sun glimmered beyond the horizon. I leaned over the gunwale and spat. Then I looked at my jiggling face in the water and counted in my head: I had been away from home for six days now. Usually I left home at dawn and came back after dusk. When I left home, my mother was on her way to a distant village to midwife some woman's baby. She told me she'd stay on to help nurse the infant for six days and then come back. Why six days, I asked her. She said that by the sixth day the infant would be strong enough for the mother to leave it on its own. She said she'd be back before midnight on the sixth day—today. I knew the way to that village, and I knew my mother would pass a stretch of the river a good distance from where we moored our boat on her way home. She'd reach that stretch at dusk, from my estimation. They called that place Cursed Spirits Stretch. Many people had drowned there. The river was wide and its current was swift.

When I was a little boy and my father was still alive, I crossed that wide river with my mother and baby brother on a rainy afternoon. Midstream, the boat began to swirl in the fast eddies, and the oarsman and his helper shouted obscenities at each other. Standing drenched from head to toe, they tried to pole and steer the boat, but its bow kept spinning. An old woman in the boat clasped her hands on her chest and prayed, and my mother hugged my baby brother in her bosom, her conical straw hat sheltering him from the rain. Then I saw the oarsman leave his spot at the stern and

fumble under the transom. He pulled out a black cock by
the neck, unsheathed a knife, and sliced off the fowl's head.
He tossed the head into the river, shoved the headless bird
back under the transom, and stood watching the current as
his knife dripped rainwater and blood. The boat spun, and
the man lost his footing and was slammed against the gunwale. His knife flew into the water. The old woman doubled
up, bowing to the wind and rain and the river. The oarsman
regained his footing and took the oar again. He pushed on
it like a madman and gabbled to his helper. I could hear
his choppy shouts in the wind, and I wasn't afraid. I knew
my mother was from the way she hugged my baby brother
so tight she seemed locked up inside herself. I wondered
what caused the current to swirl as the boatmen frantically
pushed with their poles. I peeked into the dark transom and
saw the yellow legs of the headless black cock. For the first
time I felt a tremor that wasn't fear. It was like the flutter you
get when you see something dark and mysterious, something like cutting off a bird's head and throwing it into the
river to pacify the malevolent spirits. When I looked up, the
bow of the boat was aimed toward the bank, a misty green
line of bear's breeches. The old woman kept up her prayers
until the boat reached the jetty.

It took several hours to walk home from that stretch of
river, but I wasn't too worried about the long distance. I was
worried about the river.

"Mr. Chim," I asked, and he glanced toward me from the
bubbling rice pot. "Do you care if I go pick up my mother at
Cursed Spirits Stretch?"

"Why'd you want to do that?" Chim said. "Will be a long
way if you take the road. Then how'd you plan to go back
with her?"

I dropped my voice. "I was about to ask if you'd mind taking me there. And then . . . let her ride back here in the boat."

Chim stared at me. He knew where my mother went, and the only way you could get there and back was to cross Cursed Spirits Stretch. He looked disturbed. I dropped my voice even lower, "It'd be dark by the time she gets there. That's why I asked you."

Chim glanced down at his pot of rice and said nothing. Then he looked up and said, "There's a problem, son."

His mild tone surprised me. He went on in a monotonous voice, "I can't take you there and back. You know why, don't you?"

"Yeah."

"It's not windy tonight though. No rain either. So don't worry for her."

But boats still capsized in fair weather. They didn't call it Cursed Spirits Stretch for nothing. If I owned the boat, I would do what I had asked Chim to do. Just tell my patron to ease himself into sleep while I rowed. And I'd row it, keeping close to the bank, to Cursed Spirits Stretch. Even Chim mentioned the name under his breath.

At sunset our patron returned. As he climbed onto the boat, he swung his bag off his shoulder and got out a handkerchief to wipe his brow. He stood with perfect balance as the moored boat rocked with the current. Then he sniffed at the air. "What smells so good, Mr. Chim?" he said, looking down at Chim, who was squatting on his heels at the dome entrance, turning the charcoal-blackened rice pot on the trivet. In the thick aroma of cooked rice, the pungent smell of anchovy cooked with black pepper was delectable.

"You're a man of many skills, Mr. Chim," our patron said, inhaling the aroma.

"Hehe," Chim laughed. He wasn't loud even when he laughed. It was like he didn't want to be noticed. "What's your plan for tomorrow, sir?"

Our patron sat down on the gunwale. "I'll need to go back into the hills in the morning."

"How much longer will you need me?"

"I'll release you from your duty by tomorrow." Our patron grinned a rare grin.

Chim blew the heat from the rice pot from his palms and edged his way past the man to the bow, where he pried open a plank and fished out a small-waisted jar. He palmed it with a reverent gaze and handed it to our patron.

"For you, sir," Chim said.

"What is it? Alcohol?"

"Best spirits, sir."

"Very generous of you, Mr. Chim."

"You've been with us a week now. The least I can do."

Our patron uncapped the jar and passed it under his nose. Then he closed his eyes and held the jar's mouth next to his nostrils, wetting his lips. "How'd you manage to lay your hands on this sort of rare rice liquor?"

Chim tiptoed back past the man to the dome entrance where he bent and quickly rolled out a rush mat for our patron to sit. "I made it myself."

"You moonshine it?"

"Not for sale—only for pleasure."

"I wasn't mistaken." Our patron crossed his legs under him to sit down on the mat. "You're a man of talent."

He dined, sipping Chim's rice liquor from a thumb-sized cup that Chim had placed next to his rice bowl. Chim and

I ate, sitting on the cross-plank at the bow with a clay rice pot between us. None of us spoke, but as I shoved rice into my mouth with a pair of chopsticks I peered at the man who ate in silence and sipped rice liquor with slow motions. The movements of his hand were precise, neat. Chim always asked his guests to join him when he drank. Danton, the French priest, was like that too—always cordial. But this man was drinking another man's best liquor, and he was going to drink it by himself.

Chim clanked his chopsticks against the rim of his bowl. He peered at the man, about to ask him something, but then went back to eating. Then, as the man rested his chopsticks crosswise on his bowl, Chim said, "Have you found what you've been looking for, sir?"

Our patron raised the tiny cup to his lips and sipped. His protruding eyes regarded us warily. "It's a worthwhile trip."

"Are you looking for burial spots?" I said when I saw our patron's lingering smile.

Chim glanced at me, then at the man. Chim shrugged. What the hell, I thought, we're about to be free of this ordeal.

Our patron tipped his head back and downed his cup with a flourish. He blew and licked his lips and then gave us a quick once-over. "I know you have been watching me," he said. "But I know you're decent people. I have to be discreet in my line of business—to protect my investments and my clients'. Can you keep a secret?"

Chim grinned. "What you do is none of my business, sir. Even if you tell us about the burial spot you picked, as vast as it is here, you think people like us could just walk in there and pick out what you've found?"

"You won't, but another geomancer might. And he'd better be good."

"You're safe with us, sir."

Our patron rose to his feet. He looked relaxed, leaning on his elbow which rested on the dome. I put away my bowl and chopsticks. "Sir," I said, "you mind if we take our boat to Cursed Spirits Stretch?"

Chim looked at me. Our patron looked at me. I knew our patron had only the foggiest idea where such a place was. He said, "Why?"

"My mother is arriving there after dark. I haven't seen her for six days."

"Your mother? She's there to take you home?"

"No, I'll be taking her home. She's coming back from her job."

"What kind of job?"

"She's a midwife."

"Eh. Would you be back by morning?"

"Sir, I'd never be gone."

"Wouldn't you be taking her home?"

"Yes, sir. I'll do just that after you're gone."

"She'll be on the boat till then?"

I glanced at Chim. He was cleaning up our dinner. I hadn't even asked for permission for my mother to stay, but my gut told me not to worry.

"Yes, sir," I said.

Our patron picked up the jar of rice liquor and slowly poured himself a cupful. He sipped while we watched him in silence. Finally he said, "Well, I'm going to retire early. I want to go back to the hills at dawn tomorrow. I hope I can get my sleep while you people take the boat upriver."

I looked at Chim. Perhaps his rice liquor had worked its

magic on the man. Chim motioned for me to clean up the remains of dinner. We stacked up the bowls and stashed them
away under the board where we kept our rice pots. We'd
wash them in the river later, in a quiet time.

We came upriver along the pebbled bank, gray-white at
dusk. It is safer to stay clear of the middle channel of the
river than to cross it. Maneuvering our boat up the bank, we
followed the S shape of Cursed Spirits Stretch, wide with
blue water.

The promontory jutted into the river from the foot of
the hill, where ferries were docked at night. There were no
passengers on the landing. I hoped my mother hadn't been
there and left, and Chim echoed my worry.

"Say," he said, "she could've missed us."

The miserable feeling kept me silent. I had asked Chim
to come upriver for nothing. But what made me feel even
guiltier was to have missed my mother. I leaned and spat
into the water as I thought of her walking the long way
home in the dark.

"Let me look around on the bank," I said and climbed
out of the boat. Branches of fig trees wept toward the peb-
bly ground. Perched on them were cormorants roosting for
the night. They looked at me as they stirred, some preening
their glossy black plumage. I stood on the incline of the bank
among large rocks, gazing at the bald hill. After a while I
made out the dark winding footpaths across the slopes.

I sat down against a rock. It felt warm on my back—the
day had been hot. The last glimmer of sun had gone from
the sky and my hope left with it. How long should I wait?
Tired from watching for a lantern light to suddenly dance in
the dark, I closed my eyes. The rock kept me warm. It had

white spots on its ridge, and between half-sleeps I thought someone had daubed paint on it. Then I looked closer. The spots were insects' eggs.

I inched away from the rock and sat hugging my knees, hearing the sudden plops in the river. I thanked Chim in my head. He didn't mind having my mother on his boat until our patron was gone. His kindness came from his sensitivity. He was no fool—he knew I was a good son.

Then I saw a lantern light coming down the hill and stood up, my legs numb and wobbly. I couldn't see well enough to tell if it was my mother, but moments later I recognized her gait and her slender shape in the lantern's glow. Even steps, unhurried. The glow grew brighter as she came near. I ran to her.

"Mother!"

She halted. She brought the lantern to her eye level. Hanging down the side of her face was the tail of the black cloth that was wrapped around her head. She was wiping her sweat with it.

"Tài!"

She stared at me. I felt loved. Seldom had she shown me her affection, and a slightest change in her tone of voice would give her emotion away.

"Are you here alone? Where's your boss?" She moved the lantern away from her and looked beyond me toward the river.

"He's in the boat." I told her the story of the geomancer as we weaved among rocks in the ghostly light of the lantern.

"Where's he from?" she asked, referring to the geomancer.

"He didn't want to be asked."

My mother shifted the cloth sack on her shoulder. We

went down the shingled bank, the pebbles churned. "I was worried . . .," she said. "Sometimes you can't catch a ferry at this hour."

I said I knew and told her my plan. She'd only have to stay on Chim's boat for another day until we got rid of the geomancer. Then I told her my crazy idea about asking the geomancer to find a burial spot for my father and my little brother. It wasn't for my benefit or for my children's, I told her. I wanted a place where my father and brother could rest, dry, in eternal peace. She held my arm as we slid down the bank to the ferry landing, and she said, out of breath, "Tài, don't be so naïve. You'll get yourself in trouble if you think people are that sympathetic. No one ever gives you anything for free. You must earn it."

I didn't think I was naïve. I was desperate. Their bones might not rot in soggy soil, but their putrid flesh might already have. I kept having this miserable feeling when I thought of them. I believed that their spirits remained where their bones were.

We came down to the landing, which was now crowded with moored boats and sampans. You could smell smoked fish and tobacco from the water pipes and the smells made me feel restless, like the evening had just been roused to life. My mother rolled up her pantaloons to her knees and we waded out to Chim's boat. He woke, rubbing his neck. His good eye squinted in the lantern's light. Then he sprung up.

"Good evenin', ma'am," he said, bowing to her.

"Good evening, Chim," my mother said, bowing back.

He took hold of her arm and helped her climb onto the boat. He was older than my mother, by several years perhaps, but he always showed her respect. I guessed his respect came from his awe of my late father. Before I swung over the gunwale, Chim had already spread out a small rush mat on the floorboard.

"Please," he said to my mother, "make yourself comfortable."

She placed the lantern by her side as she sat down. Chim remained standing, rubbing his hands.

"Have you had dinner, ma'am?" he said.

"I ate while I was on the road," my mother said. "What about you two?"

"We ate," I said and looked at her as she dabbed her cheek with the cloth tail of her headgear. She must have eaten the packed riceballs like most wayfarers do as they hurry between places. I looked down at her cloth sack. There must be a few riceballs still left in there. We had leftover rice, but Chim would cook a fresh pot for my mother if he knew that she had traveled on an empty stomach. Good old Chim.

"Ma'am," he said to my mother as he backpedaled toward the bow, "I'm terribly sorry for putting you up like this for the night. I still have my patron—he sleeps in there. I don't know what to do."

"Do what you need to do," my mother said, smiling. "Please get going—you'll forget all about me after a while."

Chim blinked his dead eye. I thought of my blanket I kept under the stern as Chim raised a floorboard and picked up his bedroll. He placed it by the lantern my mother had set next to her. "Please use this," he said. "It gets kinda damp in the night." Then he motioned to me to unmoor the boat.

I was set to climb off the boat and head for the stern—you don't want to pass through the cabin and rouse your patron from his sleep—when our patron emerged from the dome. He flexed his neck and then his protuberant eyes darted around until he saw my mother. The way he looked at her irked me.

Gently, my mother nodded in his direction. "Good evening, sir."

Her voice was melodious. Though the side of her face was shadowed above the lantern's glow, her looks held his gaze. "Good evening," he said glancing at me. "This your mother?" It seemed he wasn't sure because of her youthful appearance.

I nodded. Her face tilted up at him, she said, "Forgive me if I've disturbed your sleep."

"It wasn't you," he said. "The rice liquor."

He was rubbing his thumb and forefinger nervously, and then his other hand groped for the rim of the dome behind him. He leaned back on it and seemed to regain his composure. I was climbing down the boat when Chim said, "Sir, we're going to head back downriver now. You might find sleep easier when the boat is moving. Don't ask me why."

I splashed toward the stern. The man said, "I'll wait out the rice liquor. Such a warm, beautiful evening to sleep in the cabin." I spat, untied the boat, tossed the rope over the gunwale, and climbed in. The wind was on my back as I rowed, and I could hear them talk, Mother and the man. Tidbits of sound. My arms felt tired and I wished he'd sober up from the liquor so he could crawl back into the cabin and get his beauty sleep. He'd never stayed up this late. At times I heard him laughing, and his laugh always ended abruptly on a high note, like someone had grabbed his throat.

The hills were velvety blue beyond the bank. We poled the boat along until we found the spot we'd been at earlier, at dusk. I tied up the boat and looked toward the bow. She wasn't there, but the man and Chim were. Then she ducked out of the cabin.

"Tài," she said.

"Why were you in the cabin?" I said.

"He insisted that I sleep in there."

"Where'd he sleep?"

"Out there with Chim."

One of my eyelids twitched.

"He asked if I wanted to go with him into the hills in the morning," she said.

"What for?"

"Because I wanted to see the burial site."

"He'll show it to you?" I stood in the shallows, eyeing her. "You told him our problem?"

Lips crimped, she nodded. "The way he told it, I thought it ought to be seen."

"Then what?" My mistrust in the man grew. "You said no one ever gives anyone anything for free."

"Yes, I said that. And if it is like what he told me, I want to pay for it."

Perhaps she had saved some money from the days when my father was still alive. But I knew most of what father laid his hands on was spent on gambling and smoking opium. Then I thought of the person who had paid our patron to prospect for a burial site. We wouldn't get it unless my mother was willing to pay more. I said, "How much did he want?"

"I didn't ask. But I will."

"Can we afford it?" Doubt made my tone sour. "Where'd we get the money?"

She smiled calmly. "We'll pay for it with our hard-earned money."

"You mean he'd let us do that? Wait for us—"

"I'll ask him."

She went back into the cabin, and I got my bedroll and
laid my head down on it. The damp breeze smelled of or-
ganic decay, and the air vibrated with the trilling of insects.
You could hear the rustle of wings in the trees, the cadence
of oars *plop-plopping* down the river. Unless you were used
to the night sounds, sleep would be hard. I wondered if they
would keep my mother awake. A grunt came from the bow.
Perhaps the rice liquor still racked our patron's brain.

I wished we had never met him.

MOTHS TO THE FLAME

I woke to a faint aroma of cinnamon that hung in the air.

The pungent bark helped my mother's chronic abdominal pain. The bark was rare, expensive. Because the Annamese emperor monopolized the cinnamon trade, my mother told me, the Annamese laws sentenced a person to death if he was found guilty of damaging the root of a cinnamon tree.

The backdoor was left open and it was gray outside. She must be out there tidying up the two graves. In the pale light of dawn I looked at daddy's skull draped in a white cloth on the crate. When we reburied my little brother and him, we would give him back his head. Then he would be fit to seek life elsewhere.

We found a burial site for both of them. The morning she came back from the hills with the geomancer, she looked flustered. All the way to the port, she sat quietly at the bow. I wondered what had happened. The geomancer was quiet, too, as he reclined in the cabin, smoking the water pipe. Then, as he bid us goodbye, he said to my mother, "Come visit us whenever you like." *Us*? Vexed, I watched him cross the waterfront. Later when we walked home I asked her, "Did you see it?"

She nodded. A silence, then she said, "I want it for your father and your brother."

"What about him? What'd he say?"

She fell silent again. As she dabbed her cheek with the

corner of her headscarf, she said, "He wanted me as his mistress."

Dumb fart. I saw a flash of his eyes. "What'd you tell him?"

"I told him I appreciated his interest in me. But I couldn't see myself in that role." She chuckled. "He said, 'Does it mean that you will say yes if I make you my first wife?' I said, 'No, I'm still mourning my husband.'"

I felt hostile toward her. Why was she so polite with that predator? Why didn't she just tell him that he ought to use his frog eyes to look for tadpoles and mosquitoes, not for young women half his age. Perhaps he had a daughter her age. Who the hell knew?

Words came to my lips as she continued. "He said, 'I'll wait. It's almost over, right?' I said to him, 'It is. But that won't change anything.' He said, 'It won't, eh? You like the burial spot, don't you?' 'I like it very much,' I said. 'And I'll pay for it.'"

She must have some money saved up, I thought, and it'd better be a lot of money. "What'd you mean I'll pay for it?" I said, excited. "You have the money?"

"Well, no," she said. "And there's a problem. He said to me, 'It's not for sale. You see, a man paid me to find him a site. Do you know how long it took me to locate a site like this? Three months. I'd been all over this region before I came upon this place.' 'Why just this region?' I asked. He said, 'That's what he wanted. A fabulous burial spot right in this region.' I felt disturbed by his trickery, how he used the burial plot as bait. Then he said, 'I can save this spot for you. Say yes and it's yours.'"

"Forget him," I blurted out. "You know where it is. You know he has no claim to it. Why don't we just take Daddy's bones and Thái's bones and bury them up there?"

She glanced at me, shaking her head, "Tài, that site isn't anything special unless you know where the heaven-sent spot is. They said that's where the dragon vein is, where all the wonderful energy flows through. He's no fool."

"He could give you a fake spot—that bastard," I said. "He'll save the real spot for his patron. He'll double-deal you and he'll still get paid by his client."

"I thought about that." She nodded and kept on walking. "It's almost like make-believe. You cover your eyes in blind faith."

I felt helpless and I didn't like it. "What'd you say to him?"

"I told him I'd pay him here and there until it's all paid up. I told him I'd forever owe a debt of gratitude to him."

"What'd he say?"

"He said, 'Don't you want to know the price?' I said, 'What's the price?' He said, 'Two hundred piasters.'"

The words stuck in my throat. *Robber*. "Their bones will rot before we can pay enough to bury them there," I said, spat, and licked my lips.

She gazed ahead. "Tài, we'll both pay him. You'll make more money if you leave this place and go to Hanoi and work for him."

My voice shot up. "What? Me? Working for *him*?"

She looked down at her feet. "I couldn't think of any other way."

"For how long?"

"Two years. Roughly."

Two years working for that old bastard.

I didn't feel like getting up, but I knew I had to get going to

catch Chim's boat. I liked the cinnamon scent that still hung
around. You wonder how my mother could afford such
thing? Danton gave her the bark on one of his visits. He,
too, suffered stomach pains and diarrhea since he settled in
Tonkin. He had not eaten bread, only rice, like his Annamese
Christian followers, or what they cooked for him. He said
the native diet had caused him digestive disorders. Lacking
medicine, he took the advice of his parishioners. When he
drank tea he added a sliver of ginger, and he chewed cinnamon bark to help settle his abdominal pains.

I turned on my side, feeling dampness on the front of
my shorts. I wished they were black so they would hide
the stains of my wet dreams. In the morning on my way to
meet Chim, I'd stop and wash the stains at a creek. When
Xoan rowed with us because Chim was drunk on his home-
brewed rice liquor, I saw her eye the dark blots and I wondered if she knew. A year older than me, she had a woman's
figure. She was slightly taller than me and had a round face
like Chim's, a flat nose. Barefoot, she walked with a straight
back, chest thrust out, black pantaloons flapping around her
legs. Her dimpled smile and her shining white teeth gave
her a radiant look, as if she always had lights around her. A
few times when she pulled up the hems of her pantaloons
to wash her legs and feet, she seemed to show them to me.
She had nice white skin. I pretended I wasn't looking, but
when Chim was dozing on his back in the rattan dome I
took a good look at her as she swayed her body at the bow.
Her blouse was drawn back tight as her arms pushed and
pulled on the oars and her breasts jutted. I'd never looked at
a girl that long. My mother always covered her front with a
piece of garment tied back behind her, and over it she wore
her loose blouse in tobacco-juice brown. When I let imagi-

nation play, I thought about Xoan. I wondered if looking at a girl had anything to do with my recurrent wet dreams; it seemed like they started sometime after I went to work for Chim.

He came to our hut one late afternoon after my father died. He knew our family was down on its luck. If I remembered right, it was while my father's head was still hung on the banyan outside Chung village. After he had a long talk with my mother, I was told to meet him the next morning on the ferry landing just outside our village. Soon I became his helper's helper. The girl could row that big boat on both oars by herself when it had gained momentum, or when Chim decided to have a smoke. I was in awe of her. The first day, my arms ached sharply, my back hurt and I had to sit while she rowed, casually, easily. What a miracle it would be when I could row like that. But before long we rowed that boat together up and down rivers and creeks, and she told me how to avoid the shallows lined with sharp rocks that could wreck a boat's bottom, how to maneuver our course around treacherously swirling water. One day past a sandbank I saw two turtles, one picking algae off the other with its jaws. "Look," I said to her, "you ever seen em creatures do that?"

Xoan nodded. "Yeah," she said, "they're in love, so they take care of each other like us. I mean humans."

She didn't say much after I broke the news to her father that I'd leave for Hanoi in the morning. We were eating lunch outside the dome, and Chim was done with his bowl. He poured himself a cup of tea, gargled, and spat over the gunwale as if tea was bad for his health. "I hate to see you go," he said, wiping his mouth with his hand. "But you do what's best for the family. One thing, though, son: keep your eyes open and learn."

"Yessir," I said.

"How are you going to get there in the morning?"

"Oh. I'll catch a boat."

"How about this . . . tomorrow you and her . . ." He nodded toward Xoan. "Take the boat as far as the Monkey Hop Landing. That's half of your trip. You'll manage from there."

"And how'd she manage to bring the boat back?"

"I'll take it back with her." He rose and headed into the dome. "I'm getting off here. But I'll be there—tomorrow noon."

I helped him with a wicker bin. It had two handles, and the lid was tied down with hemp ropes. When we hoisted it over the ledge I could hear faint clinks inside, muffled by rags. I was about to ask him something and then decided not to. We laid it on the ground and he stood resting his foot on its lid. He saw me standing with unasked questions in my eyes and grinned. "Get going," he said.

"Thank you, sir," I said, nodding. "I'll be going now."

I wouldn't see him again until who knows when and I wanted to do something to thank him, yet I climbed onto the boat and we poled it away. We rowed downriver and passed a wooded bank where turtles had left tracks in the ochre sand the night before to dig holes and lay their eggs. The tracks went up into a clump of vegetation. I said, "I thought he never moonshined his stuff."

"Was so," she said, half turning her head from where she stood at the bow. "But you can't keep a secret for long—not when you have your drinking buddies all over you for your spirits."

"I guess he knows what he's doing."

"He does." Then she laughed. "Most of the time."

Still he could encounter trouble. But old Chim was a coot who played dumb, hiding his dark thoughts behind his dead eye and looking innocently through his good one. Maybe Xoan could talk sense into his head, like she did when she made him quit smoking.

All afternoon we ferried merchants who were traveling to distant villages, trading cotton and indigo and castor bean and mulberry. We hardly spoke to each other, and when she had to speak to me she did so with her face partially turned away. I knew she held something in her heart. When dusk fell, the last passengers got off at a promontory, and we shoved the boat back out and headed home. A mist curled over the water so I lit a lantern and hung it outside the dome. The river opened wide and the villages grew far apart. Her head tilted back, and she said, "Are you hungry?"

"Yeah. I'll wash the rice. I'll cook it this time."

"Good." She rested the oars. "Let me know when it's ready. I got the tuna marinated. I'm going to wash myself in the river."

She turned and leaned hard on the oars and I steered the boat toward the bank where the water was inky in the shade of giant figs. It was so quiet you could hear it trickling as it streamed under the boat and its oars. I scooped rice grains from a bin hidden under the floorboard, opened a jug of fresh water, and poured it into the clay rice pot. I glanced through the dome toward the bow to see what she was doing. She had let down the curtain. I felt the boat shake and heard the water splash. She wasn't on the bank. I stood looking, rice pot in hands, and saw her clothes draped over the oar, the wide legs of her black pantaloons knotted and dangling. I sat down, placed the rice pot on the iron trivet, and watched the flame licking its sooty legs. But I wasn't looking at the bluish flames.

"Tài!" her voice came up from the river.

"What?"

"Come down! Water's so warm."

"I don't have spare clothes."

"You can wear my father's clothes afterward."

"I have to watch the rice."

"Let it sit. Bring the flames down. You know how."

I knew how. I wasn't thinking of the rice, even though it would burn.

"Come on down!" she called out, mockingly.

I looked around. Twilight shrouded the bank and in the shade a black hollow pulsed with fireflies. They seemed to be watching me undress. I tossed my shirt into the stern, rolled the legs of my trousers above my knees, and then slid into the river from the side of the boat opposite the bank. The water came up to my waist. She wasn't in sight. I moved toward the bow when something grabbed my leg. I jerked on my feet and saw her break through the water, her hair matted down on her brow and the sides of her face. Her teeth shone white when she smiled. My heart was still thumping.

"Scared?" she said, flicking her wet hair back behind her ears.

"Hell, yeah. Thought it was an otter."

Then I saw her breasts, hugged wetly, tightly by her white shirt, glistening with moisture. The curves of her shoulders were round and her navel was a dark dimple. I just looked, like a dumb beast. She seemed to hear the call of my heart and moved into the lantern's glow and raised her arms to squeeze water out of her hair.

"You never seen a girl before?" she asked, laughing.

I said "no," but only I could hear it. She folded her arms behind her head and flung her hair over her shoulder.

"You never set eyes on any particular girl?"

I thought of the girl who was with the buffalo boys. Each time I conjured her up, a primitive urge flooded me. "I've run into some," I said, grinning. Most of them were old maids not even worth looking at.

"How long can you hold your breath under the water?" she said, ignoring my lie.

"I don't know. Why?"

"Try."

I took a deep breath and went under the water. Then I opened my eyes and saw her pale figure a few feet away. Bare legs. Full hips covered in a black loincloth that floated about her. Like a watery vision, dark and pale from the lantern's gleam. I looked at where her thighs met, holding on to the air left in my lungs until my head was near bursting. I shot up, blowing water from my nose, my mouth.

"How's that?" I said, gasping.

"Fair."

"Fair?"

She nodded, her eyes searching my face for something I had just seen. Then she brushed her wet hair up above her nape.

"Can you do better than that?" I said, measuring her with my eyes.

"Yeah," she said, barely moving her lips.

"Want to bet?"

"Why?"

"Because you're so sure of yourself."

She flashed a grin, white teeth gleaming. "What're we betting?"

"If you lose, you'll lose what you've got covering your body."

"My clothes?" Then she snickered. "Could be yours."

"Could be. I'm halfway there already."

She appraised my bare torso with her gaze. Then again she smiled. "Are you sure that it's fair?"

"What's not fair?"

"I have more to lose than you—if I lose. I'm not going to gain anything if I win."

"What's fair then for you?"

"Tell me again what you'll do if you win."

"You lose your clothes."

"You said that."

"But not here." I tilted my head toward the boat's dome, kept my voice level. "In there."

She pursed her lips, then nodded. "If you lose, you'll do something else for me."

"Like what?"

"Call off your trip tomorrow. And work for my father for another year."

My stomach knotted. She seemed so sure of herself. What if I lost? Go tell my mother to forget her dream, and mine, because of a bet? What would I look like to this girl if I called off the bet? There she stood. Her bosom wetly contoured by the tight shirt. A sinful bait.

"All right," I said calmly.

"A man of your word, I hope." Her lips curled mockingly.

"Whenever you're ready."

She quickly knotted her hair with a twist of her wrist

and her other hand pulled the knot tight. We sucked in air and went down at the same time. She was an opaque shape squatting on her haunches, her loincloth spread about her like a dark mushroom head, her arms crossed over her abdomen. Quickly I pressed my knees together and crossed my arms on my chest to save the air left in my lungs. Then I crimped my lips and shut my eyes. Soon my head began to swell, tingling at the root of my hair. The air in my chest thinned quickly and I shrunk to a dark hollow somewhere in my guts. Then I saw my mother's face. Her whispers melted into a viscosity in my mouth that dripped into my lungs. They were burning hot. I wanted to free myself of this dark, miserable suffocation, push up, rise. But I didn't move. I'd rather drown.

Water got into my mouth, stinging my nose like red-hot pins. Then in the blackest depth of my mind I smelled air, and when I opened my eyes I was slumped against the side of the boat. I felt her hands on my shoulders.

"Take a deep breath," she said.

I took a deep breath. I gagged and coughed violently.

"Again," she said. I sucked in air through my nose. There was something wrong with it. It felt like it was bleeding. I wiped my nose and saw no blood. From her calm voice, I knew I had lost.

"Did I win?" I said, not looking at her.

"You're still alive."

"Did I win?"

"Yeah," she said. "You won."

A dead weight was gone from my chest. Suddenly I felt very tired and hungry. The aroma of rice was in the air. It must be ready.

"Hope it didn't burn," I said, climbing back onto the

boat.

She remained in the water. I turned. "Won't you come up?"

She searched my face, swung her leg over the gunwale, her wet loincloth clinging to her thigh, and deftly dropped to her feet on the boat's floor. I squatted over the opening on the floorboard.

"Why don't you cook the tuna now?" I said, "I'm starving."

She said nothing as she stooped to enter the dome. I looked at the curtain behind her and turned to the pot, opened its lid, and let my face soak in the wet steam. The breeze came up across the river and there was a faint odor of wet timber from the opposite bank. When she came back out, she had put on her clothes. She handed me a pair of dark gray cotton pantaloons.

"Put these on," she said. "You're dripping all over the floor."

I took them from her hand. She avoided my eyes. Inside the dome I took off my wet trousers and sat on the plank bed holding them in my hands. Then I touched my nose. It didn't feel tender anymore. Something was covered over in my mind. I couldn't explain it. Did I come up from under the water against my will?

I sat there naked. I felt miserable.

The breeze fluttered the curtain, bringing in the dark aroma of fried tuna. My stomach churned as I pulled up the pantaloons, and as I put down my foot, it hit a bump on the warped floor. A tiny shock from the sole of my foot shot to my brain. It wasn't pain anymore. It used to be, in the weeks after the bamboo spike went through it. When I refused to stay home, against Chim's advice, she let me row with her and helped me change the dressing at the end of each day. They gave me a support to help me walk. It was a cane with a cross-handle, both made out of black bamboo. When I thanked Chim for it, he said that she made it for me so I wouldn't hop along like a bird. I had time to examine it afterward—how the handle fit tightly into the cane through two round openings, cleanly bored. I knew then she was a handy girl.

We sat and ate by the lantern. She had dried her hair and rolled it into a bun above her nape. She looked older this way, and the white of her neck and her throat held my gaze. Water was boiling in the kettle that sat on the trivet. She leaned down, picked up the kettle, and began to add hot water to the teapot. A thick layer of leftover tea leaves covered the bottom. Between mouthfuls of rice, I asked her when she'd be ready in the morning so we could take the boat up to Monkey Hop. By the cockcrow, she said. I wanted to arrive in the city in daylight. It was a big city. She asked if I'd been there and I said no, that all I had was the man's address. It was on Limestone Street, one of the thirty-six streets on which thrived trade guilds of all kinds. I told her what my mother told me: ask for Mr. Đinh-Hòa, the geomancer. They all knew him.

She poured tea into two clay cups and sipped hers while I refilled my bowl with rice. In the silence, we could hear water lapping at the side of the boat, the harsh calls of waterfowl across the river. She drained her cup and stowed it with her bowl and chopsticks in a rattan strainer and then rose to her feet.

"I know you have something else on your mind," she said, looking down at me.

"Maybe I do." I glanced up without meeting her eyes.

"You won the bet. I won't go back on my words."

"I didn't forget."

She turned on her heel, speaking to me with her head cocked back. "You know where to find me."

I stole a glance at her back just as she let the curtain fall behind her. The rice was stuck in my throat, and quickly I washed it down with a gulp of tea. It scalded my tongue and I spat it out. Then I glanced at the remains of our dinner in the trembling shadows the lantern cast on the mat. Out on the river, some boatwoman was singing a ballad, her lantern gliding low on the water.

I put a lid on the remains of the tuna and wrapped it with a jute cloth. Then I put the dishes under the floorboard. The teapot in one hand, the cup in the other, I entered the dome through the curtain.

She was a dark shape under the blanket on the plank bed a foot from the floor. All I could see was the glimmering white of her face. I stood hunched over her, and then sat down on the floor. She turned on her side, pulling the blanket up to her chin. Her eyes gleamed. I could hear the beating of my heart as I lifted the teapot and poured myself a cup.

"Are you going to sit there and drink and make me do this?" she said.

"No." I sipped my tea.

She watched me. I got up from the floor and sat on the edge of the bed. She dropped her gaze and I tugged at the corner of the blanket. I watched it fall, watched her pale white figure lying on her side, one leg pulled up and both arms crooked covering her chest. My throat went dry. I put my hand on her calf, felt it, remembering how I'd gazed at her calves whenever she washed her feet at the river. The thickness in my throat grew as I looked where her thighs met. She lay very still. I pushed at her leg and slowly turned her onto her back. Gingerly, she obliged. Out on the river we could hear the *clap-clapping* of the bamboo sticks the boatmen made when there was a fog.

I could smell the river, the damp silty smell still clinging to my skin, and I could smell her.

THE DEMONIC OPIUM PIPE

There was a rutted trail that went up from the ferry landing, and along the trail there were tall ridges of dried mud where porters would rest their tired bones, their pointed straw hats covering their faces, their backs bent under the heavy bales. A half moon hung on this clear night. The trail shone dimly and the trunks of the fig trees were mottled and gray.

There wasn't a soul behind me, and the river was now out of sight. After I changed ferries at the Monkey Hop Landing, I started thinking of my days ahead in the city. All day it rained, and a fog hung over the river which was rough from the wind. Its water was frothy and red from the stirred silt in the riverbed. Boats were docked under weeping willows, bobbing on the waves, and the cormorants roosting on the tree branches watched the rain falling on the water. From the jetty, as I waited for an upriver boat, I watched the pale fog drift. Sometimes the wind parted the fog and you could see the dark water. There weren't any boats coming by, and late in the afternoon the rain stopped. By dusk the fog had lifted and a glimmer of sun reddened the horizon. The jetty was empty but for me and a fisherman. He told me if I took the trail, I could find lodging for the night.

Before me stood a hut, low and long. I saw a dozen mules, each tethered to a wooden stake that lined the front of the shabby hut. The mules stepped back and forth, twitching their ears when I walked up to the hut. Through its door a yellow light wavered from an oil lamp. Inside, the air was warm and foul. There were bodies everywhere. Some were curled up in a corner, snoring, some were sprawled, resting their heads on their bundles and bales, and some lay on their sides, smoking opium pipes. I stepped over feet and hands like a nervous horse, holding my breath because of the stench of the bodies and their clothes. No one minded me.

"Boss?" I called out. "Boss here?"

"Hey, you!"

Someone pulled at my leg. I looked down. A figure in gray. Then the pointed straw hat tipped back and eyes peered up. "Keep quiet," came a phlegmy voice. "Don't you see I'm sleeping?"

He had an accent. These must be Chinese merchants, I thought. "Where's the innkeeper?" I asked in a low voice.

"Gone."

"Gone where?"

"Find a medicine man. A fellow there...got very sick..."

I couldn't tell which one. They all looked dead, except the opium smokers.

"What'd you want?" the voice asked.

"A place to sleep," I said.

"Got money?"

I glanced down at the human heap at my feet. "Yeah."

"Take my spot," the voice rose. "Pay me."

"Pay you? And where'd you sleep?"

"Out. With em mules."

"How much?"

"Fifty *sapèques*."

I almost kicked him. I stepped over him and headed out. His voice followed me. "Where're you going?"

"Out. With em mules."

"Thirty-five *sapèques*?"

I ignored him. Outside the night was cool and pale and slivers of light glimmered on the hut's mud wall which was laced with rotted, yellowed bamboo. The mules snorted. One black mule nibbled mindlessly at its rope. I walked past them, cursing their sour smell, and found a tree that stood clear of the underbrush that faced the hut. I unslung my jute bag. Sitting with my back against the tree trunk, I ate one of the riceballs my mother had packed for me. As I chewed, I could smell the crushed sesame, and it made me homesick. She ate these riceballs too when she went midwifing a day or two on foot. "Save every *sapèque* you earn," she said to me before I left that morning. I shoved the last morsel into my mouth and pulled out a canteen and drank. The tin felt cool in my hand. I liked this canteen more than anything my father left behind. He had bought it from an Algerian infantryman, he said. That was after he gave me a whipping when he saw that I had peed in it. He whipped me until he broke the bamboo rod in half. He said no son of his was too scared of darkness to go outside to pee at night. I did that, just once when I was five. I was too scared to go out back of our hut to relieve myself.

My eyes closed, my head resting on my bag, I squirmed against the hard ground under me. I turned on my side and tried to sleep. *She was rowing the boat home with her father under the steady rain, the fog blowing like gray vapor past the bow of the boat.* A longing rose in me and for the first time I knew that nothing would be the same again. The silty smell of the river had been in her hair and now I could taste it in my breath.

Something woke me. It sounded like water gurgling down a sluice. Bleary eyed, I looked toward the hut. A man

was squatting beside a mule, the black mule, holding a
wad of rag under the mule's belly while it peed. He must
have soaked the rag because he sprung up, squeezed it, and
shook it wildly as if it was a rattlesnake. He then slunk back
inside. Could those bastards be that thirsty? I lay my head
back down. The mule was still making water. The damned
beast must have drunk a whole river.

As I drifted in the silt-scented fog of my mind, I felt trem-
ors in the ground. This time I saw two men coming out of
the hut carrying someone by the neck and feet. They stood
looking around and then moved in my direction. They saw
me, stopped, and came forward. They both wore their pointed straw hats tipped back behind their heads, their calves
wrapped in dirty-looking puttees. I sat up. They dropped
the man like a sack a few feet from me and, not even looking
at me, turned around and strode back inside. I stared at the
thing, a human bundle in gray clothing. What was wrong
with him? Dead? He must be.

I sat on my haunches and fixed my stare on the body. It
lay still, the lower legs bound in tattered dark leggings, bare
feet pointing up. Too bad he died before the innkeeper could
get him a medicine man. Then in the quiet came a moan. I
listened. I stepped over and looked down. His face looked
like a wrinkled piece of elephant hide and his gray hair was
knotted in a long pigtail that drooped over his shoulder.

"Hey there," I said to him.

The eyes opened to a slit above the high, sharp cheek-
bones. I squatted down and a repulsive smell of urine hit
me. They must have washed him with the mule's urine.

"You're not dead?" I said, half convinced that he wasn't
alive.

A hand touched mine, clammy against my skin.

"Who . . . is . . . this?" he asked in his Chinese accent.

"I hope you don't die," I said. "Do you know if they sent for a doctor?"

The eyes closed. His windpipe wheezed. He was breathing through his mouth. Then he mumbled something in Chinese. I wasn't sure if he was talking to himself or to me.

"Huh?" I said.

He barely opened his eyes, the dark slits trembling, and held me in his gaze. "You a boy?" he finally muttered.

"Yeah."

"Where you from?"

"Lau."

He said nothing. Then he nodded.

"You from China?" I said.

"Yunnan."

Winters they would come in a caravan, sometimes a hundred or two pack horses, and you'd see them travel through our villages in small groups and the clinking of kettles and saucepans they strapped to their horses brought our people rushing out of their huts. They had with them cotton goods—always cotton goods—and sold them to us, the very people they had bought raw cotton from. Chim once told me the Chinese had better weaving machines that made good, durable fabric and they thus had the Annamese in their pocket. The other good they brought with them was opium. Chim said that if you want cheap opium that may kill you, you could get a bargain from them.

I glanced toward the hut and then back at him. "Why'd they put you out here?"

"Me...dying," came his wispy voice. "Save them a space in there."

"You're sick?"

He was breathing with difficulty and his eyes opened in the glimmer of the moon. He put his hand on his throat and then on his chest like he didn't know they were still there.

"Me . . . addict," he said in a whisper.

"The drug made you sick?"

"Yeah." His skeleton hand clawed at his chest. "Me . . . forty years . . . smoke opium. Now very sick."

"I don't know what I can do for you, mister."

He found my hand. The coldness from his thin, bony fingers made me squirm. "You can," he said. "Can you . . . help me?"

"How?"

"Find my granddaughter."

I simply stared at him.

"My granddaughter...she live in Hanoi..."

I thought of my ordeal in days ahead, then of his plea, and said nothing. Better not tell him that was where I was headed.

"Me...can't never see her again...me...needs you find her ...for me..."

His cold hand clamped mine as if I was his savior.

"You don't know this..." he said. "Me...have only her now...my daughter just died...my granddaughter...she must go back home...tend her mother grave..."

"You mean your granddaughter doesn't know that her mother just died?"

"She not know...we sent her here to work...so she could send money home."

I looked into his darkened face and felt his bone-cold fingers crawl up my arm. "You help me...you will?" he said.

I said nothing, and he withdrew his hand and felt around inside his blouse. He then let out a pained bleat.

"You all right mister?" I said, startled.

"Them...them..." He was choking on his words. "They took my money."

"Them? In there?" I pointed toward the hut.

"Took my money. Bad...bad."

His hands began shaking, then his body. His breathing came in spurts, squeezed out of his lizardlike neck. I watched the lump on his throat, which stuck out like an egg. It must be all the money he had. Would a dying man need money?

"Me...me want to pay you...but me...lost all money now."

In the dark the slits of his eyes fluttered like he was crying, but there were no tears.

"Mister," I said, "you expect me to find your granddaughter in a big city like that? Huh?"

Suddenly his noisy breathing calmed. "My granddaughter...she live in the Chinese quarter...that is. You find her there easy."

"She has a name?"

"Yeah...name ... Xiaoli."

Xiaoli. I repeated the name in my head. "Is there only one Xiaoli in the Chinese quarter?"

"You ...you go look for...Zhang Xiaoli, that's her."

Again I said the name in my head. "How old?"

"My granddaughter...old like you."

I tried to stay calm. "Mister, you expect me to go around the Chinese quarter hollering for this...this Zhang Xiaoli? Hey..."

"Me...me forgot to tell you...she work in an opium den ...yeah."

A breeze brought a strong ammoniac odor from his body. I couldn't tell if he wetted himself or if it was the mule's urine they had washed him with. He said hoarsely, "Mercy. You have mercy."

I felt his desperation. Years later, when I thought back on that moment, I realized his hopelessness wasn't alien to me. I said nothing, but I remembered the name. Zhang Xiaoli.

"You...you take my mule." He gasped for air, purring in his throat. "Me...have nothing left."

"Your mule, mister?" I glanced toward the mules. "Which one?"

"Black. Only one."

"What do I do with a mule?"

"Sell it." His voice was now a whisper. "So you can go . . .to Hanoi."

The whole thing befuddled me. First, how would I sell his mule around here to pay for my trip? Who would let me board a ferry with a mule? During my time with Chim, we once ferried a man with a horse, and we regretted it. Sure, we got the money we asked for, but was it worth it? The horse made a mess on our boat, peeing and crapping, enjoying itself. But then again a horse or a mule—his dumb beast over there—was no small change if you could sell it. I could walk away with the money and surely wouldn't do myself any harm. The thought of wandering into the Chinese quarter in Hanoi looking for someone I had never met, a Chinese girl slaving in an opium den—who might even look like him—wasn't something I called pleasure. I looked down at him and kept my voice even. "Mister, hey, mister."

He stirred. The smell came back.

"I need to get some sleep," I said. "I have to get going early in the morning."

"Going? Where?"

"I won't forget what you asked me."

"But...you...you take my mule...don't wait till morning."

"I need my sleep, mister."

"Them...them...they see you...you no take my mule."

Damn your mule, I thought. "All right," I said. "I'll take a nap—then the mule."

I lay back down on my old spot and immediately sank into blackness.

I woke, not knowing where I was, aching all over, and fell back asleep. When I opened my eyes again, the night was whirring with the sounds of insects, the moon hung like a pale sickle. Then I saw black things dangling from an enormous tree on the edge of the trail. They looked like hanged men. Evil-looking. Those trees sometimes grew on the riverbank, and when you passed them at dusk, the sight of their monstrous pods swinging made your bones chill. I didn't feel good as I looked at them. But I didn't feel tired anymore, so I went over to look at the man. He lay flat on his back, a dark gray shape, with his ponytail flung on the ground like a dead snake. I looked toward the hut. Better get the mule now.

There were noises inside the hut. Someone groaning. The snoring filled the air. Then someone cursing in Chinese. I stood by the black mule, resting my hand on a canvas sack flung over the mule's back. There was a big dark spot on the dirt beneath the animal, and the smell of its piss still hung around. If I took it away now, I'd go back to the ferry landing and wait for the first upriver boat to come by at dawn. Then I'd ask around for a buyer. Sometimes you got lucky—people said a mule was a handy beast. It stood there shaking its head and rotating its hairy jaw. When did these beasts ever sleep? I reached for the hemp rope that was tied around the wooden stake and patted the mule on the head.

"Let's go," I said.

The mule tossed its head up and its flaring nostrils rubbed my face. "C'mon, now," I said, pulling the animal away. It jerked its head and stood its ground. This time I slapped it on the head. The next thing I knew the mule let out a shrill bray and turned and banged its flank against the stake. It hit hard, and all the mules were roused, jerking their ropes with their big heads. Then several men came staggering out. For a brief moment they stood outside the hut like a bunch of lunatics, looking at me. Then they gestured wildly with their hands, shouting in Chinese. One man, the fellow trying to offer me his sleeping spot, grabbed the mule by its head and shouted into its ear. The beast calmed down, now standing and sniffing at the stake, and all the other mules stopped fretting. He turned to me.

"You stealing our mule?" he said in Annamese.

"It's his mule," I said, pointing toward the shabby figure on the ground. "He gave it to me."

"He gave you his mule? Just when then?"

"A while back. So I'm taking it."

"He gave you his mule—just like that?"

"Ask him."

The fellow laughed, scratching his chest. He slapped his leg and rubbed his fingers together crushing whatever he had just killed. Without saying a word, he walked over to where the old man lay. The rest followed him. I stood looking. He bent and shook the old man by the shoulder, shook and shook, and then said something in Chinese. He put his fingers on the old man's neck and then on his chest. I knew the old man was dead as the fellow walked back. He tied the black mule to the stake.

"I asked him," he said, grinning.

The rest of them didn't grin, but looked at me morosely.

"He died, didn't he?" I said.

"What'd you think?" he said, blowing snot out of one of his nostrils.

"He must've just died."

"I don't think so," he said, scratching himself behind the ear. "I think he was long dead and you knew it. That's why you were trying to make off with his mule. Heh?"

I spat. "I don't care what you think. But you don't make any damn sense."

"Me?" He jabbed his finger at his chest. "What's this dumbfuck talking about?"

"How'd I know this mule was his?"

"I don't know. But I know this: this mule ain't yours."

"So you stole his money and left him out there for dead. And now you take his mule too?"

"You're not as dumb as you look. So what if we do that? Heh?"

I glanced toward the corpse. "What're you gonna do with him?"

He hawked up phlegm and spat near my foot. "Do you care?"

The old man was right. Once these bastards were up, I could forget taking the mule. He took his eyes off me as he rummaged through the sack strapped to the mule's back. He felt around, taking a mental inventory of the items he felt. His hand came out, holding a pipe. An opium pipe. It was black with a small round bowl. He weighed it in his hand, grinning.

"You smoke?" he said, extending the pipe to me.

"Do I look like one of you Chinese addicts?"

"Good pipe. Let you have it for half a piaster."

"Give me half a piaster and I'll take it."

He squinted his eyes at me and turned to the men, saying something in Chinese and waving the pipe in front of them. They all waved it off and one of them started ranting, jabbing his finger at the pipe. Finally the man shouted at him and he shut up. With one flick of his wrist, the man chucked the pipe. It landed somewhere near the corpse. Then they turned and headed back inside.

I called out after them. "Hey, you said it's a good pipe."

"Yeah." He looked back at me. "Good pipe. Older than your great-granddad, I'd say."

"So?" I said.

"Let it be buried with him."

I looked at the corpse and back at him. "If you could sell his bones, I know you would. What're you hiding?"

"You really want to know?"

"Yeah."

"His great-granddad smoked that pipe and he died from smoking it. Then his granddad smoked it, died too. Then his dad. Now him."

I pondered this. He disappeared inside and I walked back to my spot. I saw the pipe and picked it up. It was a bamboo pipe, but thinner than a tobacco pipe. It had carvings on it I couldn't make out in the dark. These superstitious Chinese! The fellow who was ranting obviously didn't want any part of the curse. I sniffed at the bowl, winced at the dross' acrid smell. You die from smoking too much opium and you blame a pipe?

But this pipe did look evil from its charcoal black color. The pipe must have originally been yellow. The black coat was the result of the heat and smoke of at least a hundred years.

I opened my sack, pushed the pipe down, and tied the knot. At my feet, the old man's mouth and eyes were open. The frozen look on his face made me think of Death, who came to take him before he was ready to leave.

I sat down on my spot. Perhaps I should deliver his message to his granddaughter when I got to Hanoi. I could give her this pipe to remind her of him.

THE BLACK-FACED GIRL

The first time Mr. Đinh-Hòa, the geomancer and my new employer, took me to this opium den on Silk Street, I walked behind him carrying his trinkets in a round wicker basket— his pipe, a teapot, two tiny handleless cups, and sweetmeat wrapped inside two layers of brown paper. We passed shops now closed at dusk, me trailing him. Sometimes, on my errands during the day, I saw bright colorful place mats, white mosquito nets, and tailored martial robes on display. We came to this den once or twice a week, in the evening. When it rained, he came in on a rickshaw, while I walked the muddy street, hugging the basket inside my palm-leaf raincoat, bulging like I was pregnant.

It was a den for patrons who came and smoked while their rickshaw coolies loitered outside, often gambling nois- ily. Those dens and the alcohol served there were legal in the city, monopolized by the colonial government. I knew that much from Chim, who made moonshine and told me about his days working in the opium den in Hanoi where he met my father. Some evenings I saw two guards in red attire standing outside the den—this meant a mandarin was passing his evening inside. Mr. Đinh-Hòa told me to tend my tasks as quietly as a mouse, never talk to the servants who served the patrons, and never stare at the patrons while they were deep in their reveries.

I was in awe the first time I set foot inside the den. After Mr. Đinh-Hòa lay down on a low bed made of wood, I sat gingerly on the edge of it. I noticed its fine curved legs. I couldn't help but touch the carvings on them, the pale, glittering mother-of-pearl etchings of small tortoises and cranes and dwarfed trees. Then I touched the dark red satin sheet. It was cool, smooth. After a while I looked up at the yellow silk canopy dangling with tassels above me. The room flickered with peanut-oil lamps, their crystal globes a handsome bulbous shape, and they suddenly grew dim when a patron leaned out, drawing deeply on his pipe. There was an orange paper lantern that hung over the door from a cord attached to the ceiling. When I gazed up at the beautiful tear-shape, still and solitary, I thought of an ethereal world free of all pain, all worries. I breathed in a dark odor of caramel, and the room came to life with the occasional crackling of pipes.

I didn't know opium smelled like burnt sugar. Mr. Đinh-Hòa explained that only premium opium smelled that way. He said base opium had an unpleasant smell. I had no desire to know that and wondered what would happen if I kept inhaling the opium fumes. Would I become an addict like him someday?

He was very picky about his opium habit. He didn't like the tea served by the den's servants, so he had me brew it just as he began preparing his first pipe. The tea must be hot when he drank it. That was why the teapot held just a pinch of his select tea, enough to make two tiny cups. I had to brew it again and again. Three months after I went to work for him, he taught me how to prepare a pipe. Reclining on his elbow, he watched me. Unlike Chim, who never nitpicked, he liked to find fault. I'd watched him, and when it came time for me to prepare a pipe, I did what I remembered seeing.

I heated a wooden-handled needle over the lamp and dipped it into the crystal opium jar, watching the brown drug glue itself to the tip of the pin. I could sense him following my every move as I brought the needle to the lamp and cooked the sticky drop. I twirled the pin, the lamp burning a soft yellow. I watched the drop intently, and then it swelled, glistening a brown color. I picked it off the pin and kneaded it against the palm of my hand until it became putty-like. Then, holding my breath, I pushed the paste neatly into the tiny opening of the bowl. With both hands, I held the pipe over the lamp, ignoring the heat on my fingertips, and watched the dark brown opium melt into smoke. He brought his lips to the stem and drew in the smoke as deeply as he could. His eyes slowly closed, his head tilted back, and then he exhaled the smoke through his nostrils and mouth. I kept the pipe still as his lips again found the pipe stem and his cheeks hollowed as he sucked in the fumes.

He would take five draws before preparing a fresh pipe. Some evenings he smoked fifteen pipes, some evenings twenty. Between drags, he sipped tea and nibbled a caramel sweetmeat, savoring the taste as it melted in his mouth. His wife made delectable sweetmeats. Then he napped. I started cleaning his pipe. One of the knickknacks in the basket I carried was a thin iron pin that I used to scrape out the opium dregs in the blowhole of the pipe bowl. One evening I held it in my hand, tracing my finger along its slick, yellow bamboo handle, its cold lustrous pin. Its sharp point gleamed in the lamplight. You could run this thing through somebody's stomach easily. Like that drug addict who tried to drive a cleaning rod through my father's belly in an opium den somewhere in this very city. But my father had blocked it with his body by God-knows-what martial arts technique.

In the opposite corner of the room stood a canary-yellow silk screen framed in shiny black wood. Three months before I arrived, there was a murder in this den. Where the screen was now, there used to be a bed. The bed belonged to a judge who sometimes slept there in the evening. One night while he smoked, a man came in, walked right up to his bed, grabbed the cleaning rod, and stabbed him in the heart several times. He must have been dead after the first lunge, but the killer seemed bent on making his heart minced meat. Now the killer was in a dungeon awaiting execution.

Mr. Đinh-Hòa said the man was a rickshaw coolie who couldn't pay the daily rent for a rickshaw. The rickshaw boss had sent a foreman to collect the money. What the foreman couldn't collect he made up for with brute force, leaving the rickshaw coolie in coma. The rickshaw coolies got together and protested to the law, and a trial followed. But the judge acquitted the foreman. Mr. Đinh-Hòa wasn't in the den that night, but the gruesome scene must have scared away many patrons. It took a while for things to return to normal. Now, behind the silk screen, you could glimpse the girls changing their attire before they came out to entertain the patrons, a move by the den owner to revive his business.

They would come out dressed in shiny green or blue or red moiré cheongsams, but the girls weren't Chinese. When one of them came to my employer's bed, I could sometimes smell a lemon or rose scent when she slid in at Mr. Đinh-Hòa's side. Her white skin, like porcelain, made his skin look sickly and pale in comparison, and when she reached for the pipe and the pin, her dress was pulled back tight and I could see the whiteness of her upper arms where the sleeves stopped a finger-length short of her armpits. I couldn't take my eyes from her blood-red fingernails. I found out later that she painted them.

Before I came, my employer had to do all these chores by himself—he had to prepare his pipe and brew his own tea, not to mention carry all his playthings himself. Now he had me. He smoked at least twenty pipes in a night. One night while he napped, I was cleaning his pipe and a den servant came to me, and asked me to let him have the dregs I was scraping out of the pipe's bowl. I looked up at him and then at a piece of brown paper he held in his hand.

"Why?" I said. "I'll trash this myself."

"Just give it to me."

I watched him wrap the dregs carefully inside the paper. "You aren't trashing this, are you?"

He said nothing, and just eyed me. Then he put the packet in his trouser pocket and pointed at the pipe. "Any time you get the dirt out, don't dump it. Understand? I can make some money on em."

"You sell them?"

"Yeah."

"Who buys?"

"Street drug addicts."

"They smoke this crap?"

"Yeah. Smoke. Drink. Mix it with tobacco. Tonic for em."

"And good money for you."

"A sin to waste even crap."

From that night on I thought of saving up the opium residues and selling them to the addicts. But where would I find the dope fiends? And how many visits to the den with my employer would it take for me to earn money? Each patron, I noticed, smoked fifteen to thirty pipes an evening. Even a light smoker could go for ten pipes before he nodded off. If I cleaned every pipe in the den, how much could I earn selling this sort of poison? I wondered.

One evening as we were leaving the den, a drizzle was falling. You could hardly feel any wetness on your face or your hair. They called it ash rain. Fitting, I thought, because Mr. Đinh-Hòa didn't seem bothered when he emerged from the den and stepped out onto the street. Several rickshaw coolies were throwing dice on the sidewalk, whooping and hollering. Seeing us, a coolie stopped and came tottering up.

"Sir, how bout a ride home?" he said.

"I think I'll just walk," Mr. Đinh-Hòa said.

"Oh no, not in this weather." The coolie touched my employer's crêpe de chine sleeve. "Your robe's gonna get soiled, sir."

"It might, eh? But I feel like walking tonight."

He must have felt good after his catnap because he walked sprightly into the night, and I strode behind him past the closed shops. The air smelled sodden. There was a cool breeze coming from the river, and as I walked the dark street I thought that I would have brought a lantern if I had known we'd walk home like this. Most of the time he rode home in a rickshaw. Now the noise of the coolies was gone, and it was so quiet I could hear the clinking of the teacups inside the basket I carried. We walked past closed doors of thatch-roofed houses. I saw glimmers of oil lamps between the gaps in the door planks. Our footfalls spooked the dogs inside the houses and they barked. Those starved, scruffy canines were loud. Danton, the priest, once told me that those dogs possessed an uncanny memory of scents. They remembered his smell in distant hamlets of his outlying parishes, though he visited them very infrequently.

When we turned onto a crossroad that ran perpendicu-

lar to the river, a breeze came up and a muddy smell hung
in the air. This road led to a garrison. Two human figures
moved across the street in the dancing reflection of a lantern. They were barefoot and seemed to glide in darkness.
A child, clothed in rags, was pulling a blind old man along,
holding in his other hand a red paper lantern at the end
of a stick. As Mr. Đinh-Hòa kept walking, I stopped and
watched the child and the blind man heading into a dense,
wild banana grove by the roadside. The red of their lantern
dimmed, wavering eerily, and suddenly disappeared. Then
in the blackness of the grove a torch light glowed.

A group of men, at least ten, squatted around the torch.
They were Chinese. You could see their pigtails hanging
from the back of their heads. It sounded like they were hag-
gling over something. Finally they stood up, each looking at
something in his hands. Standing in the center was a young
girl counting zinc coins. They clanked as she dropped them
into her bag. She had a ghastly face, so black in the dancing
torch light it looked ghoulish. She swung her bag over her
shoulder, her pigtail dangling behind her, and strode out of
the grove.

Suddenly, out of the darkness a horseman rode up. He
rode up so quickly that everyone, including me, just stared at
him, bewildered, for a moment. Perhaps he had been there,
waiting in the dark, unseen, for his whole outfit was black.
He wore a high-collared, tight-looking jacket and trousers
that were tucked into his black boots. Even his horse was
black as an otter. He shouted something in French, and
the Chinese broke off running. The torch remained on the
ground, sputtering with blue sparks. The girl froze in her
tracks.

He slid off his horse and grabbed her by the pigtail.

Before she could even move, he reached into her bag and pulled something out. A bad feeling hit me. She must be selling opium dregs. He kicked the torch over, dragged her to his horse by her pigtail, and swung himself back up on the saddle. I didn't know what to do, but when I saw the horse trot away, the girl being dragged alongside, tumbling over her feet as her arms flailed wildly, I dropped the basket to the ground. Something broke inside. I ran. I don't know what drove me, but I ran with all my might after the horse. Something hit my foot and I dropped to the ground. A rock. With one hand I picked it up and stood, sucking in my pain. I let it fly. The black shape on the horse reeled and dropped to the ground. The girl tottered, groping like she was blind. I ran up to her. Fright burned my dry throat. Had I just killed a man?

"Run!" I shouted to her. "Damn it! Run!"

It was so dark I could only see her eyes, like tiny lights on her ghostly black face. She looked at me and wiped her eyes with the back of her hand. When I saw the pale white of her hand and wrist, something struck me as funny—she must have smeared her face with coal. I waved her off.

"Go!" I said.

I backed away from her just as she turned and ran into the banana grove. Up the road, the horse was milling around as if waiting for the horseman to get up and ride him. I took off running. Darkness was all around and Mr. Đinh-Hòa was nowhere in sight. I cut across a dirt road near where he lived and saw him walking like a pale apparition under the flickering lanterns that hung at the corners of the crossroads. My chest ached and my mouth was dry. I slowed down as he turned around. He saw me.

"Where's the basket?" he asked.

"The basket?" I said.

I dashed back. The pain in my toes was growing. They must be bleeding. I must have nearly broken them when I hit my foot against that rock. The rock. Where did I hit the man? Hell. What if he was dead? No, no. My mouth tasted like copper. *Get that basket. Don't lose it. You know how much love and care he'd put into keeping those tiny teacups speckless? The teapot, too.* His little treasure. And his pipe.

The banana grove was dark and the muddy smell floated in the breeze. The first thing I looked for was the man and his horse. Neither was anywhere to be seen. Just darkness. A feeling of relief lightened my chest. Thank Heaven, I thought. He was all right.

It was so still I could hear myself panting. I heard the gruff *glunk* of a toad. I went to the spot on the roadside where I'd left the basket. It wasn't there. I took a sharp breath, got my bearings, and faced the grove. Surely this was the spot I'd stood on. I saw the little clearing where I'd seen the Chinese men and the girl. I bent to look again. The basket wasn't tiny. It had that pale yellow of the cane. A dead weight sat on my chest. Someone must've made off with it.

Just as the thought hit me, a huge black shape silently emerged from the grove. The soft clacking of hooves filled me with horror. I was too dumbstruck to move as the horseman rode up to me, like a spirit returning to settle the scores with the living. He had my basket in his hand.

I looked up at him. Flesh and all. His high black boots were at my face level. Up close, I could smell the horse, hear it snorting. He held the basket in front of my face. He spoke something in French. His voice had a dead tone, like he'd just woken from a disturbed slumber. I understood what he said. Not the words, but the menace behind them. He had

my basket and now he had me, the one who had knocked
him senseless with a rock. Looking up, I saw a round head
covered with short, cropped hair. The hairline swooped
down in a sharp V on his forehead. Only his dark, liquid
eyes were alive.

His boot caught me squarely under the chin. It could
have snipped off the tip of my tongue. Suddenly, he hit my
face with the basket. I grabbed it and jerked it from him. I
jerked so hard that I lost my balance and went reeling with
the basket in my hands. I saw him hanging on to the side of
his horse.

I ran. The only sound I heard was the frantic clinking of
china inside the basket. Broken pieces. Hell awaited me.

LIKE WATER, LIKE CLAY

When I woke up the next morning, Mr. Đinh-Hòa was already gone. He didn't say a thing when we came home the night before. I had not volunteered to tell the bad news about his little treasure. I also, of course, kept my mouth shut about the clash with the Frenchman.

I met his wife in the kitchen and asked her where he went. "Consulting for a client," she said. "Some prospective owner of a new store wants to know if his storefront faces an auspicious direction." She was sitting on a low stool, a bowl in one hand, a spoon in the other, beating the egg whites unhurriedly and steadily like a machine. Listening to the soft rhythm of her spoon, I eyed her and could find nothing on her face that alerted me to her knowledge of my mishap. But I knew he drank tea very early in the morning and that she had served him breakfast. The last thing he would want to see was broken pieces of china as he sat down for his morning tea rite.

Mr. Đinh-Hòa's wife was a plain woman in her fifties, round-faced, with sharp cheekbones. Her nose was flat and wide. Most women her age or younger, except my mother, seemed to share these common features. You could always spot my mother's fine physiognomy in a crowd. Her skin, too, was nicer than Mr. Đinh-Hòa's wife's, having none of the pale white of those who lived most of their lives in the city. My mother's was amber, like sunlight.

Mr. Đinh-Hòa's wife never took off her black silk turban,

except maybe when she went to bed. The black cloth made her face look a sickly shade of white in the early morning. She was often bedridden, lying in bed as I tended her. Mr. Đinh-Hòa would raise his voice all over the house, demanding some trivial thing he could do or find himself.

Now, looking at her sitting and whipping the egg whites to make some kind of sugared cream, I realized why their household needed an extra hand. She had a round piece of lime plaster on the center of her brow and two more on her temples. She told me once they cured head colds and headaches. I was looking at the side of her face where she had a wart and I felt like reaching out and plucking the short black hair growing out of it. I knew they needed me. I could run errands and I could cook. I was a quick learner.

Suddenly she dropped the bowl. It hit the packed dirt floor and bounced, spilling out all the egg whites. Her hands froze in midair, fingers crooked like a skeleton's. Heaven, I thought. Chronic arthritis, her worst enemy. Twice I'd seen her drop her bowl of rice during dinner. "Slipped out of my hand," she'd say apologetically to her husband, and I'd curse silently as I noticed his scowl.

Quickly I picked up the bowl and wiped up the mess with a rag. She was trying to flex her fingers, smiling like nothing had happened. She rarely frowned. When she did, she looked more puzzled than disturbed. Why didn't she deserve good health and a good husband?

She rose from the stool, bending back her fingers. "Tài," she said, "we'll have an important guest for lunch. Can you help me out?"

Of course, I thought. She never bossed me around. "Yes, ma'am," I said. "Should I start with the egg whites again?"

"Start with that." She pointed toward a shelf on which

sat two wooden bins. "Use the fresh eggs in the bin on the right."

"How many?"

She raised four crooked fingers. I picked four fresh eggs. In the other bin were incubated eggs, the only kind of eggs the locals ate, the kind of eggs the French hated. I bought them for a sapèque each. I had bought half a dozen fresh eggs for Mr. Đinh-Hòa's wife the day before—two for a sapèque.

I cracked the eggs, letting the whites drip into a bowl in viscous filaments, and then poured the yolks into another bowl.

"What're we making here?" I asked.

"Caramel nougats."

"Mr. Đinh-Hòa loves those." He ate a whole bag she had packed for him a fortnight ago at the opium den, caramel-colored nougats made with brown sugar and chopped nuts. "How do you make those?"

"I'll show you. I'll make a whole bunch this time so you can have some for yourself."

"That's very nice of you, ma'am. You think he'd like them?"

"Who'd like them?"

"Your guest. I mean our guest."

"My husband said he has a sweet tooth. So."

"Who is he?" I said, squatting with the bowl in one hand.

"Someone very important."

"A mandarin?"

"No, no." Smiling, she kept shaking her head like that was the silliest thing she'd ever heard. "He's not a mandarin. But for the power he has, yes, he is a mandarin without a mandarin's robe."

"Then what is he?"

"An entrepreneur."

My meeting with this man would be a turning point in my life.

If you asked me what I know about fate, I'd say that fate is the arrangement the Maker has for each of us. You just have to play your part, whether or not you like it. In my case, it was a good omen that day when Mr. Cao Lai, our important guest, came. I often thought that it was no mere coincidence that I met Mr. Đinh-Hòa, the way things were arranged one after another, eventually leading me to his doorstep. Then out of nowhere came Mr. Cao Lai. I can't argue with the Maker about what he intends for me. I take what he gives, good or bad.

I remember that day like it was yesterday. I was busy all morning until noon. Our guest had arrived, and from the kitchen I could hear them talking in the house. They were in good spirits, judging from Mr. Đinh-Hòa's roaring laughs. For a sullen man like him, I wondered if this expansive cheerfulness was motivated by something else. I could hear only his voice and his throaty laughs, leaving me to think that our guest was either soft-spoken or reserved by nature. Then Mr. Đinh-Hòa's wife came to me, took me by the hand, and led me to a waist-high barrel near the kitchen entrance.

"You need to help me with this," she said, lifting the cover.

I was expecting something heavy she wanted me to pick up. When I looked down, my jaw dropped. A gray snake lay coiled inside.

"It's...a snake," I said to her.

"A rat snake," she said. "Dead."

"It's poisonous."

"It is. I need you to cut off its head, and then I'll tell you what to do next."

"Yes, ma'am."

The snake felt heavy and cold in my grip. I lay its triangular head on a cutting board while she held a bowl nearby. With one clean stroke I brought the cleaver down. The head fell. She grabbed the body and quickly brought the bowl over. I knew what she wanted to do, so I lifted the snake and held its body straight up and saw blood flowing into the bowl. When the blood stopped she reached up, seized its body, and worked her hand down its length, squeezing repeatedly. By the time the snake's body was drained of blood, the bowl was filled with a red liquid as bright as pomegranate pulp. She picked up the bowl with both hands, looked at the curdled blood, now a darker red like firecrackers, and said to me, "While I'm serving this to them, you skin the snake and take out its gall bladder."

"Gall bladder, you said?" I asked, completely puzzled.

She pressed her fingertip against a spot on the snake in the middle of its body. "Take a small knife. Make a decent cut and you can take it out. Then put it in a cup for me."

The whole thing had me unsettled. What unusual person craved this?

"They drink snake blood straight up, ma'am?" I asked before she walked out of the kitchen.

"With warm rice liquor," she said, stopping momentarily. "I have to mix them together before I serve it."

"And . . . what're you going to do with the gall bladder?"

She glanced back over her shoulder. "Keep it in a cup and soak it with that liquor." She motioned toward a red clay jar among all the knickknacks that filled another shelf.

"You'll have to show me how to cook this thing."

"You won't. Our guest will just swallow it whole—with liquor."

After she was gone I went about my chores and then ate two bowls of rice with pickled bean curds. I made those myself and got compliments from Mr. Đinh-Hòa's wife for their taste and smell. Those bean curds usually had a strong odor from fermentation, much like some of the French cheese her husband would eat now and then. But besides an airy, prickling sensation in the mouth, mine had just a whiff of a tangy smell. Then Mr. Đinh-Hòa's wife returned and asked me to dice the snake meat the way she wanted. As I chopped, she heated a skillet until it smoked and then coated it with a slab of lard. The thick chunk melted instantly with tiny pops. As it puffed gray smoke, she dropped a handful of almond slivers and sliced mushrooms on the skillet. Now it gave off a biting smell. A dash of soy sauce produced a rising balloon of smoke, and she tossed in the meat. Her hand spun the skillet just as it started popping frantically. She set it down on the flame until it sizzled and smoked again. My mouth watered.

After she had gone with the smoking dish, I helped myself to a fresh bowl of rice and a good portion of snake meat. Chewing, I let the taste spread in my mouth. The meat was tender, light. As my tongue began to remember the chicken-like flavor, I thought if she let me prepare it the next time, I'd add hot peppers and basil and a lot of green onions.

Mr. Đinh-Hòa's wife went back and forth between the house and the kitchen as the afternoon wore on. I washed the dishes. She would drop in to fetch a jar of rice liquor, one after another. I heard Mr. Đinh-Hòa's voice and ringing laugh. Though I didn't keep track of how many jars of liquor they drank together, I counted those left on the shelf and estimated it was about the amount Chim would drink one night by himself.

The dishes done, I decided to chop some firewood. After hacking an armful of wood, I stopped and whetted the blade. I whetted it until the blue stone gave off a smoky odor. When I tested the blade's sharpness with my fingertip it felt hot. I had to sharpen this machete often because it was light. Heavier cutting tools need less sharpening. As I stroked its edge, the cold metal on my fingers brought to my mind the coldness I once felt on my granduncle's saber's blade. It was a heavy saber, and its cutting edge gave me goose bumps when I touched it with my fingers. What made my flesh crawl? Not the fact that its blade had lopped off so many heads. What made me shudder, I remembered, was the thought of its once being stained with my father's blood. Now, as I stroked the machete's freshly honed blade, I felt that I hadn't thought of him as much as I should have. Rather than missing him, I'd thought of the way he died. Every time I did, I felt horrible. Then I thought of the man who put my family through this hell. I thought of that man a lot. I used to picture his face as a composite of those faces just before their possessors died on the execution ground. Cowardly, wretched-looking. Where was he now?

I loved my father the way I loved my mother, but I didn't feel the same tenderness for him. Maybe men shouldn't have that. It makes you weak.

I leaned on the machete. Voices drifted in from the main house. Were they all drunk now? The small courtyard between the kitchen and the main house was bright in the mid-afternoon sun. A Chinese voice called out, "Dumplings, steaming hot before they're gone! Last call, last call!" His

bamboo clappers kept cadence with his calls as he passed
the house. I gazed at the cistern in the center of the courtyard. The brick, which I scrubbed every day to kill the moss
that grew on it, was a muted red in the sunlight. Rooftops
and walls beyond. A pale blue sky. Somewhere in the citadel
lived my granduncle, still working, past his prime. I should
go to see him one of these days, according to my mother.
I listened to the bamboo clappers now in the distance and
the Chinese vendor's singsong voice. That old Chinese man
who died outside the tavern must loathe me for not keeping
my word. Wearily I shook my head.

Mr. Đinh-Hòa's wife came back in, stopped, and looked
at the pile of firewood.

"You're so conscientious," she said. "Have you eaten?"

"Yes, ma'am. I helped myself to some snake meat."

"Come with me."

I leaned the machete against the wall. They must be set to
see their guest off. Such a long lunch. I followed her across
the courtyard into the reception room. There was a three-
paneled screen made of lacquered rosewood at the entrance,
shielding the outside view. Iridescent, inlaid mother-of-
pearl shimmered on a panoramic view of woodcutters and
forests and herons taking wing over rolling hills and crested
mountains and drifting clouds. The first time I cleaned this
screen, I took a short break and studied the scene. The panels made up a singular scene and, gazing at it, I felt like I
was the Maker watching over my own creation. Then, while
my gaze followed a creek that meandered through forests
and hills, I spotted a tiny sand turtle sunning on a bank all
by itself. Most people wouldn't notice it. But it was there, a
pleasant surprise.

The room was dim, redolent of pipe tobacco. My nose

picked up the sweet odor of rice liquor. I didn't drink, but rice liquor, particularly the kind Chim brewed, had that devilish odor that made my mouth water. I stood by an urn behind the screen. Sitting on top of the urn was a stone tiger, black-striped, watching the entrance with its narrowed, mean-looking eyes. At the table Mr. Đinh-Hòa sat with one leg drawn up to his chin, fanning himself leisurely. I saw his guest's back. He was pouring himself liquor from a clay jar.

"Here you are," Mr. Đinh-Hòa said roaringly.

His guest turned. The first thing I noticed about him was his black hair. He had a head full of it, long and black and parted in the middle, down to the side of his jaw. Seeing me, he tossed back his hair to clear it from his eyes. Then his left eye blinked.

"So this is the boy you were talking about," he said, his thin lips curled up into a grin.

"Tài," Mr. Đinh-Hòa said, "come and greet Mr. Cao Lai."

I took a few steps forward as Mr. Cao Lai swung around to have a better look at me. Yet the way they both appraised me with their curious eyes made me feel oddly disturbed. I looked at him, his broad, round forehead, his very dark, thin eyebrows, a slightly hooked nose, well-proportioned to his hollow face. He was about my father's age but not as masculine. In fact, he looked like a lead actor in an opera.

"My due respect to you, sir," I said, bowing slightly to him.

"What happened to your face?" he said just before he sipped.

"Smallpox, sir."

"You were lucky."

"Yes, I know. Many died in my village."

"Lau? Yes?"

"Yes, sir." I didn't feel like talking about it. The sentimentality of remembrance didn't bring back the dead and, worse, made you feel maimed.

"I heard what happened to your family," Mr. Cao Lai said. "Mr. Đinh-Hòa and I had a good talk about your excellent service. I'll let him tell you more about it."

Then he smiled. His teeth were even, white. I found his voice soothing. I wondered if he ever lost his temper.

Mr. Đinh-Hòa folded his fan and tapped it against the palm of his hand. "What we were talking about is this: Here is Mr. Cao Lai, my most respected client and also a noteworthy businessman. He was the one who commissioned me to prospect a burial site. Tài, what happened is, when Mr. Cao Lai heard of your family's misfortune, he had a change of heart. You see, your father died because he committed a crime, but he wasn't an ordinary criminal. A lot of people feared him and yet respected him. I'm one of them. Out of that respect, I made a promise to your family and, in return, receive your service. Now, regardless of what happened, Mr. Cao Lai still has the final say over what I was entrusted to deliver. The burial site is his. And we're here today to discuss the matter, and after much thought have come to a conclusion. Mr. Cao Lai will honor my promise to your family in exchange for your service."

I was very confused. But words flowed so smoothly from Mr. Đinh-Hòa's mouth that I thought I was listening in on somebody else's family affair. I looked at Mr. Đinh-Hòa and then at Mr. Cao Lai without a clue about what to expect from him as my mind worked things over. I had a thought and said to both of them, "Can my mother and I still own that burial site?"

Mr. Đinh-Hòa shook open his fan and held it in midair. "Mr. Cao Lai is a man of his word. Bless yourself and show him your gratitude."

Like an automaton, I bowed deeply to Mr. Cao Lai. I didn't know what to say so I said nothing when I straightened my back and stood up. One employer was as good as another, but if you knew Mr. Đinh-Hòa like I did, it could only be better. Both men rose at the same time. I could see that my new employer was lanky in his loose pants and blouse, both immaculately white. The round buttons running down the front of his blouse were shiny like black pearls and fastened by ivory loops stitched in coral-pink thread. From the back room Mr. Đinh-Hòa's wife appeared, working her way along the edge of the table and picking things up as quietly as a thief. As Mr. Cao Lai went out the door, he paused on the step, glanced back at me and said, "I will go to Lau with Mr. Đinh-Hòa tomorrow to see the burial site. If I'm satisfied, I expect to see you at my residence after I return."

For a moment I felt weightless. Watching him leave, I remained by the stone tiger. What awaited me?

A clink of utensils made me aware of another person's presence in the room.

A PLACE INSIDE MY SOUL

My father may have been a criminal, but he was a well-liked criminal.

I had told Mr. Đinh-Hòa exactly that a few days after I arrived at his residence. He came to ask me what I knew of my father, what led to the feud between the two villages of Chung and Lau, and what I felt toward him both as a father and a "robber"—that was his word. I couldn't make any sense of it. How could I have known his scheme then? By the time his client returned from a long stay in China, Mr. Đinh-Hòa must have known enough about my father to spin a good story. Then, when I heard him profess his "respect" for my father, I knew he aimed to cheat Mr. Cao Lai, his most influential client, out of the prospected burial site and—to my abhorrence—my work as a servant.

I wondered if a man like Mr. Cao Lai could be deluded by such a lie. He advanced Mr. Đinh-Hòa some money to find a burial site, but Mr. Đinh-Hòa offered it back, saying that he would be looking for a site other than the spot in Lau, because it should belong to the widow of a bandit he called "a people's outlaw." I never believed that Mr. Cao Lai was fooled. Not him. His long narrow eyes, which made him look like he was always half asleep, never betrayed his thoughts.

It was a long lunch that day. What came out of it was this: Swayed by Mr. Đinh-Hòa into a mutual respect for my father's greatness, Mr. Cao Lai agreed to cede his right to the

burial site. I wondered if the snake's gall bladder he swallowed that day had clouded his judgment. But there was
more. The trip to Lau to see the burial plot pleased him. But
Mr. Đinh-Hòa, the stubborn old mule, was bent on declar-
ing himself the "benefactor" of my family. What did Mr. Cao
Lai do? He bought the site. Now he became our family's
patron. He also wanted me to work for him, but Mr. Đinh-
Hòa confessed that his family needed a helping hand, me to
fulfill his wife's duties. So Mr. Cao Lai bought out my two-
year service from my employer. Could generosity lead men
to an unwise business decision?

I wondered why he would need my service. Two years
of service was worth as much as the sum he paid for that
burial site. That doubled Mr. Đinh-Hòa's profits and gave
him three months of my service. Well, actually he only paid
me for two months. He docked an entire month's pay—my
last—for what I did to his tea set.

My new employer was a fair-minded man. He said to me
on my first day as his employee, "You're not here as a bound
boy. You and your family owe me nothing. I paid off your
two-year service with Mr. Đinh-Hòa, but rest assured that
I'm not robbing you. You're free to go if you so elect after
two years. I do hope you'll stay."

That was democratic. But here let me tell you what he
said next. He said, "When the time comes, I'd like to pay
your mother a visit. After all, it'd be an affront to her not
to speak out about my act. Besides, she ought to have the
proper documents of ownership to protect your family from
any unexpected false claim. In fact, the deed of the property
takes effect in two years' time. Meanwhile, send the news
home—tell her everything that's transpired. If you can't do
that, I can send someone on your behalf."

I didn't want to look so helpless—a miserable feeling—and something crossed my mind. "My granduncle will do that, sir. He lives in the city."

"What's your granduncle doing in the city?"

"He's the executioner, sir."

Mr. Cao Lai brushed back his hair with his long fingers. "You don't mean to tell me that when your father faced execution . . ."

"My granduncle executed him."

"Well, well." He threw back his head.

I looked down.

"Did your mother tell you this?" he said.

"No, sir. I was there with my mother and my little brother. We were to bring his body—and his head—back to our village."

"He will be reburied at the new site. He'll command a fantastic view. You ought to see the site. You, your mother, your brother."

"I don't have a brother anymore."

His narrowed eyes opened a tad wider. "Why is that?"

"Smallpox, sir. It spared me but got him."

"Will he be reburied there too?"

"Yes, sir." I looked down and then up at him. "Me and my mother want them to be reburied side by side."

"How much do you know about your father?"

"A fair amount, sir."

"He had quite a reputation."

"Yes, sir."

"You know how he met his end?"

"Yes, sir."

He appraised me with an impassive eye. "What do you know?"

"One of his men betrayed him to the authorities, sir."

"But to face execution, he must've committed a horrendous crime. Had he?"

"He had, sir. He and his gang burned down a good part of the Chung village. Houses and granaries, sir. Darn near killed their chief. But the fellow managed to make his way out of his burning house."

Mr. Cao Lai stroked his stubbled chin. "He wasn't looting them, was he?"

"No, sir, he wasn't. Didn't take a thing from those Catholics. He was just out for revenge."

"Revenge? Someone wronged him?"

"No, sir. My father, he'd stand up for you if you came to him for help. So when there was this terrible thing happening in our village, our elders had no one else to turn to for help and they came to my father."

Mr. Cao Lai fixed his gaze on me. "What happened?"

"There was a murder. But no clues, sir. Our elders were set to go to the canton chief for help. But you know what, sir? If the canton chief failed to catch the murderer, he'd be demoted. Sometimes a canton chief winds up hiring a bounty hunter and prays that he'll catch the murderer. What happened was our elders didn't want to put the canton chief in a bind, so after they went back and forth arguing, they came to my father."

"I want to hear what happened next."

"Yes, sir. There was this man's body they found in a sugarcane field. A thief from Chung village. They knew that much because they had caught him once before. On the side of his head there was a bloody hole like he was struck with something nasty. So when they gathered around with my father, they all said that the poor thief must've been killed in the cane field. But why in the cane field? Nothing there to steal until harvest time, but that was months away. Then my father went off into a clump of sugarcane to relieve himself. He saw a flock of ravens shoot up into the air and then he saw a dead dog. A bitch with her teats still swollen with milk. They went back and forth arguing again. His dog? Or someone else's?" I paused. Mr. Cao Lai, rapt, looked on.

"My father asked them to go into the village and find out who had the puppies. 'What for?' they asked shaking their heads. 'Just bring them here,' my father said. At sunset the men returned with two crates of puppies. When the first crate was opened, the three puppies all ran up to the dead bitch and sniffed around at her teats. Then all turned away. They put them back in the crate and let loose the next litter. You know what, sir? The four puppies bumped each other for the bitch's teats. At dusk they surrounded the house the men had taken the puppies from. When they searched the barn, they found a hoe with blood on its blade. The owner said he had killed no one and had also lost his dog. Then my father pulled him aside, told him if he had killed the man, it was an act of self-defense. Besides, the dead man was a known felon. My father told him about the Annamese law: five years in prison if one kills a burglar. But if the man confessed, his sentence might be reduced to one year. After some thinking, the man said the thief poisoned his dog and broke into his house where he caught him. He killed the man and dumped his body and the dead dog in the cane field."

"Then what?" Mr. Cao Lai asked, tilting his head back.

"Chung's village chief appealed to the governor. He was a Catholic, sir. Then the governor went to the judge and the judge put the man in prison for five years. Here's the problem, sir. The man was a farmer, and so after he went to prison his family was in bad shape—wife and two little kids. She couldn't farm, and she'd go broke hiring someone to till the land and do all the farm work he used to do. The village elders all felt humiliated, like they had just lost a war to the Chung Catholics. But the one who took it personally was my father. He felt they had wronged him badly. And there's this thing, sir. To attack the village of Chung—that's what he aimed to do—wasn't like a walk-in. It's stockaded and there are those watchtowers. You can't get in if they don't know you. But my father, he was pretty wise. You know what he did, sir? Well, he bought off someone from Chung, and one night that fellow opened one of the gates and let in my father and his gang."

Mr. Cao Lai squinted his eyes at me. "Who told you all this?"

"My father, sir—when he was in a real good mood. He'd sit there drinking and telling me and my mother and my little brother things he did."

"I'd heard he was quite a character."

"You heard, sir?"

He pinched his brow between his eyes. "When I was up in Kwangtung."

"My father was in China?"

"You didn't know that? Well, that was a long, long time ago. Maybe before you were even born. How old are you?"

"Just turned seventeen, sir." I felt curious now. "What was my father doing in Kwangtung?"

"He was whoring around, gambling and getting drunk, win or lose. He was a big gambler. It looked like he'd settle down to live there."

"Settle down?"

"He was always with this Chinese girl."

I wondered if he was married to my mother then. "You saw him? With her, sir?"

"In and out of those opium and gambling dens." Mr. Cao Lai rested his hand on the mouth of his teacup. "My father ran some of them."

"Are you . . . Chinese, sir?" I could detect no accent in his voice though.

"Ah. Well, my father is Chinese, he married my mother when he traveled to Hanoi to sell stuff. She's Annamese."

Something struck me funny. "You ever met my father, sir?"

"No." He pushed his teacup away. "But he was one of our regulars."

"I mean here in Hanoi."

"No." He picked up the teapot, sloshed it around, and put it down. "Once I saw him in one of the opium dens in the Chinese quarter."

I thought of something and it came out before I meant to say it. "What'd you think of my father, sir?"

His lips pursed, Mr. Cao Lai regarded me out of his narrow eyes. "I don't have any opinion of him. I didn't know him personally."

I looked at him as he was pouring tea. His white satin blouse shone in the soft light suffusing through the slatted window shutters. The cuffs of his satin pants stopped short of his ankles. His wool slippers were black, their soles white. He had that orderly presence of a man in charge of himself. No, I could never imagine he was the sort of fellow who'd make an impression on my father—and true also the other way around.

After one sip he cupped his hand around his teapot. I took a step and reached for it. "Sir, let me make a fresh pot.

Your tea is getting cold."

I turned. He said, "Do you like living in the city?"

I stopped, looked back over my shoulder. "It's all right, sir. I adjust well."

"Everybody should have a place called home. I hope you don't feel out of place here."

"Yes, you're right, sir—about a place called home."

I met his gaze briefly. I appreciated his concern for my welfare. The "here" he referred to was his residence. But I didn't want to disappoint him by telling him that I had made up my mind. I was soon to let him know my decision.

I was free to go if I so chose after two years.

THE QUICKSAND

One day when I was coming back from an errand for Mr. Cao Lai, I decided to head into the citadel and pay my granduncle a visit.

I passed the Chinese quarter and went down Sugar Street to the citadel's eastern gate and stepped out into an open space bright with steel-white heat. On the sides of the bridge, sentries were lounging under the trees' shade. The heat stirred like haze. A French guard was dozing in a cane chair. He was pale, listless. This heat must have robbed him and many of his people of their ruddy complexion. Even the Algerians suffered it, and they were once children of the African sun.

A procession was coming out of the gate. The guard woke and rubbed his eyes. Ahead of the cortege walked an Annamese soldier in blue tunic, holding up a red banner lettered with Chinese characters. Decapitation. *Hell*. The same red banner announced when my father was to die. The procession passed by. Behind the herald was my granduncle—the executioner. His blue tunic shone in the sun as he walked barefoot, wielding his saber upright with both hands against his chest. He wore the same outfit the day he beheaded my father and his gang. The white stubble was shaved on his copper-toned face. Trailing him in single file were three condemned men dressed in coarse white cloth, each wearing a cangue of burled wood. Behind them, soldiers in blue tunics walked in two columns, long spears keeping the crowd at a safe distance.

I gazed at the condemned men as they passed, their heads bent and their hands roped behind their backs at the wrists. Then the rear of the column went by. I spotted the mandarin sitting in a hammock under two flat-topped white parasols, but his face was blocked from view by the soldiers.

An urge overtook me and I stepped out onto the road and followed the cortege. It was a large crowd that was gaining in number, and I could see my granduncle's head for one brief moment before he disappeared. The crowd followed the rampart of the old town of Hanoi, along the moat in which lily pads skimmed the brown water. Their leaves were a soiled yellow. We passed a solitary persimmon tree that stood like an enigma created by God. Bare feet stirred the red dust. Patches of black, white, brown lambent in the dizzying heat. Human voices droned. "That man can chop a head so clean, bet you they feel no pain." "Did you see him the last time? He chopped his own nephew's head." "Yeah, I saw the whole thing. . . . That poor sergeant . . ." The two women's cartwheel hats bobbed with their heads, and their blood-red lips were swollen from betel juice. My throat felt dry. I dropped back.

Ahead the white parasols floated in the sun, so white they seemed like a mirage. I thought of the moment when I watched my father just before he died, and my stomach churned raw. What kind of excitement was this—watching somebody's head fall?

On the dike the condemned men walk in single file, each with a huge cangue around his neck. The banter and laughter made me feel sick. Red dust shimmered. Sweat ran down my legs like a spider crawling inside my trousers. I knew I'd made a mistake.

I turned around and walked back. What had they done? I wondered. Were they bandits like my father and his old gang? Thieves? Murderers?

The sun was full in my face, and my eyes hazed over from the vapor that rose from the moat.

Poverty, misery.

One day over a year ago, a drifter came to my village looking for work. He was in rags. He wouldn't beg. No one had anything to give him. No work. No food. The plague had robbed many people of their livelihood. Some even warned one another to guard their dogs for fear that the drifter might snatch them up. One morning I saw a crowd of people by the roadside. Everyone was watching the drifter who was on his knees eating column cactus. He broke off the spines, long and sharp, and then, like a dog, brought his mouth to the fleshy edge of the leaf and sank his teeth into it. Then he chewed. You could see his sharp jawbones. He didn't even look at us, as if we were ghosts. He chewed and bit and sap leaked out the corner of his mouth. When he couldn't bite because of obstructing spines, he broke them off one by one and then bit off the flesh. Suddenly he spat. There was blood in his spit, and from the cud in his mouth he pulled a thorn. He sat, not looking at us, picking his teeth with the spine, as if he'd just gorged himself on pork and white rice.

The next morning on my way to the riverside I cut across the rice fields on a dike. The air smelled sweet just after harvest, and the stubble fields were yellow as fresh straw. Silhouetted in the sun were lumbering buffalos as brown as mud. Near the dike was a small group of buffalo boys clad in shorts, bodies dusty, crouching over a man. The drifter was lying on his back, clasping his hands on his belly. It was split open. He tried to rise and, halfway up, stuffed his spilled intestines back in. Blood smeared his hands, his stomach. The scowl on his livid face made you think his wound was more a nuisance than a pain. He trembled as he stood up. Then he began to walk, legs bowed, both hands cupping the gaping slash. The boys followed him. I trailed them. I wondered where he was headed. Each step he took left a bloody footprint behind him, and soon blood was dripping freely down his legs. Where the dike forked there was a small pool. A strong odor seeped through the air. The man sank slowly to his knees, his hands clutching his stomach, and began lapping water. The water was stagnant, thick, and brown. The boys and I watched. Soon the water turned redder and blood pooled on the ground beneath him. He remained bent at the edge of the waterhole like he'd gone to sleep. The boys shook him. He was already dead.

He had wandered into the rice fields, picking fallen grains after the harvest. Most of them had long been pecked away by ducks and field rats. He must have roused the water buffalos. One of them gored him.

Hunger. No place to live, no work, no food. I thought of my father and those misfits of the same lot who found one another and formed gangs of thieves, bandits, murderers. Now each walked across the dike with a cangue around his neck as the consequence of his crime.

Dazzling blue sky. I blinked the sweat from my eyes. The horde of humans in green, blue, and dusty white, and a black silhouette. I looked up, shading my eyes, and gasped. Coming toward me was a black horse, glistening with sweat. On it was the French horseman clad in an entirely black uniform. I saw his cropped hair and sharp hairline, shaped like a V on his brow. The horse's neck brushed my face. Its hide, its sweat smelled like wet leather. His hand swooped down and grabbed me by the hair. I jerked away. He held me in his viselike grip, and I felt the burning pain in my scalp. My eyes were blinded by the sun. Just then, I punched his horse in the eye. It neighed and rose on its forelegs, and it felt like all the hair had been torn from my head and, staggering, I felt the shock of being free. I ran.

I ran toward the corner of the citadel. All heads were turned, and I flew by them. As I swung around the corner I saw him looming up. Guards stood watching. None moved a muscle in the stifling heat.

The stone bridge. A cross street. The city in haze.

I heard the horse's hooves behind me. My lungs were bursting. I smelled dust, my nose stung. *Don't let him catch you and drag you by the hair along the street.*

I came to a narrow dirt street lined with mud huts and hucksters, squatting between their big baskets. Sweet smells of fruits. The horse snorting. Some female vendors screaming. I leaped through a space between two women, knocking their tea-tray hats off. The horse and the man missed me by a handspan. I ran down the dirt street.

A butcher was shouting about his delicacy, shouldering a bamboo pole on either end of which was suspended a wooden shelved bin. There was a glistening roasted piglet atop one bin. I rammed him so hard he danced backward and the suckling pig flew off the bin. The horse trampled the butcher's merchandise. I ran around a gang of coolies, each with a rattan basket strapped on his back. In the baskets, the fowls—chickens and ducks—squawked and quacked as I spun the men around, turned, and streaked down a cross street.

Now the dirt street was gone, and I ran on the blue-

stone ground toward a high stone wall and through a half-
open gate into the Chinese quarter. The quick clacking of
the horse's hooves echoed behind. From tall bamboo poles
along the street colorful pennants fluttered, men with pigtails leaned like corpses on the poles. The heat smelled of
fruits and herbs and smoke. People milled on the street. I
saw parasols and lid-like hats and overhanging roofs. Under one roof a throng of Chinese porters lounged in the
shade. Each sat hugging his huge reed basket, bent forward,
dozing in the dead, still heat. Several feet from them on a
corner stood a girl in a white blouse. Alone, she was leaning
against the wall, her hands clasped on her abdomen and her
face shadowed by the overhanging tiled roof. A pretty face.

I turned the corner and ran down an alley. Dappled sunlight and shards of a broken vat lay strewn across the dirt.
They crunched under my crepe-soled shoes. Then I stopped.
The alley dead-ended with a wall—set in it was a blood-red
door framed with wrought iron. I turned around.

The black horse and its rider slowly entered the alley.
It was so narrow, the horse completely blocked the alley
entrance. The Frenchman let his horse pick its steps. He
looked at me, calm. His swooping hairline made a sharp V
just above his hooknose, and the skin of his well-shaven face
was paler than ash.

There was a creaking noise.

The wrought-iron-framed door opened inward enough
for one person to squeeze through. The girl in the white
blouse stood like a mirage. She shouted in Chinese and I
looked at her and she grabbed me by the hand and pulled
me hard. I tumbled inside, hearing the door slam shut behind me. She ran across a courtyard and I ran with her. There
were fruit trees heavy with scents, guava and jackfruit, rock-

work trickling with water and a cuckoo calling in a tree. At the other end of the courtyard was another wall, another red door framed with black wrought iron.

She opened the door, which gave a melancholy creak. Another alley bright in the harsh glare of sunlight. A cross street up beyond the alley entrance. A rickshaw went past. She said something in Chinese, pointing toward the street. I simply looked at her. She was about my age and slender. Wavy hair framed her oval face. Skin like white porcelain. Ink-stroked eyebrows. Her eyes were clear, and her pupils were peppercorn black.

She spoke again.

I shook my head.

"You're . . . not Chinese?" she spoke in Annamese with her Chinese accent.

"No," I said.

"What did you do to him?" She strode into the alley toward the street.

"He remembered my face." I kept up with her.

"What you did?"

"Something awful." I spat at the wall. "I don't know why I did it." I told her what I had done.

We reached the street. A rare breeze brought a smell of noodle soup, and my stomach groaned. She glanced quickly in the direction of the place she first saw me. I knew what she was thinking: Don't get caught again.

"Hurry," she said. "He'll come back. He will."

I checked the street and turned to head up the other way.

"That street," she said, pointing toward a cross street— Cantonese Street.

I looked back at her. "What's your name?"

"Xiaoli," she said.

I walked quickly to the cross street, turned, and looked
back again. She was gone. I kept on walking away from Sail
Street, following a Chinese girl in black calf-length pantaloons with a black umbrella spread over her head. Her
plaited braid swung with her quick steps. Xiaoli with a
pigtail. Her Annamese had that funny Chinese accent. Father must've spoken it well. He'd lived in Kwangtung. Was
she born here in Hanoi? This girl's back has Xiaoli's girlish
curve. What does she look like? There she crosses the street,
gliding in her black felt slippers, and disappears into a narrow shop. You can't see her now because of the glass display
cases shadowed by the low-hanging roof. Sunlight falls in
a gold-colored bar across the front steps. What's she doing
in there? Hung on hooks in the glass cases are glistening
roasted ducks and entrails of pigs, twisted and pale. Where
the people stand waiting, the tight sidewalk has spider-web
cracks in its bluestone. Now an old man in a white cotton
blouse comes floating up, his hands folded behind his back,
his round-rimmed spectacles slipping from the bridge of his
flat nose. He seemed to be taking a leisurely walk to a street
barber who sits waiting on a narrow bench outside a shop.
His tools are a long-blade razor that can be snapped into a
bamboo handle, clippers, a faded strop in dun. I watched
the store front and the girl didn't come back out. After a
while I turned and walked back to Sail Street and entered
the alley.

I touched the black wrought iron of the door. Hot. It
smelled of the sun's heat, strong and rusty. The alley was
quiet. I hit the door with my fist. Caught between the iron
bars, my knuckles went raw, red. A cuckoo was calling lazi-
ly in the courtyard. If they heard me, they probably thought

it was the Frenchman.

I went back up the alley, licking my bleeding knuckles. Behind me came the melancholy creak of the door.

Framed between the narrow gap was a shriveled face the size of my fist. The crone's rheumy eyes were wet, watching me until I came close to the door. Then she blinked and bared her gums as if trying to get her words out, but all I could see was a dark hole studded with some black seeds, what was left of her teeth.

"I want to see Xiaoli," I said.

She simply watched me.

"Xiaoli," I said.

She muttered incoherent sounds.

"Xiaoli," I repeated. "I want to see her."

She pulled back. The door was almost closed when she peered out again through the tight gap.

"Xiaoli?" That was the only sound coming out of her mouth.

I nodded.

"No . . . Xiaoli here." Her halting Annamese came with saliva dripping on her chapped lips.

"I was with her," I said, agitated. "Here. Here."

"No . . . Xiaoli here."

The door closed.

I walked back up the alley. For a moment I didn't know where I was. Then I smelled noodle soup. It hung thick. The street became familiar again, and I didn't feel like going anywhere. Xiaoli. The name came back. It was the name I remembered from the old Chinese opium addict.

It must be a common Chinese name.

THE FACE OF ANOTHER

At night the glowing lamps the coolies carried in their convoy flickered like friars' lanterns along the moat. Leaving the citadel, they crossed the bridge. Flanking them with rifles and bayonets was a French platoon that marched in silence.

I trailed the coolies, carrying crates and bins. There were two child coolies walking in front of me, each bent under a loaded pannier. They must have been under ten. At ten, their parents sent them out in the street with a bamboo pole on their shoulder and two cane baskets to haul any load that needed to be hauled. They all had a big callus on the ridge of their shoulders from hauling these weights.

It was one of those nights that Mr. Cao Lai didn't need me. He was playing mahjong at a mandarin's residence inside the citadel. It would be sunrise when he was through. Dogs barked in the thatch-roofed huts, and after a while they stopped. In the quiet you could hear the murmurs of the Buddhists' prayers and the *tok-tok-tok* of the *mõ*, a wooden fish-shaped percussion instrument that made a deep, soothing echo. The coolie convoy took a cross road heading toward the garrison and I walked on. I walked past the Chinese quarter under tall gum trees with a smell of day-old dust and betel juice and horse manure long baked in the sun. Over the gate the faint lines of electric wires crisscrossed. *Does she have electricity in that big house?* The red door framed with black wrought iron faced me coldly each time I came back. It'd been a week. *You can't go back home and work the boat trade with Chim and Xoan. You thought you could leave Mr. Cao Lai if you so elected and be free. Why this?*

Soon I approached the banana grove, dense and wild by the roadside. A breeze stirred the banana fronds and then I saw a glimmer of torch light. I felt tight in my stomach and reached for the knife tucked behind my cloth belt against my belly. He could be waiting in there on his black horse, but I wouldn't be helpless this time. I crossed the road so that I walked along the edge of the banana grove. If he charged out on his horse, I'd spring like a hare into the grove. Then I stopped. A noise of something falling. From where I stood, I could see two men, one watching the other. The one who stood watching held a torch at shoulder level. It must have been made of some kind of gummy wood, for it crackled with red sparks. The one wielding a saber with both hands walked back and forth between two rows of bananas, examining each trunk with his head tilted to one side. Both wore thigh-length blue blouses edged with red facings. The red stood out in the torchlight, and the blue looked black. The man who held the saber wiped his hand on his wide-legged trousers and just as I squinted my eyes, I saw a flash and heard the crisp sound the saber made as it sliced through a banana trunk. Then I heard a whoosh as the trunk toppled.

I ran into the grove. "Granduncle!" I shouted.

Another banana trunk fell, tumbling backward, its fronds rustling on the way down. The saber raised in midair, Granduncle stopped. He looked frozen and stood like that until I came near. He touched his black turban. The other man moved the torch toward me. His torchlight made dancing shadows on Granduncle's leathery face, which was covered with white stubble. The black hollows on his face and his jutting cheek bones made Granduncle look like a ripper.

"What on earth are you doing here?" he said.

"I've been in the city . . . working," I said. "I meant to visit you, Granduncle, but . . ." I barely remembered where he lived from the crumbled piece of paper my mother wrote the address on.

Granduncle peered at me. His hard eyes were graphite black, his wrinkled face made sinister by his pointed chin and a hooked nose. I understood. I told him what took me to the city and, listening, he slung his saber across his shoulder and jabbed his thumb in the direction behind his back where the lake was.

"That's where you're staying? Nice quarter."

"It's not my place," I said. "Are you preparing for another execution?"

"Yeah."

"Who will die?"

"This guy, he killed a judge."

"The rickshaw coolie?" I remembered the story Mr. Đinh-Hòa told.

"Yeah."

"When?"

"At noon tomorrow."

I could picture hordes of thrill-seekers. The noise. The red dust.

"I'll visit you sometime, Granduncle."

"Yeah," he said, sheathing his saber behind his back.

Granduncle never asked why. Even when he found me in the forest with my mouth stuffed with leaves. He worked the saber scabbard over his shoulder and head and handed it to the other man.

"Here," he said, turning and walking toward the road.

I followed him, listening to the crackling of the torch behind me and the sound of the other man noisily hawking up phlegm and spitting. On the roadside the man beat the torch out on the ground and crossed the road in the direction of the citadel. We stood back in the dark.

"You go on home now," Granduncle said. "Late."

"Aren't you going home too, Granduncle?"

"Nah." He began walking toward the Chinese quarter.

I felt drawn to that place like a magic curse had been put on me. Soon there were noises, and the lights of oil lamps that hung on pointed posts on crossroads corners danced with the breeze. Their smoke made my heart beat faster with unnamed wishes. Though it was late, the streets smelled of hot fat and your nose twitched at the odors of cooked cabbage, radish, ginseng. Past an alley there was a whiff of opium, the caramel odor that I knew well.

"Go home," Granduncle said, adjusting his black turban.

"Granduncle?" I said.

He simply looked at me.

"I have the deed of the burial property..."

"Where is it?"

"I'll bring it to you—it's for my mother. Can you..."

"Just bring it to me. Now go home."

"I'm going."

Granduncle turned and disappeared into the dark alley. He looked out of place in his soldier's formal attire. He didn't have a pigtail. Let him have a good time.

I walked up Sail Street, to the corner where she stood on that hot afternoon watching me chased by the French horseman. Across the street, leaning against a bamboo flagpole, was a skeleton of a man. You don't know he is there until he

raises his toothpick of an arm and feels his scalp. Maybe she
will drift by when you least expect it, or maybe she's sleeping. The rock garden was so quiet you could hear an owl's
hoot and the trickling of water among bonsai in the rock basin. Then I heard a creaking of a cart on four little wheels. A
man was pushing it up the street and on one side of the cart
hung a lantern. The side is painted with red Chinese characters. I couldn't tell what they said. Perhaps they tell of his
trade. I could see a pair of ducks, brown with fire and glinting with grease, hung upside down on a rod. Their insides
dangled in the glimmer of light. Is he heading home? I could
hear his cart creaking farther and farther away, and across
the street the skeleton seems part of the pole, gazing neither
at the street nor at the world. Can men sleep standing?

I turned and looked into the alley that led to her place.
Something stirred in the darkness. My eyes squinted, I saw
a human figure squatting and heard the sound of running
water. Now it came out of the alley—a woman in a black
flared skirt. She didn't even glance at me, and I only caught
a glimpse of her face, her black hair pulled tightly back and
clasped behind her head. I watched her glide to the next corner and into darkness. The skeleton was leaning his head on
the pole and you could see that his mouth was gaping and
his turtle-like neck was stretched out to keep his head from
falling off his shoulders. What's he dreaming? Is he dreaming of a girl with porcelain skin, a tiny red mole at the corner
of her mouth?

My feet carried me to the next corner where an odor of
late-night noodles came drifting, and with it came the odor
of opium. Squalid dens were squeezed into those dark alleys. Dimly I thought of the old Chinese addict and of his
niece and my promise to him. I remembered his despair and

felt my betrayal of him. Someone slunk out of the alley and headed toward the river. A thin body gliding in calf-length trousers, wide-sleeved blouse in a dark color like the night. A pigtail flung across her shoulder. I quickened my feet as she disappeared into the night. The smell of the river was in the air. It was muddy and foul with waste, fish and bamboo scraps, rotten cabbage and orange peels. There were lights on the quay.

She crossed the street, and I stood back under an Indian almond tree. Sampans and junks and small steam ships dotted the water's edge, and the quay lay trembling in the yellowy light of the lanterns. On the gangplank, the coolies stood naked above the waist. Some sat slumped against the rail and some lay like corpses on top of coiled ropes. She came up on the gangplank and stood near a lantern. They surrounded her. I felt a quiver in my stomach. I looked around. No, there's no place around here for him to hide, him and his black horse. Then the clanks of zinc coins changing hands. Each paper packet they get is gold. You add a scrap of opium, the sticky leftover, to your tobacco and you swallow the smoke. Or you soak the burnt residue in some kind of cooking oil until it gets pasty and then you smoke it. And the air is tinged with an unmistakable stench, not of caramel but of putrefaction. As quickly as she came, she left, gliding down the gangplank, silhouetted against the glow of the lamps. Her face was so black she was faceless, and I held still, watching her until she reached Sail Street. I kept a distance from her and now she ghosted down the street past flickering corner lamps. The odor of noodles seeped into the air. Then she turned into an alley.

I felt a prick in my heart.

There was nothing in the alley but a wall at the dead end.

A wall with a red door framed with black wrought iron.
   The door opened, then shut.
   My heart throbbed. *Xiaoli.*

DADDY'S KNIFE

Lin Gao was mute. He could not read or write. Before Mr. Cao Lai took him under his wing as a servant, Lin Gao's name was Ti-sái, "pig crap." He was named so by his parents to ward off evil spirits.

There were times when I thought he was dead as he slept in his hammock, when his mangy black dog wailed on and on by his side. Eyes shut. Dark welts in half-moons under them. Creases crisscrossed his face like a parchment swatch withered with age. The mouth agape, a black hole, toothless, with only a stump of his tongue. It must have hurt when they cut it off. He wasn't born mute. But he'd been mute as a stone now for over twenty years. Mute and half-crazed from what they'd done to him. Blindfolded him and took him to a place stockaded with bamboo stakes. There was a hut inside. There was a shovel, a hoe, a rake, a hammer, a trowel, a hand-forged knife. A chisel, a handsaw. Tools for a jack-of-all-trades like him. He took his pay, his blood rushing by the large sum, and then began building a tomb. Deep, hollowed into the earth. A black dog guarded the hut, watching him as he toiled in the pit. Rain. Heat. Food came at midday, once a day, the only time he heard human footfalls on the worn trail. Behind the hut was a tall eucalyptus, the tough sickle-shaped leaves of which he crushed to salve his cuts every now and then. There was a hollow in its huge base. That was the dog's den. It slept and urinated in the same spot. It growled when he tried to scale the fence and, once, he was nearly over it when the dog leaped and sank its teeth into his leg. Both man and beast fell, one on top of the other. His calf was oozing blood like he had driven two pegs into it. He hobbled for weeks afterward. At night he listened for the dog's snores but heard none. It was so still he heard the eucalyptus sigh. Once he limped out of the hut into a blackness so black he couldn't even see his own hands. He paused when he felt the dog's muzzle on his calf where the wounds were scabbing. He felt pressure until he made it back into the hut. He remembered the hillocks, rising and falling—the only time he saw what was beyond the stockade he remembered from the calf wounds. The stillness and the sighs of the eucalyptus made him crazed. At times he heard the midday sounds of cartwheels on the trail carrying sand, water, and brick, and those the dog made as it chewed bones and lapped up his crap. He didn't have to shovel dirt over it, for the dog was always watching him to leave the spot to claim his waste. The chambered tomb took shape. Then one day at noon, they came. They inspected his work. The earth-level entrance was an ironwood door framed by brickwork. Pull the wood latch and raise the door and there were brick steps going down into the bowels of the earth. They went deep in the hollow with torches, examining his handiwork, banging on the brick walls. The thickness of the walls muted the sounds, and after a long time he saw the light of their torches coming up. You're going back, they said. As they blindfolded him, he stood quietly, letting them do their job. No, he knew nothing of who they were when his turn came in the line of coolies looking for work. *Can you read?* No. *Write?* He had shaken his head. *What can you do?* Masonry, carpentry. *Good enough*, they said. He hadn't seen anything when they took him away, blindfolded, in a horse-drawn

cart. He saw nothing. Except, later, the hills, the eucalyptus.
Once he started the tomb, he knew nothing of the time that
had passed, except that his clothes were so tattered after so
many washes. Each time as he dried them in the sun, he sat
naked on his haunches, watching the dog watching him. It
was always ready when it saw him in that posture. Now he
couldn't wait to see the city again. It was on such a day that
he suddenly felt himself being tied from behind. Hands, feet.
Pushed to the ground on his back. *Open your mouth*, a voice
said. Obediently he did. *Stick out your tongue*, the voice said.
More! Just then a hand seized his tongue. His head jerked in
panic. A hot flash flared as something painfully sharp sliced
across his tongue, and he screamed a muffled scream and
gagged and his tears flowed. Blood tasted salty, metallic on
the soft inside of his mouth. Blood ran down into his throat
so much he choked. They pulled him up, pressed his jaws to
hold them open and stuffed his mouth with a wad of something neither soft nor firm. It smelled dry, dark like tobacco.
Bite down, the voice said. He did as told, ears ringing, face
wet with tears, body shaking like a windblown scarecrow.
He lay on his side, hands and feet bound, mouth gagged.
The creaking of cartwheels, the clopping of horse's hooves
drifted in and out of his sleep. Lights came and went. He
knew dimly the passing of the day. Once when he woke,
there was a silty smell in the air. They untied him and together crossed a river in a sampan. He could hear voices and
knew he was still in Kwangtung. Then they walked him up
a jetty and kept on walking until there were no more human
voices. *Do not take off your blindfold till we're gone*, a voice
said. Footsteps padded away. A long time passed. He did
not dare move when he heard a dog barking. He panicked.
He jerked the blindfold off. Their black dog was running

toward him. He couldn't move, and just sat helpless. The dog came, panting, its black coat and legs dripping water. It licked his hand as if it was his own dog.

He took my hand that gripped a knife. He jiggled my wrist, made a sound in his throat like a frog, and bent my wrist with his knotty fingers. I flexed my wrist. Sunlight glinted on the knife edges. Both edges were sharp and the blade was thin. He stood beside me, wriggling his wrist with an imaginary knife, and then brought his open hand to shield it. From under his hammock, the old black dog watched, rheumy-eyed.

He padded to the edge of the garden where there was a banana patch. They looked out of place in a well-kept garden like this, but if you knew Mr. Cao Lai, you knew they belonged. Lin Gao wrapped foods like sweet rice and mungbean cakes in banana leaves and steamed them. You could smell the aroma the leaves left on them like a fragrant skin. Now Lin Gao bent his wrist back and forth, taking me by surprise with his looseness. One knee bent and, bracing himself on his other knee, he thrust his invisible knife and the hand that cupped it followed. I watched. Then I watched him, this time with my knife in his hand, flex his wrist a few times, flick the knife just to get my eyes to roll back and forth, and then, with one quick stroke, sink the knife into an upright banana trunk. No sound. He did it again. Not a sound. I imagined what it would be like to be the banana trunk.

Above his head was a banana frond, its ribbed underside yellowed from the sun. His blow struck the broad base of the leaf, splitting it open. A glint of sunlight shot through the crack. He handed me my knife.

Bowlegged, his mouth gaping, he stood watching me.

I adjusted my grip on the knife's handle, tight but not stiff. I flexed my wrist. I knew I had to be loose limbed but firm with my strokes. I sank the blade into the banana trunk. It hissed. He slapped me on the arm. Then he took the knife, drove the blade silently to the hilt, and the sap seeped out, clear white. I took my knife back and bent my wrist, but this time kept my elbow closer to my side, concentrating on the wrist, the hand. I could hear my stab. I pulled out the knife and plunged it into the trunk again. I stabbed and stabbed until my face was hot and wet with perspiration and my arm grew tired. The hisses grew whenever I swung my arm, so I stood back, studied the punctured trunk, and fixed my gaze on a spot. Then I stepped up and stabbed. I could almost hear it.

He pointed at his bare feet and slid one foot forward, his open hand over his heart, and his stabbing hand shot up from his hip.

I went back to stabbing the trunk and worked my limbs over and over, and at one point in the act of stabbing, I began feeling them go together when I thrust the knife. I went around the tree to find fresh spots and soon the trunk was pockmarked and leaking sap. I sat in its strong smell, leaning against the trunk. Lin Gao had gone back in.

I wiped the knife blade against the hem of my trousers. The steel blade was so thin it made you think you could bend it like a blade of grass. But touching it, its steely hardness surprised you. The blade had a luster and shot a glare when you held it in sunlight, and yet it turned dark when you looked at it in the shade. Daddy's knife. I ran my fingertip along the cool, thin blade and touched its tip where the razor-sharp edges met. Older folks said when a knife has tasted blood, its color changes. I couldn't tell. What did it look like when a blacksmith was done forging it? They said the more blood taints it, the more it wants. Daddy slit somebody's throat open in an opium den. How many men had he killed with this knife? *This is no innocent knife.* The only things nice about it were its hilt and its sheath. They were pale yellow ivory with red flecks and veins.

I slid the knife into the sheath, and heard it click shut. Where the hilt met the sheath's opening, it was banded with a metal clasp that had a small ring. I had run a short string through it. When I went out at night, I tucked the sheathed knife under my cloth belt and tied the string to my belt. Sunlight was gleaming like silver splinters through the split in a banana frond. Someday I could slice it the way Lin Gao did. It takes a long time to obtain the skills that Granduncle and Lin Gao have. You don't wield a knife unless you know what to do with it.

In the cool shade I felt drowsy. The slow-leaking sap bubbled with tiny hisses. I tried to imagine how much sap there was in a banana trunk. The scent of roses came in on the breeze. I knew the smell. It came from those iridescent beetles in our garden. They might give off no odor when you pick them up, and then suddenly they perfume the air as if you were sleeping on a bed of roses. The smell pricked my heart. At night I prowled the Chinese quarter, hoping to see her. I knew I wasn't supposed to be out at night, leaving my patron unattended if he happened to need me. If he caught me sneaking out once, or twice perhaps, he'd surely terminate my employment like he did with my predecessor, a boy my age with ambition. Now I heard he was working for some rich family in the Chinese quarter. I begged Lin Gao to lie to our patron if he called for me at night during my absence. "Tell him I'm in the outhouse," I said, and then wondered how he'd describe such a thing to Mr. Cao Lai. I went at night to the quay every chance I got, when the streets started quieting down and the Chinese coolies gathered on the pier to have a good time. Each time I stood in the dark shade of the Indian almond tree and watched them. I waited. Waiting. Sometimes it was a long time before the coolies broke up. She must have been there earlier. Had she? Where was she?

One moonlit night my worst fear came true. The street was quiet and I could hear the boisterous Chinese coolies on the quay. One of them went to a lantern, lit his cigarette, and leaned over the rail, coughing up phlegm, and spat into the water. Then came the soft *clop-clopp*ing on the paved street. It was one of the few paved streets that was busy in daylight, with victorias and sometimes malabars, the Indian buggies that look like a coffin on wheels. In the pale moonlight a horseman went by. The black horse and black rider quietly passed. I pressed myself against the tree trunk, quietly cursing my idiocy for wearing gray trousers. He was a stone's throw away, and the moonlight shimmered on his contours and those of his horse like they were lit from inside.

Don't come now don't don't, I thought to myself, and my stomach hurt at the thought of him grabbing her pigtail and dragging her along the street if he caught her. Up on the quay there was shouting and laughter. The horseman rode on quietly into the night.

For several nights I had to escort Mr. Cao Lai to places where he dined and drank with his hosts until very late, and by the time we left, the streets were quiet. Our footfalls scared the dogs inside the mud-thatched houses and they'd bark in frenzy. Someone would snap at them to hush. On Salt Street, which led to the river, the air was cooled by the breeze and smelled of seawater. Mr. Cao Lai slowed his pace as we passed a row of brick houses.

"They make salt in there," he said. "See those?"

In the back of the houses, piles of salt glimmered white. Mr. Cao Lai took different roads each night to get home. He despised riding in a rickshaw. On a cross street, he gestured with his hand toward the shops with low-hanging roofs. "Coffin makers," he said. As we passed by them, he stopped before a shop that had a gilt plaque hung on the door. I noticed it must have been a Chinese-owned shop— the characters written in red on the plaque were Chinese. Out of curiosity I asked him what they meant. He spoke it in Chinese and then said in Annamese, "The Coffin Shop of Mr. Wang."

When we resumed walking he said that he was having a coffin custom-built by Mr. Wang.

"Who for, sir?" I asked, thinking of someone in his family, someone old.

"For me," he said, throwing back his head that was covered with a mass of long black hair.

I laughed. Mr. Cao Lai did have a sense of humor every now and then. But he said, "Mr. Wang happened to have this rare material—aged black wood—that kind won't rot even in water for a hundred years." He cleared his throat and spat on the sidewalk, and I thought of my father and my little brother. A coffin made of black wood. They would be dry for a century even in that soggy soil. So Mr. Cao Lai had seized the opportunity like a good businessman should. One might think it was odd, but the Annamese didn't live very long, so we were prepared when we got old enough to think of death. Mr. Cao Lai said, "It ought to be an extremely solid type of wood—incorrupt, that is. You might not be buried right away after you die, eh? Not because you are delayed by all that fancy burial rite. You must wait for the hour. And there you lie in a coffin, waiting. Weeks, months. The hour of the burial is everything. And that's why the wood to make a coffin, not just any coffin, ought to be flawless." He combed his hair back with his long fingernails and studied his nails in the dark. "I spent half a morning with Mr. Wang to inspect the timber. Looked for burls, lumps. I found it to be knot-free, to my delight."

I thought of my little brother wrapped in his straw mat that was his coffin. Rich people like Mr. Cao Lai took care of themselves exceedingly well, down to the minute details of the burial hour and the burial ground.

"Have you got a burial ground selected, sir?" I asked, already knowing the answer.

"No."

In fact, he did. And out of his good heart he gave it to our family. Since then he seemed to have forgotten it because he was so busy. A burial ground like that took a long time to find. But why was it in our region when he wasn't even living there or nearby? I remembered what Mr. Đinh-Hòa told my mother. He said his client wanted a burial site in the region of our village. Perhaps where it was didn't matter.

"Sir?" I said, glancing at him.

He glanced back at me and kept on walking.

"Were you born here in Hanoi?" I said.

"In Kwangtung."

"But you chose a burial site here . . . and in our land."

"Some areas are blessed. You go there and look for favorable spots for burial."

I thought about it. "That'd be very inconvenient for your family to visit you, sir—when you die."

"I don't have a family."

I fell silent. We walked on home, and I couldn't help but think of Lin Gao. When people like him and Mr. Cao Lai die, it'll be a lonely death. It might not matter where he's buried then.

One night we were back at the mandarin's residence inside the citadel. It was near midnight when Mr. Cao Lai summoned me. His face was ghastly. He was sitting in a red lacquered chair of rosewood, holding a straw basket in his lap. It was lidded and covered with a brocaded red cloth.

"Take this home with you," he said.

I took the basket as the mandarin in his black-tulle robe looked on from across the shiny black table. We hadn't brought it. It must be a gift. I bowed to both of them. The air felt wet with a sweet smell of liquor. The room was blue with tobacco smoke, and the wall behind the mandarin had a large painting in rice paper of birds and herons and water.

Holding the basket by its handles, I hurried out of the citadel and headed for the Chinese quarter. The streets were quiet, and an empty rickshaw went by. The lanterns on street corners flickered in the wind, which bore an odor of musk and ginseng. Bodies squirmed in darkness, sheltered between the shops' partitioning walls, bodies rolled up in bundles under the lee of the wall with gaping mouths and eyes open in their sleep, staring into their own blackest dreams. I peered into dark alleys and stood on the corner where she once stood, and after a while I went up the street. There were no more lanterns, just a glimmer from a half-moon. I stopped. Thirst made my throat dry. I squatted on the street, set the basket down, and lifted the brocade cloth and lid. There was something pale inside. I picked it up and looked. A human skull. I stared at the dark eye sockets, and they stared back. I held the skull up against a sliver of moonlight and looked at the blackened teeth. I remembered one of the skulls owned by the buffalo boys had blackened teeth. Even ash and many washes in lime would not change the color of lacquer. A gift? Who did this skull belong to?

Disturbed, I rose and quickened my pace. Soon I saw lights behind dark crowns of trees. On the quay the coolies were shouting and laughing. As I crossed the street to the Indian almond tree there was a sudden smashing sound. One of the coolies rose from the planks, raising his fist. You could see an opium pipe in his clenched hand. He was half naked, his torso oxblood and his arms sinewy. He kicked the broken neck of a lamp with his bare foot, and it shattered against a wooden pile. The other coolies hollered, jabbing their fingers at him as he brought his other hand up to his mouth. I saw a glinting shard of glass. You could hear him crunch it with his teeth as if he were crunching ice cubes. Then he chewed. His companions laughed and gawked and spat, and the dazed coolie chewed on. There were red threads coming out of his mouth and you could see him trying to swallow with difficulty. When he finally did, his head jerked and the other coolies' bantering suddenly subsided.

Then I saw her.

Out of darkness she emerged, lithe, quick-stepping, a cloth bag flung across her shoulder, her pigtail bouncing. She moved swiftly onto the quay. Like ants to sugar, they swarmed around her. The stuporous coolie stood mumbling to himself. The wind blew the lanterns to and fro, and the flames bent and came back, throwing a tremulous shadow across the quay. A barge was coming into the dock. I caught a glimpse of her blackened face between thrusting arms and snatching hands. The zinc coins clanked. I set the straw basket down and walked out to the quay, my eyes fixed on the disturbed coolie.

He tucked his pipe into his trousers, bent, picked up another broken piece of glass, and fed it into his mouth. He crunched it, chewed. Then he stopped. His arms flailed. Blood was coming out the corners of his mouth as he teetered toward a lantern. All the coolies were oblivious to him before he came crashing into them. He flung his arm and grabbed her by the shoulder. The wind came up and shadows danced. The other coolies cursed and shoved him back, and zinc coins fell clanking. I grabbed him by the arm that held her. His arm was hard. He yanked her toward him, and she fell smack against his chest. The coolies broke up. He had his hand in her bag as I pummeled his face. His head didn't even move. All I saw were the slits of his eyes, his bulging teeth and a shaven head, pale to the top where his hair was plaited in a long pigtail. I saw a knife in his hand. He grabbed her by the neck, ignoring me, as though he was angered she had kept him waiting. I pulled out my knife. She was helpless in the vise of his grip, and her arms flailed. I slid up just as his knife came across her throat. I drove the knife into his naked stomach. I felt it hit something. I felt the impact on my wrist all the way to my elbow. He dropped his knife, his empty hand clawed at the air. I pulled the knife out, and he fell to his knees, sitting with his head down. Suddenly the planks shook. The horseman emerged from the far end of the wharf where the barge was moored. As soon as I saw him and heard the quick *clop-clop*ping of the horse's hooves, I shouted to her, "Run! Run!" The coolies ran. We ran off the wharf, she ahead of me, headed for the dark street corner where she had come from. But he caught up with us just as we hit the street. He grabbed her by the pigtail and lifted her off her feet. I heard her cry. He reined in his horse and turned around, and I caught up with him. I saw his dark sleeve and I saw her, dangling, off the ground. I thrust my knife up and it went into his forearm. He shrieked. His horse swung in a circle, sending her tumbling to the ground. My knife was dislodged. She sprung up, running, and I ran after her.

She took several turns, squeezing through narrow alleys and then she was back out on the streets. My ears buzzed, my breathing came in gasps but there was no *clop-clop*ping from behind, only our quick footfalls. In a dark alley she stopped running and slumped against a wall. Gasping, I walked up to her.

"You again!" she said, huffing in Annamese.

Her face was so dark only her white teeth showed in the soot-black alley. I dropped my hand that clutched the knife. I could feel it shaking. Then I said, "Xiaoli?"

She was silent, and simply looked at me.

"Your name is Xiaoli?" I said.

"How d'you know my name?" she said in a heavy accent.

"You told me." I didn't want to tell her that I had spied on her.

"I never told you my name."

I nodded. "But you told me when you were not like you are tonight."

She said nothing. Then she looked down at my hand that held the knife. "You killed him, yes?"

"The Chinese coolie?" I said, pained.

"Him." She touched her throat and looked at her fingers.

"He cut you there?" I hoped he hadn't died.

"Yes."

"Wet your finger with your spit," I said, licking my fingertip. "Put it on the cut."

She did what I said. Then I spoke slowly to her, "What you did is very dangerous."

"Don't I know that?"

"Then why keep doing it?"

"Why are you asking?"

I shook my head. I would feel vulnerable if I told her. She didn't know me. To her, I was a stranger who happened to save her twice.

"You work in an opium den?" I said.

"Yes."

"Where?"

"Here."

"In one of those alleys?"

"Them."

"What alley?"

"You will come?"

"I don't smoke opium."

"I know."

"So where is it?"

She thought for a moment and then spoke. Her hands drew invisible directions. I heard the name Sail Street, a cross street somewhere with no name, but there was an old woman on the corner selling silk from early morning till dusk. Off the cross street was an alley with shops and houses. The den had no name.

"Ask for me if you are lost," she said.

"Ask? Who?" I said.

"The silk woman."

"The woman who sells silk?"

She nodded. Then she said, "She doesn't talk. She knows me."

"Ask for Xiaoli?"

"No. They call me White Lily."

"She understands? Say White Lily in Chinese."

She said it slowly and swung her cloth bag onto her back. "I must get on home."

"I'll walk with you," I said.

"Put your knife away."

I hesitated. Its blade was still wet with blood, and I didn't want to wipe it on my trousers. I gripped the knife, remembering the sick sensation I felt when I stabbed him. Then it came to me that I had left the straw basket behind. I could not go back to the quay now. I slid the knife back into the sheath tucked behind my belt. My heart was heavy.

"You live in that house?" I pointed in the direction of the alley we were heading toward.

"I work there," she said. "I'm a maid."

"There—and in the opium den?"

"Yes."

"You sneak out at night—to go to the den?"

"What?"

"They let you out? The family you work for."

"They own the den."

She touched her throat again and looked at her fingers. Even blackened with soot, her face was gentle, with soft lines flowing from her well-shaped nose to her lips and chin. I felt a warmth deep in the pit of my stomach and the warmth turned to queasiness. Did he die from the knife wound—a man against whom I bore no ill will?

"You work there every night?" I said as we entered the alley to her place.

"Yes. I only bring supplies." She glanced quickly at me. "And clean the pipes."

"The Frenchman will get you someday."

"He already had."

I felt her rocklike stubbornness. "Will you ever leave that place?"

"What place?"

"The opium lair."

"When I save enough. I will go back to my mother."

"Your mother?" We stopped at the red door. "Where's she?"

"In Yunnan."

A hollow in my stomach seized my breath. "Why?" I said.

"Mother is very poor."

"And your father?"

"No father. Only Mother and Grandfather."

"Xiaoli?" I felt a shortness of breath.

She looked at me, her hand in her bag.

"What's your family name?"

"Zhang." Then she smiled a rare smile. "You have a name?"

"Tài."

Suddenly I felt very tired. She opened the big door with a bulky key and then dropped it back in the bag. It clanked against the zinc coins. She pushed the door open and went in. The door creaked, and she stopped in the opening.

"You don't speak Chinese," she said. "No?"

"No." I could speak a few words that I learned from Mr. Cao Lai. But her words made me feel warm again deep down.

She closed the door just as I said, "When can I see you

again?"

She kept the door open just a crack. "I don't promise."

Then she closed the door.

I turned and walked up the dark alley, imagining her walking in the opposite direction across the quiet rock garden. Could I bring myself to tell her the sad news her grandfather had asked me to deliver? She was supposed to go back and tend her mother's grave.

Perhaps not now. But I would tell her. Just then I knew I was lying to myself.

THE SILK WOMAN

Twilight. The earth felt warm when I groped for my knife. It wasn't on the ground. I sat up under the banana tree, bent, and looked. Then I looked across the garden toward the kitchen and saw Lin Gao moving between the cast-iron stove and the brick shelf. Could he have taken it while I was sleeping? He was putting away pots, pans, and kettles that cluttered up the bluestone floor, for Mr. Cao Lai said they would collect mold if they sat on the floor. I watched him pick up the big straw broom in a corner, the black dog's den, and start sweeping. He swept and scrubbed it three times a day at sunrise, midday, and at sunset. He cringed whenever Mr. Cao Lai appeared in the kitchen. Each time he looked things over, Mr. Cao Lai would even inspect the ink drawing of Zao Jun, the kitchen god, propped up in a nook above the cast-iron stove. You never saw Zao Jun covered with grime. Perhaps it had nothing to do with the god who blessed a household with harmony. It could have been Lin Gao's self-portrait in the god's place—he still would have had to keep it grime free.

I walked the ground among the banana trunks. My eyes still stung from lack of sleep. Something pale green stirred among the grass blades and a grasshopper suddenly sprung up in the thin twilight. I looked at the banana trunk and then walked around it. Could I have left it stuck there after my stabbing frenzy? There were dark cuts and torn fibers hanging loose on the trunk. The sap felt sticky when I touched the nicks. This sap had cleansed the knife blade though. *Had I not stabbed him, she would have been dead.* Yet his blood didn't stain the blade. It had a dull shine. Perhaps blood had given it that muted shine.

When I came into the kitchen, the smell of warm broth made my stomach churn. I stood behind Lin Gao. Holding the straw broom, he looked up at the kitchen god that was held between two pieces of red-rimmed cardboard. He scratched his chin when I tapped his shoulder.

"Where's my knife?" I said.

With his mouth open like a little dark hole, he shook his head. Then his gray eyes shifted to a tray of food, and he motioned with his hand toward the main hall.

"Mr. Cao Lai back?" I said, knowing what my duty was.

Lin Gao nodded with a throaty grunt, sweeping his hand repeatedly at the tray. Mr. Cao Lai must be waiting. He had been gone all night and all day. At dawn when I left the house and headed for the quay to retrieve the basket, he was not back. A blue haze hung on the quay and the dirt streets were wet with dew. To my dismay, there was no sight of the straw basket. Who took it? What would someone do with a human skull?

I picked up the wooden tray by its cane handles. There were a bowl of steamed rice noodles next to a covered bowl of smoking broth, a plate of thin slices of pork, and a plate of green onions and fresh bean sprouts. A pair of ivory chopsticks lay between the bowls, and a tiny drinking cup with no handle sat next to a small vase of rice liquor.

I crossed the paved courtyard in the dim light that the red lanterns cast from beneath the eaves over the walkways. If Mr. Cao Lai hadn't found out about the missing gift, he would soon know. When Mr. Đinh-Hòa found out that I had broken his prized tea set, he said not a word, but quietly took away a whole month's pay. I remembered my misery. What kind of punishment would I get from Mr. Cao Lai?

The main hall felt cool and the black wainscoting glimmered from the glow of the oil lamp that sat on a lacquered black table. Leaning back in the chair, Mr. Cao Lai's face was shadowed by the silk screen behind him. He was so rapt in studying something he held in his lap that he didn't look up as I put the tray down on the table.

"Sir," I said, "May I serve you while your noodles are still hot?"

Without looking up he said, "Go ahead. Pour me a cup of liquor."

He reached for the cup and sipped, peering up at me while I picked up the bowl of steaming broth with both hands and poured it slowly over the dry noodles. The warm, rich smell made my mouth water. Then I stood back in the shadow beyond the lamp's glow. He leaned forward and, before picking up the chopsticks with his left hand, placed something down on the table next to the tray.

It was my knife he had been studying.

Every nerve in my head felt taut. My temples throbbed. Had he taken my knife while I slept? Lin Gao didn't even tell me.

With his chopsticks in his left hand, Mr. Cao Lai deftly picked up the slices of pork and transferred them to his steaming bowl of noodles. Then he pinched the green onions and bean sprouts and dropped them into his bowl. He stirred the noodles, blew, and began to eat. He lifted his bowl and drank the broth. I could tell that he wanted me to wait for whatever he had to say. Then before I could gather my thoughts, he spoke as he held the bowl's rim close to his lips, "Where is the basket I asked you to take home?"

"I lost it, sir," I said softly.

"How?" He glanced at me, still holding the bowl in mid-air.

I dropped my gaze, unable to speak because of the tightness in my throat.

"You can tell me."

Lying to him would perhaps exonerate me. But there lay my knife at his elbow. It rattled me that he must know something.

"I lost it somewhere near the quay, sir," I said.

"Just lost it?" He put down the bowl and casually reached for his cup of liquor.

"Something happened, sir."

He gazed at me after taking a sip. Even in the shadow beyond the lamp, I felt bare.

"What happened?" he said.

"I stabbed this Chinese coolie."

"Why?"

"He was attacking a girl on the quay."

"A girl?" he raised his voice sharply. "Just a girl? Someone you know?"

"Just a girl, sir. He was about to cut her throat."

Mr. Cao Lai sipped his liquor pensively. "And what happened to the basket?"

"I ran," I said. "I came back to the quay before it was light this morning. It wasn't there, sir."

"You stabbed him with this knife?" He held it up for me to see.

I nodded.

"Your knife?" he said, turning it in his palm.

"Mine, sir."

He said nothing, and then his gaze fell on me. "Who gave it to you?"

"My father." I leaned my head to one side. "He didn't give it to me. He left it behind—after he died."

"Fine knife." Mr. Cao Lai's lips curled into a grim smile.

"I'd been looking for it," I said. "I didn't know you had it."

"I didn't take it from you." He palmed the knife, then opened his hand, then closed it around the knife again.

"Lin Gao did?" I said.

"His dog fetched it to me."

Words came to my lips but I could manage only a grin. The old black dog? I didn't doubt what he said, but there must be an explanation for everything.

"Why to you, sir?"

"Maybe he's a wise dog. He smells death. And he knows who to go to."

I let out a slow sigh.

Mr. Cao Lai leaned back in the chair and again studied the knife, sheathed in its ivory red-flecked case. His shadow gloomed on the silk screen. On its five panels were paintings of the Eight Immortals, each holding an object that symbolized one of the eight conditions of life. I knew they symbolized longevity only from what he had once explained to me. I never gave it much thought—my life span. Perhaps it was the rich man's preoccupation.

Then Mr. Cao Lai said, "I know what happened."

I said nothing.

"You also injured a French lieutenant," his voice was toneless. "The French authorities came upon the scene before the Annamese did. They found a dead man and the basket that belonged to me. That is all true, isn't it?"

"Yes, sir." I felt gray. The man was dead.

"If the Annamese authorities had gotten there more quickly, they'd have found the basket and I wouldn't have lost it. And my mandarin friend, the Annamese chief of justice, wouldn't have been so upset."

"He gave you the basket?"

"It's what inside that matters."

I pursed my lips, nodding.

"You seem to know," he said, narrowing his eyes to slits.

"I know what was inside."

"You weren't supposed to."

"Yes, sir. I was very thirsty. Thought there might be something in there to drink . . ."

He shook his head sadly, brushed his long black hair back over the top of his head and examined his long fingernails. In the silence, I said, "Must be someone special to you, sir?"

He kept looking at his fingernails and seemed not to hear me. I decided not to ask again.

"A man I once knew," he finally said.

I looked down and then up. "Dear to you, sir?"

"No. An enemy."

I couldn't tell my exact feeling when he said that. I took risks to get my father's skull back, and there was a reason for it. What was Mr. Cao Lai's reason? How did the man meet his fate before he became a mere skull in a basket? Something broke inside me.

"Didn't you know," Mr. Cao Lai said tonelessly, "you were helping a girl who peddled opium? It's forbidden by law. Have you got any sense at all?"

I understood his point. The colonial government had a monopoly on opium and alcohol. One could only sell them with a license. Moonshiners like Chim were flouting the

law. But I thought of the logic behind Mr. Cao Lai's state-
ment and said, "Sir, I was helping her. I had no idea what
she was into."

He set the cup down. "That's between you and me. But
the law says you're a murderer and a criminal."

I felt like a cornered dog and I didn't like the feeling.
Worse, I felt that he was toying with me. What about the
skull given to him? What had he done?

"To me it's not a crime, sir," I said. "The situation might
make it look like a crime."

He poured, leaned back, and sipped. He touched his lips
with his fingertip and scratched the side of his nose leisurely
with his long nail. He was sitting there like a judge. I fought
against my helplessness.

"I can protect you," he finally said. "But you must change
your appearance."

I frowned. "Change my appearance?"

"The French authorities are going to post a criminal's
sketch—yours—in the city. It might not look like you, but
why flirt with danger?" He leaned forward, closed one eye
and looked at me with the other. "Shave your head—just
like a Chinese. You don't have much hair, so forget a pigtail.
Just shave it all. Wear a Chinese cap, a Chinese blouse."

"All that?" I said, exasperated.

"No worse than having your head lopped off if they catch
you." He pushed the tray away. "You can take this now."

I picked up the tray and my gaze fell on my knife. He
saw that and said, "Leave the knife with me."

I glanced up at him. "Why, sir? It's my knife."

"It'd be best if it remains with me—and by that I mean
it'd keep you out of trouble."

"Sir, I don't look for trouble any more than it looks for me."

"Less likely if you don't wield a knife."

"But it's my father's knife. I can't let anyone keep it, sir."

He gazed at me placidly. "You can trust me."

"I don't mean any disrespect, sir."

"Good."

I stood in one place, waiting. We both looked at the knife without saying a word. I could hear the sharp *click-click* the bats made out in the courtyard. I felt no anger or animosity toward him, but I would never lose my father's knife. After a long silence I heard him smack his lips and say, "The knife is yours."

His tone was subdued.

"Thank you, sir," I said, and picked up my knife and the tray and walked back down the dim hallway in the soft glimmer of black wainscoting, past the round latticed openings on the wall. On each of them was a human figure in long robes with a bat hovering above. Mr. Cao Lai said the bats were good omens.

The house had no ancestral altar, no shrine of buddhas. Each time I entered the main hall it would leave me with an odd feeling, and I could never overcome it.

Was he an atheist or a man with no roots?

Days went by so quickly I hardly remembered at night what I had done each day, but what I never forgot was the feeling that hit me the first time I put on my blue Chinese blouse, buttoned down the right side with loops, and stood looking at the wide sleeves with their cuffs turned back to show the darker blue lining. I had to wear it when I went outside, the Chinese blouse and the Chinese black cap to hide my shaved head. The cap had a red pom-pom on top. They

made me feel separated from myself. I had not seen her for
what seemed a long time, and one afternoon, sick with longing, I asked Lin Gao to give me an errand so I could get out
of the house.

I walked quickly for several blocks, and then ran like
a man possessed until my lungs ached. My cap slid down
from the top of my head, and I slowed my pace, striding
breathlessly in the heat of the dusty streets. I saw the gate to
the Chinese quarter. One side of the street lay bright in the
late afternoon sun, and the other side was dark under overhanging roofs. It looked like it belonged to another world.
I walked on the slanted shadows of bamboo poles, straight
and tall, stepped on shadows of the flags, and walked up
Sail Street. She said to just keep on walking until you see
a cross street with no name. I could hear her clear, heav-
ily-accented voice and see each gesture she made with her
hands. I passed one cross street after another, stepping away
from the edge of the street each time a rickshaw came running by, its wheels squeaking. The smell of noodles hung
on one corner as if it had always been there. On another
corner sat an old woman with a small teapot and teacup
and a bamboo basket in front of her. She wore a black cap
like mine, and she had a long plait of hair hanging down her
back. She was gazing at the street as I came by. Her basket
was open. In it was a pile of pale yellow silk. I sat down
on my heels, greeted her in my rudimentary Chinese and
pointed toward the cross street. She looked. There were
overhanging roofs and blue smoke rising from the clay vats
on narrow sidewalks where women were cooking meals
for their family. I spoke her name, White Lily. The woman
gazed at me. I said the word *A'pin*—opium—and spoke her
name again, hoping to strike a note with the old woman.

She turned her face toward the cross street, her serene eyes looking into the saffron glow beyond the hazy blue of wood smoke. I looked, not knowing what I was looking for, and she went back to her basket. She sorted through the silk pile and pulled out a swath of red silk. Slowly, she closed one hand and then opened three fingers. She folded the swath so gently it seemed to fold back into itself, feather-light and crimson red. She looked so small in her gray blouse, sitting with spread legs in purple trousers with hems that fastened above her ankles. I headed down the cross street, confused and lost, past the women cooking their meals in clay vats. I saw an alley and, farther down, another one. I kept on walking until I came to the next alley. It had a brick gate and two red doors. On them were Chinese characters brush-stroked in black ink. The doors were open. Down the alley, the walls between doors were painted with lime that flaked in chunks. Sloping roofs met and shaded the brick walk. A child cried, utensils clanked, and there was a fragrance of burning incense. When I came out of the alley through another brick gate on the other end, I turned up the street and walked back to where I had come from.

Late one night, after he had his supper, Mr. Cao Lai sent for me and told me that he had to meet someone in the Chinese quarter. He asked me to bring along my own mat.

"What for, sir?" I said.

"To spend the night there," he said.

I donned my blue Chinese blouse and picked up my Chinese black cap. I grinned as I looked at the two red pompoms and then chucked the hat onto my bed. Nighttime, who needs a hat? My bamboo mat felt light after I rolled it up. An old mat, it had gained a brown-red color. Mr. Cao Lai used a bamboo mat too, for it was cooler than the straw mat that I saw on Lin Gao's plank bed. I strapped the mat on my back and went into the main hall. Behind the silk screen was a door that led to Mr. Cao Lai's sleeping quarters. I heard a faint melody, light and soothing, as if someone was playing a musical instrument. Suddenly it stopped.

He came out quietly in his satin black shoes, dressed in Chinese clothing like mine, except that his blouse was white silk fastened on the side with coral-colored cross-stitches.

"What was that music, sir?" I said, knowing of no musical instrument in the house.

"Music?" He frowned.

"I heard it."

"I didn't."

"I didn't imagine it, sir."

"Then you didn't."

His curtness told me not to ask more. We crossed the courtyard and mounted the five steps to the entrance where a brick screen shielded the view. I had gotten used to seeing this plain masonry in a Chinese house. From the street, all one sees is the brick screen. The entrance door was not on a straight line with the inner quarters. After the door I would turn right to go to the living quarters. Mr. Cao Lai said the Chinese believed that baleful spirits traveled in a straight line, so the screen would halt their advance into one's home.

Mr. Cao Lai stood waiting at the main door while I went and fetched two rickshaws. What a luxury! He rode in one and I in the other, following him. It was very late when we went through the gate into the Chinese quarter. The rickshaws sped past a late-night food peddler pushing his cart slowly, like a malnourished spirit in the dim light of the lantern that swung to and fro on the side of the cart. We went past alleys, the dark nocturnal cemetery of the living, and in them stirred figures of sleeping humans, staggering somnambulists with staring eyes. Where is her lithe figure clad in black, gliding through the darkness? Could she be at the den at this hour? Worse, could she be on the quay or somewhere else with those addicted coolies? Who's this Chinese man he's supposed to meet?

When the rickshaws turned a corner, their wheels clacked and bounced on the bluestone and I sat upright, watching alleys go past. We stopped at the alley with the red doors. I tripped as I stepped out of the rickshaw.

My bamboo mat slid off my back when I came behind Mr. Cao Lai, both of us standing in front of the massive closed doors. On each door was a black iron knocker—a ring looped around a human head in iron with bulging eyes and flaring nostrils. I couldn't help but think of the guardian spirits that were worshipped in our village shrine. Mr. Cao Lai opened the doors with a long key. Over the creaky sound of the doors being pushed open, I could hear the beating of my heart.

A dog whined. There was a murmur of prayer, a sound of splashing water. Then we came to a brown wooden door. The door opened into a narrow, dimly lit hall. The red glow of the lamp was hazy with smoke. I stared into the warm murkiness. Small peanut-oil lamps flickered in their crystal globes, illuminating half-naked bodies that leaned on cushions on the mats. Mr. Cao Lai stepped carefully between the mats, saying not a word, and I kept close to him as we picked our way past the burning lamps that sent spirals to the ceiling. There was a sweet caramel odor, warm and intoxicating, that made one drunk. At the end of the hall, there was

a bead curtain that clanked when one went through it. The
world behind it glowed in soft illumination from the paper
lanterns, round and yellow, that hung from the rafters. Silk
parasols in guava green, aqua blue, and bright lilac leaned
in the gossamer-thin light at the heads of narrow, low-lying
beds of carved wood. Bodies reclined in eddying plumes,
the opium crackling over low-necked lamps. On one bed lay
a man in white Annamese pajamas. I knew he was Annamese from his chignon. He stopped drawing on a pipe and
glanced up at us. He was pale-skinned, with sharp cheek
bones. His moustache drooped to his chin into a short, thick
beard.

"Brother Lai," he said with a smile to Mr. Cao Lai.

He was certainly an Annamese—he had black lacquered
teeth.

"Brother Lý," Mr. Cao Lai said, sitting down on the facing bed.

I stood with the mat still strapped to my back. Mr. Cao
Lai gestured with his hand. "Put that in the corner," he said.
"Have you ever prepared a pipe?"

"Yes, sir."

"Good. Make me a pipe."

They chatted while I heated the pin above the lamp. Then
I dipped its tip into the jar of opium and twirled the wooden
handle. They paid me no mind. Over the low-burning lamp
I cooked the pale brown drop until it began to swell like a
bud and I could smell a dark, warm smell. The bud felt hot
against my fingertips when I rolled and kneaded it on the
tray. In the crackling of pipes, the room and the smokers
seemed indistinct. Shapes and souls ceased to be, nothing
mattered but the pervasive placidity. The two men talked
in soft voices. The man, Lý, was the village head of Chung,

our nemesis. In our Annamese custom, if a man holds a title, he goes by the name of the title he holds. So as the village chief, his title was *Lý truong*. I was distracted from kneading the opium drop when Mr. Cao Lai turned to me and said, "Don't mash it. That's enough."

"Yes, sir," I said and carefully glued the sticky paste to the small orifice of the pipe's bowl. I handed him the pipe, and both men leaned forward at the same time, placing their pipes over the bulbous lamp and drawing deeply with a hiss. Unsettled, I watched Lý. My late father almost got him when my father and his gang broke into Chung village. Had he succeeded, the *Lý truong* wouldn't be here tonight. The pipes crackled. The men drew sharply again and again and then leaned their heads back on the cushion. I picked up Mr. Cao Lai's pipe and prepared a fresh one, taking my time while he rested. By the third pipe, Lý raised himself up on his elbow and said, "Would you care for some tea, Brother Lai?"

"Red tea for me, Brother Lý."

Lý picked up a pear-shaped bell on his tray and shook it repeatedly. I wondered why he, but no others, had a bell on his tray. Someone came out from the back of the room and knelt beside Lý's bed while I was heating a drop of opium. I heard a girl's voice, heavily accented, speaking in Annamese. "What is it that you need, sir?"

"Tea," Lý said. "My regular tea. And red tea for Mr. Cao Lai."

"Mr. Cao Lai! Good evening, sir."

My hand froze holding the silver pin above the lamp. She was looking across the beds as she spoke and her face was a pearly white in the translucent lamps.

"I haven't seen you for a while, Xiaoli," Mr. Cao Lai said

from his repose. "You have grown."

"You still drink Qimen tea, sir?"

"Yes, indeed. You surprise me."

She rose and left. I watched her until she was gone behind a door. Black blouse, black trousers. Her long pigtail swung as she slid through the door. Perhaps she didn't recognize me because of my shaved head. Perhaps it was my Chinese blouse.

She came back with a small tray and set a teapot and a tiny cup on Mr. Cao Lai's tray and then did the same for Lý. When she turned around, the cuff of her sleeve touched my face and I wanted to speak her name, though she never looked at me, as if I wasn't in the room. It hurt me. At the same time I hadn't come to grips with what was taking place before my eyes. How did Mr. Cao Lai come to know her? Yet I didn't want him to know my business with her, not after I killed a man on her behalf.

As she poured tea for Lý, Mr. Cao Lai said to her, "You sure look like your mother, Xiaoli, the older you get."

"I haven't changed that much, sir," she said, turning her head over her shoulder. "Just taller, and my hair is so long now it bothers me sometimes."

"Your mother will have a hard time telling who you are when she sees you again. I would myself had I not seen you in between."

"When she sends for me, I will go." Xiaoli paused and smiled. "I must pay Mr. Lý my debt before I can go anywhere."

The man, Lý, raised his teacup to his lips, sipped, and peered up at her. "In due time you can go visit your mother. For now you are needed at the house."

I felt a heaviness in my chest. When could I tell her the

news about her mother—and her grandfather? There was
no one else left for her back home, but she might still go
back to tend her mother's grave, much as I was bent on reburying both my father and my little brother. Distance made
no difference. Your heart would tell you what to do.

As I took the third pipe from Mr. Cao Lai's hand, I
watched her back. I could touch her—she was an arm's
length away. Was she a bound girl indentured to Lý? Like
me, she had no father. It surprised me to see an Annamese
like Lý own a big house and an opium den in the heart of the
Chinese quarter. How was he able to break into the brother-
hood of the prosperous Chinese association?

She rose and, without a word, left the room. Before I could
gather my thoughts, she reappeared, moving between beds,
now silhouetted, now lit against the lamps' illuminations,
like a spirit feeding methodically on the living. I knew what
she was doing and my stomach churned. I could hear the
scraping her hook made in the pipes' hollows as she cleaned
each pipe. How could she not notice me? Was I nothing but
a stranger to her after I had killed a man for her? Was she
that heartless?

By the time she had cleaned all the smokers' pipes in the
room—but not those in the anterior room for second-class
smokers—it was past midnight. A bag slung over her shoulder, she came and bent over her employer's bed and told
him she was leaving. Without even glancing in my direction, she went through the rear door.

I could picture her sliding through the darkness of the
night and finding herself surrounded by a horde of unruly
Chinese coolies and addicts. She could take care of herself.
She must have done this many a time to be so sure of herself. But all it took was one mishap. It had happened. She

survived.

Sometime after both men were asleep on their beds, I went out the front door and stood in the alley. It was so dark I could hardly see my own hands. They locked both alley entrances when the den was full, and only the alley tenants could enter with their own keys. The night was cool, and stars glittered like diamond chips in the immense black sky. I stood until the grayness in my heart was gone and then went back in. I spread my mat out in a corner and fell asleep.

It was a short sleep. I suddenly woke to a tapping on my shoulder. Mr. Cao Lai was already up. He asked me to get ready to leave and told me to bring back two rickshaws. Outside, it was half light and a gray mist hung. I walked out of the alley and up the nameless side street to the corner and waited. In the stillness came shuffling footsteps. A shapeless figure came looming up in the mist, and when it came near I saw that it was the old Chinese woman who sold silk. Not even looking at me, she sat down on the stone curb, put her bamboo basket by her side and lifted its lid. A teapot, a cup. She sat with them in front of her, like she was waiting for someone to come and drink. The only one out at that hour was me.

MELODY OF A BYGONE PAST

A few nights later, we left the mandarin's residence very late in two rickshaws. Mr. Cao Lai was tipsy, I could tell. From deep in the citadel, the rickshaws snaked their way out on narrow dirt roads, dark under tamarind and flame trees. Watching the coolie's back in the dancing light of his lantern, as his blue blouse pulled tight against his jutting shoulder blades, I began to pity him. The *quan án*, chief of justice, owned a rickshaw rental business in the city. He was the one who gave Mr. Cao Lai the skull of his enemy as a gift. I surely wanted to see where he kept his fleet of rickshaws. It was a thriving business for the owners. The rickshaw coolies, like the two pulling us this night, were their human horses. They survived on what they could make after paying their employer the daily rent in advance. In between fares, they smoked opium—the dregs that Xiaoli sold to the addicts in paper packets. Even dregs were unaffordable to some coolies, so they bought the water the dens washed pipes and picks in. Then they boiled the water and drank it. Some drank moonshine heavily to keep them on their feet.

Mr. Cao Lai had sought a favor from the *quan án*. He asked his backing so that Mr. Cao Lai could open a franchise for rice alcohol, licensed by the colonial government. The *quan án* congratulated Mr. Cao Lai on this night: he had been awarded the franchise. Then, after the good news, the *quan án* forewarned Mr. Cao Lai about moonshining that was costing those alcohol franchises a great deal of profit. "Troubles are brewing, my good friend," the *quan án* said, "unless we can exterminate those moonshiners."

I sat there listening and couldn't help but think of Chim, my former employer and mentor. These days I didn't have time to think of anything but Xiaoli. Everything else receded. I didn't care where I came from, didn't care about friends and those who cared for me from my Lau village.

The *quan án* said even some alcohol franchises bought moonshine and resold it to stay competitive. He said the bootleggers brought rice alcohol into the city from surrounding villages in oxcarts. Each cart was loaded with farm produce, and hidden under it were containers of moonshine. "We sent agents to several villages," the *quan án* said. "We'll buy from whoever sells those spirits and we'll get to those who made them." Mr. Cao Lai said, deadpan, "Cutting off the snake's head might solve part of the problem. You will punish those moonshiners with penalties so severe, they will be crushed. The condemned will never break the law again."

When the rickshaws went on the bridge that crossed the moat, the air had the cool fragrance of lotus blossoms, pure and clean and purest at nighttime. A night bird cried. The last time I saw Chim was at Monkey Hop Landing where he saw me off and then took his boat and rowed home with Xoan. He had an empty wicker bin. Gone were all his jars of moonshine. He might have mended his ways now, for Xoan's sake. Her plea did make him quit smoking. Fortunately, I thought, Lau wasn't one of those villages surrounding the city. It was a day-long trip by boat or half a day on horseback, like the trip Granduncle made the time my little brother died.

The clattering of the rickshaws' wheels on paved roads distracted my thoughts. The rickshaws sped along Bamboo Street, their lanterns swinging to and fro like two eerie orbs, and the river's smell was warm and strong like the smell of silt. We had just passed the Chinese quarter, and the odors of hot fat and late-night noodles came drifting ghostly in the breeze, and I groaned. The rickshaws skittered toward the curb—they were running in the path of an oncoming horseman. He did not yield as he plunged ahead, and I swore I could touch the horse's rump with my hand. Black horse. Black rider. I turned my head in his direction. There he was, farther up the road, a dark shape sitting on his horse, not moving. He was just sitting still. Then the horse turned, and he sat gazing down Salt Street. This late in the night brought back the scenes on the quay, in the banana grove.

"Hey! Stop!" I shouted to the coolie.

The coolie slowed down, looked back. The horseman suddenly lurched as his horse took off. I jumped out, ran. I could hear the horse's hooves clacking on the bluestone, and I ran with the smell of the river warm and thick in my nose and my lungs ached. I saw him pull up in front of the brick houses where they kept salt. Torch lights wavered in the yard. Heaps of pale white salt glittered. The man, the horse blocked the entrance. Then I saw her, dressed in black, face blackened, in the center of a crowd of Chinese coolies. The Chinese held up their torches to see better. They all hushed, waiting for the Frenchman's move. I planted my feet, my teeth clenched. I was no more than ten feet behind him, hand gripping the sheath of my knife. The torches spurted and popped and blue sparks flew. He nudged his horse with his heel and it came forward. The Chinese backed away and she too moved back, partially covered by them. The Frenchman let out a sharp cry, and his horse lunged into the crowd. All the Chinese ran except one. The lone Chinese man stood his ground in front of the salt pile and sank a knife into the horse's throat. I couldn't see him anymore, as if he had been engulfed by the horse as the animal slumped on its fore- legs. The Frenchman slid off the saddle, and in his hand I saw a pistol. He stepped up as the Chinese man struggled to pull out his knife, now locked in the horse's neck. But he managed to pull it out, with such a force that it knocked him back against the salt pile. The Frenchman leveled his pistol and shot him. The gunshot echoed, my guts throbbed. He holstered his handgun, bent, and picked up the knife. Then he turned to his horse, lying with its head on the pile of salt. He looked down at the dead Chinese man and at the knife that killed his horse. Just then he saw her darting to the entrance. He swiveled on his heel and missed her by a handspan, and we both ran to her. He grabbed her by the pigtail, swinging her so hard that she wailed and kicked out her foot. I came at him to wrench her from his grip, and I saw his knife aimed at my stomach. I grabbed the blade. My knees locked, my hand screamed with pain, and I felt him seize me by the back of my neck. I was helpless as his knife went into my body. My breath was cut off. The only thing that kept me standing was my will. *Don't die!* My head hit his shoulder, and I willed my hand that clutched the knife to drive it up into his chest. I grunted and felt his whole weight fall down on me. Something was forced up from my convulsed stomach, and I tasted blood.

He fell against me and knocked me backward. My knife became dislodged from his chest. I saw salt piles, white against a black sky, and I could taste more blood in my mouth now and I gagged, trying to breathe. She squatted

down beside me, her eyes searching my face as if she wanted an answer. Then she saw my cut hand cupping my stomach. The handle of his knife was the only thing outside my
body. I saw her looking down, a face black as the sky above.
Then she cried. Footfalls. Faces. The shaved heads. The gray
blouses. Like they all came together in the same picture. She
cried hysterically. She shouted in Chinese, and the Chinese
coolies, frenzied, talked among themselves. Someone ran
out to the street with a torch. She dropped her gaze to my
hand that still clutched my own knife, unclasped my fingers,
and then tried to sheathe it. After she secured it under my
belt, she cupped her hand over mine on my stomach. Her
other hand wiped the blood that had started leaking from
the corner of my mouth. I couldn't see very well because
of a wet film over my eyes, and my nose felt soggy. I had to
breathe through my mouth. Beneath me the earth shook. I
heard the clacking of wheels. She cried out as someone bent
over me, "Sir, it's you!"

I sensed a strange familiarity in the face that looked
down at me before a name came back.

"Who are you?" Mr. Cao Lai said.

"It's me. Xiaoli, sir."

He asked her something in Chinese, and as she told him
between her sobs what had happened, he looked down at
me and said, "Oh, fool, oh, you hopeless fool. Do you want
to waste your life?"

She pointed at the knife still stuck in my stomach, sobbing and saying incoherent words in Chinese. He shook his
head, his long black hair falling over his face, and bent closer to my face. "Got to get you some help," he said. "You'll
bleed to death if we pull out the knife."

I had a searing thirst just like the time the smallpox hit me.

"Mr. Cao Lai," she said, sniffling. "Take him to our place."

"No," he snapped. "I'm taking him back myself."

"But our place is only a short way away. He's bleeding..."

Mr. Cao Lai turned and ordered one of the rickshaw coolies to bring his vehicle up.

"Sir," she said, her voice scratchy, "we have a physician at our place."

"Physician? What sort of physician?"

"He tends to the old lady, Mr. Lý's mother."

"A physician, eh?" Mr. Cao Lai inhaled sharply. "Let's make sure he can save the boy. Then I'll take him home."

"Not tonight, sir. Things like this take days. I have seen it."

"Say no more." Mr. Cao Lai stood up, gave a curt order to the rickshaw coolies.

They lifted me off the ground and lay me in the rickshaw I had been riding in. The Chinese watched. Mr. Cao Lai spoke sharply to them in their language, and they stood there not saying a word. One by one, they came to their dead friend's side. Then Mr. Cao Lai got in his rickshaw, and I saw everything move back. Soon I heard the clacking of wheels and felt a sharp thump. My stomach felt rent, and I bit down hard. It was worse than having smallpox, when your whole body is sometimes singed with fever and chilled with cold. The delirium seizes your whole body, but it isn't like this, when your mind knows only one bad wound and won't quit telling you about it.

I clasped my hands around the hilt of the knife in my stomach. It was wet. I smelled the stench of blood as I breathed through my mouth. Hot breath, as I had when I was sick with smallpox. I saw something moving alongside the rickshaw. Bleary-eyed, I could make out her slender figure in black running, running.

There is a whirling mass. It glows red-hot. It dims, everything goes black. You float in it. No arms, no legs. You know it is you, but you don't have a body. You see the swirling mass, perhaps you are it. Perhaps it is outside of you, for you are but a thought. You feel the engulfing heat, yet it can't consume you. You know it. You don't have a body.

For one moment before coming out of that blackest mass, there was a soothing, peaceful melody. A long bar of sunlight fell across the plank bed from the latticed window high above, where a patch of blue sky hung. This wasn't my place. I could tell. The plank bed was raised on a platform. It had a headrest, a footrest. I was lying on a thin floral quilt. I was alive. I had a body. Its midsection was wrapped heavily in white cloth under a gray blouse they had put on me. My head rested against a round wooden pillow covered in blue linen. The melody. It came out of Mr. Cao Lai's sleeping quarters that night. I thought I was home. Was I hallucinating?

I slept, woke, and slept again. Each time I woke, my abdomen and my hand twinged. When I moved my body, it screamed. Once I woke, I caught myself groaning. She was sitting on the edge of the bed, holding a clay bowl in her hands.

"I brought you medicine," she said.

I looked at her. Her ponytail was flung over her shoulder, touching her abdomen. Her dark blue blouse had a sheen on it. I tried to find words. She was real, no more a furtive figure gliding through the night. At my silence, she moved the bowl to my lips. I sipped the first taste of liquid and winced. She held the rim of the bowl near my lips, her fingers long and tapered, and I could see the white facings of her sleeves' cuffs. I leaned forward and took another sip, this time holding it in my mouth until the herbal smell stung my nose. I gulped it down. She watched me calmly, patiently. I took hold of the bowl and her hands as they held it.

"Let me —" I said and felt a sharp twitch in my left hand. The bowl spilled onto my chest.

Quickly she wiped it with her hand. "Don't use your hand," she said. "Rest it."

They had put something yellow like turmeric on the palm of my cut hand and fingers. The yellow powder had caked on the slashes, but it hurt sharply when I made a fist. I sipped and swallowed with difficulty, and each time I gazed up I met her eyes, steadily watching me. Her pupils were peppercorn-black, her eyes so symmetrically shaped and clear that I felt thick in my throat again, like the very first time I met her. For the last sip I took, I had to lean my head back as she tilted the bowl almost upside down, and it covered my face completely.

"Xiaoli," I said, gagging, liquid dripping from my lips.

"Oh, I'm clumsy," she said, and burst out laughing.

"It hurts when I laugh."

She looked suddenly solemn. "You saved me three times."

"Don't say it."

"Why me?" Her face clouded over.

"You weren't hurt," I said. "Everything else doesn't matter."

"It matters." Her voice shook. "Three died. Not one. Not two. Three."

Her accented voice trailed and she cried. She just told me something I dreaded to remember. I felt like moaning.

"Wish none of that happened," I said. "You'll never feel the same again."

"No. You won't ever. Especially you."

"Especially me," I said pensively.

"I saw pictures of you on the street..."

I simply gazed at her.

"The face does not look like you," she said, taking me in with her gaze. "Why did you shave your head? Ah, I see..."

I ran my good hand over the top of my head, feeling the stubble that had grown back.

"What happened to your face?" she said, trailing her gaze.

"Smallpox. You know what that is?"

"Small . . . pox?"

I explained. "Chills, fevers, pus . . . lots of it. My little brother died from it."

"You had a brother? Ah. Any sister?"

"No. Just me and him."

"Where are your father and mother?"

"Just my mother. Daddy, he wasn't so lucky . . ."

"Small . . .pox?"

"No." I turned my face away because of a twinge of shame.

"Do you know him?"

"I know him. Why?"

"I don't know my father."

"Why is that?"

"He left my mother when she had me."

I thought of her grandfather, what he asked of me, and felt sick.

"Your father still in Yunnan?" I said. "Or dead?"

"He went back to here. Mother told me."

"To where?"

"Here. This country."

"He's not Chinese? Or he had business here?"

"He is like you. Not Chinese."

I hated those who ran away from responsibilities.

"How did you end up here?" I asked, taking in her gentle features for one brief moment while she looked down.

"Ah," she said, crimping her lips.

I could see her thick lashes flutter. She seemed to be searching for something to say. Finally she looked up. "This . . . merchant, yes, merchant, gave my mother some money, borrowed money, yes. I was eleven. I went in a boat with many women and little girls like me. They made many of us take opium, so we don't cry while we are at sea. . . ."

"Who's this merchant?" I said. "Lý ?"

She flinched. "No. It does not matter. But, well, he told me I was to work for Mr. Lý."

"He sold you to Lý?"

She said nothing, just looked at me, and then nodded.

"You work and no pay?"

She shook her head. Now I understood why she was so bent on selling opium dregs. I told her who Lý was. She said she knew. The big courtyard house was where he entertained guests. The only permanent residents were the matriarch—Lý's mother—the Chinese physician, the old Chinese woman—the gardener—and her. She said Lý would come when he had business to tend to. Often he arrived with his daughter.

"Is he here? Lý?" I said.

"He left with his daughter. The morning after he was at his opium den."

I narrowed my eyes at her. "So you saw me there that

night?"

"I saw you."

"With my head shaved and in my Chinese clothing?"

"I knew it was you."

I met her gaze. Each time I felt thick in the throat. "I came here once. I asked for you. But the old woman said there was no Xiaoli here. I thought she lied."

"Everyone knows me as White Lily. Are you hungry?"

"Hungry?" I felt quizzical. The pain seemed to be the only thing I felt. It was a malicious omnipresence.

She smiled as she rose. "I'll bring you something to eat."

I heard a cuckoo in the quiet. Its throaty, lazy call brought me back to those hot summer days in my village when I would take my little brother with me, looking for the cuckoo in a bush or a thicket. *Why it?* he asked. *I want to kill it,* I said. *Why?* he asked. *These birds,* I said, *they drop their eggs in other birds' nests so they don't have to raise their own babies. They do that? But why?* he said, completely puzzled. *Because that's their nature,* I said.

Through the latticed window, the streak of sunlight had become longer across the floor. Watching it, I wondered about the time of day. Then I noticed that they had also put a fresh pair of cotton trousers on me. Mine must have been covered with bloodstains. I felt hot in the head. Who changed my clothes?

She came back carrying a small bamboo food steamer. It had two decks, round, veined with gray stains from steam and heat from cooking. She lifted the lid of the top deck. In it were two white steamed buns.

"I made them," she said, handing me one.

It was warm as I held it in my good hand. Steam was coming from its silky skin. "I eat one," I said. "You eat one."

I chewed. It tasted sweet, with a bamboo fragrance cling-ing to its skin. I watched her take a bite, forgetting my dis-comfort. In the quiet we ate.

"I need to wash your wounds later," she said.

"You? Why?"

"The physician said you must change it twice a day. Or you might get infection."

I swallowed what was in my mouth and opened my cut hand. "What is this yellow stuff?"

"That? Ah." She squinted her eyes, thought, and said something to herself in Chinese. Then she raised her face at me. "I don't know what it is here, in this country. It's a round fruit like an egg. Its flesh is yellow and thick."

I thought of the mamey sapote. "*Cây trung gà*," I said.

"That's what it is. They grind the seeds into powder. It heals cuts."

It must have, I thought. They didn't bandage my hand. "I don't remember anything after I passed out in the rick-shaw."

"We didn't know if you would ever wake up again." She dropped her gaze to my midsection. "You lost so much blood, you would have died if we had not gotten you back here in time."

"I know," I said. "Thanks for taking care of me."

"I washed your clothes. They had much blood on them." She gestured with her hand toward the courtyard. "I will patch your blouse when it's dried."

"You're very kind, Xiaoli."

"Because of me you almost died."

"Don't say that."

The cuckoo called again. A desolate sound in the quiet.

"I must wash your wound now and dress it," she said.

"Is it afternoon now?"

She nodded, picked up the steamer and left the room. She came back shortly with a brass pail of water and a handkerchief and a roll of white cloth draped over her forearm. Without saying a word, she slid up to me and began removing the pins that fastened the strip of cloth around my midsection. She unwrapped it deftly, lifting me up with her hand pressed against the small of my back. I held my breath, watching her hands, and then the wound. It was covered with the yellow powder. She wrung the handkerchief and gently washed the powder away. My chest heaved. A faint lemon scent got in my nostrils. It wasn't from the water or the powder. By then I could see the gash, red and raw, and her fingers dabbing it with the fresh yellow powder she took from a pouch in her blouse pocket. When she unrolled the fresh cloth strip, I pushed myself up from the bed with both hands and let her wind the strip around my midsection. Her face was serene as she dressed my wound. She never frowned. Her skin was so clear, her nose straight and so finely shaped. I noticed the nick on her throat. He could have killed her had I not killed him.

"Who changed my clothes?" I said quietly.

"Me," she said, glancing quickly at me, then dropping her gaze.

I gulped, but she did not see.

"I will change the bandage again tonight," she said, buttoning up the side of my blouse.

"How long will I be staying here?"

"Until you are healed." She washed her hands in the pail. "When you can walk again."

"Where's your room?"

"Here."

"This room?"

She nodded and flung her ponytail back over her shoulder.

"I can sleep anywhere else but here," I said. "You don't have to put up with me."

She crimped her lips and smiled. "I don't think like that."

"Where d'you sleep?"

"Anywhere in the house but here."

I grinned. She rose and the lemon scent rose with her.

"You rest now. Sleep, you are still tired. It's very quiet here."

Something struck me. "Do you play any type of musical instrument?" I said.

"No." She shook her head. "You asked because you want me to play something for you?"

"No. I heard some melody when I woke. Beautiful sound."

"Ah." She canted her head to one side and said nothing as she left the room with the pail.

Alone, I tried to sit up, dreading the thought of being bedridden. Already I saw how I had disrupted my service to Mr. Cao Lai. How would he view me now after I had become a liability to him? He could terminate my employment like he did the boy before me. He could void the deed to the burial ground. I let out a deep sigh and suddenly remembered Chim's words. *If you act with pure thought, happiness will follow you like a shadow that never leaves.* I knew he must have borrowed those words from someone, but I knew I didn't kill those men because of malice or hate.

She came back into the room while I was feeling gloomy.

She sat down on the edge of the bed and gave me what was in her hand.

"Open it," she said, smiling.

It was a pocket watch, round and silvery. The cover was engraved with flowers around the fringe, and in the center there was a bird hovering over two nestlings. I flipped open the hinged cover. A melody rose, clinking into the air. Listening, I felt the weight on my heart lifted. All the time I gazed at a woman's face that was on the inside of the cover. Her hair was brushed back and clasped with a white flower. She had such soft and gentle features that her beauty made me think of Xiaoli, though they did not look like each other.

The melody wound down to tiny jingles and ended.

"Who's she?" I said, not wanting to close the cover.

"My mother."

"I couldn't tell. Well, it's a picture."

"She has not changed. She always looks like that."

Her words pricked my heart and I closed the watch with a sigh.

"Why you sigh?" she said, concerned.

"Nothing. I wish I had a watch like this. It takes everything off your mind. Lovely tune."

"She said it was made for her. You do not get things like this out there."

"Who made it for her?"

"My father. She said he loved her so much he carried it with him all the time. Then he gave it to her because she loved it."

"Why did he leave her then? If you ever love someone so much . . ."

"Yes. But she never told me why. She just gave me this watch."

"She wants you to remember her," I said, placing the watch in her hand.

"Whenever I hear the melody . . ."

I could almost hear in my mind the melody that came out of Mr. Cao Lai's chamber that night. He had denied hearing it.

THE HORSEMAN IN BLACK

By mid-morning of my third day in Xiaoli's room, she came in and told me there was a rickshaw waiting outside to take me back. She was befuddled, for the physician had cautioned her that I was still frail, unable to walk without bleeding. When she took the plate of dumplings from my hands, she said if I could not make it, she would send the rickshaw away. I listened, warmed from within by her words. For one brief moment I could see that it did not matter if I stayed or went. Nothing would ever change again because we were together. But I knew Mr. Cao Lai, and I did not want to go against his wishes. So I told her that my employer needed me and asked her not to worry about me. Then I changed back into my old clothes while she went out to talk to the rickshaw coolie. I did everything sitting up on the plank bed, feeling a twinge in my abdomen each time I twisted my torso. In the cloth bundle in which she had wrapped my belongings, I saw my knife. I picked it up and looked at it. Then I pulled it out of its sheath. The slender blade gleamed, spotless. Had I left it in Mr. Cao Lai's care, I would have been helpless and most certainly dead by the Frenchman's hand. Would it thirst for more blood?

She returned. With her, to my surprise, were a rickshaw coolie and Lin Gao. The old man stood watching me, his wrinkled face impassive. Then he walked up to me and put his gnarled hands on my midsection and looked at Xiaoli. She told him something in Chinese and he nodded. She gestured with her hands while she spoke, and he too made hand signs. I couldn't tell what it was about until she went out of the room and came back with a large paper pouch. In it were herbs that she had received from the physician to make drinking medicine for me. Lin Gao opened the pouch, pinched shreds of herbs, and smelled them. He held his hand up like a cup and made a pouring motion. She nodded. Then she handed him a roll of white cotton strip and he took that. The men hoisted me off the ground, each with an arm over his shoulders. I was standing straight up like a scarecrow as they carried me out. Another rickshaw coolie was waiting outside in the alley. As they laid me down in one rickshaw I looked at her. She bent down over me.

"He will make the medicine," she said. "You drink it twice a day. Every drop of it."

"When can I see you again?"

"A-Mei knows you, if she hears you. . . . She can't hear very well."

"I can't come during the day. I can go to the opium den. You're there every night, arenn't you?"

"Not every night."

Already I saw a chasm between us. Laying my hand over hers on the rim of the seat, I said, "I just want to see you."

She nodded. One side of her face was in the sun and I could see the tiny red mole at the corner of her mouth.

"Go to the street corner where the silk woman sits," she said. "Ask her if I left any message for you."

"I had a hard time understanding her."

"It will come to you if you let it. Can you do that?"

I nodded. I had no choice. "How about you tie a red cloth around the bamboo pole on that corner?" I said jokingly. "Tell me to wait for you there."

"Yes."

"You'll do that?" I raised myself up.

"I will."

She stood back as the rickshaws pulled away.

For several days I was bedridden. In the mornings, Lin Gao brought me the medicine in a bowl and in the evenings another fresh bowl of bitter herbs. He changed the dressing at midday after cleaning my wound and repeated the process at night. One night after bandaging my abdomen and salving the cuts on my hand, he sat on the edge of my bamboo cot and picked up the knife I kept by my side. He unsheathed it. At the door the black dog rose from its rest, came and sniffed at Lin Gao's hand that held the knife.

"Hey, *Lao* Gao," I said, pointing at the dog, "he took my knife while I was asleep out there?"

Lin Gao sheathed the knife, unsheathed it, then glanced at the dog. Finally he nodded.

"And brought it to Mr. Cao Lai?" I said in disbelief.

He held the knife up, turning it back and forth to inspect the blade with a marveled look on his face. Then he nodded.

"Why?" I said, eyeing the dog. "Why did he do such a dumb thing?"

Lin Gao looked at the animal, whose eyes were half blind from cataracts. He looked at me and scratched his head. Finally he made a series of grumbles in his throat while his hands went left and right with confusing signs. I stared. When he was done with his explaining, he picked up the discarded dressing and the brass pail and walked, bow-legged, out of the room. The dog trailed him like a blind dog following a scent.

I never questioned why he had abruptly ordered me back to spend my convalescence in the house. I thought of all the possible reasons and finally concluded that he did so for my own welfare. He could have sent me home, like he was discharging an invalid. He surely had the right, considering I had put him in this plight in which he had to protect me as a criminal. But he never said a word about my reckless nature, not a word about the money he paid the rickshaw coolie whose vehicle was soaked with my blood. He put Lin Gao to tasks I would normally do, namely escorting him all over town—opium dens too. Poor old man. Then *Lao* Gao had to cook and take care of me.

While I lay on my cot thinking about all these things I had no answers for, I felt an emptiness so complete I wished I could will myself to her place, lie down on her bed, my face pressed against the wooden pillow that hinted of her scent, hear her voice, see her walk, lithe and graceful. I rose. The house was quiet. The black dog was somewhere in the kitchen across the courtyard, perhaps sleeping. He was so old his hair had fallen out and his skin was mangy. I took several small steps between my cot and the door. My knees nearly gave, but I didn't feel the twinges in my stomach. *Walk. Don't lie down.* I paced back and forth, and when my legs grew tired, stopped, resting on my feet. My knees were burning. I stood leaning against the doorframe to catch my breath, my face warm and perspiring, and then walked slowly to the courtyard with my knife in my hand.

The sun was hot, the courtyard shimmered, and shadows of shrubs and dwarf trees shrank. In the kitchen the dog lay sprawled on the bluestone floor by the cast-iron stove. I

could see his thin rib cage heave. The corners of his closed
eyes were yellow with mucus. He didn't hear my footsteps.
I stood over him, then lowered myself and placed my knife
at the tip of his paws.

I moved back toward the stone bench where Lin Gao kept
an iron pot filled with rainwater. I sat and waited. After a
while the dog stirred to life, lifted his old head and yawned.
I could see his tongue loll about and hear his jaws snap shut.
Momentarily he tucked his muzzle between his forelegs, his
eyes fluttering like he was about to doze again. Then his
wet, black muzzle twitched. I watched him. He scrabbled to
his feet, jabbed his nose at the knife and sniffed. As I sat staring in rapt attention, he bared his teeth and snapped up the
knife. He turned and I followed him out of the kitchen and
across the courtyard into the dim hall. His paws made tiny
sounds on the hardwood floor as he went into Mr. Cao Lai's
room. There were his slippers neatly laid side by side outside the door, so neatly arranged in the same spot every day.
I waited until the dog made his way out, moving slowly, his
head lolling. He passed me like I wasn't there and went out
into the bright sun.

I retrieved my knife. I wished I had understood *Lao* Gao's
wild gestures, his sole form of communication.

I told Mr. Cao Lai a few days later that I was ready to go
back to serving him. I had drunk up all the herbal medicine,
and though I was still wearing the dressing on my stomach,
I didn't have much pain there or in my hand. He made me
walk the length of the hall back and forth and said that my
gait was still unsteady. "Let your body heal completely," he
said to me. "Then I have plans for you."

I thought about what he said and, like before, I had no

answers. But I did know why I felt so empty all the time.
On nights when it was very late, I couldn't fall asleep, for I
knew she was somewhere out there, peddling opium dregs.
Just thinking of her made me feel thick in the throat.

The morning after Mr. Cao Lai and I had our talk, I left
the hall and went to the kitchen. Sitting on the stone bench,
Lin Gao was puffing smoke from his bamboo water pipe.
You could hear the water purring in the big old pipe as he
drew deeply on it and then leaned back with his eyes closed
and let out streams of smoke from his nostrils and his mouth.
At his feet the dog lay, twitching his nose. He always came
when he smelled the tobacco smoke. He used to lap up Lin
Gao's crap, and had become the man's old faithful friend. I
wondered what else Lin Gao was addicted to.

He watched me, his eyes half closed, behind curls of
smoke. I sat down by him.

"*Lao* Gao," I said, turning sideways to look at him. "Can
you help me?"

He made a hand gesture that told me to come out with it.

"Are you going to the marketplace soon?" I said.

He shook his head and jabbed his bamboo pipe toward
the main house and then made a drinking motion. He
watched my reaction, his mouth agape. Then he went into
his hand signals again, stood up, walked hunched like he
was escorting someone, and then threw back his head to
drink from an imaginary cup. Suddenly it dawned on me.
He was telling me that he and Mr. Cao Lai had been to the
rice liquor store, the franchise he was awarded. Very busy. I
understood. He sat back down, tapping the pipe against his
shin to knock out the dottle. I put my hand on his gnarled
hand.

"Can you go to the Chinese quarter for me?" I said.

He opened his mouth and answered with a grunt.

I told him about her. He nodded. I said there was an old Chinese woman who sat on a corner of Sail Street and a side street with no name. I told him that she was the only one sitting on that corner. A teacup, a teapot in front of her, a basket of raw silk by her side. I said she would have a message for me, except that she never spoke. Then I patted him on the back of his hand and said, "Like you, *Lao* Gao. Can't speak."

He grinned. His face went soft, and he made a purring sound in his throat and gesticulated slowly in a feminine way. Something began to open up in me.

"Her name is Xiaoli," I said. "I'm in love with her."

He grinned broadly and his laugh was but a rough cry.

"*Lao* Gao," I said, pleading, "ask the woman if Xiaoli has any message for me."

He kept grinning and pointed at his chest where his heart was and smiled. Then he began stuffing dark tobacco into his water pipe. The dog saw this and turned around, laying his old head on *Lao* Gao's bare feet. He lit the pipe and gave it to me. I shook my head. He grabbed my hand and made me take the pipe. The first draw went right to my head like a stinging shot. I hacked. He watched me until I regained my breath and then took the pipe from my hand and drew deeply from it. The water sang merrily. As he drove smoke out of his nostrils and mouth, he handed me the pipe. The dog seemed to sense something awry and let out a groan. I took a draw, feeling the smoke go up my nose to my brain, feeling it mushroom. I held in the smoke. Then I let it out, through my nose and mouth. My eyes watered. I felt buoyed up. Perhaps this was how one got into this simple pleasure and then never got out of it.

Late in the afternoon Lin Gao returned from the market-place with a cane basket on his back. The dog lifted his sleepy head from the floor and watched him. I asked Lin Gao if he wanted me to cook the rice. He nodded. I took the iron pot filled with rainwater, and poured some of it into a cooking pot. I scooped rice grains from a wooden barrel with a clay bowl and poured them into the rice pot. I set the pot on the stove, opened its smoke-stained door, and began lighting the coals. Without any draft, they lit easily. He was hanging up the cane basket on a hook nailed to a lengthwise wooden strip on the wall. Nothing was allowed to sit on the floor. That was Mr. Cao Lai's creed. Shelved bins for stowing things away. Everything else was hung on the wall—straw sieve, frying pan, iron skillet, funnel, ladle, boning knife, cleaver. When he turned around he had something in his hand. He walked bow-legged to me and gave me a strip of red cloth.

"What's this for?" I said, closing the stove's door.

He pointed east and west and put his hand on his heart. I felt a jolt.

"From Xiaoli?" I said.

He grinned.

"The old woman gave this to you?" I said.

He nodded.

Blood rushed to my head. I couldn't believe that he went to the Chinese quarter.

"What else?" I said.

He looked at the ceiling, gesticulating. There was noth-ing on the ceiling, only the sky above it. I stared at the cloth strip. It came back to me.

"She said to wait for her there tonight?" I said.

He pointed to the ceiling or perhaps the sky beyond.

The evening was long. After we ate in the kitchen I helped
Lin Gao sharpen his cleaver. While he was sweeping the
floor, I whetted the square blade against the steel rod, one
side and then the other, whetting it slowly down the length
of the rod. I did each side ten times, sliding the blade's edge
back and forth across the steel. At one point I sensed his
presence behind me, but I ignored him. Then there was the
sound of water singing in his water pipe, and the blue smoke
floated by like smoke from a cooking fire. I held the blade up
and pressed my fingertip against its edge. My finger tingled
with the heat from it. I brought the cleaver to Lin Gao. Laying down his pipe, he picked up a broken broom handle that
leaned against the stone bench. He stood it up and brought
the cleaver down, splitting it in half. He handed the cleaver
back to me with a nod. I hung it on the wall hook by the hole
in its handle. Then I took down the boning knife and honed
it. I found every knife he had and sharpened it, and then I
retrieved the ax that he used to chop wood, and I honed that
too. It took much longer to grind the axe, for it was heavy
and bulky. But I didn't mind. I must keep myself busy. By the
time I was done with all the cutting tools, the steel rod was
burning hot and Lin Gao was asleep, sitting on the bench
with his bamboo pipe still smoldering in his hand.

It was getting late. I walked out into the garden. There
was a full moon and the garden was pale yellow. I stood
listening to the sounds coming from the street. After a
while there were no more sounds. It got so quiet I could
hear the whirring and sawing of insects and Lin Gao's hacking coughs. He was up now, checking on the fire in the iron

stove. Then came the sound of the stove's side door clanging shut. I saw him carrying a paper lantern as he headed through the courtyard to his room near the entrance door. I waited. The moonlight was a yellow shawl, and everything paled in its hue, the banana fronds, the blades of grass, all shimmering like bones.

I closed the entrance door quietly and walked down the street, passing under the dark leaves of old gnarled trees whose trunks were hollowed with age. At the end of the street I turned toward the lakeshore where rickshaw coolies picked up late-night clients. My knees began to lock up and my stomach spasmed. As I stopped to catch my breath, a rickshaw came up the moon-washed road.

"Sail Street," I said, flopping down on the seat.

I tried to close my eyes and rest, but I kept opening them. The sweat had dried on my face and I felt cool from the lakeshore breeze. Darkness cloaked the shore, save for the dancing light of lanterns from the rickshaws that went by every now and then.

I paid the coolie and watched him turn around and head back to town. The corner lanterns wavered in the breeze, throwing shadows on his bare back. I stood leaning against the tall, straight bamboo pole, looking down the sidewalk that was crammed with barrows leaning against stalls. I took out the strip of red cloth. Had she tied it around this bamboo pole each night? The bluestone of the side street glowed from kerosene lamps inside the houses. A red dot flickered where a man squatted outside his abode, smoking a cigarette. Rickshaw after rickshaw went by, flashing through the glow of lanterns. The coolies' naked torsos gleamed white. In one of the rickshaws was a Chinese man clad in white trousers and a brocaded tunic in deep blue that shone in the lantern's light. Looking at him, I thought of Mr. Cao Lai. The way they dressed, the black toques they wore, tasseled with a red ball, their braided hair sometimes laced with a silken cord to accent its look. A woman in a wide-sleeved blouse materialized out of nowhere on the cross street. She walked with an umbrella over her head. The sun had gone down long before, but she still held the parasol over her, like a solitary creature that belonged to neither the world of darkness nor the world of light.

The man who smoked the cigarette rose, squashed out the stub with his heel, and went back into the house. The door shut with a small echo. It was a long time now between each passing rickshaw, and when they passed they would holler at each other. You could hear the creaking of wheels until they died away. Soon none went by at all. A glowing lantern would move up the empty street when a pedestrian appeared and then it too disappeared beyond the dark street corners.

I went down the side street until I reached the alley that had the red doors. I pushed on them. They didn't give. I stood back and looked them over. Not a soul around. Maybe someone would come out. No. They would not come out until morning. I leaned against the doors, resting. A dog howled. A sound of splashing water. A pail clanging. After a while I left and walked back to the corner feeling like a child who cried for something he could not even name.

I saw her waiting on the corner. A black, solitary figure. I knew it was her.

"Xiaoli!" I called.

She turned her face when I came up. She had not painted her face, and my heart sang with joy.

"You went to the den?" she said.

"Thought you wouldn't come. Which way you come from?"

"The other side of the alley. I went out the back door."

I looked at her. Her face was a pale white in the moon-light.

"You waited here every night?" I said.

"I knew you would not come," she said. "I never thought you would heal that quick."

The thickness in my throat returned. "You know why I tried to heal quick?"

She gazed at me and smiled faintly. Then she said, "I knew you got my message."

"Lin Gao got it for me."

"I know. The old woman told me."

"Told you? You came to the den early tonight?"

"No. When I came I didn't see my red string on the pole." She turned and pointed at it. "I told her if you came and asked for me, she should give it to you. How did you get here tonight?"

"In a rickshaw."

"You could save the money. What did you pay?"

"Fifty *sapèques*." I sucked in my breath. "I'd walk if I could. Are you done for the night?"

"Yes."

Just then I noticed her bag slung over her shoulder. "Can I walk you home?"

She nodded, then said quickly, "But I have to meet with them first."

My heart sank. "Them? The addicts?"

"Yes. Them."

"Where?"

"In the . . ." She seemed lost for words. ". . . the banana

grove."

That was where I saved her the first time.

"You don't have to go," she said, fumbling in the bag for something.

"I'll go with you. You don't know what those thugs might do."

"They are not thugs. I know them."

"You forgot the fellow trying to slash your throat."

"If I had come earlier that night, he would still be alive."

She was smearing her face black. How much soot could a skin so fine take before it lost its beauty?

We left the street corner. She moved with an easy stride, and I tried to keep up with her. We cut through one alley after another and came back out on the street. My stomach began throbbing with a dull pain. I acted unconcerned, but my forehead broke out in a heavy sweat that ran down my face. I clutched my abdomen.

"You hurt?" She stopped.

We were near the banana grove. I could see it in the short distance, and I remembered this dirt road, the horror when the Frenchman charged in on horseback.

"I gotta get used to this," I said, panting. "I mean the long walk."

"I'll wait here with you. It's not bleeding, no?"

I slid my hand under my blouse and felt my stomach. I shook my head.

"It might be a cramp," she said.

Before I could agree, she bent slightly, put her hand on my abdomen and pressed the heel of her palm against my midsection. "Breathe deep," she said, and worked her hand in a circular motion. I didn't know if it was the rest, the breath I had regained, or the blessing of being with her, but I no longer felt the pain. I told her so. She straightened up and flung her plait over her shoulder with a toss of her head.

"Let's go," she said, her gleaming eyes fixed on mine.

We came up the moonlit road and followed its narrow shoulder, which butted against the banana grove. She slowed down and looked into the dark clumps of trees and suddenly stepped off the road. We saw flickering flames deep in the grove. I kept close to her, wanting to hold her hand, but suddenly she was slashing her way through the grove, parting banana fronds with her hands. Our feet were tangled in weeds and the tall grass. Soon the sap of banana fronds stung my nose. My legs were lead heavy. Glowing torches lit up a corner of the grove.

She came to the fringe of the light, and the Chinese coolies stopped talking among themselves. Seeing me, they hooted, slapping their hands on their thighs. One of them started jabbering, pointing his finger at me.

"What do they want?" I called to her.

She glanced back over her shoulder. "He said you were not dead, my bodyguard."

"They know me?"

"They know who you are. Do not worry. Mr. Cao Lai warned them not to tell."

"What is he to them?" I stepped up and stood beside her.

"They know him," she said quickly. She left me and went to them.

They were a frenzied mob. There must have been twenty of them. They all wore baggy gray pantaloons, half of them naked to the waists. Their torches popped and crackled, and blue sparks flew and danced like fireflies. They had shaved heads and tattooed arms and chests covered in grotesque shapes of serpents and phoenixes and dragons breathing fire. Zinc coins clanked. When they all got the drugs, they rushed out of the grove. A pall of black smoke trailed them. We came out on the road after the stampede was over. Down the road we could hear their voices and see the trembling glow of their torches. We began to walk back in the direction we came from. In the stillness came the *qwonk* of a toad.

"How do you feel now?" she said, turning her blackened face toward me.

"About what?" I said.

"Do you still have pain?"

"No."

"Can you walk far? You still have to get home."

"I can walk."

"Get a rickshaw," she said.

I said nothing. In fact, I had no more money on me.

"You don't have money?" she said.

"Don't you worry." I grinned.

I turned my head to see what she was doing when I heard the clinking sound of *sapèques*. She opened her hand, holding it close to her face in the pale wash of moonlight. She handed me the coins.

"Tài," she said.

She said it softly. The first time. I swallowed the thickness in my throat.

"You can walk," she said. "But not tonight."

"I can't take your money," I said.

"You feel bad?" She smiled, then laughed. "If you bleed you won't see me again for a long time."

"I'll pay you back." I opened my hand gingerly.

"No. Do not."

"No easy money for you—every *sapèque*."

"Do not worry." She watched me put away the zinc coins in my blouse pocket. "What do you do with your money?"

I pursed my lips and thought. Should I tell her the reason I came to the city?

"Why do you ask?" I finally said to her.

"Because it tells me what kind of person you are."

I laughed. I just couldn't help myself at the way she accented each word.

"It's true," she said, smiling. "So tell me."

"I save some for myself," I said. "Save most of it for Mom."

I said nothing more, looking down at the pale ground as I walked.

"Something else on your mind?" she said softly.

Her voice soothed me. Why was I so cautious?

"You believe in good fortune that burial brings you?" I said, knowing how hard it would be to explain. "Say, you die and you're buried in a certain place. Do you believe this place could have effects on your bloodline afterward. . . ."

"Feng shui? Yes. I believe in *yin* and *yang*."

"It's not superstitious."

"No. Karma is not superstitious. Perhaps you and I share karma."

I glanced at her just as her smile faded away.

"So," she said, "your family shares it even when only one member dies."

I thought of what Chim told me about the man who was killed by lightning while he was out in a field with a goat. "How does it change your children's luck?" I said. "Where you're buried and all that?"

"Your karmas are connected," she said. "So *qi*—energy— stored in your burial ground is shared with your children.

Qi of *yin* and *yang*."

"I believe you," I said with subdued admiration for her. "You know this feng shui very well."

"I listen a lot to Mr. Lý's mother. Before she does anything, she talks to a man who knows feng shui."

"A geomancer?" I said.

"Yes." She hung her head to one side. "Why do you want to talk about this?"

"'Cause that's why I came to Hanoi. I work to pay for a burial site for my father and my little brother."

"Ah. You want to rebury them."

Her mind worked fast, I thought. I said, "My mother had them buried in the back of our hut. Soggy soil. You should see how rotten it is during rainy season."

"When do you get enough money to pay for it?"

"Two years." I spat on the ground. "I've been here six months now."

"It must be a special site." She nodded to herself.

I told her of my encounter with the geomancer who came to the region of my village scouting for a burial site, and that I used to work as an oarsboy for a man who one day told me a story of how a man's burial site brought incredibly good fortune to his offspring. I told her that because I trusted the man I worked for, I believed in his story. I told her the complications of the deal and how I became a servant first for the geomancer and then for Mr. Cao Lai who paid off my two-year service to the geomancer, plus the fee to claim the site. The biggest difference between working for the two men was ownership of the burial site. With the geomancer, I would have to work for him for two years before we got the burial ground. With Mr. Cao Lai, my mother and I held the deed in our names, though I had yet to see it myself. Also, thanks to Mr. Cao Lai's goodwill, my mother and I could rebury the bones of my father and my little brother without a wait of two years.

"So he bought you off," she said.

"Bought and sold," I said. "We are alike."

"Except that you have a year and half left. I have several."

"Why?"

"I was eleven when I was sold to Mr. Lý. I was not much of a help, so my service did not count much toward our debt."

"When did it start counting?"

"Three years ago."

I thought about it. "How old are you now?"

"Eighteen." She turned to look at me. "How old are you?"

"Seventeen."

"You want to be rich, yes?"

I cocked my head and looked at her. "I never thought of that."

"But you did," she said. "You bought a burial site and now you slave yourself for two years."

I laughed. "I didn't do it for myself. I had bad thoughts about them lying down there in the soggy soil."

She looked at me, her blackened face lustrous from the moon. Then she said, "I believe you."

I felt good hearing it. I felt like she was part of me and knew me.

From behind us came a *clop-clop*ping of horse's hooves. I pushed her off the road and turned around. A horseman in black was riding up on a black horse. As he passed us, I saw his face. That unforgettable face, chiseled in hard lines, cropped hair with the sharp V of the hairline that stopped short in the middle of his forehead. He was sitting straight-backed, looking as if he saw nothing but the empty road ahead of him. I could hear the horse wheezing as they went past. Man and horse shimmered. And like a quickly thinning haze, they were suddenly gone.

FALLING STAR

The following night I met her on the same street corner, and we went to the banana grove. After she was done selling her opium, we left the grove and walked down the empty road. We kept looking back, but the sound of horse's hooves never came. She told me not to be afraid, for I did not kill him with malice. I said, *How would he know that?* She said, *Do not worry about him. If you kill him with a bad thought, pain will follow you until you pay for it in full.* Her words comforted me, for I knew I never held any grudge against those men. Yet it happened, and I wondered why I was put in such a predicament. I asked her that. She said, *It is your karma.* Then, smiling, she added, *It is our karmas. You were put in a fix because you met me.* I thought about it, and it chilled me.

When she opened the red door to go into the house, she turned to me and said, "Would you like to sit in the garden?"

"I would love that," I said.

There was a wood bench by a rockwork basin. I sat there and waited for her. She disappeared into the house through a side door that had a small, round mirror above the doorway. Later, she told me that a mirror over a door guarded against malign spirits. We did hang a pot of taro in front of our hut during the smallpox plague. I was told that each hut with an infected family must hang a taro pot outside to warn people off. But Mother told me the taro pot kept bad spirits away. In the end my little brother still died.

The full moon washed the blue-tiled roofs with yellow light. The quiet made my heart throb with an unknown trepidation. She came out soundlessly like a cat. She had a tin can in her hand, and her face was clean of black soot. I couldn't help but gaze at her as if I'd never seen her before.

"I sit here every night when there is a full moon," she said as she sat down beside me. "I want to see if the silver carp will come up."

I looked toward the rock basin where she pointed.

"What silver carp?" I said.

"It lives in there," she said, flicking her gaze toward the basin. "If you are the one who sees it jump from the water when the full moon is just above it, something wonderful will happen to you."

She sipped from the tin can and then handed it to me. I drank. Cold and fragrant and sweet. I shivered. She said it was *hong cha*. I knew the tea. Mr. Cao Lai drank it. Lin Gao was the only one who knew how to brew it to his meticulous taste. She said she added some white sugar and lemon and left it in a thick clay pot in the cellar where they kept fresh herbs and vegetables for the household. I peered up at the sky. In its dead blackness the moon hung so bright its halo was a shade paler.

"When the moon's right above it," I said, pointing toward the basin, "I'll close my eyes if that carp jumps."

"You need luck, more than me," she said and lifted her chin to the sky. "There's the Big Dipper."

I knew what it was, for I used to watch the night sky when I was an oarsboy. But as we looked up at the cloudless sky she told me about the Big Dipper and told me to look across from it. She showed me Cassiopeia, and when I said I saw it, she pointed between the two constellations.

The North Star glittered like a diamond chip.

She drew a sharp breath. "Such a beautiful sight!"

A shadow crossed the dark garden. We watched a cat saunter off the brick walk into the darkness, its eyes two shining marbles.

"Watch the night sky," she said. "Sometimes you see a falling star. It might tell you someone close to you just died."

"Maybe I missed one before my little brother died."

"If it falls in the direction where someone you know lives."

"I've seen them falling while I was out on the boat at night. They always fell toward the mountains." I handed her the tin can. "You ever seen one?"

"Yes."

"Where did it fall to?"

"North. My home."

"China?"

"Yes."

"How long ago?"

"Months ago."

"But many people live there. What're the odds?"

"But not many people see a falling star."

"What made you think someone you love died when you saw it?"

"I just know. My grandfather might have died."

"You haven't seen your mother and your grandfather?"

"I saw Grandfather twice. Every three years."

"Here?"

"He came to the opium den. He is an addict."

She sipped. A plop came from the rock basin. We both looked. Perhaps a frog had jumped in. In the lull you could hear water trickling from the rocks. How much longer could I keep the truth from her? I loathed myself.

"Someday I'll go to China," I said. "To see what it's like."

"Like here. Only bigger. Much bigger."

She placed the tin can in my hand. I took it and put it between us on the bench.

"You learn Chinese," she said. "Like I learn Annamese."

"My father could speak Chinese. He was in Kwangtung many years ago."

"What was he doing there?"

I didn't know what to say. She must have seen my hesitancy and said, "You never told me how you lost him."

I nodded. "'Cause I was ashamed."

"Ashamed of your father?"

"No. I'm not ashamed of him. But I'm not proud of him either."

"Because he had done something you're afraid you might do yourself?"

"Something like that."

"Like what, then?"

"He was a bandit."

"He did not die from smallpox. But you said he was not so lucky."

I couldn't help but grin. She never forgot anything I told her.

"No," I said. "He wasn't so lucky. He was caught with his gang and they were all beheaded."

Her lips parted like she was about to say something, but she said nothing.

"Nearly two years now," I said.

I told her that he was betrayed. I told her that as long as

I lived his decapitation would live in my mind.

"You saw it?" she said, tilting her head sideways to look at me.

"Yeah. Me, Mother and my little brother. We had to bring back his body."

I told her it was my granduncle who beheaded him, since he was the executioner. I told her that Granduncle helped raise my father when my grandparents died. Then I told her how I set out to retrieve my father's skull from the buffalo boys, an attempt that nearly cost me the use of my foot. While telling her this lurid story, I felt wrathful. For a long time now I hadn't felt it, the acidity of vengeance. Maybe when you harbored it for so long, the pain would torment you as if you had killed someone—the pain would follow you until you paid in full. I told her this.

"Who betrayed your father?" she said, eyes narrowed to slits.

"I don't know." I looked at her calmly.

"You do not want to know?"

"Would you? If you were me?"

"Yes."

"Then?"

"Then I'd do what my heart told me."

"What d'you think it'd tell you?"

"I cannot tell you." She clasped her hands on her lap. "I cannot tell you what I would do if the same thing happened to me."

"I don't know either. But it keeps eating at me. His name does."

"You know his name?" Her eyes opened wide.

"Granduncle told me."

"Your granduncle knows him?"

"No. He heard from my father's men."

"Those he beheaded?"

"Yeah."

Neither one of us said a word after that. Another plop came from the basin. We looked. She said it was perhaps a tadpole. She said she could tell almost every sound in the garden at night. I reached for the tin can and so did she. Her hand clasped mine. I looked into her eyes and she did not move her hand.

"If you like the tea," she said, "I will give you a jar to take home tonight."

"I'll bring it back tomorrow night so you won't get into trouble."

"Do you want anything to eat when you leave?"

"I'll eat anything you care to give."

"How about steamed buns?"

"I was about to say it." I let out a short laugh, but stopped when out of the corner of my eye I saw a figure standing in the side door. A diminutive figure in pale white. She turned to look.

"Wait here," she said.

I watched her lope toward the white shape. She stood at the door with her back toward me and put her hands on the figure. After a while the figure turned and went back into the darkness of the house.

The rock basin glowed. Over it hung the full moon.

"That was A-Mei," she said, sitting down.

"She reminds me of Lin Gao," I said. "They're in their own world most of the time."

"She forgets her name sometimes and she walks around the house at night. Sometimes all night."

"It's late," I said.

"You need to get home." She rose. "I will be back."

She passed through the soft light of the moon over the rock basin. You could not hear her footfalls, for she glided. I breathed in the stillness. It was damp with the scent of trees and moss and the vegetation in the old earth. A plop. I looked just as a large fish jumped out of the water. Silvery and gleaming, it plunged back down into the dark water with a clean splash. I sat, bewildered. I looked toward the house.

Perhaps I should have been the one who left and she the one who saw the silver carp jumping to catch the moon.

THE FOLLY OF MAN

I had been shocked before but never as badly as when I found that our entrance door was bolted with a lock the next night. It was never locked, day or night. I was leaving the house, holding the glass jar she had given me to take her tea home in. I stood looking at it, now empty, imagining in vain that she would soon be waiting on the street corner. I was outraged.

He must have known that I had slipped out at night, but Mr. Cao Lai handled everything discreetly. That night I lay awake until the glimmer of the moon was gone from the window. In my splintered dreams I willed myself to go through the bolted door and the wall, and fly through space until I saw her on the street corner. I felt so happy when I took her hand in mine and walked down the nameless street, past corners lit with lanterns under a bright full moon. When I woke with the dream still warm on my eyelids, I realized that I had been so ecstatic to see her I forgot to tell her about the silver carp.

In the morning Mr. Cao Lai told me that we would leave for Lau, my village, the following day.

"I have the deed to the burial plot," he said. "I'll give it to your mother in person."

He mentioned nothing about the locked door. I thought I ought to be happy, hearing the news of the visit to my mother. But I felt wretched. It clouded my judgment. To end my misery of waiting, I asked him for his permission to go out late at night when he no longer needed my service. He mused on it, combing back long strands of black hair with his fingers.

"I can't let you do that," he said finally. The corner of his mouth twitched.

"Even when you don't need me in the evening, sir?" I said.

"Do you mind telling me where you go at night?"

"To see Xiaoli, sir."

He didn't look surprised. I believed he knew.

"Do you realize how much damage you've done since you've known her?" he said.

"I know, sir," I said, dreading the way he appraised me with his narrowed eyes.

"You don't want to put her employment with Mr. Lý at risk, do you?"

"No, sir."

"Then stop seeing her."

His words were like ice.

That evening when I ate dinner with Lin Gao, I asked him about the lock. From his hand gestures I gathered that Mr. Cao Lai kept the key. I thought of the trip in the morning and decided against breaking his rules. I'd rather suffer than risk what my mother and I had long wished for.

The cactus hedge around our house in Lau was green, with green leaves and white flowers. The malabar began quaking down the dirt trail I had not seen in many months. Through the square hole of the window of the horse-drawn carriage, I could see the hedge taller and thicker, hemming in the narrow footpath. Its soil had turned redder in my absence.

"Will you wait here, sir?" I said to Mr. Cao Lai.

"I'm not going anywhere," he said, brushing back his hair with both hands.

Somehow we had fit his wooden coffin into the four-wheeled carriage. During the half-day trip, he sat with a straight back, his hands on his knees, his eyes closed, resting. He talked to me only once. When we returned, I was to help out at his new state liquor store. I mulled over what he said. Everything was trivial, for my heart was somewhere else. I looked out the square holes at women in straw-yellow hats, bent in rows in the fields, planting pale green rice seedlings in the muddy, ankle-deep water. A drizzle fell. The windows were fogged up. The sky beyond it was blue and gray. I imagined Lin Gao had gone to the Chinese quarter and given the silk woman my message: *Tell Xiaoli not to wait for me until she hears from me again.*

A voice drifted from a hut behind the hedges, and then there was the sound of water splashing. In the stillness of the afternoon, a wooden ladle banged an earthen vat.

The air was moist and fresh after a passing shower. As I walked up the footpath, I saw a green gecko sunning on the old gray rock slab that I used to hone our kitchen knives on. The cement steps that led up to the narrow porch were still wet, perhaps from my mother's scrubbing.

From the open kitchen, closed only on the side of the hearth, I watched her pick peppercorns that came down in deep green jade from a vine around the trunk of an areca. She wore a white blouse and black pantaloons, and a polka-dotted kerchief held her hair back. She deftly dropped peppercorns into a tin can next to an earthen vat at the base of the areca. She lifted the lid and ladled water with a wooden spoon and drank. Nothing had changed. The same old brown spathe tied around the areca's trunk, the end dropped into the vat, collected rainwater. The areca was so old its trunk was powdery gray. The ash in the hearth smelled warm. The fire in the blackened embers had yet to die. The same dirt floor in sooty black, the same iron trivet, charred from years of cooking, the same bamboo tube we used to blow embers into a flame, its trunk veined with smoke stains, its end singed from daily contact with fire. The small woman stood with the ladle in her hand and poured the water left in it onto a patch of red peppers. A wind blew, rattling the trees, and she closed the lid quickly. I saw wisps of kapok fiber, white as cotton, coming down from the blue sky. I called out to her.

She looked back inside and then, as if gliding, came to me soundlessly and took my hands. "Heaven," she said, her lips pale. "Why didn't I know you were coming home?"

I said I wished I could have told her. As I spoke, I looked down into her wet eyes and the imprint of the rush mat on her cheek, and my heart throbbed with tenderness.

"How have you been, Ma?" I asked, hearing my scratchy voice.

She gazed at me without speaking and then asked why I lost my voice. From tiredness, I told her. She bent, looking at my hand, the one badly cut by the Frenchman's knife. She touched it gently with her fingers and looked up at me. "What have you done to yourself, Tài?"

"Nothing," I said, withdrawing my hand from hers. "Don't you worry, Ma."

"Why did you shave your head?"

"Mr. Cao Lai wanted me to look neat."

"Who's Mr. Cao Lai?"

"I work for him now. Not Mr. Đinh-Hòa."

"What happened?" she said softly. "What happened to

our agreement?"

I dropped to my knees and we squatted, face to face. I didn't have the guts to lie. "Let me tell you the whole story," I said.

She gazed at me, listening, as I told her of my tempestuous time in Hanoi, how my service changed hands, how the deed of the burial ground came to us. I told her of my troubles with the law after I killed two men to save a Chinese girl, and how I had fallen in love with her. I told her she was the one who in turn saved my life from the nearly fatal knife wound. I told her who the Chinese girl was, and about the secret I kept from her, the promise I had broken with her late grandfather. I told her I didn't want to lose the girl, so I never told her of her mother's death at home. If I did tell her, I might never see her again. Then I told her why we were here. I told her that our wish had come true.

She took hold of my hands and in her almond-shaped eyes I could see how much she loved me. She didn't have to say a word. I couldn't help but drop my gaze.

"Tài," she said, "you never told her the truth because you didn't want to hurt her."

"No," I said, "I never want to hurt her."

"But the truth is the truth. She must know it. Does she love you?"

I said nothing.

"Your father came to me," she said evenly, "in the same way you came to her. Much violence. He told me who he was, a bandit. He told me he had killed many people. He said he had a wild life, most of it rough and stormy and vile. But he said he loved me and he was ready to give up what he had and start over. You have his violence in your blood. You also look more and more like him, the older you get. So

I believe that this girl will one day love you if she doesn't
love you now. You came to her with all your heart the way
your father came to me. You'll receive her love in return."

"What did he have to give up?"

"His wild life in China."

"In Kwangtung?"

"Yes. You know?"

"Mr. Cao Lai told me that's where they ran into each
other."

"Is he here to stay for the night?"

"No, we're going back soon. He's a busy man."

Then I told her of Mr. Cao Lai's plans for me when we
headed back to the city.

"Now," she said with a sigh, "that is ironic."

A dark tone in her voice made me frown.

"Here you're selling state rice liquor," she said, "and
your old boss is locked up in prison."

"Mr. Chim?" I gasped.

"His moonshining caught up with him."

"Prison? Where's he now?"

"In Hanoi."

I thought of Xoan. I shook my head. "Have you seen
Xoan?"

"No," she said. "Heaven have mercy on him."

For one brief moment I felt so frail, so formless. I understood that the power to act was part of a man's will to live.
That was what I didn't have. I rose to my feet and told her
that I would bring in our guest.

While the coachman sat on the ground and ate a lunch
that was wrapped in a banana leaf, I led Mr. Cao Lai to
the house. My mother received him at the door and gently
asked him to be seated. He sat down on Daddy's old chair of

oak wood, aged and stained brown. She took the remaining chair. It was rickety on its rear legs. I sat down on my old bamboo cot, which she had pushed into a corner to fill up the empty space once occupied by my little brother's cot. We had taken it apart to build a crude coffin to bury him in after wrapping him in his own straw mat. She told me to make a pot of tea. I boiled water in the brick hearth that Daddy built. Squatting on the packed dirt floor, my back toward them, I watched the flames licking the bottom of the tin pot on the trivet. Mr. Cao Lai was telling Mother his reason for visiting her, telling her of his great respect for Daddy, whom he called "a people's brigand."

"That his name, Madam?" he said.

"My late husband's name, yes," my mother said.

I turned my head as he pointed toward the altar. On the wooden table that had replaced the old crate stood narrow teak tablets. On them were Chinese characters in brush-strokes of black ink.

He rose from the chair and walked to the table that sat against the wall. Behind the wall was Mother's sleeping quarters. In front of the teak tablets, on a woodblock, was Daddy's skull, uncovered. She must have forgotten to drape it with the white cloth. I felt insulted. In silence I kept my eye on Mr. Cao Lai.

He stood at the table, his shoulders hunched. In the dimness, only his white blouse and pantaloons shone. He spoke without turning his head. "Who did the calligraphy, Madam?"

"Our village schoolteacher," my mother said.

"Quite impressive."

"Do you read Chinese?"

"Yes. My father is Chinese."

"Oh." My mother smiled.

He gazed at her momentarily and turned to study the skull. The water boiled, hissing. I poured it into the teapot and heard him say, "They called him Black Tiger. No one ever bothered with his real name."

"Did you know him well?" my mother said, turning her body in the chair.

"He hardly knew me. My late father ran an opium den in Kwangtung and this man—your husband—would come in now and then."

"That was a long time ago."

"Twenty years. A long time."

He sat down in Daddy's chair and pulled from his blouse pocket a paper pouch tied with red strings. He hunched forward and extended it to my mother.

"Madam," he said, "here's the deed to the burial ground."

She took it. He watched her with reverence, something Daddy never showed when he was around. When she was done reading the deed, she held it in her lap momentarily and read it again. I brought out two teacups, placed them on the low, round table between them, and poured each of them a cup. I felt his gaze on the side of my face, for I was blocking his view. I poured slowly. Then I set down the teapot and arranged the cups so that when he reached for his with his left hand, he had to twist his body and not look her in the face. Carefully she slipped the deed back into the pouch.

"What you've done for us," she said, "we won't ever be able to pay back."

"You won't have to, Madam," he said, tossing back his head slightly. "He had quite a reputation. I'm only paying my belated respects."

"But you don't know much about him as a person," she said casually, but with a hint of curiosity.

"I know people who knew him." He pursed his lips and then his face relaxed into a smile. "The number is not small."

That drew a smile from her. I agreed in my mind. I had never seen Daddy alone for long. He attracted people and thrived among them. She sipped her tea pensively, as if she was trying to find words. Perhaps she was shunning his gaze. I stood with the teapot in my hand.

"Can we plan on reburying them, sir?" I said to him.

"Ask your mother," he said.

He knew how to redirect attention to the person who deserved it.

"I thought this month would be best," she said. "Before the rain sets in."

"You should find a propitious date and hour," he said. "I think you should, Madam."

She drew a deep breath. I knew our tight spot. Would we have to hire an astrologer?

"Madam," he said softly, "do you remember Mr. Đinh-Hòa?"

"I remember him," she said.

"He's also a good astrologer," he said. "I can have him pick the date and time for you."

She blinked as she lifted her face to him. His calm countenance had a soothing effect on her, and on me.

"You have done a lot for us," she said, shifting her gaze from his face to mine. "Tài, can you help me move their bones when we're ready?"

Before I could answer, he said, "I'll send some coolies.

You need not be burdened with this sort of labor."

She nodded and looked down into the teacup in her lap.

"Have you considered tombstones?" he said monotonally. "With their names on them?"

I tried to think of a stonecutter in the village when my mother said, "I've thought of that, but for now we can do without them."

"Just tell me what you want done on the slabs," he said. "I'll get them done in the city. They'll be ready. I promise."

"I'm very grateful," she said. "My late husband and my younger son, too."

With his left hand he put his teacup down on the table and brushed back his hair with the other.

"I hope I can say that when I die," he said with a chuckle. "You see, having a grateful heart makes you feel blessed. You can buy a burial site. You can lie in it in your death. But do you feel blessed? I don't know. I doubt if there'd ever be any benediction coming from that. Perhaps someday someone might bless me out of pure kindness. When I die, that is."

He smiled. I thought of how the burial plot changed hands. Yet without our chance encounter, it would still be his. He was a bachelor. Who else in his lineage would benefit from the *yin-yang* hole in which his flesh rotted?

"When that day comes," my mother said with a faint smile, "you shall be blessed. Your good heart won't ever betray you."

He dropped his gaze to the table where his teacup sat. He reached for it and raised his face to her. "Why don't you come and visit Tài? I'm sure he misses you as much as you miss him."

I knew she knew that.

"I plan to," she said. "When the time comes."

He said his house was one street from the lakeshore and told her the address. Then he rose from his chair, saying he must head back to the city. He declined her invitation to stay for a mid-afternoon meal. He asked me to work the reburial plan out with my mother and give him what we wanted for the inscriptions on the tombstones. He said that ought to be done first. He told me he would be waiting in the coach.

After he left, my mother said to me, "All I want is your father's and brother's names on the headstones. That's all I want."

"I'll tell him that," I said.

She looked lost in thought. I felt that she was still overwhelmed with what just happened. Then she put her hand on my shoulder and said, "When you get back in the city, can you find a way to visit Chim?"

I drew a deep breath. "How?"

"Don't you forget what he's done for you."

"I never will, Ma. You don't have to remind me of that."

"Good."

"It's been bothering me too. Him in prison."

"Approach Mr. Cao Lai. Tell him that I ask for his help just one more time."

I told her that a good friend of his was the *quan án*, the chief of justice. But I didn't tell her the special gift the man gave him—the skull. Neither did I tell her of his hard line on moonshiners, those who set out to hurt his liquor business.

METAMORPHOSIS

In the center of the back courtyard was a pond brimming with water. In its mossy bottom was imprinted a blue sky that trembled when the breeze blew. Tiny ripples pushed the green lily pads languidly. Perched on them were red dragonflies, shiny and still sleeping.

On one side of the pond at the end of the spacious courtyard stood a wall, and beyond it were the *tông đôc*'s living quarters. He was the governor of Hanoi and had two of the highest mandarins under him: the *quan bô* and the *quan án*. The first was his chief of finance, the latter his chief of justice, who was also a good friend of Mr. Cao Lai. Surrounding the *tông đôc*'s complex were high walls, and there was an armed guard wearing a white helmet at the gate. While Mr. Cao Lai went to the gala in the audience hall, I stood waiting in the back courtyard until an Annamese guard came to fetch me. He led me across the ground to the far end, opposite the wall. We came to a chain of mud huts that bowed under heavy thatched roofs. The huts had no windows except a small wooden square, peppered with holes, in the only door. The shadows pooled away from sunlight under overhanging roofs. The gloom harbored a musty odor of decay.

The barefoot guard ducked his head to enter a hut. I followed him into the dim light of a kerosene lamp that hung on a peg by the door. The air shivered with a putrid smell of things long fermented and unwashed. The guard stood his lance on the ground while I tried to see through the murkiness.

"He's somewhere in there," the guard said in the heavy accent of one from a backwater. "Don't mind them mouthing at ya."

He closed the door behind me. I began to make out the shape of the space, long and high. The ground was hard-packed earth. Someone coughed. Someone snored. The stench of puke and feces hung powerfully in the simmering air.

"Hey, you!" a voice twanged across the space.

I strained my neck to look, then took a few steps toward a bamboo post in the center. The posts ran the length of the space, supporting crossbeams, and the roof, resting on them, was a foot clear of the walls. Fire-colored lights flickered through the gap. On the floor naked bodies were sprawled and, looking down, I saw that they were fastened to a large plank with holes in it. Some of them had their ankles locked in a hole, some their wrists. Each wore a bamboo cangue around his neck.

"Yeah, you! Com'ere!"

I saw him. On his forehead was a Chinese character marked in black ink. He had a thick beard like a French missionary's. Both his hands and feet were locked in the stock. In the murky light I could see his eyes gleam. A furious caged animal.

"Who the hell are you?" he said, raising his face at me from the floor.

"Never mind who I am," I snapped back.

Just then a hand grabbed my ankle. A stubbled face peered up at me. The face was a hazy image before it became familiar.

"Mr. Chim?" I said, dropping to my knees.

"Tài?" His breath withered the air.

"Yeah. It's me."

He was one of those inmates locked to the plank by the foot. He was half sitting, half lying with one leg jackknifed. There was nothing on his body except a black loincloth.

"What brings you here?" he said, squinting at me.

I looked at him, at his long hair matted on his skull, at his sickly opaque eye. On the center of his forehead a Chinese character was inked in black. His head looked small, for the cangue around his neck was big. It wasn't long ago that he was a freewheeling human, and sky and water was his universe.

"They gave me permission," I said under my breath. "So, here I am."

"Good." He cracked a grin. "Tell me, who gave you permission?"

"The *tông đôc.*"

"Say what?"

"You see, I work for this man . . ." I lowered my voice and told him that the man I worked for knew the *quan án*, and that this chief of justice received the governor's permission for me to talk to an inmate. Then I pulled back to look at him and said, "You've changed. But I knew it was you."

"You've changed too. Where's all the hair?"

"It's too hot in the city."

"You look like a Chinaman."

He was referring to my clothing. I looked at his brow. "What is that thing?"

"My number. Don't know what the hell it is in Chinese."

"What'll happen next?"

"I'll go to trial."

"All of these people here are waiting for that?"

"Yeah."

"After that? Where will they send you?"

"Somewhere that's not here."

"This is hell."

"Could be worse. I heard the death cell is simply inhuman."

I tilted my head toward the fellow with the thick beard. "Why is he all locked up?"

"He bit off a guard's ear one day. Just last week he threw a chamber pot full of his crap at another guard. The guy was bringing in lunch for all of us."

"What did he do?"

"Before? Was a bandit. I heard he collected heads that he cut."

I glanced at the devil just as he fixed his gaze on me.

"You got a cigarette?" he said to me, twisting his large body in my direction.

"No."

"You here to sneak him cigarettes, ain't ya? Heh?"

"Say what you want."

"If I catch him smoking later," he said, meaning Chim, "I'll crack his skull."

"With what? Your mouth?"

"Com'ere, little shit."

I stood up just as Chim grabbed my hand. "Ignore that son of the bitch."

I fought down my irritation and sat on my haunches, my chin just above Chim's cangue. It was so hot, the stench seeping through the thick air made my eyes bulge.

"So what went wrong with you?" I dropped my voice as I asked Chim this.

"Got careless. Trusted wrong people."

"Like my daddy."

"Except he was respected. I was despised."

"What about your boat business? What'd that leave Xoan?"

His expression froze in a scowl. "Ain't no more boat."

"What did you do with it?"

"Sold it."

"How does she make a living?"

"How? How the hell could she row that damn boat with a child in her belly?"

My jaw dropped. I stared at him. "Pregnant? She's pregnant?"

"Seven months and going. Didn't you know?"

"No. How could I know?"

"Yeah. Time flies. Seven months since you left."

My head felt like exploding. He regarded me with his good eye. I didn't have to ask who the father was. Neither did he. In that brief silence my whole being was caught on fire. When I looked into his eye, I could see the judgment he had reserved for me. Perhaps he had been consumed by a single thought: to see me again.

"How does she get by?" I said, feeling the bile in his look.

"I got some money stashed away. I told her from day one where to find it if they nabbed me."

"She told you to quit this damn moonshining business, didn't she?"

"Don't start!"

I leaned my head over his cangue so our foreheads touched. "I'm trying my hardest to see if they can reduce the charges against you. I'm a nobody. But I've got somebody to help."

"I ain't counting on any help except on my meal once a day."

"Yeah. Not when you live among these louts. Don't you lose hope."

"Got none to lose. I'm no dreamer."

"Don't you want to see Xoan again?"

"Do I? Do you? Yeah!" his voice shot up and seemed to wake the comatose inmates around him.

I shriveled in his stare. I knew I deserved his wrath. Or perhaps he was just venting his ire at his lousy fate. Then I said without even thinking, "I will see her, Mr. Chim."

He kept his gaze on me a moment longer, and then his good eye softened.

"I know," he said. "You ain't running away from her, though I did suspect that. I know you."

I tried to grin.

"You know what she almost did?" he said, chortling. "When she found out she was pregnant, she told me she'd go and talk to your mother. I said hellfire no. Told her what kind of girl would go and do that? Told her if you love her you'd surely come back someday. 'How would he know that I'm pregnant?' she said. I said if you had enough sense to know how a baby is made, you would know." He spat at his free foot. "Tài, you ever thought of that?"

"Yeah." That was a lie, and I muttered it.

"Wish I could be there for her. Oh hell."

I dropped my gaze. Suddenly the stench came back, and the heat crawled on my skin. I was so consumed with guilt that they hadn't bothered me.

"I'm leaving, Mr. Chim." I rose to my feet.

"Won't you come back?"

"If I get another chance."

"We have much to talk about. I hope you and your mother can someday give your daddy a nice place to rest."

"I sure hope so."

"You come back, you hear?"

"Yeah."

I looked at his haggard face. Hope? If I stood there any longer I knew I'd tell him the truth from my heart. I remembered hating the man who left Xiaoli's mother and her baby. I remembered hating the cuckoo bird for the same reason. And now I knew I was no different from them. But then I never told him the one truth that left me crumbling. To be able to see him and have his crime pardoned, I had agreed to Mr. Cao Lai's condition. He had said to me, *If I can get this man out, you are never to see Xiaoli again.*

ANCIENT WORDS

The scent of wood smoke before sunset brought back memories of the smell of cooling ash in the hearth in my home. I saw my mother—her face, her hair, even smelled her scent which came from memories of childhood. Then I saw another face. The faces shared something, something unnamed yet dear to me. It linked their souls. I was close to them but wasn't a part of their souls. I was merely a child to both. I was a worshipper of deities. In the night I got up and went for a bowl of water and came back to my cot. I could almost smell the lemon that she washed her hair with. It was on her wooden pillow. It had stayed on my skin, seeped into my soul for two days and two nights as I lay in her bed with my knife wound. I took out the black opium pipe and, holding it in my hands, felt closer to her. The pipe no longer looked sinister. The dead man was no longer a burden of memory. I lit the kerosene lamp. A hundred years of use had coated the pipe an ominous black. There was dross in its every pore, the bowl black inside and out from venomous morphine. In the black you could still make out the carvings, you could feel their muted presence against your fingertips down the length of the pipe. Mountain peaks cloaked in clouds; a gaur bull with massive curved horns, its dewlap hanging down between its front legs; a tiger lapping water at a waterhole. I turned the pipe, and there were stringed chilies and bundled ears of corn and human figures and oxen in the fields. There was nothing left to see on the pipe except what was on the stem toward the mouthpiece, a poppy flower and small Chinese characters. They were engraved in three lines, two characters on each line.

Was this the soul of Yunnan, her birthplace?

He spent a whole week training me as a clerk in his new liquor franchise. It took me some effort to learn how to use the *suan pan*. I learned it quickly. It could be that Mr. Cao Lai was a good teacher. But I knew this: I'd rather be anywhere than in his house. I'd rather be with the liquor nuts every day than follow him everywhere like a mute.

On the seventh day I witnessed an unusual transaction that had nothing to do with a liquor purchase. It was noon when a Chinese man came into our store. A coolie was behind him with a heavy cloth bag on his bare back. The man was well-dressed. He wore a white vest that showed through a glossy tulle blouse, white stockings, and black French shoes. He clapped shut his huge umbrella once he was in the store. Mr. Cao Lai had been waiting at the counter. On it he set a square woodblock. I had never seen it before. Shiny reddish-brown mahogany. Someone must owe him a huge sum of money, but I didn't know what he was doing with the mahogany woodblock. As I stood watching, he took one silver piaster from the coolie and tapped it against the woodblock. He tossed the piaster into a cloth bag he had at his feet and took the next silver piece from the coolie. I didn't count how many silver piasters he tested, perhaps over a hundred. It was a long time before he was done. There were three pieces he set aside. The Chinese man took them back. False currency. Mr. Cao Lai wrote an IOU using a brush he dipped in an inkpot and handed it to the man. Though I couldn't read Chinese, I admired his calligraphy. After the man and his coolie left, I asked Mr. Cao Lai how to tell a good silver piece from a false one. He took out one piece and bounced it off the woodblock. It clanked crisp and clear. "There," he said, and bounced it one more time. "Just remember that sound."

He left the woodblock with me and said, "Use it whenever somebody gives you piasters." But I hadn't seen any piasters in our daily transaction since. Most people came in to buy rice liquor in small quantities and all I collected was zinc coins. Still, I marveled at how some counterfeiters could put lead in the silver pieces and save the silver for themselves.

After noon it was quiet. In the dry heat, everything stood still. Yellow and hazy. Even stray dogs were finding shade somewhere to cool off. I bought two cubes of fried tofu from a peddler and ate it with the cooked rice Lin Gao had packed for me. During this lull, I thought of her.

"Tell her I'm not allowed to see her," I told Lin Gao after I made a pact with Mr. Cao Lai.

He opened his mouth and uttered a small sound like a toad's. I watched him put his hand on his heart, and I said, "Not anymore. Just tell her."

Now, looking out the store into the simmering heat I saw him in my mind, walking bowlegged to the corner on which the silk woman sat. There would be no more news that told itself in a piece of red cloth tied around the street corner's bamboo post. I put my rice bowl in a wicker container and took out the teapot. I leaned on the counter, drank my tea, and gazed into the glare on the wall of a store across the street. If I looked long enough into the blaze, I could see myriad tiny spots of yellow and red and white. The red was poppy-red, so fierce, like anger; the white cool as ice; the yellow was soothing next to the reds. Tamarind trees stood in pale yellow along the street, the sidewalk was hazy. In that haze Lin Gao appeared.

He shuffled up the sidewalk, bareheaded, white hair falling on his forehead. He never carried an umbrella. Did Mr. Cao Lai send for me?

I looked at his gaunt face. He didn't even sweat. He opened his mouth and made a drinking motion with his hand. I poured him a half bowl—the legal liquor. With one gulp he set the bowl down on the counter and motioned for another one. Afterward he blew snot from his nose onto the floor and handed me a square piece of brown paper. I looked at the small Chinese characters in black ink and grabbed his hand.

"Xiaoli sent this?" I said, flushed inside with red-hot elation.

He nodded.

I tapped his hand gratefully. I asked him if he wanted another drink. He shook his head and made a sign for me to read the note.

"I can't," I said, shaking my head. "I wish you could read so you could tell me what she said."

He grinned crookedly, hand on his heart. Perhaps someday I could learn enough Chinese and read him my love notes. I watched him leave, shuffling back down the street in the still, dead heat. The shadows of things were small pools on the ground. I held her note in my hand, and my guts throbbed. These characters held a treasure. That had been my thought when I copied the characters on her grandfather's opium pipe. I had asked Lin Gao to take the words written on a cutout of porous wrapping paper and give it to the old Chinese woman. Now I gazed at her words in response. Cross-strokes, cursive strokes, squared strokes. I traced my finger on each short line. *What do you want to tell me?*

Distracted, I ran my fingers up and down the *suan pan* board. The rosewood beads clicked. When he first taught me how to add and subtract with these beads, I was lost. Then he made me do it when someone came in to buy rice liquor. He watched while my mind worked like lightning. There were ten vertical rods in the board and a horizontal rod that divided the board into two sections. *Heaven* was the top section—each rod there had two beads, each bead meant five in value. *Earth* was the bottom section—each rod there had five beads, each bead meant one in value. I memorized them. I took the coins from a customer's hand and flicked at the beads. *Click. Click. Click.* When I handed back the change, I caught Mr. Cao Lại shifting his gaze away and begin polishing his long fingernails with his thumb.

I shook the board. All the beads clanked, spinning off the horizontal rod, and reset themselves. Someone came in the store. Mrs. Đinh-Hòa. She leaned her red umbrella against the counter and took out a handkerchief and dabbed feverishly at her face.

"Tài," she said, still panting, "I haven't seen you in ages."

"Me neither," I said, pleased to see her. "You look good, Ma'am. How did you get here?"

"I walked." She wiped her forehead with the folded kerchief. "Well, I was on Hemp Street when I ran right smack into Mr. Cao Lai. I didn't know he owned a liquor store. Good heaven. So here I am."

Our liquor store was on Cotton Street, which was an extension of Hemp Street, on the south side of the citadel.

"What was he doing on Hemp Street?" I said out of curiosity.

"He was coming out of the French Resident's house. You ever seen it? The old Chinese house with tall flag poles out front?"

I shook my head. She liked to talk. When I was working for her husband, I used to be her listener. Sometimes I went off behind her back, and she would keep on talking. I reached for her hands.

"Are they getting any better," I said, "or worse?"

"Only when it gets cold." She flexed her arthritic fingers and glanced at me. "You've changed!"

"Yes, ma'am." I laughed. "I look Chinese but I don't know a word of Chinese."

"Your boss can teach you."

The smirk on my face drew a frown on her.

"Did I say something wrong?" she said.

"No, ma'am. He's too busy for the petty stuff like that." Could I ask him to translate her note for me? "Mr. Đinh-Hòa, he knows Chinese, ma'am?"

"Certainly. Why do you ask?"

"I was thinking there might be someone who can help me . . . well, I've got this note written in Chinese. But, never mind, ma'am. What'd you need from me?"

"Oh." She opened her bag and handed me a glass jar. "He needs it filled."

I recognized the jar I used to take to a liquor store near where they lived, and filled it for Mr. Đinh-Hòa. He never liked the foreign taste in the state's distilled liquor. As I measured it with a ladle before pouring, I said to her, "He still drinks this stuff, ma'am?"

"Well, he wouldn't if he had a choice." She leaned her

weight against the counter. "A few times I bought him state liquor, but it was mixed with village moonshine. He raved about the brewed moonshine. But you know what? They're cracking down on those stores that violate the rules."

Chim's moonshine must have overwhelmed him the first time he tasted it on our boat. I thought of that day as I put the stopper on the jar. I tallied up the sale. She weighed the jar in her hands and then worked it back into her bag, which was padded with straw.

"Now," she said, peering up at me as I stood behind the counter, "what is it that you need? This Chinese letter?"

"Not a letter, ma'am," I said. "Some words I need translated."

"Can I see em?"

I watched her as she read the note. It was a personal note, and I had it out in public. She looked up from the note and said, "Hm, interesting. Some Chinese girl that won your heart?"

I wrung my hands. "Someone I know. What does it say?"

"It says, 'How did you know the names of my grandfather and my great-grandfather and my great-great-grandfather? Where did you get these names? Why are you not allowed to see me anymore? Does it have to do with these names? Does it involve Mr. Cao Lai? You must tell me.'"

She stared at me. "Well?"

My head rang with strange sounds. I didn't hear her.

"Troubles with the girl?" she said, her eyes darting side to side.

"No, ma'am. Just something dumb I did."

"Doesn't everyone your age? She speaks Annamese?"

"Yes, ma'am. But she can't write in Annamese. That's

why we have this problem."

"You can come to me." She clutched her bag and picked up her umbrella. "I'm going."

"Thank you, ma'am," I said. "Thank you very much."

I watched her cross the sunlit street, and after she was gone, I looked down at the note. If I knew those Chinese words on the opium pipe, I would have saved myself from the dreaded truth. Now she had caught a glimpse of it. And that could mean losing her forever.

THE MONK AND THE SUTRA

Twilight was brief. Turbaned women were coming home with empty straw baskets on their heads. The wild-mulberry woman, her head wrapped in a black kerchief, her pannier swinging at her side, walked barefoot and silent into the last glimmer of sun. A child sounded his bamboo clappers. Behind him followed a blind man, resting one hand on the child's shoulder and carrying a monochord in the other. Shortly after they went past the store at dusk, night fell.

I tied the bag and zinc coins clanked as I swung it over my shoulder. Before pulling down the shutter, I lit the isinglass lantern over the door. It would burn through the night despite wind or rain. The sign flickered on: *Régie Alcool.* When I turned around she was crossing the street. In her hand was a yellow paper lantern. It had been three days since her note reached me. I had been silent.

"Tài!"

I couldn't hear her footsteps. She always came that way. Nimble feet in thick-soled, black Chinese shoes with curved tips. She held her lantern away from me, and it swung to and fro on a thin bamboo rod. I opened my mouth, but words didn't come out. Instead I looked at the white facing that edged the buttoned front of her black blouse. She wasn't clad all in black. Maybe she wasn't going out later to sell opium.

"Did you get my letter?" she said with a smile as she looked into my eyes.

"Lin Gao brought it to me," I said, unsure of what I was saying.

"Did you read it?" She let out a small laugh. "Can you read it?"

"No, I can't." I smiled, then stopped. "But I asked someone."

"Where did you get those names?"

I avoided her gaze. Clear almond-shaped eyes like my mother's. The glow of her lantern held my attention. The bluestone sidewalk was lit in a small turmeric-yellow sphere.

"Xiaoli?" I met her serene stare. In it an unknown world awaited me. "I got them from your grandfather's opium pipe."

"My grandfather?"

"Before he died."

Her eyes looked darker as I told her how he died. She knitted her fine, thin eyebrows. Surprise swept through her eyes.

"Did they bury him?" she asked.

"I believe so." My guts turned at the thought of those scoundrels. They had had no intention of burying him.

"You know where it is, yes?"

"Yeah. Well, you can always ask the innkeeper."

"You should have told me sooner." She chided me silently with her narrowed eyes.

I shook my head. "After what happened . . . to you, to me . . . I didn't have the guts to tell you."

"Then why did you do what you did? You sent me the names . . ."

"Every night I couldn't see you, I talked to the pipe. I saw the words, I became curious. What are they? I wanted to know more."

She crooked her forefinger and bit gently into its joint. "If I had known sooner," she said, her tone soft, "I could have sent home the news."

"Home?" I blurted out. "Yes, home."

"My mother could arrange to bring his . . . remains back home."

"Yeah."

"I should do that."

"Do what?"

"Send home the news." She looked down at her feet, and rested one foot atop the other. "I know merchants who go back to Yunnan every other month."

They would bring back the news that her mother had died. *Keep your mouth shut or she'll hate you for not having told her.*

At my silence, she said, "You didn't tell me why you are not allowed to see me. Why?"

I didn't know why either. I told her it was Mr. Cao Lai's decision, and it appeared to me that he didn't want me to interfere with her job at Mr. Lý's. She looked puzzled. The way she crimped her lips pinched my heart. Yet I couldn't tell her of the promise I had made to Mr. Cao Lai because of my relationship with Chim. I had done enough irreparable damage.

I met her gaze. We stood in the same spot until a torch light passed by. A coolie carried it at arm's length, running alongside a rickshaw. Its rubber wheels made no sound on the dirt road. We couldn't see the passenger's face. A French passenger, perhaps, or a wealthy local. They rode in rubber-wheeled rickshaws. The iron-wheeled rickshaws were for common people.

"You still go out and sell that stuff at night?" I asked her softly.

"Yes," she said with a sharp inhalation. "But not to-night."

"Why not tonight?"

"I have to help a monk."

"You help . . . what?" I couldn't hear clearly because of her accent.

"A-m-o-n-k," she said it slowly this time.

"A monk? A Buddhist monk? There is no Buddhist pa-goda in the Chinese quarter."

"He is not Chinese. And it is not in the Chinese quarter."

"Help him? What kind of help he needs?"

"He has to make books so they . . . stay around."

"Oh. So they won't be extinct."

She tilted her head to look at me.

"They will be gone forever," I said, "if he doesn't do what he's doing."

"Yes."

"How does he make them? How can you help?"

"Do you want to see?"

"Sure," I said. "Sure."

Soon her lantern was the only light on a dirt road that took us to the western side of the citadel. In the quiet, the *sapèques* in my bag clanked together. She laughed a small laugh when I said to her that every time I met her, she was with a bag that jangled with zinc coins. Then I told her it was on this dirt road on that sultry day that I ran into the French horseman. "How?" she asked. I told her I was go-ing to watch a gang of bandits beheaded. I told her about the procession meandering its way to the execution ground, about my change of heart. That day I saw her standing on a corner in the Chinese quarter while I was running for my

life. She said she still did not understand why I wasn't allowed to see her, and then at my silence, said it might have
nothing to do with her job at Mr. Lý's, for the matriarch,
though sick, was a reasonable woman, and Mr. Lý wasn't
running the house. He only came up from his village on so-
cial or business occasions. Then she said there was something else she hadn't told me that she should. Hearing her
tone of voice, a dark feeling came back to me. It had been
there since I met her, dark, shapeless and pervasive. She
said it could be that by knowing her, I would soon find out
that Mr. Cao Lai had sold her to Mr. Lý. I stopped. "Sold?" I
said. She nodded, and we walked on. Mr. Cao Lai, she said,
bought Annamese women and children by preference. They
were victims of the Chinese Black Flags. The bandits sold
them to merchants like Mr. Cao Lai who in turn sold them
to rich families in China. Numbed, I listened. She said poor
Chinese girls like herself who wanted to get out of poverty
in the mainland were sold to wealthy Annamese families
in Tonkin. Her words gripped my throat like a vise. I said
nothing as we went on, the sounds of insects clicking in the
grass. As she passed the lantern from one hand to the other,
she asked why would Mr. Cao Lai care what I knew about
his business. With a knot in my stomach, I said I had no
answer. She raised her lantern and pointed it toward the
muddy bank going down to the moat. White egrets stepped
silently in the wet mud, heads cocked, watching with one
eye for fish. Seeing the lantern's light, the birds tipped their
heads, regarding us. A night bird called down the embank-
ment, which was pale with withered grass. On the pond a
pagoda was perched atop stone bedding.

I was standing before the pagoda's peculiar structure
when she set her lantern on the ground, rolled her pants to

her knees, and removed her shoes. She looked back at me.

"Are you just going to stand there?" she said.

I did what she did. We waded into the pond until we were knee-deep in water. Her lantern shone on a network of weathered, brown wood beams, sloping sharply, leaning against the black rocks. Out of the pond we stood under the steep, battered roof dotted with pale gray lichens. An old monk came out.

"Xiaoli!" he said in a light voice.

"Were you expecting me, sir?" she said, smiling.

"I saw your lantern. It could only be you." He set his bespectacled eyes on me. "Is this your friend?"

"Yes," she said, raising the lantern so the monk could have a better look at me. "That's Tài. He's Annamese like you, sir."

"So you're here to help?" the monk said as he turned to walk back inside.

"Help?" I said. "Yes, sir."

Despite its ruinous condition—the monk pointed out gaping holes in the roof—the place was habitable. We ducked under the sagging gate where a domed bell that had long stopped tolling dangled in midair. An oil lamp lit the dank, dark interior. There was a single round window above a corner where a three-legged stool stood. I stepped over a wooden crate in the center of the room. She set her lantern on the stool while the old monk rummaged in the crate. Here he lived among books piled in columns along the walls and stacked on wooden shelves. Misshapen books with their corners and spines torn or missing. I stood in the mildewed air and listened to constant scuffing sounds behind the piles of books. Something leaped out from a corner and ran past the monk. A rat. The old monk was oblivious

to the disturbance. Finally he stood up with an armful of
wooden plates and called out to Xiaoli.

She brought him a cloth bag, and he placed the plates
carefully in the bag. She told me he reproduced the ruined
books from these wood-block prints.

"So they will not become extinct," she spoke each word
slowly and smiled.

"And how do you help?" I said.

The monk chortled. "She copies the sutras for me."

He paused and picked up a wooden plate from the crate
and handed to me. I turned it over and saw tiny Chinese
characters engraved on the surface.

"These plates," he said, "are worn out after so many
prints, they cannot be used to reproduce books anymore.
Those books over there, rats have been eating them. Before I
lose them all, I must preserve the sutras."

"Copy them from the plates by hand, sir?" I said.

"By hand, word for word," he said and peered up at me
from behind his spectacles. "Can you do that?"

I looked at his shadowy face, his round spectacles. Then
I looked at the plate in my hand. "Do that? I don't know
Chinese, sir."

"You don't need to."

She chimed in. "Yes. You don't need to know Chinese to
copy Chinese characters."

I felt stupid. I nodded.

She went to the lamp-lit corner and came back with another cloth bag. The monk began sorting through the wood-
en plates while she held the lantern over him. He looked at
each plate, and, if it was agreeable to him, he placed it in the
bag. I reached for one and tried to read the Chinese characters in the lantern's trembling light. Each character was as

small as those printed on one side of the *sapèque*. The plate was full of them. Then I looked at what was in the bag.

"How many books do you have to make?" I asked the monk.

"All of them," he said.

I looked at the piles of books. As I looked back at him, he was gazing at a rat's shiny round eyes peering up at him from a dim corner. Perhaps he had a clever way of going about it.

"How long does it take to make one book, say, like that?" I picked up a tattered book, blew off the dust and held it up for the monk to see.

"A few months," he said, taking the book from me and returning it to its shelf.

"You must work every day—and by yourself, sir?"

"Until my eyesight gives out on me."

"What about equipment?"

The old monk smiled a forgiving smile and held up his bare hands. I laughed. The rat scooted back behind a pile of books.

"I used to be an engraver when I was your age," he said. "I engraved many of these plates myself when I was a young monk. But now my eyes cannot do it anymore. Young people like you and Xiaoli can make a difference."

He pushed the round spectacles up on his forehead and looked at me. His gentle smile made me nod like a simpleton.

"You come back when you are done with those," he said, patting the bag reserved for me. "Both you and Xiaoli will be copying the *Diamond Sutra*. Try not to make mistakes."

He bent and tried to push the huge crate into a corner. I walked up to it, picked it up, and realized how heavy it was.

I didn't want to show him that, so I crimped my lips, heaved it up and, using my thighs as the support, carried it to the lit corner. As I bent my knees, the weight pulled me and I doubled over. Something tore inside my stomach. The glare before my eyes wasn't from the lamp. Half bent, I clutched my abdomen , my forehead perspiring.

"What is wrong?" she said from behind me.

"Nothing," I said, tossing back my head.

"Your stomach, yes?"

I shook my head to clear the drumming. I felt her hand over mine on my stomach.

"Sit down," she said.

She made me lean back against the crate and rest my head on its rim. I peered up and saw the old monk. She told him of my old wound. He nodded, picked up the oil lamp from the stool, said he would give me something to take. She brought her lantern, placed it by my side and knelt.

"Are you bleeding?" she said, and opened the front of my blouse.

"I hope not," I said.

She ran her fingers over the scar, now a purplish line, and then she lay her palm on it. It felt warm. I held still. In the lantern's light her face glowed with a porcelain sheen. When I put my hand over hers, she kept it there and I felt peaceful. I felt as though I had just come back from some distant world. I could feel a longing, thin and wispy like a curl of mist, even in her presence. I thought of her undressing me, washing me and changing my clothes while I was unconscious with the knife wound. Maybe her care for me helped bind our souls together.

"You must have been very reckless when you were a child," she said, tilting her face to me. "No?"

"Why do you say that?"

"You have another scar as big as this."

"What scar?" Then my gaze froze on her face. "Oh, that scar."

"How did you get it?"

"From riding a water buffalo," I said, held by her gaze. "When we got to this pond I went in for a swim. Well, I didn't slide off the buffalo's back. I jumped over his head. Yeah. He snapped his head back and his horn caught me there."

That scar was later covered by my pubic hair.

"It could have been worse," she said, smiling.

"Yeah, it could have. That's what my mother said."

"What did you do when that happened?"

"Put mud on it. Clay mud. And lay there till it dried. Bleeding stopped. I didn't tell my mother. But later she saw my shorts all torn up in the front and I had to tell her."

"Can she speak Chinese like your father?"

"No. But I never heard my father speak a word in Chinese."

"He told you he could?"

"Mr. Cao Lai, he told me. Said he met my father in Kwangtung way back."

"What was your father doing in Kwangtung?"

"Living with some Chinese girl. Had a wild life."

"Learn Chinese like your father."

"I'm beginning to."

"By copying the sutras?" she said with a glint of humor in her eyes.

"I'll do it 'cause you do it." Then I grinned. "Show me how to write your name."

"Then what?"

"I'll carry it with me. Like you carry your mother's pocket watch."

The old monk came back with a mug in his hands. It had no handle and felt hot when he made me hold it.

"Drink this," he said, rising to his feet.

His acorn-brown robe stirred the air with a musty odor.

"What's this water, sir?" I looked up at him.

"Lotus node. In case you bleed inside."

I drank. The drink had a bitter taste and smelled like parched leaves.

"Rest for a while," he said. "Where do you live?"

Near the lake, I told him. He told me to spend the night in the pagoda. I grew alarmed and told him why I could not.

"I will tell your employer myself," he said. "Don't risk walking home. And forget the bag, the plates."

She closed the front of my blouse. "It might be just a tiny tear."

He asked us if we had eaten dinner. We said no.

"Can you eat fermented tofu?" he said.

"Yes, sir," I said.

After he left I held her hand in mine. "You can't stay. You'll be in trouble."

"I will leave after our meal."

I smiled at the way she said it. I told her how to say it properly in Annamese.

"I miss speaking Chinese," she said, clasping her other hand over mine. "No one in Mr. Lý's household speaks Chinese except A-Mei. But she doesn't talk."

"Neither does Lin Gao. So I learn signs he makes with his hands." Something came to my mind. "Xiaoli?"

She leaned her head sideways. "Yes?"

"There was something I asked Lin Gao. He made signs—I didn't get it. Like this." I had memorized his hand motions when he explained to me why his black dog took my knife to Mr. Cao Lai.

She hung her head and swept her plait over her shoulder to her front. She repeated my last motion by clenching her hands and bringing them together. "Tell me what you asked him."

I told her.

"He was saying the dog brought the knife to its owner," she said.

"I'm the owner," I said.

"If you are the owner, it would be like this . . ." She made some motions that went toward herself.

I shook my head. But I saw it with my own eyes when the dog picked up my knife and brought it into Mr. Cao Lai's sleeping quarters. Perhaps Lin Gao knew more than he wanted me to know.

I looked into her eyes full of shadows, at her pigtail gleaming black on her black blouse. I touched the plait with my fingers. A thickness swelled up in my throat. An affection darkened with anxiety.

"Tài," she said.

"Yeah?"

"What is with Mr. Cao Lai?"

Her soft hands in mine took away the trepidation. Keeping my voice low, I told her what happened when he found out about my late-night outings with her. A locked entrance door. A stern warning. I told her about the skull—an enemy of his—that he received as a gift from the *quan án,* which I lost on the night I killed the Chinese maniac and wounded the French lieutenant. Rapt, she listened. I told her he was also the one who helped me and my mother realize our dream. Without his generosity, we could never rebury my father and my little brother.

The lantern popped, the flame dimmed, and her face became shadowy. I could feel her fingertips tracing imaginary lines in my palm.

"Do you still want to see me?" she said softly. "No matter what he said?"

I heaved myself up. Should I tell her my pledge with Mr. Cao Lai to stop seeing her in exchange for Chim's freedom?

"Come to his liquor store before I close," I said. "Whenever you can. I'll tell him that I gave the monk my word to copy the sutras. We can be at the pagoda together."

"You will become a . . . scribe." She hesitated, and then smiled.

"I didn't tell you about the silver carp. I saw it jump after you went in."

"Good fortune will come to you." Her eyes gleamed.

"It already did," I said and brought her hand to my lips.

Early the next morning when I left the pagoda with the monk and arrived at the liquor store, Mr. Cao Lai was there. Taken aback at the sight of me and the monk, he asked where I had been the night before. The old monk explained. Despite that, Mr. Cao Lai opened the cloth bag and inspected its content. He read one plate, then another before nodding at the monk with a congenial smile.

"The *Diamond Sutra*, sir?" he said.

"Yes," the old monk said, acknowledging it by putting his palms together on his chest.

"Only a few people could treasure it." Mr. Cao Lai smacked his lips. "And none could put it to use."

"Thus I have heard."

Mr. Cao Lai laughed. "That is the Buddha's famous line in the sutra."

I could see the mirth in his eyes, and for one brief moment I didn't dislike him. Before taking leave, the old monk told me to keep drinking the lotus node decoction and copy the sutra only when my mind was uncluttered.

Mr. Cao Lai looked more at ease after the monk left. He asked me about my incident and then picked up the rhizome, black and dried, from inside the bag. Seeing that I was walking gingerly, he told me to sit on the stool and went to boil the sponge-like tuber.

"Did the monk tell you to drink it before a meal?" he said while brewing the node.

"I don't remember, sir."

"Always drink it with an empty stomach." Then he shook his head. "You never cease to amaze me."

"I'm sorry, sir," I said.

"This new venture of yours might be a good distraction."

"I'm not distracted," I said calmly. "Though you might see it that way, sir."

"Then what is your motivation?" He narrowed his eyes. "If it wasn't the monk, but a priest who asked you to copy the New Testament, would you do it?"

"I don't see the difference, sir. If it's an old priest who takes on such a thankless job, like this monk against Father Time, I'll help him if I'm asked."

"Are you in for a long haul?" He grinned. "Inspiration is short-lived."

"I never quit in the middle of anything." I began to hate this interrogation.

"I'm glad to hear that. Just don't let it interfere with your work here."

"You don't have to worry about that, sir."

He checked on the brewed herb and carefully poured the content into a small clay bowl. As he placed it in front of me on the counter, he said, "Yesterday I sent a messenger to tell your mother about the date and time for the reburial. It's a week from today."

"A week? We still don't have the gravestones."

"They'll be ready in two days—the way your mother wanted it." Then he tapped his fingers on his forehead. "The coffins! They'll be ready at the same time."

"My deepest gratitude to you, sir," I said, touched by his kindness and awed by his thoroughness. "What about the burial time, sir?"

"Shortly before midnight."

"What if it rains?"

"The hour is fixed. Treat weather as an afterthought."

"Can I be there? I want to be there to help my mother."

"No. I have four coolies for the job. And I'll be there to oversee it."

"You will be there, sir?" I arched my brows.

He nodded and then brushed back long strands of hair from his forehead.

"You're very kind, sir," I said. "It'd be exhausting to make the trip back in the middle of the night."

"We'll stay for the night," he said, stretching his hand and looking at his long fingernails.

"Our hut isn't big enough for six people."

"The coolies will sleep outside. I don't mind sleeping on your old cot."

I managed a smile. "Thank you, sir. My mother would be honored."

I took small sips, wincing from the biting taste. I glimpsed his hand going into the bag and heard the clacking of wooden plates. He was absorbed in reading the plate. For a merchant, he had a broad knowledge of things. But the *Diamond Sutra*?

"How did you meet this monk?" he said without taking his eyes off the plate.

I swallowed the drink and it scalded my throat. "I saw the pagoda one day. It looked so weird I explored it. That's how I met him."

"You hardly have time during the day to make such an excursion."

"Before you put me to work here, sir."

"You know his name? His title?"

"No, sir." I gulped and lowered my head to hide my jitters.

"Does he know yours?"

"Yes, sir."

"Have you ever written anything in Chinese?"

"No, sir."

"You simply volunteer your time and effort just because . . ." He shrugged. "But it's good that you want to learn Chinese. If something befuddles you, just come to me."

"Thank you, sir."

As he leaned over to pick up his white umbrella behind the counter, I said, "Is there anything new about Mr. Chim, sir?"

"He'll go to trial in a month. That's quick. The average wait is six months."

"Any chance that he might be freed, sir?"

"There is always a chance in this world." He hooked the umbrella on his forearm. "But chance in turn depends on other things. Doesn't it always?"

"If you say so, sir."

It rained in the afternoon. From inside the store I watched rain fall in sheets across the empty space framed by the door. Rain blew against the door and drummed on the roof. There were no customers. I took out the sheets of paper I bought at noon, a brush, an ink dish. I began my work. Late in the afternoon in the gusting wind and rain, Mr. Cao Lai came back. He said he anticipated a slack in business, and I confirmed it for him. He saw what I did with my idle time as he perused the inked sheets. After he put down the sheets on the counter, his gaze lingered on my face.

"Shave your hair," he said. "It's coming back out. Where's your cap?"

"I left it at home."

"From here on treat it as your most valuable possession." He glanced at the street. "Your picture is still out there."

"Why can't I wear my own clothes? And there are all kinds of Annamese hats. Why can't I just wrap a turban round my head? Why a Chinese cap?"

"Your Annamese clothes and headgear? You'll end up in the death cell quicker than you thought."

I said nothing, stewing with resentment.

"You just need to look Chinese." He threw a sidelong glance at me. "It's not as easy as you think."

He walked out into the rain with his white umbrella raised above his head. His loose white blouse and baggy white trousers clung to his body in the crosswind. I lifted the bowl and drank, hating its strange taste. I left the counter, walked to the door, and tossed its contents out onto the sidewalk. I stood there until my resentment simmered down. *Would you act rashly like that if she was the one who made the drink for you?*

There was no twilight. Darkness came with the sound
of rain. In the wet blackness a lantern burned as the child
led the blind man past the store. Winds carried the sound of
bamboo clappers from down the street long after they were
gone. Inside, darkness filled the store. I gathered the sheets
of paper and carefully slid them into the cloth bag, keeping
them with their parental plates. The rain let up. In the lull, I
heard a crack of thunder. I placed the bag under the counter
and then, on second thought, pulled it back out and flung
it over my shoulder. Outside a fine rain was falling. After
I lit the lantern over the door, I opened my umbrella and
stood and smelled the wind-blown rain. It smelled of wood
smoke. Down the street, a lantern swayed in a blurred yellow. The light moved diagonally. Her slender figure on the
sidewalk, clad in black, came into my field of vision.

"Xiaoli!"

She leaned her black umbrella against the shop door, and
raindrops slid from its spokes into the lantern. The flame
shuddered with a wet hiss.

"I brought you something to eat," she said as her hand
went into the cloth bag—like mine.

I took the steamed bun from her hand. It was warm inside the container. "What about you?" I said, cupping the
bun in my hands. "Have you had anything?"

"I ate."

I wondered how she was so timely this time and last. We
could have missed each other by just a hundred steps, van-
ishing around a street corner. I mentioned that to her.

"I watched the shop before I came up," she said.

"Oh, for Mr. Cao Lai."

"Do you still feel pain?"

"I haven't thought about it." I stopped chewing. "I did a

few sheets of the sutra. Business was slow during the day."

"Do you want to walk with me to the pagoda?"

I swallowed what was in my mouth. My eyes watered. "Let's go."

It was drizzling when we took to the road. She folded her umbrella, and we walked under mine. She laced her fingers in mine and held the lantern on her side. Droplets of rain spattered on the lantern and occasionally hit the flame. It sputtered. I told her that my family finally had the chance to rebury the bones of my father and my brother and added that Mr. Cao Lai would be there to see it through. She asked me if I believed in Mr. Cao Lai's altruism—she described what it meant before I told her the word—and I didn't know what to say. Then, thinking back on his personal care for me during my difficult time, counting my most recent accident, I said that he was, though difficult, a good man. I asked her how he bought her. She said he loaned her mother money at the time her family was living hand to mouth. But, unable to pay off the debt, her mother was forced to sell her. She saw him many times when she was a little girl living in a village near the old town of Lijiang in northwestern Yunnan. She said he kept coming by to see her mother, but she kept turning him away. One day he went back to Kwangtung.

"Kwangtung?" I said.

"Yes," she said, where he had met her mother as a maid in one of the opium dens that his father owned. She heard from her mother that he later left China and was bound for Annam because his father cut him out of his will. A compulsive gambler who fell from grace, she called him. One day, she told me, he came back on account of his father's death. He was a merchant of some sort, and from that day on he was often seen going back and forth across the border.

Around the bend where tangles of vines and shrubbery caught our feet, rain was falling harder. Wind blew through cane brakes, sweetening the air with an odor of floral decay. Inside the pagoda it was pitch dark. Her lantern's light fell over bins and crates and trailed a conical yellow sphere on the floorboard. The air was damp. Everywhere you turned, the mustiness stung your nostrils. The mildewed air was so thick it was brittle.

"Where's he tonight?" I asked her when we found the corner with the three-legged stool.

"He went to town," she said. "For a death . . . memorial service?"

"Will he be back tonight?"

"No. He has a remarkable voice when he chants the sutra. People want him."

She placed her bag on the floor and motioned with her hand for me to leave mine next to hers, where the monk would collect them. A wind blew through the door and the lantern's flame danced wildly. Beyond the entrance the bell turret was a ghostly white. An earsplitting thunderclap shook the floor. I told her I saw something like this the time I was lost in the forest, half mad from the evil smallpox. Chewing leaves to keep my teeth from knocking, running into creeks to drive the demonic heat out of my body. I told her about the yellow monkey that brought me the pumpkin that gave me back strength to dodge the storm. I told her I was nearly killed by a boar trap. The boar took my place and was knocked several feet when the arrow went through its thick body. I told her before I ran out of our hut in the early light of that morning I was near death, in a delirium. I saw Daddy come to me. He was a black shape, evil-smelling, and it was then I decided to come back to life.

She moved the lantern into the corner where it burned, now yellow, now blue, and she lay inclined on the floor, resting her head on the rim of the wooden crate. The side of her face went dark, only the white of her throat glowed. When I lay down by her, her hands came up soft and warm, touching my face like she wanted to feel the remains of the smallpox scourge. I held still, forgetting myself. Warm, fragrant heat clung to her skin. The curve of her throat sloped into the valley of her shoulder. Wind came sweeping through the door, the air infused with a tinge of wet moss. Her curved back, hollowed to kiss the fingertips. Patches of light on her feverish skin, white worms writhing in the sky. From the corner, the lantern's flame sputtered and dimmed.

THE YIN WORLD OF LOVE

On nights before Mr. Cao Lai departed for my village, she would meet me as I left the shop. Sometimes it rained, for it rained often now, just before the Moon Festival, and along the unlit streets her raised lantern would shine on the breathtaking, bright red poinciana flowers. On a dark corner, children were catching fireflies in glass jars, and they waved at anyone who passed by. When we looked back, the dark corner was blinking with glow worms. She said it was summer when she arrived in Annam. Summer was the months of tropical storms and heat. The sea was rough during the whole journey. The warm breeze was dry, the sky blue. The coastline came into view, and then disappeared. Sand-yellow, ochre, then brown. An older woman stayed close to her. The night they approached Tonkin, she lay awake. She lost track of time between sleeping and waking. In her sleep, she heard the murmur of the sea, the shrill call of a gull, the sound of waves. Summer blue sky, white lines of distant shores. The sea smelled acrid and warm like unwashed bodies. The sky grayed when rain clouds gathered. Then the sky and the sea became one, so immense she felt like a grain of sand. That night, unable to sleep, she put on the shawl her mother knitted for her. Its wool smelled fresh. She pressed it to her face, inhaling the scent. The older woman asked if she felt sick. She feigned sleep and closed her eyes to hold back her tears. She understood then what it meant to leave her mother for good.

Eleven was a beautiful age. Carefree and happy just being with her mother. At the riverbank, she watched people
washing clothes, beating them on the steps. Women and
children picked soapberries along the bank stepped with
flagstone. She watched children her age pick out round
seeds, brown and shiny, and put them in their pockets. She
asked her mother why they collected them. She told her that
they pierced the marble-like seeds and strung them together
to make necklaces. She watched two boys, perhaps brothers,
crushing soapberries and throwing them into the shallow
water. Moments later, fish floated up. She came near and
saw the fish afloat in the current, their scales gleaming silver. She asked what kind of fish they were.

"Minnow," the older boy said.

"Can we eat them like food?" she asked.

"Don't taste very good. Use them as bait."

"Can I try?" She took a handful of soapberries from the
boys, walked to the river's edge and tossed the broken fruit
into the water. The boys watched her as she gazed at the
river. She felt a surge of excitement, knowing that she must
be pretty for them to stare so raptly. The water was frothy,
flowing downriver from the landings where women washed
clothes. She saw her mother still waiting on the bank, her
little figure brown in the afternoon sun. She thought the
fish must have gone home to sleep since none came for her
soapberries. She glanced at the boys standing behind her.
"Where did they go? They don't like the fruit any more."

"They don't eat em," the older boy said. "The foam kills
em."

She looked down at the water again. "I don't understand." She decided to walk upriver to her mother. But as
soon as she left the boys called out, "Hey, come back. Fish.

Fish."

Fish drifted on the current. All minnows. One boy said there must be a school of them moving through. They spotted other fish, green-backed, silvery-sided, among the minnows. "Smelt! Smelt!" the younger boy shouted. She asked if they were good to eat, and the boys, snatching them up, said yes.

"Can I have some?" she held out her hands and they dropped three smelt, wet and shuddering, into her cupped hands. She headed upriver, her back stooped, afraid of dropping the fish, and when she looked back downriver at the two boys, they were bending over the water's edge. The older boy looked up and saw her. He straightened his back, shading his eyes against the red sunset. When she looked again, he was still watching her with the setting sun in his face.

In those days, she wrote her mother every other day, saving sheets of porous paper and giving them to Lý's mother at the end of the week to send home. The matriarch loved her penmanship and studied each letter. She told her, "Xiaoli, my handwriting on the best day doesn't come close to your calligraphy. You express your thoughts beautifully."

In those days, their letters took a few months to come and go. She almost cut into the first letter she received from home when she hastily scissored the envelope. A sheet of yellowed paper bore her mother's writing, the ink smeared on each downward-slanted line. The letter had no date. It took a while for her to recognize her mother's voice in the handwriting. Her mother had written the letter over several days and left gaps between her thoughts, always preceded by the line, "I'll come back later."

One night, unable to sleep, her mother sat up and began knitting a white sweater with a lavender hibiscus on the front for her. "It'll look pretty on you, darling. Tonight when I got up and went for a bowl of water, I passed your cot and could almost smell the honey locust I used to wash your hair with. Old smells in the house. I use them to tell my way around the house at night. The one I most want to smell is the scent of your skin the nights you slept with me."

The letters from home came once every three months, one sheet each time, different ink colors from letter to letter. "I buy ink pellets only when I need to write you," her mother wrote. "Whatever the store has that day." She saved all the letters her mother wrote. She studied their colors and the tiny notched edges, imagining their journey from one relay mail post to the next by carts, by runners, traveling on rivers and creeks to Annam by basket boats, from town to town until they reached her. If only she could stuff herself into an envelope and go home!

Between copying the *Diamond Sutra* and doing her household chores, she wrote home to her mother. In the early days, the writing paper was so porous and veined with bamboo fibers it pricked her hand. In those days, she would be homesick when something familiar would come to her at some time in the day or night. The sound of a woodpecker drilling a tree outside the window made her think of the *ah-oh* of the mourning doves at home.

I listened to her stories that told of distant lands, and I knew she could tell me anything in her soft, accented voice. She said the wall of her school, next to the much faded blackboard, displayed an old map of China. On the chalk rail were wooden compasses, a metal triangle, a square, a protractor. The school was poor, so the students took turns looking for white clay to make chalk for the teachers. On

the day her turn came, her mother went with her to distant tracts of paddies where the soil was gray. They would
wrap clay clods in a hemp bag and dissolve them in water at home. When the clay settled, her mother taught her
how to roll it into finger-shaped sticks and let them dry
so her teacher could use them as chalk. Sometimes when
school supplies became scarce, she went with her mother
to the hills to scour bog myrtles to make ink. With a basket
hooked on her forearm, she left home with her mother while
the morning sun was still mild. She had never seen the bog
myrtle fruit until she saw their purple flowers coloring the
brow of the hill. She plucked the berries, took them home,
and mashed them. She boiled the liquid until it turned dark
purple. The homemade ink lasted three days and gave off a
strong smell. Some of her classmates' ink lasted much longer because they mixed it with scarce alum, which cost more
than rice. So every three days she would go back to the bog
myrtle hills. She resented the bog myrtle ink. Its foul smell
made her miserable. Her mother held her against her breast
a long time and told her to have faith in Heaven, faith in the
order of things to be bestowed on mortals who cared and
believed. She kept her mother's words in mind and believed
in a faith that could defy even death.

One autumn day, rain fell all morning. Then it rained
again into the next day and the next, a damp wind never
ceasing. Coming home from school in the afternoon, she saw
a village messenger beating a gong as he raced up and down
the dirt road. "Each house, each man, five bags of sand," he
hollered. Flood again, she thought. But this one could be
bad, because the village had already mobilized all the men
from fifteen to fifty years of age to guard the dike.

When she got home, her mother was putting on her woven rope raincoat, ready to leave the house. "Where are you going, Mother?"

"To the village cooperative," her mother said. "Come with me. We have to buy sand and jute bags and carry them to the dike tonight."

As she closed the door, a black spider fell dangling in the doorway. "Wait here," her mother said and went back inside. At the ancestral altar, she lit a joss stick and prayed. Xiaoli watched the spider. It stopped descending and seemed to wait for her to go away. She swatted it and it wriggled on the doorstep.

Her mother put on her straw hat and took her by the hand. "Let's go," she said, "before it gets dark."

"Why'd you have to pray?"

"The black spider is a bad omen."

"Of the flood?"

"I prayed for us to be spared."

She helped her mother carry the jute bags and sand home. They made five sandbags and hauled them to the dike in the twilight.

On the dike, villagers were banging pans and gongs and beating drums. Megaphones called people to spots along the dike that needed to be fortified. She clung to her mother's arm as they jostled through the crowd. Papaya torches lit the night and the rain smelled of burnt leaves.

Men and women worked to reinforce the dike. Wives and daughters came to help their husbands, fathers, brothers. The sky was black, the river and the dike lit only by torches. The drums beat steadily. People moved about like ants, dragging sandbags across the rain-slick dike to places that had to be buttressed. After midnight, the river crested. The megaphones blared out orders: "Dike about to break.

Run!" Water surged through gaps in the dike, and people splashed through the current toward higher ground. The frantic beat of drums knotted her stomach. Torches were tossed away, sizzling in the floodwater. Ashes floating like fireflies carried the burnt smell of papaya.

Water rose swiftly to their chest. They reached a hillside shrine, but people were already packed inside. They sat on the steps in the downpour, watching people crouched in the darkness under trees. Her mother cradled her, shielding her head from rain.

"Same kind of flood when I just had you," she said, ". . . when you were barely a month old."

She raised her head. "Was Father with you? In the flood?"

"No. He went back to Annam."

"Why? What did Father do? You never told me."

"He works for the greater good."

"What does that mean?"

"He works for his country—in a dangerous line of business."

"But if someone kills Father, who will take care of us?"

"You always have me, darling. And I always have you." Her mother smiled at her affectionately. "Now, just rest. It's going to be a long night."

She closed her eyes, imagining a river that was like the rush of water surrounding them. A thunderous noise blasted through the air. Then shouts— "Dike broke!"—followed by cries in the dark. She shut her eyes, imagining a river, this wild river, overflowing her village, drowning livestock and pets. She thought of her house, then dimly of what her mother said about her faceless father before she fell asleep in her mother's arms.

One day her mother came home late from her tobacco-
stripping job in another village. She worked odd jobs. Nothing lasted long. Knitting shawls for people until her fingers
and hands ached. She had calluses on her hands that she
could not even pare with a knife. When there was no work,
she set up a stand selling ginger sweetdrops in the alley outside their house. Xiaoli saw her coming in with glazed eyes.
The bog myrtle ink smelled sour, and the brush she wrote
with smeared it across the porous paper. The bamboo fibers
had ruined it. Tiny splinters from the writing paper went
into the heel of her hand. Her mother examined Xiaoli's
hand by the light of the oil lamp. After she pulled the bamboo splinters from the heel of her hand, she padded it with
a handkerchief. Her face looked grim, her fingertips brown
from tobacco leaves. She said, "Xiaoli, I'm sending you to
Annam." Shocked, she looked at her mother who took her
bleeding hand into her own. "I owe people money." Her
mother's shoulders felt soft and bony, and when Xiaoli wept
into her chest, she smelled sweat and tobacco.

In bed later that night, Xiaoli listened to the stillness,
to the sound of oxcarts creaking along the road, but after a
while she heard nothing. The air was hot after three weeks
of dry weather. So much water had evaporated from the
pond that you could see the mossy bottom. The rush mat
was warm, and her mother was still awake, lying on her
side. Her hair covered half her face. Her eyes gleamed.

"What kept you up so late?" her mother said.

"Do you want me to go to Annam, Mother?"

Her mother's chest heaved and she said nothing.

She spoke into her mother's chest. "Will you miss me
when I go, Mother?"

"I will," her mother murmured.

"I know deep in your heart you don't want me to go, do you, Mother?"

"My heart will say no, but my head and mouth will say yes."

Her mother stopped speaking.

"Mother?"

"What, dear?"

"Where will you get the money to buy my ticket?"

"You'll be on a boat. I don't have to pay."

She rubbed Xiaoli's back for a while and then picked up a palm-leaf hand fan and fanned her daughter. Slowly Xiaoli felt herself disconnecting from her mother and slipping into a dark vacuum with nothing to grab, nothing to pull herself back with, and in that vacuum she cried out "Mother" and woke. Her cheek still pressed against her mother's bosom, she felt her mother's warmth and then a stifled sob from deep in her mother's chest.

MR. CAO LAI

It rained the night before Mr. Cao Lai returned from Lau. It worried me that rain also might reach the region of our village. Wet earth, water-filled holes. And what I had often imagined came back—the corpses' remains unearthed from the wet clayey soil would have to be scooped up, not just bones, but also rotten flesh, for it had been only two years since their burial. Rain would make the trip to the mountains a daunting task.

Mr. Cao Lai looked like he hadn't slept much when he returned. Stubble lined his jaw and his skin was pale as when he was drunk. It was dawn when he came back, hours before I would leave for the liquor store. I asked if he needed rest. He said no and instructed me to prepare a hot bath for him. Before going to the bathhouse, he asked whether a messenger had come during his absence. When I said no one had come, he looked relieved. I went to the kitchen and told Lin Gao to make a bowl of hot noodles and heat a jar of rice liquor. Halfway through the courtyard on my way back to the main hall, I heard rapid knocks on the entrance door.

A messenger wearing a conical palm-leaf hat stood outside by a horse that looked like a pony. Seeing me, he turned and went to his saddle, a crudely made wooden seat that sat on a red tasseled cover. He pulled out a long tin tube with both ends capped and sealed. I thought he must have come a long way, for his leggings were flecked with soot and his bare feet yellowed with dust. He said he would wait to take the document back.

It took Mr. Cao Lai a long time to come out of the tub after he read the document. Wet footmarks trailed him back into the main hall where he sat and composed a letter, his hair tangled and wet like kelp. He didn't touch the bowl of noodles that sat steaming on the tray in front of him. He drank his rice liquor and kept on writing. When he called me in, he was rolling up the parchments and sliding them into the tube. He asked me to bring him the bar of red wax he always used for sealing envelopes. Then he lit the oil lamp and held the capped ends of the tube against the wax bar over the glass globe until the wax melted. He watched the color of the wax until it lost its red tinge, picked up a square seal, and pressed it firmly into the cooling wax.

I took the sealed documents back out to the messenger. The wax had hardened and Mr. Cao Lai's seal had left two raised characters in Chinese. At the sound of the door opening, the bay horse twitched its ears and blew its nose. Its unshod hooves were yellowed from road dust. I asked the man how far he had come. He said he came from Lai Châu, northwest of Hanoi, close to the border with China, and it had taken him four days on horseback. As he put his foot in the stirrup, ready to mount his horse, I asked who sent the message. He swung onto the saddle and, tilting back his hat, said he was not allowed to discuss it.

I came back in. Mr. Cao Lai had changed into his customary white silk blouse and trousers, loose and light. He hadn't touched his noodles.

"Do you want me to reheat it, sir?" I said.

"No need," he said and picked up the chopsticks.

I poured him a cup of rice liquor. The jar was nearly empty. He motioned with his hand for me to leave it on the tray and began to tell me that my father and my little brother were now interred at the new burial site. It had been an arduous effort due to bad weather. The porters, he said, had to carry two coffins on foot to the nearest creek. The two hired boats, then took them to the river and to the mountains. He and my mother rode to the mountains in a malabar. He said when they were ready to bury the coffins, to his surprise, the ground in both excavations was only damp, despite the heavy rain. It was past midnight when they left the mountains, so he took my mother back and bade her goodbye. He was to return to the city.

I thought of the messenger and understood his change of plans.

That evening I walked home alone. She didn't come. I hoped she did not go out to sell opium. The evenings we spent together, we just walked through the city streets, sometimes with a shoulder bag clicking with wooden plates, and sometimes just wandering until her lantern burned out. We would then stop and light a new candle. It was the most wonderful time I had ever had. The night before Mr. Cao Lai returned, we came back to her place in the rain and stood embracing each other outside the red door with her umbrella tilted back. Rain fell on our shoulders, on our napes. She asked if I would like to come in, and I hesitated for fear of being seen with her. But then I met her gaze and it coaxed me into nodding like a child. She blew out the lantern, and we walked like thieves across the courtyard, which was lit sporadically with white trembling flashes. The air was torn with claps of thunder. The house was cool, quiet. We slid across the tiled floor, dimly lit with an all-night kerosene lamp, the air redolent of an herbal scent, moist in the rain dampness. It followed us to her room. The room was dark,

save the occasional glimmers of lightning outside the latticed window. Her pillow held the scent of her skin, and
in the dark it burned with the warmth of our bodies. There
was a noise at the door. We kept ourselves still. After a while
she said in a hushed voice that it was the house cat. I said,
"You ever wear your hair without a plait?" and she said,
"Yes, but rarely," and asked me why I wanted to know. I
said that my mother wore hers around her head, and it was
so long it hung down her back to her waist, and that the
only time she let down her hair was after her bath when
it flowed to the ground like the banyan's aerial roots. She
smiled at my description, her teeth white in the dark. She
found the twists of her plait and undid them with her fingers and ran them through her hair, letting it fall over the
pillow. It spread like black satin, and her whole body was a
pale white. She opened her arms and held my face against
her chest. Her skin was cool and her heart thumped against
my ear. She asked if I had known any woman before her.
Yes, I said, wanting to be pure at heart in her aura. "Tell me
about her," she said. I became a storyteller and she a curious listener. She asked if I loved the girl, and I said no and
took her hand and pressed it against the side of my face as
though to calm a sudden dark, alien agitation that stirred
in my heart. "Do you love me?" she whispered. "Yes, I love
you," I said, but the palpitation in my heart beat on. "Do
you love me no matter what happens?" she asked. "No matter what happens," I said. "One day," she said, "I will go
back home. Will you go with me to Lijiang?" "Yes," I said, "I
will go wherever you want me to." Then I closed my eyes. I
saw a red poppy.

When I returned in the evening I found no one in the
house. I went out to the dark courtyard and lit the lanterns.

A drizzle fell, wetting my skin. I went into the main hall and then the kitchen and back out across the courtyard to Lin Gao's room, next to mine. In the last room, always empty save an old table and two broken chairs, I saw something that caught my eye through the half-open door. Draped under a long, tasseled red fabric was a huge coffin resting on a pair of trestles. This must be what Mr. Cao Lai had ordered from Mr. Wang's coffin shop. I lifted the fabric and ran my hand along the coffin. Smooth and cool, the dark wood shone. Its corners were sculpted with a lion's head, and a blooming, knoblike lotus was carved toward the bottom on each side.

Late that night in bed I heard them coming back. The sounds of shuffling feet and things moved around in the coffin room lasted past midnight. Morning came, and I found the room padlocked. Mr. Cao Lai must have had it rearranged for the permanent storage of his own coffin. With a casket like that, nothing could get to you after you were laid to rest. Moisture, earthworms, maggots. You would rot on your own.

Three days passed quietly. During the day I kept myself busy transcribing the sutra, and when evening came I looked outside for the light of her lantern. For two nights she didn't come, but on the night of Moon Festival, she came unexpectedly after I had left the store. I heard her call my name up a cross street. I turned and saw the light of a lantern. My heart wept with joy. We stopped at a street corner, and I took out a moon cake wrapped in waxed paper. Had she not come, I told her, I would have had to eat it alone. I asked her what the four Chinese characters embossed on the rust-colored wheat-flour crust said. "Mid-Autumn Moon Cake," she replied. We leaned against a wall between two shops and each ate our share. She said she had always loved this pastry, filled with red bean paste and lotus seeds. Up Hemp Street we passed closed shops with unsold toys still dangling on strings in the display windows—colored paper lanterns printed with flowers and animals. I looked at the children's toys bright in the shops' lanterns, and I saw her smile while she gazed at them. Her face was tranquil. I saw the gentle lines that flowed from her nose to her lips, the arch of her throat, the satiny white of her skin. A procession of unicorn dancers pranced down the street. We stood back in the lee of the shop walls as they went by. The unicorn head bobbed and weaved in the cadence of the drums, its long body a flowing ribbon of red cloth. The first firecrackers that went off startled her, and she laughed. Trailing the unicorn were children carrying their octagon-shaped lanterns. She pointed and said, "Look, the revolving lanterns." They glowed red and yellow as they passed by, and I could see the silhouettes of eight warriors on horseback go around and around. She asked what made them circle, and I explained to her that the lantern's candle created hot air that propelled the figures. I walked with her into the dark alley to the red door of her place. She blew out the light and hugged me. We stood as one in the dark for a long time, and then she broke off and entered the door without looking back. I stood beneath the dark vault of sky. A feeling came over me as old as the earth, as if I had been here eons before, as air, as dust, or as the scent that clung to her.

On the fourth day, in mid-afternoon, Mr. Cao Lai stopped by his liquor store while I was tallying up a sale. He picked up a paper bag from the coal stove where we would heat the liquor for customers. After the customer left, he said, "You haven't used up the lotus nodes. Why?"

"I'm fine, sir," I said, not wanting to tell him that I hated
its detestable taste.

"Any wound will heal if you take good care of yourself."

"I don't have any more pain," I said, though I still felt its
spasms now and then when I exerted myself.

"We'll be leaving for Chung village in four days."

"Chung village?" The name of our foe shocked me.

"I have a business proposition for Mr. Lý. I thought having you along would help during our trip."

"Who will take care of the store?"

"*Lao* Gao."

"Does he know how to use this?" I pointed at the abacus.

"He knows everything a Chinese person needs to know
to do business." Mr. Cao Lai smiled proudly.

"How long will we be there?" I didn't want to speak the
name.

"We'll stay overnight at Mr. Lý's. When we return, we'll
stop by your village so your mother can join us on the way
back to the city." He cleared his throat. "I sent your mother
an invitation to come for a brief stay with us. She accepted
it. I forgot to tell you."

"I see."

"I also sent her a good supply of cinnamon bark. The
very best. She doesn't have to depend on that French priest
any more. Danton? Jules Danton?"

"Yes, sir. A good man. He speaks Annamese better than
me."

"Your village is anti-Catholic. How do you feel about it?
When a Catholic priest kept riding through your village just
to visit a widow and give her cinnamon bark?"

His grin irked me. Who was he to pass judgment on my
mother? He was tactful about it, though.

"My mother doesn't depend on the priest for the medicine. With or without it, she's fine, sir."

He nodded and seemed pacified. Then he glanced at me. "Do you like city life?"

"I'm getting to like it, sir."

"I know. You seem like you're cut out for it. Well now, when your mother is here, take a couple days off and show her around the city. City life can take your mind off many things. I feel honored that she accepted my invitation."

"What room will she stay in, sir?"

"West room." Then he punctuated his words with his hand. "Make sure everything is in order, everything immaculate."

"I'll do that, sir." I cracked my knuckles, left hand, then right. "I saw that you got your custom-made coffin a few days ago."

"That's right." He tossed back his head and laughed. "You won't see me lying in there any time soon, if that's what you think."

"Oh no, sir. When I saw it I couldn't help but think of this fellow in my village. He had a coffin made for him. Kept it in his house for many years. He outlived everyone in his family. Guess what, sir? His wife, when she died, was buried in that casket."

"Now," he said, chuckling, "that's fortuitous."

"Why is that, sir?"

"Some people have a coffin built for them because they believe that it would deter death. This symbolic death sitting in their house."

"Do you believe in that, sir?"

"I believe in death. Not in its symbol."

Four days later, we arrived at Chung in mid-afternoon. From inside the malabar, through its small window, I looked at the tall, dark banyan outside the village gate. Those bastards from Chung. I wondered what had happened to the rest of the skulls. The thought of it caused a tic in the sole of my foot. It seemed a long time since that night when I fell into their trap. Chim said I was damn lucky to be able to walk normally again. He said if the nerves were damaged, the foot was gone. Perhaps I was a fast healer. The knife wound didn't kill me.

The lookout in the watchtower was a different man, not the lout I talked to the last time. I remembered his face well. Once the gate was opened, a guide was waiting on horseback and the carriage pulled away. I told Mr. Cao Lai that the village banyan was where they hung my daddy's head, hung it until its flesh was pecked away by vultures and eaten by maggots. He asked how I got my hands on it, and I told him. Told him how they violated my daddy's skull by pissing in it. Told him about their clever trap and how my rashness got me harmed. Told him if Chim and his daughter hadn't come to my rescue that night, I wouldn't be here now. We were sitting on the wooden bench, elbow to elbow in the cramped carriage. He turned to look at me and said, "You're impetuous. But you always make your presence felt with your heart." His eyes weren't narrow like they were when he wanted to appraise you. Rather, they looked at me serenely. For the first time I thought that he had beautiful eyes.

The malabar followed the winding roads, the coachman yelled, children laughed and shouted, and the carriage whisked, bounced. It then came to an abrupt stop.

Around us were tall areca palms surrounding a blue-stone courtyard. Mr. Lý's house sat at least two feet above the ground, which was covered with white pebbles. The red-tiled roof came down, sharp and curving, overhanging the veranda. One walked up to it on a flight of five stone steps. Lý stood waiting on the top step. He wasn't as tall as Mr. Cao Lai. You noticed him because of his small, well-trimmed white beard and eyes that had fire in them when they looked at you. His sharp cheekbones drew attention to his piercing eyes.

He took us through a hall, walking in his soft-soled leather slippers that made no sound on the concrete floor. Next to Mr. Cao Lai's white blouse and trousers, Lý's gleaming black-tulle gown made him look solemn. I could hear voices beyond the hall and then we emerged from the hall's dimness into sunlight. The hall's colonnaded open side was in the cool shade beneath the overhang. Three rows of long tables, draped in red cloths and flanked by wooden benches, were in full sunlight. Bottles of wine, covered pots and crocks, ivory-colored chopsticks laid crosswise on blue plates, blue porcelain bowls with a gold-colored band round the rim. This must be a feast.

I looked at the children in baggy trousers sitting in groups of threes and fours on the grass. I looked at the boys and girls my age milling in the dappled shade of frangipani. A face I saw, then another, made my throat suddenly dry. The two of them. The buffalo boy who schemed to hurt me was there with his girlfriend. They saw me. I knew immediately that they recognized me. I wore no Chinese cap, no Chinese blouse, but was wearing instead my old gray shirt and indigo knee-length pants like I did on the day I came to this Catholic village to reclaim my father's skull. Then beyond the tree shades where tall hedges of bear's breeches screened the view, I saw the pointed tops of conical hats painted red, white, and blue in concentric circles. Tonkinese soldiers.

I looked around and saw Mr. Cao Lai standing in the company of Lý and two Chinese men. They stood out with their brocaded black caps, pearly wide-sleeved jackets and satiny black trousers. The yellow silk of their pom-poms shimmered on their fuzzy contours.

The four of them sat at a shaded round table between the teakwood columns and, at Mr. Cao Lai's permission, I went to sit among strangers at one of the long tables in the sun. The aroma of grilled meat made my mouth water. Keeping my head down, I ate. Rice vermicelli and grilled pork and shrimp. They sold this on the streets in Hanoi. You picked sliced carrots and cucumber slivers and radish and mixed them with crushed peanuts. You doused the mound with thin, sugary fish sauce that was mixed with a dash of lemon. The servants came down the tables to serve tea, each carrying a large, silvery teapot. When I sipped it, I looked across the table and saw the boy looking at me. His hair was long like Mr. Cao Lai's, always with a strand or two falling on the forehead. Next to him was his girl. She wore her hair in a plait like Xiaoli, her skin bland white in the sunlight. She was talking to another girl at her elbow, and then she glanced in my direction before I could look away. When the servants brought beef fondue to each table, they lit the coals under the fondue pots and surrounded them with plates of sliced beef. You could see hands and chopsticks flying in clouds of steam. I rose from the table. I wanted to leave. But where?

A paper screen was standing in front of Mr. Cao Lai's

table, long enough to shield the men from open view. Servants stood behind each man and fanned them leisurely. The white feathers of the fans were like raw silk, like stork's feathers. I walked up and stopped when a servant brought out a monkey on a brass pail. Yellow-haired, it sat like a little melancholy baby with life already taken out of its body. It looked exactly like the yellow monkey that brought me a pumpkin in the forest. Could this be its baby?

The servant placed the monkey and the pail in the center of the table.

"Will it jump off?" Mr. Cao Lai asked.

"No, sir," the servant said. "He's dead drunk."

Lý grinned, patting the monkey's little head. "He's got a *sheng* of rice liquor in his body, enough to last him in his next life."

The two Chinese men guffawed. These men surely understood Annamese. Now they all leaned back in their rosewood armchairs and watched. The servant pulled out a knife from his blouse pocket. Short handle, long blade. The blade was similar to the blade of my knife, grass-blade thin, pointed. Those behind the men stopped fanning. The little monkey looked around like a baby curiously taking in the world with his innocent eyes. With one hand, the man clamped the monkey's mouth shut and pressed its head against his abdomen. His other hand went around the top of the monkey's head so quickly the body didn't even jerk by the time the top of its head was gone. Then the little body twitched and shivered. The mouth opened, slack-jawed, and the eyes clouded. The little monkey was still alive.

I stood rooted to the ground. Something shattered inside me.

The servant pushed the pail to the center of the table,

picked up a plate—Mr. Cao Lai's plate—and deftly scooped part of the white brain with a spoon. The monkey slumped over, and its face hit the pail's rim. Each man was served with a plate on which was a little white mound. Then each looked at the others until Lý proceeded by picking up the condiments with his chopsticks from the tiny saucers in front of him—pickled ginger, coriander, roasted peanuts—and laying them on top of the white mound. Solemnly, he rested his chopsticks on his plate, picked up a spoon, and scooped up the tofu-like glob. He brought it to his mouth. The rest watched until he swallowed and nodded his approval. The Chinese men laughed, and Mr. Cao Lai joined them.

As they ate, the dead monkey sank into the pail, its unsightly, opened head falling forward. Pink, pulpy.

The servants again fanned the men. A server went around the table refilling their cups with rice liquor. I headed to the hall. Now in the cool, dim hall that echoed my tiny footfalls, I took a deep breath and slowly exhaled. One moment my heart was a fire-red ball of anger, the next it was ice. I felt empty. Sad. Where did they catch the helpless little monkey? In the forest of my village? Those bastards.

Past a corridor I stopped and stepped back to look. Then I walked into the corridor and looked down at all kinds of canvas sacks tied with hemp ropes. You could see the shiny cartridges in several sacks. It must have been twenty sacks full of ammunition. I saw long bamboo bags with handguns and rifles in them. They lined the length of the corridor to where it opened onto a side courtyard. There was a big tent rigged up by a dwarfed pine tree, and inside the tent were rows of wooden crates. In each crate were stacked greenish balls. They looked like cannonballs. But I saw they weren't cannonballs when I came near.

"Hey, keep off!" someone shouted.

Coming toward me was a Tonkinese soldier in a red jacket and knee-length blue trousers. There must be more of them behind the bear's-breeches hedge. He tilted back his conical hat with the tip of his rifle and shooed me with a forceful motion of his hand. "Look here," he said, "you're not allowed in this area."

"Yes, sir," I said, backing out of the tent. "What are those balls anyway?"

"What do they look like to you?"

"Cannonballs. But, hell, I know they aren't cannon balls."

"Opium."

"Oh." I took in the color. "Looks odd. Are those leaves? The wrappings?"

"Yup. Poppy leaves." He seemed easy now. "Protect the opium inside."

"The stuff they sell in the opium dens?"

"Ah, no. Raw stuff. Have to go through several steps for get them ready for . . . con . . ."

"Consumption?"

"That one."

I hung my head back. Something struck my mind as odd. "Is it legal opium?"

"Legal? State opium?" He scratched the tip of his nose with his dirty fingernail. "There ain't no state opium here. All these."

"And they showed up here just like that?" I grinned.

"Hehe. No. But you're not supposed to know that either." He motioned with his head toward the banquet. "Why don't you go join your friends over there, eh?"

"Yeah," I said, nodding, and turned and walked back

through the corridor. But instead of going back to the feast, I walked out to the front court. The bluestone courtyard was empty except for one soldier standing guard at the bottom of the stone steps.

"Did you see the malabar man?" I asked the soldier.

"The coachman?" He cocked his head to one side to look at me.

"Yeah. Him. Where's he?"

"We sent him back."

"Back where?"

"Hanoi. He's long gone."

"Heck. Why? He's supposed to wait. He leaves when we leave."

"We? Who are 'we' you're talking here?"

"Me and Mr. Cao Lai. He's the guest of honor."

"Ah." A dark look passed over his face.

"Well?"

"You just have to wait around. Say, till all the eating's over."

"You don't know who sent him back, do you?"

"Just wait till they're all done eating."

"Sure."

I walked to the fringe of the courtyard and stopped at an areca tree that had a powdery gray trunk. I sat down behind the trunk where the soldier couldn't see me. From the border of areca trees, the land sloped gently until it met a pond. Beyond the pond lay rice fields, pale green and hazy in the late afternoon sun. The gnawing in my stomach began to abate. The sky grayed. I closed my eyes in the breeze that came often now. There was a heady scent of areca flowers in the air. It might rain before nightfall, I thought, floating in a daze. The breeze carried the sound of church bells across the

rice fields, across the pond. When the sound died, an emptiness stayed in the air. The sun was no longer in my eyes, and
shadows gained on the incline. I heard in my half-sleep the
deep *moo*s of buffalos coming home from the fields.

Something told me I must wake up. When I did, I saw
the blue-trousered legs of a soldier in front of me. He was
the sentinel.

"Come with me," he said, bending to scratch his bare
calf.

"Is it over?" I rose, dusting the seat of my pants.

"Just about. Your boss sent for you."

They all must be drunk by now, I thought.

I followed the man through the hall, now dark, for it was
near sunset. Past the corridor cluttered with gun and ammunition sacks, we turned into a room, parting the bamboo
bead curtain that was painted with a clear blue sky, white
clouds, and a pair of white-plumaged storks rising to air.
There were men sitting on one side of the room—Lý, the
two Chinese men—beneath two pairs of rosewood panels,
one pair painted with turtles and cranes, the other with cou-
plets in beautiful Chinese characters, perhaps with oppos-
ing meanings—the wordplay that had fascinated scholars
for centuries. On the other side sat Mr. Cao Lai. Hung above
him on the wall was a sword, long and curving, sheathed
inside an iridescent mother-of-pearl scabbard. There was a
table between them, low on carved legs. On the table sat a
cane basket, much like the one I lost.

They weren't talking or drinking. The soldier stood behind the three men, and they all watched me as I approached
Mr. Cao Lai. It was so quiet in the room I could hear my own
footsteps. Something was horribly wrong.

Mr. Cao Lai motioned with his hand for me to come closer. He waited until I bent with my ear at his mouth and said in a whisper, "You must go home immediately. Get everything out of the bottom of the coffin—and keep them somewhere else, not in the house. *Lao* Gao has the key." "What happened, sir?" "Just go home." He placed in my hand one silver piaster coin and said, "They will take you in a boat to Monkey Hop Landing. You can manage from there." Something broke inside me. "Will you be safe, sir?" "You'll hear from me, I promise."

Lý gestured with his hand toward the basket on the table, and the soldier walked up to it, picked it up with both hands, and jerked his head to tell me to leave. The bead curtain clanked softly as we left the tomb-quiet room.

Past the corridor still littered with sacks, he looked back at me. "Wait in the front court."

"Yeah," I said. "Sure."

As he walked into the corridor, I said to him, "What's in that basket?"

He stopped, turned, and eyed me. Then he shook his head with a resigned look on his face and lifted the lid. A man's head. Long strands of black hair still matted on his forehead. Blotches of dark red bloodstains caked like dried paint on his face. A gob of it still clung to his thick moustache. His eyes were open. An empty look in them as if he didn't know what happened.

I suppressed a sigh and said quickly, "Whose head is that?"

"Don't ask, just wait out there."

I went down the stone steps and stood looking at the darkening sky. The breeze came up stronger now, and the areca trees shuddered. I sat down on the bottom step, crossing my arms on my knees. Suddenly I felt cold.

I heard footfalls behind me, from the direction of the hall. I didn't bother to turn. Then a hand touched my shoulder. I looked up. The buffalo boy's girlfriend. Something about her made me think of Xiaoli. Perhaps the way she wore her plait, or perhaps the way she moved. A panicked look in her eyes, she spoke to me, "Are they going to take you away in a boat?"

I didn't speak. Couldn't speak. Then words came. "Yeah."

"You must be very careful. They're going to hurt you."

"Who? The soldiers?"

"No. My boyfriend and his chums."

"They'll take me away in a boat, you said?"

"No. Someone else. But he'll stop somewhere. Just watch out... Do something then. Or..."

She shook her head repeatedly. I stood up. The soldier was walking out through the hall. I looked at her, for her face since that night in the paddy field had quietly lived in me until it became Xiaoli's. I dropped my voice, "Why d'you want to help me?"

"I'm a friend of Xiaoli."

"You know her?"

"She works for my father."

"You're Mr. Lý's daughter?"

She nodded. Then, just as the soldier emerged from the hall, she said quickly, "Don't let them hurt you."

I looked at her long and hard, and then turned to the soldier. He led me across the courtyard out to the road and we stood waiting until the guide rode up on horseback. I swung up on the saddle, and he heeled the horse and put it into a trot. Soon there was light ahead. Over the gate shone an electric lamp. These bastards were technologically ahead of other villages, for they were the biggest Catholic village in Tonkin. I remembered the dirt trail that led to the river. It was dark along the trail until the horse pulled up at the jetty. There was a lantern post now before one walked onto the dock. The guide turned his horse around, and I stood until he disappeared around the bend. Beyond the amber sphere of the lantern, the jetty was cloaked in blackness. I walked on to the end of the pier, and my hand touched the knife tucked behind my belt. I pulled on the front of my blouse. It was getting chilly.

I made out a narrow boat moored against the pile. A dark face from the boat looked up and said, "Git on in!"

I dropped down onto the stern. Both the stern and bow were covered with a rattan frame, nailed to the ledges on both sides so one sat high on it rather than sinking into the open space. He untied the boat and began rowing with one arm. He reached down with his free hand, picked up a smoldering stick from the brazier at his feet, and lit a cigarette. His paddle churned the water, and soon it was the only cadence in the stillness. He maneuvered the boat around sandbanks in darkness. He knew the course of the river very well. In the dark glowed the red dot of his cigarette, the air damp and acrid with silt and tobacco smoke. A chill rose from the river. Past a bank tangled with brushwood and vines, a flock of herons shot out in a heavy rush of wings. They glided like white paper cutouts, and their wing-beating grew faint and fainter in the distance. The river was growing choppy; several tributaries flowed into it. There was a sharp curve, and he poled it skillfully until the bow was level with the current. But I noticed that the boat was moving toward the bank and, before I became aware of what was going on, its bottom scraped the gravel. This wasn't a landing but a vine-covered slope with a cleft on the incline for a footpath. I could feel the tightness in my stomach. The river was wide, but I could swim across if I had to.

"Why are we stopped here?" I asked him.

He stepped out of the boat, took a drag on his cigarette, and flicked the stub into the water. Without saying a word, he climbed up the slope.

"Hey," I called out to him, "aren't we going to Monkey Hop Landing?"

"Shut up!" he said, barely turning his head.

I felt it was coming but I decided to stay put. It wasn't fear I felt any more, but a dark, baleful, demonic urge to kill. I drew my knife, clutched it under my thigh, and waited.

Soon a light came over the top of the slope. A lantern hovered. Dark figures stood looking down, and then down they came until they reached the graveled ground. The buffalo boy wore a brown collarless shirt and white trousers. The lantern glowed behind him as he stood looking at me.

"Well, well, skull thief," he said, flicking back stray hair on his brow.

He had mean-looking eyes.

"Will you do what I ask, skull thief?" he said with a grin that stayed.

"That depends," I said.

"On?"

"How I feel."

"How do you feel now?"

"Pissed."

"At who?"

"Being here."

"Oh. Why don't you step out of the boat? Right now."

"Why don't you step in?"

"What for?" He snorted.

"I'm not going anywhere."

"Ain't that right? Yeah. We have the whole night. So. . ."

He sloshed through the ankle-deep water to the boat and stood looking down at me. Then he stepped in. I lunged at him, drove the knife up the inside of his thigh. He screamed. We almost fell, and I grabbed his hair to steady myself and felt the knife blade wedged in his flesh.

"Sit," I mouthed the word against his ear.

His hands groped around like he didn't know how to sit, but he did sit, perching on the ledge. Already his forehead was dripping with sweat and my hand was wet with his blood. I glanced toward them and shouted, "You, boatman!"

He stepped toward the boat with a sneer on his face.

"Row it!" I said. "Or stay there and watch him bleed to death."

The boatman got in, acting as if he had been drugged. I bent my knee, half kneeling, to steady my hand against the buffalo boy's thigh. The churning of gravel. The boat groaned and creaked until it found the depth of water. The buffalo boy's head lolled. Sweat was running down the side of his face. I yanked his hair.

"I'm gonna pull out the knife," I said. "Take off your shirt."

His jaw clenched, and he looked at me like he didn't understand.

"Take it off," I said slowly. "Piece your fucking self together."

His arms flailed as he took off his shirt. They bumped my elbow and wrist of the hand that held a handful of his hair. My forehead began to sweat. I said into his ear, "Now, fix yourself."

I pulled the knife out in one steady motion. He doubled up, shrieking. His sharp cry echoed across the still river. The light-colored cloth of his pants had already darkened while he tried to wind a sleeve of his shirt around his thigh. Then he tried the other sleeve. Then he sat, hunched on the ledge, holding his thigh with his bloodstained hands.

"Ain't that bad," I said, tugging his hair. "When you feel a bamboo spike going through your foot, that's pain."

He kept his head down. I could hear him curse under his breath. I motioned with my head toward the bank. "You," I said to the boatman, "bring it over there."

"What the fuck for?" he said coldly.

I fixed him a stare. "If you don't, this scum is gonna lose his dick." I lowered my voice. "You pissed in my daddy's skull. Remember, boy?"

He didn't answer. I pushed the tip of the knife under his chin. He stretched his back, but refused to lift his face to look at me. The boat's bow swept a half circle in the water as it moved toward the bank of a steep drop. I spoke into his ear, "'Cause your girlfriend is a nice, decent girl, I'm gonna let you keep your dick. But I happen to have a long memory. I kinda remember you said something about my face. Small-pox face? Pimpled face? God stamps my face with scars so I can't hide? Well, I don't hide. And I don't set traps, I don't waylay innocent people. But I want you to remember me. As long as you live."

Gripping his hair, I cushioned the back of his head with my forearm and brought the tip of the knife down his cheek to his jaw line. The boat hit the sand with a sharp jerk, and he fell tumbling back over the ledge. He lay half submerged in the water like a heap of pale clothing washed ashore.

"Move out!" I shouted to the other fellow.

Bending my knees, I gripped the side of boat with one hand and held my knife at my hip. I inched toward the boatman, pushing the smoking brazier with my foot ahead of me. He avoided my eyes and rowed hard with both arms. I watched his arms' movement. The oar rested in the oarlock. To swing it at me, he would have to stand up to free it. I knew it well when I rowed Chim's boat. I waited. In midstream, I said to him, "Stop!"

He paused mid-stroke. I pushed the brazier until it hit his feet.

"Put both feet in it," I said, my arm holding the knife cocked at my elbow.

"What the fuck..."

"Put them in," I said, staring into his dark face.

He looked down at the brazier. It glowed a dull red. I picked up a smoldering stick, brought its end between his eyes. Gingerly, he lifted his feet.

"Now!" I shouted.

He yelled the moment his feet went in the bed of smoking coals and twigs. He raised them, gasping.

"Jump!" I said, pushed the smoking stick into his face.

He rolled sideways over the ledge and into the water. His feet kicking, he flipped onto his stomach, and his arms swung and swung like a windmill as he swam ashore. I took the oar and steered the boat straight in the current.

It was a long way to Monkey Hop Landing, and the first drops of rain began to fall.

THE REMAINS OF BONDAGE

I thought of my mother when I got back to the city. It was getting light, and the streets were still wet from the earlier rain. She must be up by now, expecting us. The awful wait. What lay ahead in the days to come? Like a ghost, I walked into the house, clinging to what I saw, old things, old feelings.

The first thing I did was to find *Lao* Gao. He was already up, sitting in the kitchen, puffing on a hand-rolled cigarette he held between his lips. The old dog was lapping water from a wooden bowl. The fire was burning in the iron stove, and a pot simmered as a wooden ladle leaned against it. The dry smell of grain. The fresh morning air. On Lin Gao's wrinkled face was printed a yellow coin of sunlight.

I sat down next to him, told him what happened in Chung village. I told him to expect the worst, having nothing any more to fall back on, not even a roof over our heads. He looked down at his gnarled hands, moving his fingers that pinched the cigarette. I sat in silence. After a while he looked up at the ceiling, perhaps at the sky beyond, and nodded to himself. There was nothing he could do, but his muted reception got me thinking.

"*Lao* Gao," I said, "have you got a place to go to?"

He brought the cigarette to his lips and then brought it back down. He shook his head with a crooked smile.

"You can stay with me and my mother. I'll take care of you."

He turned his face and looked at me. His eyes were serene. He looked down at the old dog, now snoring at his feet, and reached out with his hand to stroke its head.

"Yeah," I said, "him too."

He pointed to the pot on the stove and made a hand motion to ask me if I wanted to eat. I nodded, but then told him what Mr. Cao Lai had asked me to do. Lin Gao rose to his feet, took a final drag on his cigarette, opened the iron stove's door and tossed in the stub. Mr. Cao Lai never tolerated seeing mashed cigarette stubs anywhere in the house.

We went to the coffin room, and Lin Gao opened the padlock with a long key. He flung back the red cloth cover, and I could now see the luster of the coffin's blackish-brown wood. He took out a shorter key, inserted it into the lotus-flower knob, and turned the key. Watching him, I realized that one of the flowers on the sides of the coffin was meant to be a drawer knob. The deep drawer had several tin tubes, the kind made for storing documents. A large metal chest in silver. Lin Gao used another small key to open the chest. He didn't look surprised when he opened the lid for me. Inside was a black, velvet-lined compartment filled with rows of pasteboard cylinders. Stacked in them were gold and silver coins. I wasn't surprised either. Many of the silver coins in the chest must have come from the payment brought to Mr. Cao Lai's liquor store. I remembered the three fake coins. I went through each tin tube, pulling out the papers, looking at them, at dense black characters inked in Chinese. One of them was a map, with colors shaded in red, blue and gray, and lines and triangles that looked like terrain symbols of some sort. I asked Lin Gao what the papers were, but he just made undecipherable hand gestures that left me nodding and shaking my head and in the end feeling nothing more than a pang of hopelessness. I thought of Xiaoli. She could help.

At my instruction, Lin Gao helped me move all the items in the coffin out to the kitchen. I sat on the stone bench with him, cradling my head in my hands. Where would I hide the money and Mr. Cao Lai's personal papers? I asked Lin Gao. He went into some elaborate pantomime, even lugging the chest out of the kitchen and then towing it back. I grabbed his arm.

"*Lao* Gao," I said, "can you leave a message with the silk woman? For Xiaoli?"

He pulled the chest into a corner and pushed it against the wall next to the wooden rice bin. Then he grabbed the tin tubes from me and walked to the pile of straw behind the iron stove. One by one he buried them in the bottom of the pile. He looked back to me and nodded.

"Tell her I must see her tonight. Tell her it's urgent. If she can't come tonight to the liquor store, I'll be in the Chinese quarter tomorrow night."

I watched him drape the chest with a canvas bag and then place a round tray on top. I told him I had to open the liquor store. He brought his water pipe and its accessories and laid them on the tray.

Xiaoli didn't come that evening. Nor did she come the next night. With Mr. Cao Lai's money from the liquor store, I paid a messenger during the day to deliver a message home to my mother. I sealed it in a tube I took from Mr. Cao Lai's sleeping chamber. I told the messenger to bring back the tube with my mother's message.

After closing the store after dark, I went home and ate with Lin Gao in the kitchen. Told him I'd be going to the Chinese quarter later. Then I walked out to the dark court-yard. A drizzle misted my face, the boughs of the young

ylang-ylang tree were perspiring. We hadn't lit the lanterns
for several evenings. Did we need to light them at all? For
whom? The money in the chest. I shook my head. Mr. Cao
Lai's petty cash. Where did he stash his fortune? In properties he owned? In those paper documents? Me, I'm slaving for him to pay off the debt on our burial ground. And
her. Enslaved since eleven. Perhaps she was taking up her
old habit again during those evenings she didn't come. Out
there selling opium. Each *sapèque* she earned only brought
her closer to unknown dangers.

There was a firm knock on the entrance door.

I wondered who it could be at this hour.

I unlatched the door and stood face to face with her.
She wore a black outfit with the usual bag flung over her
shoulder. I threw my arms around her, closed my eyes. Her
hair was damp. She smelled like wet fern. I asked if she felt
cold and she shook her head and touched her face with her
hand.

"Where's your umbrella?" I asked.

"I forgot it tonight. I was rushing out to get medication
for the matriarch."

"The old woman is sick?"

"The last few days."

"You took a chance to come here?"

"No. I knew."

"Knew? Ahh. *Lao* Gao."

"Yes. What happens now?"

I told her that the arrest of Mr. Cao Lai at Lý's residence
left us with a dilemma. Then I pulled her inside and shut the
door, and as we crossed the courtyard, I told her what Lin
Gao was trying to tell me.

He grinned at us from behind the bluish veil of the water pipe's smoke, patting his stone seat for her to sit down. She spoke to him in Chinese. He rose and went to the pile of straw and dug out the tin tubes. I sat cross-legged on the floor, next to the sleeping old dog, watching her examine the papers. After a while she turned to me and said, "These are debt papers."

"Whose debts?" I said.

"People owe him money. Many of them."

"Lots of money?"

"Yes."

"Ask him what to do with the money chest."

"Take it home. Leave it with your mother."

My lips opened but I couldn't find words. He was wise. If they seized the house, they would seize all of its assets. I could leave the city for my village and come back the next day, leaving Lin Gao in charge of the liquor store during my absence. I thought as she rolled up the papers neatly and slid them one by one back into their tubes. Her face looked thin, tired. Her bag was beside her on the floor.

"Are you going out to sell tonight?" I asked her.

She didn't answer. And then she nodded without looking at me.

I got up and went to the chest. After unloading everything on top of it, I lugged it back. I asked Lin Gao for the key, and while he fumbled for it in his blouse pocket, I asked her what the debt was that she owed Lý.

"I don't know," she said, turning to face me. "I don't know how much money my mother borrowed from them. But they told me that I will pay it back in ten years."

"Ten years?" I said calmly. "And you've been here six years. Ask Lý's mother about the remaining part of your service."

"To buy out my bondage?"

"Unless there's another way."

"With Mr. Cao Lai's money?" She dropped her gaze to the money chest.

"He can add your years to mine. I'm not stealing it from him."

Lin Gao made a short guttural sound. He was grinning like he was amused at hearing what I said. Perhaps he understood what bondage meant. And for him, it was a lifetime.

"Tài," she said softly.

I gazed at her. She was an innocent child again when she called my name.

"Please don't do that," she said. "It only hurts you."

"Xiaoli," I said, "You can't go on selling opium night after night. You must stop. Stop."

"I want to," she said, barely audible. "Don't you know I want to?"

"Then stop. Please. So you can go home again."

"I am counting each day. Don't you know? I see her often in my sleep. Like we find ways to be with each other."

"Xiaoli," I said, "she's dead."

"My mother?"

"Yeah. Your grandfather told me. He asked me to tell you to come home and tend her grave."

The look in her eyes froze. Then she lowered her head and brought her hand to her mouth. She tried to stifle her sobs, and her shoulders shook and shook. I put my arm around her and, leaning my head against hers, said, "I'm sorry I didn't have the heart to tell you. I didn't want to see you go." I touched her face, damp with tears, feeling the despair that wracked her body.

She calmed down and took a cup of tea from Lin Gao's hand. He squatted in front of us, watching her sip the tea. He nodded. There was nothing we could do but keep silent. Her body sagged in my arms, she gazed into the empty cup. The three of us watched the same cup, until the old dog scrambled to his feet and went to drink his water in the wooden bowl.

"I must get home," she said hoarsely.

"I'll walk you," I said.

I helped her up. I told Lin Gao not to lock the entrance door, and I took his umbrella and left.

For a while we did not speak, just walked holding hands. We heard the *tic-toc* of raindrops on the umbrella and the wet footsteps. At times we would pass lanterns that hovered on street corners, and sometimes a torch burned brightly when a dark figure slunk past.

"Don't go out tonight," I said, canting my face toward her.

"Are you afraid for me?" Her face was a glimmer as she turned it toward me.

"Yeah."

"Sometimes I still ask what I already know. Are you mad?"

"Wish I could be there with you every night. I'm not mad."

"No, you are not. I have never seen you mad."

"But I could be. And I was when I was coming back from Chung village."

"Because of what happened to Mr. Cao Lai?"

I nodded. I told her that I hurt two people, the boatman and the buffalo boy. Then I mentioned the boy's girlfriend.

"Isn't she a friend of yours?"

"I taught her Chinese. She taught me Annamese. We

used to play around the house whenever she came up with
Mr. Lý."

"You told her about us?"

"Yes."

"Will you ask them?" I whispered.

"I will ask the matriarch."

"Tonight?"

"Yes."

"Let me know tomorrow. I'll keep the money here till
then."

She tightened her grip on my hand. I could feel her sharp
fingernails dig into my palm. What would be waiting for
her at home? Yunnan. Town of Lijiang. Home? You cannot
call a place a home when there is nothing but emptiness
around you.

"Xiaoli."

"Yes?"

"Will you come back?"

"I do not belong here."

"I know."

"It is a long way back."

"How long?"

"It took nearly a month by boat from Lijiang to Hanoi."

"You can go by steamer now."

"Steamboats? I have seen them. They are faster. You can
go on a steamboat very cheap. Well, if you stay in the lower
decks."

I had seen them on rivers. Huge riverboats with stacked-
up decks. The lower decks could hold up to two thousand
passengers. They said it cost six hundred sapeques a head
for the lower-deck class.

"You don't want to travel in a lower deck," I said.

"It will cost too much if I don't. I only need a space."

"I know."

"It's not your money. How can you pay it back?"

I chuckled. "Will you come back? At least for your grand-father's bones?"

"You will have to show me where."

"Yeah."

"Do you want me to go back?"

"I want you to."

"Because it is the right thing to do, is it not?"

"Yeah. It is."

"That's why you did what you did, so you can rebury your father and your brother in a better place. Yes?"

"Yeah."

Rain was falling harder. I felt it on my face, like pinheads that could not hurt me.

THE FORTUNE OF THE DEAD

The night before I dreamed of a red poppy flower. It had no scent. When I woke up I remembered its blood-red color.

Each day I waited to hear of her departure. Four hundred silver piasters to settle her debt with the Lý clan. The sum of her debt. The sum of bondage and time. Now she was free, a new leaf. Now she never had to count each day again. When she left, the remains of the day would be mine to count. I gave her several gold piasters which she took to a Chinese trading house to exchange for Chinese currency. Each gold piaster was worth fifteen silver piasters. Each coin she carried home with her was lifeblood of her new life. I entered into a ledger what I took out of the money chest.

On the fourth day, I was in the liquor store when Lin Gao came in with a soldier. The sight of his conical hat appalled me. Hadn't I seen enough of them at Lý's house? Without my asking, he told me to come with him to see Mr. Cao Lai—he was granted permission to speak to me. I left Lin Gao at the store and mounted the pony-sized horse with the soldier. The short-legged horse had a big head, unshod hooves. It ambled down the wet street past stores and a market and then galloped toward the citadel.

"Can you slow him down?" I yelled to the back of the soldier's head.

"Can't," he yelled back. "He ain't born to trot. Shame, eh?"

"Why this way? Aren't they all at the governor's place?"

"Prisoners?"

"Yeah."

"They're there. Until they got judged upon and they got taken somewhere else."

"Mr. Cao Lai got judged upon, you mean?"

"Yeah."

"Where's he now?"

"In the citadel."

"Then what?"

"Wait, I guess. You can't do much in a death cell." That took the wind out of me.

"When's that gonna happen?" I said, raising my voice a notch.

"Decapitation? Dunno. Ask him."

The cell had an iron door and no windows. A palm-sized opening in the door let in slivers of light from the corridor.

His figure was gray in the dark room, several feet across and about ten feet in length. It was even smaller than our coffin room. On the cement floor he sat, legs locked in the stock, hands too. He had a light beard now, hair falling over his face. Said he wasn't alone until two days before when they took out three inmates and beheaded them. My grand-uncle must have been busy lately.

I squatted beside him and could smell his strong sweat. The room breathed the odor of rancid bodies here before and gone. I asked him why all this. He pondered. Then he told me that he fell into Lý's trap. That grabbed my attention. He a victim of betrayal? Yes, he said, nodding. Sometimes, just when you begin to trust people, I thought. I remembered the ammunition, guns, opium balls. I mentioned them. That was part of our deal, he said. Opium from Montgzé in China smuggled in across the border cost one fourth the price sold in Hanoi. But the mule train of opium had to pass through the Lai Châu outpost. The name Lai Châu reminded me of the messenger on horseback the morning Mr. Cao Lai returned from Lau. Dressed like coolies and led by one man outfitted as an Annamese soldier on horseback, the caravan was allowed passage through the outpost. They killed the sentinel and proceeded to murder several more, one of them a French commandant. They took fifty guns and over thirty thousand cartridges. Many of those were to be sold to bandits in the plains. They were pricey commodities.

I sat and listened. Somehow I could not separate him, the mastermind of organized crime, the racketeer, the extortionist, from the person I used to know. He was clearly one of the business gentry. What was Lý doing in such a scheme? I asked. He was, Mr. Cao Lai said, to take delivery of the goods brought down from Lai Châu. He and his two Chinese business partners were to process the raw opium and sell it in Hanoi at four times what they paid for it. But Lý was a master of deception, Mr. Cao Lai said ruefully. He orchestrated the deal to have Mr. Cao Lai acquire the goods from the mercenaries and then took sides with the authorities. They overwhelmed the bandits in Lai Châu with the Mùòng tribal chieftain's help. They assassinated the bandit leader the night before the attack. His head, Mr. Cao Lai said, was brought back intact in a straw basket. Then they faked a document and sent it down to Hanoi to obtain Mr. Cao Lai's signature—not only his signature, but his detailed plan to have the goods transported to Chung village for the rendezvous at Lý's. I thought of his ruse. But one does not scheme against someone unless he has compelling motivation. So I asked him. "I had one of his old friends killed—and you lost his skull," he said. I asked why he had him killed. He said nothing. I listened to his quiet breathing. I thought he might be dozing. "The man knew too much about me," he said finally. I nodded. In fact, I did not understand the full meaning of it, but I knew he wouldn't elaborate. Yet I knew one thing: Lý decided to strike first before he got struck down by surprise. The price of knowing too much about a person.

"Have you done everything I asked?" he asked, tilting his head toward me.

"Yes, sir."

"Where are they now?"

"Still at the house, sir. But we hid them in the kitchen."

"Take them somewhere else—before they evict the two of you."

"I'm planning to take them with me to my village. My mother can be their custodian."

"Do not lose the papers."

"The debt papers, sir?"

He nodded with a faint smile. "You might think it's funny talking about debts. Here I am. The last one on the death row to go."

I inhaled deeply. The room's unpleasant odors made gooseflesh break out on my arms.

"I understand sometimes you can't let go, sir," I said softly. "Sometimes even the dead keep coming back to haunt the old places, people, and things they don't want to let go."

"So I heard." He chuckled. "I can't speak for any of them, dead or about to be. But I hope I won't be bothering the living."

"When is your . . . last day, sir?"

"I don't know. They like to do three at a time. It could be any time now if there are two more."

"You have any wish before it happens, sir?"

"Wish? That's something I never have much use for."

"I see. But that's good. If it happens, it happens."

"That's very true."

"What will we do with your body, sir?"

"Do? Why would I care at that point? Just a corpse. Well, a headless corpse."

"Sir, you have a beautiful coffin made just for you. Would it make sense that we bury you in it?"

"I didn't have it made with that in mind. I'll be satisfied if you can safely take away everything you found in that coffin."

"Sir?"

"Yes?"

"I did take out of your chest a lot of money. But sir, I keep a ledger of what I owe you. And Lin Gao, he knew what I was doing."

"What did you need the money for?"

"I bought out Xiaoli's service for Mr. Lý."

He nodded, turning on the seat of his pants perhaps to get the cramps out of his limbs. I asked him if I could do anything to help relieve his discomfort, and he shook his head.

"All this will disappear any day now," he said. "In fact, I look forward to it."

I asked why he didn't wear a cangue. He flexed his neck, saying it was taken off him after his good friend, the *quan án*, came to visit. He said the killing of the French commandant, more than anything else, led to his death sentence. His Annamese friend, the *tông đôc*, with his governor's authority, had to pronounce the sentence on him. The French Resident, whom he also knew, signed the decree.

"What do you want me to do with the papers, sir?"

He took a sharp breath, pursing his lips. "I want you to go see Mr. Acong in the Chinese quarter. Lin Gao can take you there. With Mr. Acong's help and influence, you can collect at least half of the debts. Even at that, it'd be a victory."

"But all these debts were signed by you as creditor. If you die, sir . . ."

"We go by an unsigned, unspoken code. I want you to remember this: for every debt Mr. Acong collects for me—well, in name only—you give him ten percent. You keep the rest."

Overwhelmed, I looked at the floor. Still, I felt unsettled.

"Sir?" I sought his eyes, now closed like he wanted to rest.

"I'm listening."

"Sir, I don't matter much in your life. I never will. I'm not even related to you. And if you don't have any relative or anyone else you feel worthy of your fortune, you must have a very good reason why you want to put it in my hand. I'm sorry to speak my mind, sir."

"That's what I like about you."

"Then why me? Why not . . . *Lao* Gao?"

"He never needs much. You can give him some, though. He's very loyal."

"I can see that. I told him if he has no place to go, he should come live with me and my mother."

"You have character."

"So do you, sir."

"Another thing."

"Yes, sir?"

"The map." He cleared his throat. His breath was hot with fever.

"What d'you want me to do with it?"

"Nothing. It's a map I drew myself. Where I keep my wealth."

"It's safe with me, sir. Unless you want me to destroy it."

"It doesn't matter. You won't need it, once I tell you." He leaned his forehead against the stock. He looked spent. Then he said, speaking into his chest, "Debt and wealth. If you think I'm planning to collect them!"

"Sir," I said quietly, "it must hurt you very bad."

"It certainly does." He leaned back his head, facing the low ceiling with his eyes shut. "All my wealth, you can find it inside the two tombstones, one for your father, one for your brother."

My head hurt. I just stared at him in the dark.

"I don't mean to disrespect the dead," he said in a whisper. "But I can't tell you why. In those two tombstones is the fortune I brought with me from Kwangtung. My family's fortune. It wasn't given to me. I was the family outcast. After my mother died, my father had a mausoleum built for him. It was built in the back of his estate. A thousand acres of land and forest and hills. Since there was no one else but me in our family's lineage, the old man decided to have his fortune buried with him when he died. He had the catacomb built first and then the mausoleum. Everyone knew about the mausoleum, few knew of the catacomb. The one he hired to build it did not know what he was building. Or if he did he would have no way of telling it. First he was picked for the job because he was illiterate, an out-of-town handyman, then he was blindfolded and transported to the land. The day he finished it they cut off his tongue, blindfolded him and took him back where they had found him. When my father was dying, I came back. In his will he made me the caretaker of the estate. He refused to tell me where he hid his fortune. After he died, I went to look for the man in the town where they had found him. I searched every street, every alley, every tavern and restaurant, the quay, the boarding houses. A faceless, nameless man. But I knew he was mute. And there was something else I looked for. My dog. I had raised him since he was a puppy. He was a guard dog. Keen on scent, smart on brain. They made him guard the man during his labors. I lost my dog—they said he'd gotten so used to the man he had guarded that he ran off with him after they brought him back to town. One day in that town I ran into my old dog. I found the man. I took him back to the estate, now mine. But much had changed since the mausoleum was built. New landscape with gardens and pathways. Though I told him what he had built must be close to the mausoleum, he couldn't tell where it was. But he did recognize the tall eucalyptus tree. Then the dog came and sniffed around the base of the tree. Sniffing, walking around it. Then he lay down. The man said the dog used to sleep at the base of the tree. He said he was sure that was the same old tree he used to see day in, day out. Then he began to trace his steps from the tree to a spot where there were now a water fountain, planters, an arbor of climbing roses. I had the whole section cleared out, and we found the hidden entrance. I recovered my father's fortune—it must be a curse to him in his eternal peace. I brought everything I found to Hanoi where I had a business. I also brought with me the man and his dog."

I felt a chill run down my back. I sighed deeply and said, "I never knew that our old dog was yours. He acted odd sometimes. One time he took my knife while I was asleep and brought it to you. Do you remember, sir?"

"It was my knife," he said tonelessly.

"Your knife?"

"I used to cut his dewclaws' nails with it. Then while I was in Kwangtung, I lost it in a card game."

My whole body felt stiff. I could sense what was coming.

"During that card game," he said quietly, "your father had a winning hand. The last stake he raised, I was out of money. But I matched it—with my knife. He examined it, liked it, accepted it."

"You said you didn't know much about my father. Or did you, sir?"

"Socially."

We sat in silence. I felt like whirling dregs that couldn't sink to the bottom. After a while I said, "Sir, you never told me why you chose to bury your fortune in the tombstones."

"For a reason. But I can't explain it."

Then he was silent. I, too, remained silent. Finally he turned his face to me and said, "One more thing."

"Yes, sir?"

"You must be wondering why I discouraged you from seeing Xiaoli?"

"Yes, sir. You told me."

"Well," he coughed, "that was just a pretext. The truth is I never want to see a serious relationship between you and her. A boy-and-girl relationship. She is your half-sister."

My arms and legs went numb. I wanted to speak. Instead I stared—not at him or at the dark space beyond him. Not even that.

"Your father lived with a Chinese girl who worked as a servant in one of the opium dens owned by my late father. He didn't marry her and eventually left her to go back to Annam. He didn't even see his daughter born."

I looked down at my feet, my heart rent.

"You did the right thing, though—buying out her service to Lý. You let mother and daughter reunite after all these years."

"Her mother died, sir," I spoke to the floor. "I broke the news to her."

"You love her, don't you?"

"Have you ever loved someone, sir?"

He squinted his eyes to look at me, and then his face re-laxed. "Yes, I have."

I listened. I could feel my heart beat, hear it. It told me an answer I did not want to hear.

XIAOLI

She wore a straw hat, a white blouse and black trousers. At dusk a drizzle was falling on the quay. She had with her a dark blue suitcase. She carried over her shoulder the old cloth bag I used to see with her on those evenings. The river was wide. Electric globe lamps shone bluish along the edge of the quay and tiny lights glowed in the portholes of the steam ship. The other side of the river was a thin line of green, and beyond, a glimmering horizon before dark. Moments later night fell without twilight.

She did not say much. At times she feigned a smile.

"Last night I went for a walk until the soles of my feet blistered," she said. "It rained, then stopped. I came back to my room wet from head to toe. I sat on the edge of my bed and opened my watch. The music played while I looked at the face of my mother. When it stopped I pressed it against my cheek and then opened my suitcase and put the watch away. I looked at my clothing, two sets of earrings, a necklace, a brooch, and several silk scarves, a few of which were given to me by the matriarch. Years earlier I had only a few blouses and trousers to wear all year round. I closed the suitcase, then sat, absorbing the silence, the loss."

On the water, sampans were roped in groups of four and five, and the lanterns were lit. Silhouette of a family sitting under the rattan roof as they shared their evening meal. "When I get there I will write you," she said. "Yes," I said. "Yes." The lampposts were dripping water in the drizzle. I

"You do not have to say the words. Just open yourself and say your truest feeling."

"I will say your name."

"Will that bring me closer to you?"

"The same way it does when I hear you say my name."

"Tài."

"Yes. It makes me feel very peaceful."

"Does it? When you pray, just say my name."

"Xiaoli."

"Do you love me?"

"Yes. More than anything."

"I will wait for you."

Her faint smile trailed. Did her mother wait for my father to come back? Did he lie to her, saying he would come back? A dark soul entered me, wet with rain, maimed. I heard it calling.

On the quay, rickshaws began to pull in. Hurried footfalls along the quay. The sounds of suitcases on the gangplank. The sound of the horn. Its wailing brought us into each other's arms. She tilted back her straw hat and smiled a melancholy smile.

"I won't cry," she said.

"Go," I said.

She picked up her suitcase and walked up the gangplank, passing between the two lampposts in a halo of bluish light. Halfway up she turned, waved, and wiped her eyes.

That evening I ate with Lin Gao and told him my plan. I wanted to sell everything in the house before it was confiscated. I asked him to take me to the Chinese quarter to see Mr. Acong when morning came. Perhaps through him I could find an auction house to help sell the household dog came and lay sprawled at his feet. He passed me the pipe and, without hesitation, I took a deep drag, holding it until my head swelled, and slowly exhaled. The dog raised its head and watched. When I blew out a fog of blue smoke, it tucked his muzzle between the paws of its legs. We passed the pipe back and forth, sipping tea, smoking in silence. It must have been my twentieth pipe when my eyes watered and I saw Lin Gao's hand try to take the pipe away from me. I refused to let go. It must have been my thirtieth pipe when a hand offered me a cup of hot tea, and I drank it like water. My tongue seemed gone. It must have been my fortieth pipe when the room was no longer itself but a desolate ground, blue with fog. I hear voices calling out to one another, shuffling footsteps of frail specters, a lantern hovering by itself in midair. The wind blows through desolation and tall eucalyptus trees sway and sigh. From a cluster of trees emerges a horde of black-garbed beings. They stumble and bump against one another soundlessly, and I can see the bones of their skeletons through their formless attire. Some among them are headless bodies walking around and around on the same spot, looking and looking. Nearby, chained to a tree, is the skeleton of a dog. He jumps at the poor apparitions only to be yanked back by his chain. It must have been my fiftieth pipe. I lie down on the moss-covered ground while the phantoms walk over me, seeking something perhaps forever lost to them. A red poppy blooms, a hand-span from my eyes. I see each petal open. I am no longer flesh, I am bound by nothing material. I am a mere thought, unable to lift my own hand to touch the flower.

I had met Mr. Acong several times. He was much older than I thought, perhaps as old as my granduncle. He wore deep scar that slanted from the inner corner of his eye to the outside of his cheek. I never asked why it was there. Each time I met with him at his house, I would leave my shoes at his door for cleanliness, exactly like I did at Mr. Cao Lai's house. Mr. Acong perused the debt papers, made notes, and then told me, based on the debts' collectible dates, that I would get most of them back in a year and a half. I told him ten percent of it would be his fee. He did not object to it, but asked what I would do with the money. Sensing my ignorance, he counseled me on how to use money to earn money. He said to me that it was the business way. I imagined that was how Mr. Cao Lai had earned his money—by lending it. After those meetings, I reached a decision. I turned over half of the money in Mr. Cao Lai's money chest to him and let him manage Mr. Cao Lai's wealth, which was now mine. I decided against telling him of my remaining assets. I wanted to see how well he could manage my investment.

A month later I took the rest of the money back to my village. The first thing I did was tell my mother everything, everything except the curse of my blood kinship with Xiaoli. I told her I had money to rebuild our house and build a cache in it to store the treasure hidden in the two tombstones. Before I left to go back to the city, I went to Chim's house. Xoan was near term with her baby. We talked about her father, and I found out that he went to trial and was now serving his six-month sentence by doing labor somewhere in a coal mine. I told her that was a very light sentence. Without fanfare, I expressed my feelings about having a good relationship between wife and husband. I said my heart wasn't in our relationship. Without it, there was no love. She said nothing. It seemed she had expected it. Surely she must have expected it. She had been silent for a long time. She was pregnant with our child. I told her she was a tough girl. When I departed, I left with her half the money I had taken home.

The day after I returned to the city, a soldier came to our house with a writ sealed inside an ivory-toned envelope. It said that we must relinquish the house two days after the execution of the household head. That was the next day.

Since there was almost nothing left in the house after a weeklong auction, I went to Mr. Wang's coffin shop and asked him if he also offered funeral services. He sent me to his son-in-law two doors away. When I got there, I changed my plans. I told the proprietor that I wanted the remains of Mr. Cao Lai cremated. Then I went back to Mr. Wang and made a deal with him. He would keep the coffin he made for Mr. Cao Lai on his premises until I had rebuilt our house in Lau. Then he would deliver the coffin there. It would sit in our house, awaiting the death of my mother or me. Like Mr. Cao Lai, I believed in death itself, not in its symbol.

At high noon the next day, a retinue of curiosity seekers followed the three condemned men to the execution ground. Heralding the cortege was a red banner that said in Chinese characters: *Tram Quyêt*. The crowd followed the old rampart of the old town of Hanoi past the solitary persimmon tree, past the odd-looking pagoda standing askew on the stony bedding like some dark, sinister relic. Was the old monk inside at work on the woodblocks of our transcriptions?

When the human column veered from the road onto the trail, it disappeared in tangles of vines, shrubbery, and a hazy shade of green. The air echoed with the shrieking of parakeets. In the distance lay a little pond, smooth as a mirror, and slicing through it were lily-trotters, gray and as small as a fist. The column stopped. The soldiers went to work on pounding a row of wooden stakes into the ground. The onlookers inched toward one another. I saw Danton, the French priest, a lone figure standing back against an outcrop, alone in his black robe, wearing a black hat like Death itself. I saw my granduncle begin preparing his first man— Mr. Cao Lai. I watched him. He looked much thinner with a full beard. All the while he looked down at the ground. A strange feeling turned my stomach. I felt like crying.

Just before Granduncle daubed the back of Mr. Cao Lai's neck with the red cud of his betel chew, he pulled up the watch chain. He worked it free of Mr. Cao Lai's neck and tossed it on the ground. I watched. When the head fell, a soldier ran up with a wicker basket, picked up the head, and dropped it inside the basket.

Moments after the crowd had cleared out, the men from the funeral house picked up Mr. Cao Lai's headless body and put it in a pine coffin. I went to the stake to which he had been tied. I looked in the grass. I wanted to retrieve his last possession. There it was, stained red from spilled blood. It was a pocket watch, round and silvery. Its fringe was carved with flowers. In its center a bird hovered over two nestlings. For one moment I thought I was holding Xiaoli's heirloom in my hand. I opened its cover and the melody played. There was a picture of a woman inside. Not Xiaoli's mother. My mother.

The night before we moved out of the house I smoked the water pipe with Lin Gao until my head went numb. He took the lantern and crossed the courtyard to go back to his room. I sat in the courtyard, washed pale in a full moon. It was so quiet I could hear the creaking wheels of oxcarts in the streets. After a while I stood up, opened the door

and went out. I walked to the Chinese quarter, the streets
pale like yellow silk. When you walked near a house, a dog
would bark. I wished I could hold all the sounds in a glass
bottle, all the smells on a silver spoon, all the sights in a crystal vase, so I could live my past once again. On a street that
led to the citadel, a column of coolies passed by, their lanterns flickering like it was Moon Festival when she was still
here. Could a man like Mr. Cao Lai know what joy it was to
carry a moon lantern and sing *Ode to the Moon* with other
children? When did he see my mother the first time and fall
in love with her? Only later did I learn of the watch that my
father gave her when he married her. She made him wear it
to keep her in his heart. She knew him too well. Untamed,
impetuous. Could a man like Mr. Cao Lai scheme against
my father to get what he was after? Though the monetary
reward for my father's head was very large, it was, perhaps,
not his real motive. Was it him, a man whose real name was
Lam? I wasn't sure any more. I thought I disliked him, at
times hated him. But if I could hold all the sounds in a glass
bottle, surely I would like to hear him play the melody, feel
the anguish of loving someone and knowing very well that
it was forever an unrequited love.

I walked the streets until I came to the nameless cross
street where I saw a piece of red cloth tied around the bamboo pole. I untied it. It must have been there before she left,
forgotten like many other stories. Or perhaps the old silk
woman wanted to send somebody a message. Me?

I put the red cloth in my blouse pocket and walked back
along the road that went past the banana grove. In the quiet, I suddenly heard the soft *clack-clack* of horse's hooves,
turned, and saw him riding up at a trot. He passed by at an
arm's length from where I stood on the edge of the road,

and rode like he knew exactly where he was headed. Horse
and man were bathed in the moonlight until they vanished.
I looked into the dark, whispering coppice for the lights of
torches, for a crowd of unruly addicts and coolies. For a girl
clad in black wearing a long pigtail. In the susurrus of the
leaves I heard the weeping of my heart.

When morning came, we left the house together—me
with a suitcase, Lin Gao with a jute bag and his dog. I had
given him a good sum of money and bought him a ticket. He was bound for Yunnan. I told him someday when I
came to visit him and Xiaoli, his dog might not be around
anymore. He grinned a toothless grin and jabbed his finger
at his chest. Him neither. When he took the ticket from my
hand, he made a motion like he wanted me to join him for
the journey. I shook my head, smiling. Someday. Perhaps.

We waited on the quay until the steamship sounded its
horn. I took his knotted hands in mine and wished him a *bon
voyage*. Then I patted the old dog's head, looking down into
his rheumy eyes, knowing this was the last time I would
ever see him. They went up the quay, he walking stooped,
bowlegged, and the dog ambling with difficulty up the incline. I looked until they disappeared through the ship's
door and then turned and headed back into the city. I heard
the ship's horn again and something inside me broke.

I turned back and, pulling my suitcase behind me, ran
toward the ship. I ran like a late arrival. There was no one
else on the gangplank but me. I saw standing at the door to
the ship a man wearing a white uniform and a blue visor
cap. He gave me his hand and I took it at the final sound of
the horn.

KHANH HA was born in Hue, the former capital of Vietnam. During his teen years he began writing short stories which won him several awards in Vietnamese adolescent magazines. He graduated from Ohio University with a bachelor's degree in Journalism. *Flesh* is his first novel. He is currently at work on another novel.

Visit the author at: http://www.authorkhanhha.com